OF RAGE AND RUIN

THE DCI PETER MOONE THRILLERS BOOK 4

MARK YARWOOD

This novel is entirely a work of fiction. The names, characters and incidents portrayed in it are the work of the author's imagination. Any resemblance to actual persons, living or dead, events or localities is entirely coincidental.

BiscuitBooksPublishers © Mark Yarwood 2024

The author asserts the moral right to be identified as the author of this work Published by Amazon Kindle All rights reserved. No part of this publication may be reproduced, stored, or transmitted in any form or by means, electronic, mechanical, photocopying, recording or otherwise, without the prior permission of the publishers.

For all the nurses and staff
at Derriford Hospital's Medical
SDEC Unit, for all
the wonderful work you do.

EXCLUSIVE OFFER

Look out for the link at the end of this book or visit my website at www.markyarwood.co.uk to sign up to my no-spam Monthly Murder Club and receive two FREE and exclusive crime thrillers plus news and previews of forthcoming works.

Never miss out on a release.

No spam. You can unsubscribe at any time.

ACKNOWLEDGEMENTS

Once again I need to thank a few individuals who made possible the writing of this the fourth DCI Peter Moone book. First of all, I shall thank Inspector Paul Laity, whose advice on police matters has been, as always, invaluable.

Secondly, I want to thank John Hudspith, my editor who always puts up with my 'fluff'. And a big thank you to Aline Riva for all her proofreading skills.

As always I shall mention my mum, dad and brother for all their love and support. But I mostly want to thank my wife and daughter and, of course, little Mittens, my writing partner, for all their love and support. They know I'm weird and except it.

PROLOGUE

'That's you all set up,' the man said and stepped into Caroline Abbott's kitchen, a big smile stretching his face. He was a nice chap, she thought for the hundredth time that morning. He reminded her of her nephew who now lived in Scotland, and, in a way, it was as if he was here with her.

'I'm glad you were able to sort it out,' she said, smiling. The kettle had just boiled, so she put a teabag in her cup and poured in the water. 'I'm not really very good with technical stuff. I guess I'm getting old.'

He laughed and shook his head. 'You're joking. You're not old.'

She laughed and blushed a little. 'Well, I'm well into my forties now. Some people consider that old these days.'

'Then they're stupid. They don't appreciate people that have lived longer than them and have learned a lesson or two.'

'Well, I haven't learned much about laptops, have I?' She laughed. 'Are you sure you won't have a cup of tea?'

He looked at the cup she had set out, seeming to go into a dream for a moment. He shook himself out of it as he said, 'No, I'd better get going. I've got things I need to see to. Thanks, though. Anything else you need doing round the house, just let me know. You've got my number.'

'I have. I'll see you out, then.'

He held up a hand. 'No, you enjoy your tea, Mrs Abbott. I'll see myself out.'

'OK,' she said, deciding not to correct him and remind him that she wasn't married. He smiled again, then she watched him turn and leave. He walked out of the kitchen, and she heard the front door open, then shut. What a shame he was gone, she thought, and how charming he was. She really did think he was like Charlie, her nephew, in so many ways. She took the milk from the fridge and poured plenty into her tea. She put the milk away and stood resting against the kitchen work surface, holding the mug with both hands. In a moment, she would have to get some work done. It was nice working from home, but there were so many distractions.

She looked up, hearing what sounded like a footstep in the hallway. Then there was another.

'Hello?' she called.

The kitchen door slowly opened, and her heart pounded. The door fully opened and she saw him standing there, blank-faced, staring at her.

'I thought you'd left,' she said, a little relieved it wasn't a burglar. 'You scared me.'

He looked at the floor. 'I'm sorry.'

'It's all right. Did you forget something?'

'I tried to leave.'

'Is the door locked?' she asked, even though she'd heard it open and close. 'It's a bit temperamental sometimes.'

'I really, really tried to leave.' He looked up at her, staring at her strangely, not blinking. Now he didn't look like Charlie, her nephew, not at all, she thought, not any more. But she couldn't understand why.

'What's wrong?' she asked. 'Are you OK?'

'No, I don't think I'm OK.' He reached into his jacket pocket and brought out a hammer and held it at his side. 'I don't think I've ever been OK.'

She put down her tea, staring at the hammer, hearing the strange tone of his voice. 'Dave...'

'That's not my name.' He stared at her again, and then his eyes seemed to travel over her. 'I see you're wearing tights.'

She looked down, then up at him, her heart rate speeding up, panic starting to rise into her chest. 'I think maybe you should leave now.'

'That's the thing. I tried to leave. I told you, I tried to go. Now, I'm going to need you to take off your tights.'

'You need to leave! Right now or I'll call the police.'

He lifted the hammer and held it for her to see. 'Take off your tights. Now, please. Don't make me hurt you.'

She stared at him, her heart pounding, her body starting to tremble. 'Please leave. I don't know...'

'Tights. Now. Don't make me ask again.'

It was the way he said it, the tone in his voice that made her tremble and start doing what he asked. She half watched him as she pulled her skirt up and tried to take her tights off without exposing herself to him. Awful thoughts filled her mind. Why did he want her to take off her tights? She prayed he was just some kind of pervert.

'Give them to me,' he said and held out his free hand.

She balled them up, then edged closer to him, holding them out. He snatched them and lifted them to his face. He took a deep breath, closing his eyes for a few seconds. Then those eyes opened, and they burned out to her as he moved closer. He stopped for a moment as he placed the hammer on the counter, then took the tights and tied a knot in them.

She backed up, shaking her head, hardly able to take in a breath as he stretched the tights between his clenched fists.

'Be a good girl,' he said. 'Don't give me any trouble and it'll all be over quickly. Give me any nonsense and I'll make you suffer.'

CHAPTER 1

Somehow the endless winter, the deep burning cold and iciness of it had become spring. At some point that second season of the year had evolved into a sticky and muggy summer. At least it wasn't raining for once, he thought. Time seemed unforgiving to DCI Peter Moone, with no sense of mercy, he decided as he opened the bottle of white wine he had brought with him. He looked across the kitchen and saw Inspector Kevin Pinder sitting at the small table, nursing a bottle of real ale. Butler was next to him, laughing at something he had just said. More than likely a bad joke, or rather a *dad* joke, he thought as he pulled the cork from the bottle.

'Trust you to pick a bottle with a cork,' Butler said and tutted. 'They do come with screwtops these days, you know?'

He made a face at her, which she replied to with her middle finger. He poured a couple of glasses, his mind rewinding to the events of a few months ago, all the deaths that had occurred and the inquests that slowly followed. The authorities had looked into everything and decided there were no other persons involved in the deaths of DSU Charlie Armstrong and Chief Superintendent Laptew. Armstrong had been murdered by DC Banerjee in a fit of jealous rage. Banerjee had been the victim of an honour killing committed by her cousin, even though he vehemently protested his innocence. Moone believed him, but no one wanted to listen.

Kate Armstrong, DSU Armstrong's widow, had been murdered by Wise in a moment of madness and shame. After he had killed her, he took his own life because he couldn't face what he had done, and the publicity and trial that would surely follow. Chief Superintendent Laptew had killed his wife and then himself. No reason had been found for him to have committed such a terrible act, although there were rumours of several work affairs. It had all been neatly filed away because neither Bristol nor Devon and Cornwall police wanted any more bad press. It was political. It always was. Carthew had got away with it again and now she was heading back in their direction.

'Are we getting this party started?' Butler asked.

'Molly and Harding aren't here yet,' Pinder said.

'Harding can't make it.' Moone poured himself a glass of wine. 'He's gone away today with his wife. Anyway, this isn't supposed to be a party. We've got a serious matter to discuss.'

Butler huffed. 'Says the man who necked several tequilas last time we met up. He doesn't even like tequila. Did you see his face after he drank the first one? Like he'd sucked on a planet-sized lemon.'

Moone nodded and gave a half-hearted laugh as the two of them cracked up. He thought this was as good a time as any to drop the nuclear bomb. 'Thing is, she's heading back to us.'

They both stared at him, their heads springing up like dogs that had heard the biscuit tin opening.

'What?' Butler asked. 'You're winding us up.'

'I don't think he is.' Pinder took a sip of beer.

'I'm not.' Moone gulped down some of his wine. 'I heard it from our new DSU, Boulton.'

Butler sighed and then held out her hand for a drink. 'I thought she was heading off to Scotland?'

Moone sighed. 'Well, that was never going to happen, was it?'

'I'm going to need a large glass of bleeding wine, then.'

Moone handed over one of the glasses he'd

poured. Their fingers touched when he gave her the glass, but she didn't show any signs of noticing. It was the first time they had made physical contact since her dad's funeral. There had been a strange sensation surrounding them that day as they drank in the social club situated a short way from where he had lived in St Budeaux. Butler had of course had too much to drink and encouraged Moone to do the same. There had been lots of hugging too, and when he was about to put her in a taxi and send her home, she had kissed his cheek. It had been a badly aimed kiss and caught him on the corner of his mouth. His heart had pounded, and she had stopped to stare at him for a moment, a look in her eyes that told him she wanted to say something.

'What?' he had asked, words bubbling up in his chest.

'Nothing.'

'Go on.'

Then she had smiled. 'Thank you, Peter Moone.'

'For what?'

She shrugged. 'Who knows?'

Then she'd climbed in the taxi and he had heard her calling out, 'Home, driver!'

The doorbell rang, breaking Moone out of his tepid pool of memories and he headed to the door of the flat. It was a white door in a flat mostly painted magnolia. It was quite small, tidy, with a nice modern kitchen. It was Butler's place. She had moved out of her ex's home, which he was somehow glad about, but didn't understand why.

'Hello,' DC Molly Chambers said and held up a bottle of Prosecco. 'Is this OK?'

'Sure,' he said and stepped out of her way. 'I was just telling everyone that this isn't a social club and that Carthew is on her way back to us. But never mind.'

Molly faced him, her cheeks reddening. 'Is she really?'

He nodded and walked past her and into the kitchen.

'Well, we need to come up with a plan,' Butler said, after a sip of her wine. 'Play her at her own game.'

'Oh, right,' Moone said. 'So we murder a bunch of people, blame it on someone else and hope that somehow that does the trick?'

Butler made a face at him. 'Then what do you suggest we do, London boy?'

'Did Taylor Swift write that song, London Boy, about you?' Pinder laughed, but Butler stared at him.

'How the hell do you know the name of a Taylor Swift song, Kev?'

Pinder grinned. 'You know, I put the radio on, songs play...'

'Who's she going to kill next?' Molly said, her face tight, no sign of amusement. They all lost their smiles.

'I mean, if she wants to be in charge,' Molly continued, 'then chances are she's going to try and murder Boulton or the new Chief Superintendent. Isn't she?'

'Chief Super Kate Hellewell,' Pinder said and nodded. 'I can't wait to see what she makes of Carthew.'

Butler huffed. 'Don't hold your breath. She'll probably be taken in too. Probably a right cakey mare.'

Moone was about to add something when his mobile phone started ringing. He sighed, knowing that there was usually an unpleasant reason his phone made any kind of noise in the evening. He took it out and saw the station was calling. 'DCI Moone. Yeah? Oh, I see. Yep, we'll be there soon.'

'Don't tell me,' Butler said. 'A case of domestic violence? A fight outside a pub? Or has that biker gang tried to knock off one of their own again?'

Moone shook his head. 'Dead woman. Looks suspicious. Come on, we're on call.'

'This is going to be weird,' Kev said, shaking his head as he sipped his beer.

'Why weird?' Butler said as she got to her feet.

Pinder shrugged. 'First murder investigation since, you know...'

'What?'

Everyone stared at him, but it was Butler who said, 'Spit it out, Kev.'

'Since Parry committed... I still can't get my head around it. He didn't seem the type.'

Butler exchanged looks with Moone as she said, 'No one seems the type. There you go. Come on, let's get going.'

Neither of them said a word for most of the journey to the crime scene which was situated somewhere in King's Tamerton. Butler drove, while Moone sipped his hurriedly home-made flask of coffee, looking out at the night sky. He turned his head when he spotted Weston Mill cemetery and looked at Butler to see her reaction. She kept her eyes on the road, but said, 'What is it, Moone?'

'Nothing.' He tasted his coffee and almost spat it back into the cup.

'Is it what Kev said?' She glanced at him.

'I suppose. I just keep thinking about what we did.'

'What we did was prevent a load of scum walking free from prison. He killed himself, end of story. It's not like we...'

'I know. Just a big secret to carry. They still haven't completely closed the file on it.'

'They will. Just keep your cockney trap shut.'

Butler pulled into King's Tamerton Road, a long stretch of houses that looped around and rejoined the main road a mile away. Most of the homes had been built after the Second World War as prefabs and should have been by rights pulled down long ago. Now with a layer of plaster on the exterior and a lick of paint, they had developed into permanent residences.

The blue lights flashing into the night told them where the murder scene was. Uniforms were on patrol outside Number 92, a prefab like the rest, but it had had an injection of cash and love and kindness. The crime scene tape was already in place, twisting a little in the slight breeze. After Butler parked up, they got out, and Moone stared over at the other homes and the neighbours who had come out to observe what had occurred. Some of the uniforms were talking to them, taking notes. Moone could see the odd mobile phone being raised in the air and he sighed.

He arrived first at the house and showed his ID to a slender, dark-haired inspector who was standing at the gate.

'Inspector Matt Elphick,' the Inspector said and pointed towards the house, its windows lit up with the strobing blues. 'The deceased is a woman in her late forties, lived alone by the looks. Found her driving licence, and it says her name was Caroline Abbott.'

Moone nodded and turned to see a couple of SOCOs setting up a white tent over the front of the house. 'Who found her?'

'Lady who lives two doors down,' Elphick said. 'She's in her seventies with heart trouble, so we've got a paramedic in with her. Might have to take her to Derriford.'

'How come she found her?' Butler asked, folding her arms over her chest. 'Bit late for popping in, isn't it?'

Inspector Elphick nodded. 'True. She said she'd texted the lady a couple of times to check if she wanted her garden doing. Apparently, they have the same guy come round and do their lawns. Anyway, she didn't get any reply. She's usually pretty sharp at replying. So she went to knock and saw the porch door was ajar. So was the front door. She found her in the kitchen. You'd better take a look, although the SOCOs have been taking plenty of footage. Listen though, she's a bit of a mess. At least her head is.'

'I see,' Moone said, nodding. 'OK, thanks for the warning. We better go in.'

Moone and Butler went over to the SOCOs and got fitted up with forensic outfits, then went in through the tent and found themselves in a carpeted, narrow hallway, stairs to the left. At the back of the house, through an archway, was the compact kitchen that looked as if it had been modernised quite recently. The ceiling and windows were lit up as a white-suited SOCO knelt and took photographs of something at the end of the kitchen, presumably the body. Butler stayed back as Moone edged down the hallway, moving himself around to get his first view of the victim.

There she was, lying on the lino kitchen floor, legs together, arms placed on her chest, almost as if she was on the morgue table already. Moone took out his notebook and wrote it down. Then he raised his eyes to her neck and saw the thin ligature that had been tied around the victim's throat, leaving a deep red mark dug into her skin. The reality of it all hit him and he tasted the vomit at the back of his throat as he raised his eyes to her face. She was almost unrecognisable as human, he thought and looked away for a moment. He took a breath, then looked back again, taking in her puffy, swollen eyes, her head that was a deep purple colour and seemed two sizes too big. Her hair was splayed out and dark with dried blood.

He turned to see Butler standing, arms folded, in the doorway.

'Here we go again.' She raised her eyebrows, then turned away. 'Another sick bastard for us to deal with.'

'Was she found like this?' Moone asked the room.

A figure in a white forensic outfit turned and looked at him, then Butler. 'Are you the detectives?'

Moone nodded to the middle-aged, goatee-wearing man who looked a little silly with his hood pulled tight around his head. Moone couldn't help but think of kids sent off to school in their new winter coats, all tucked in by their mums. But then Moone realised he looked just as silly when he caught sight of his reflection in the darkened kitchen window.

'Yes, she was like this when we got here,' the SOCO said, then bent over a silver case he had rested on the kitchen work surface. 'You'll have to find out if the person who found her moved her. Some people do, sometimes. Or cover their faces, and close their eyes. Makes our job more difficult, but I guess it helps them feel like... well, they helped.'

'I suppose.' Moone stepped around the body, getting a closer look. He crouched down and tried to get a better view of the ligature. He looked up at Butler. 'Tights.'

She stepped in. 'What?'

'Tights. He's used tights to strangle her. I wonder if they belonged to her.'

'Or the sicko brought them himself. Might've even been wearing...'

Moone shot her a look and she glared back at him.

'Did you find whatever he beat her with?' Moone asked, looking at the SOCO.

'No,' the SOCO said, raising his shoulders. 'We're still processing the scene. It's funny,' the

SOCO said as he went through some equipment in his case.

'Oh, it's hilarious,' Butler said, sarcastically.

The SOCO shook his head. 'No, I mean... sorry, I'm Martin Barker, the new crime scene manager.'

'DCI Moone, and this is the oh so subtle, DI Mandy Butler.' Moone smiled, then stopped when Butler narrowed her eyes at him. 'What's funny, Martin?'

Barker folded his arms, the sound of fabric scrapping against itself filling the air. 'Well, there's something very familiar about this. The strangulation, the position of the body. I feel like I've seen it somewhere before or read about it.'

'A previous case?' Moone asked, looking at the body again.

Barker shrugged. 'I don't know.'

Moone sighed. 'How long has she been dead?'

'You'll have to ask the doctor who was here. Dr Jenkins, I think she said she was called. She went next door to look after the woman who found her, a Mrs Margaret Jarvis.'

'OK. Any signs of forced entry?'

'None so far. Looks like she let her killer in.'

'Thanks.' Moone looked up at Butler and gestured to the door. 'Let's go see the neighbour.'

They were let into the house by a red-headed female uniform and, for a brief moment, Moone found his breath sucked out. She resembled Carthew in her younger, seemingly more vulnerable days. Except, of course, she hadn't been vulnerable at all; she had been a wolf dressed as a lamb.

She was heading back to Plymouth. His stomach tried to garrotte itself as he entered the small living area that was taken up by a large brown sofa, a big TV and an armchair that Mrs Margaret Jarvis was sitting in, sipping a cup of tea. Another female uniform was seated on the sofa, close to her.

'Hello, Mrs Jarvis,' Moone said, and the elderly lady looked up. 'I'm DCI Peter Moone, this is DI Mandy Butler.'

'Sorry, my lover,' the woman said. 'I won't remember your names. Maybe you can write them down. My phone's here somewhere.'

'It's OK, Mrs Jarvis,' Moone said and sat down next to the uniform. 'We just need to ask you about what happened this evening. I'm sorry you've had to go through this.'

The woman waved a hand. 'Oh, you wouldn't believe what I've been through. I could tell you a few stories. Listen to me rambling on. Do you want a cup of tea?'

The woman started to get up, so Moone

held up a hand. 'You stay where you are. We're fine, thank you. I need to ask you what happened today. Why did you go round there this evening?'

'Well, it's like I told the other fella. One of your lot, he was. I went in, 'cause I'd texted her and she didn't reply. She always replies pretty much straight away. I wanted to know if she wanted Gareth to mow her lawn and also, did she want to come round and plant these new flowers I'd got. Then when I didn't hear from her for ages, I thought I'd knock on the door. The door was open, so I went in. Oh, my lord, didn't I take a turn when I saw her lying there.'

'Did you touch her?' Butler asked, arms folded, leaning on the door frame.

'No, dear. I thought to myself, don't touch anything, Margaret. I watch Vera and all that stuff on the telly. I knew not to touch anything. Is that right?'

'You did great,' Moone said. 'Can you tell me anything about Mrs Abbott?'

'A little bit. I know she was married at one time. To a Mr Abbott, she kept his name. They never had kids. Don't know why. I assumed she couldn't. That was her old mum's place, but she moved in about ten years ago, I think it was. Done it all up. Nice kitchen. All the mod cons. Not like my kitchen. Needs a lick of paint. But then again, I think I need a lick of paint.'

Moone smiled. 'No, you don't. Did she have

a boyfriend?'

'No. Well, there was one fella a few months back. I saw him coming by the house a while back, but that fizzled out, she told me.'

'Has he got a name, this fella?' Butler asked.

'Can't remember, love,' Mrs Jarvis said. 'I think she said he was in the Navy or used to be. Yes, I think he used to be in the Navy.'

'Did you notice anything missing?' Moone asked.

'No, I wouldn't know if there was. Oh, I know she had a new computer or something delivered the other day. I remember her saying she wasn't sure how to set the thing up. Well, I was no use, was I? I don't know about computers and stuff. I like my telly and my word searches.'

'Me too.' He smiled. 'Can you also give us a number for this lawn guy, Gareth?'

'Oh yeah, no problem, my lover,' she said, looking round, then pointing to a mobile phone on the nearby coffee table. 'Pass my phone, would you?'

He passed it with a smile and wrote down the number when she read it out. Moone stood up when he saw Dr Jenkins poke her head around the kitchen doorway, gesturing for him to follow her. 'I'm sorry, Mrs Jarvis, I've got to go and talk to my colleague. Take care of yourself.'

Moone walked into the kitchen and found Dr Jenkins looking down at her mobile phone, tapping away at the screen. She looked up, smiled, and put her phone away. She tightened her ponytail as she stepped closer to him.

'I think she'll be all right,' Jenkins said, nodding towards the next room. 'She's a tough old bird.'

'She seems it. How long has the victim been dead?'

'I'd say about five hours. She was found around nine tonight. Obviously, I'll tell you more after the post mortem.'

'I'm guessing you won't know which killed her, the beating or the strangulation?'

She frowned. 'Sorry, not right now. Chances are, it was a bit of both. Like I said, I'll let you know later. How are you?'

'I'm good. Back in the murder business after a few months with nothing major happening. You?'

She nodded, losing her smile a little. 'I'm still in shock really. I still can't believe Dr Parry took his own life.'

Moone felt the taste of puke in the back of his throat again. 'I know. Neither can I. If you need to talk about it, I'm always around.'

She put a hand on his arm and squeezed a little. 'That would be nice. Maybe we could have coffee or something.'

He looked at the hand, his heart giving an

extra thump. 'Yeah, coffee, that would be good. I'll text you.'

She laughed. 'You'll see me at the post mortem sometime later.'

'Yeah, of course.' He felt his face burn, then his eyes jumped to the archway that led to the hall where the moody eyes of Butler were glaring at him.

'We're wanted outside if you've finished,' Butler said, her voice strained.

'Sorry,' Moone said, then followed her along the hallway and out into the front garden where Martin Barker was standing, his hood now removed, revealing messy, light brown hair.

'I remembered where I've seen this before,' the SOCO manager said.

'Good,' Moone said, noticing Butler was still giving him the evil eye. In fact, he felt it was rather sinister. 'Where?'

'Well, I Googled it, and read there were two unsolved murders just like this. Two women were found strangled with their own tights. Happened here in Plymouth.'

'When was this?' Butler asked. 'I don't remember.'

'It happened nearly twenty years ago,' Barker said, looking between them with his eyebrows raised. 'Isn't that weird?'

Moone sighed. 'Yes. Very weird. And now it's happening all over again.'

CHAPTER 2

He closed the door behind him and stood in the bare hallway of the grand old house. The house that belonged to his wife, left to her in a will. The house she never visited. He looked down at the bare wood floor and the footprints he had made in the dust. He breathed hard, almost panting, his hands still trembling with the rage that had engulfed him, followed by the pleasure that quickly followed. It had been so long since he had enjoyed such a feeling of ecstasy and pure unadulterated rage, and it felt like an old lover returning home. How had he survived all this time without it?

He had to think clearly. He told himself to concentrate, to see over the cloud of pleasure that made his vision almost blurry. Already, the anger and the desire had begun to pulse in his neck, the words going over and over in his brain, the things she had said to him before his hate had engulfed him. He could easily pick up a hammer and rush out into the street, he thought, and the beat of that inner voice started to play in his ear. He saw himself rushing to one of the houses over the road. He knew a woman lived at Number 24. She was too old, but she would do. He saw himself bringing down the hammer, again and again.

No. He told himself to behave. There would be another chance to feel the beautiful rage pounding in his brain, his chest, to feel like magnificent wings were spreading out from his back as everything in his world was coloured deep red and that part of him, that perfect monster, took over. He was a monster, he was aware of that. That much had been made clear to him when he was a young boy, and he did the things that brought him joy and others such horror and shame. Over the years he had learnt to fit in, to not act in the way he wanted, to not give in to his desires so readily. Put on a mask, he told himself and other people wouldn't seem so disturbed by his actions. Pretend to like what other people like.

He walked through the old house, turning on the lights, searching for something but not quite sure what. He kept moving, going from room to room, looking in at all the stuff he had collected over the years. The back room was filled from floor to ceiling with computer equipment from bygone years. People threw it away and he hoarded it, stacked it up in the room, with some deep sense that he could use it for something one day. Something important. Whatever that something was had remained elusive.

In the back bedroom, which he kept clean and tidy and where only a double bed sat at the centre of the space, he saw the huge poster he had sent for, the one with the solar charts and phases of the moon. He reached out his hands and pressed them onto the waxed paper, feeling the shiny smoothness under his palms. There was so much power there, within the cosmos, charging around space and time. He himself was like a black hole, a thing that had imploded and such power, fury and destruction threatened to pour out of him. He felt the destruction constantly, a pulse and beat in his brain, a soundtrack or constant voice telling him, begging him to suck everything in and crush it all to nothingness.

He stood back and lowered himself to the bed. He lay down and stared upwards, imagining all of space before him.

He heard the beep of his phone and sat up. He took it out and got his messages up and saw an unknown number had contacted him.

'Hi, I'm Sarah,' the message read and he trembled a little. 'I heard from my friend that u do odd jobs. Do u do painting and decorating?'

He stared at the message, another random person contacting him like the last. Fate, some would call it. Kismet. The universe calling out for his kind of chaos. Her name was Sarah. His head spun for a moment, his heart pounding.

'Yes, I do painting and decorating,' he replied, hardly able to type properly. 'Send me ur address and I'll come and give u a quote. I'm pretty cheap.'

He put down the phone, then searched his overalls and found a pack of cigarettes and a lighter. He put one between his lips and lit it. He took a deep lungful, then blew out the smoke, sucking it up his nose and out through his mouth again. Then he closed his eyes, feeling the burn of his rage sizzling behind his skin. He would not be able to contain it for too much longer.

Then he came to his senses and looked at the thing in his hands. He dropped the cigarette to the floor. What was he doing? He didn't smoke.

Sometimes you do. After you've finished with them.

His phone beeped again. He picked it up and read the message:

'Can you get some tomatoes on your way home?'

No kisses.

'Of course. Anything for you xx.' He waited for a reply but nothing came, so he put his phone away, stripped everything off his body, and then went completely naked to the shower on the third floor. He stood in the bath, facing the shower head as the pipes coughed and spluttered. Icy cold water sprayed into his face, followed by the burn of scalding hot. He scrubbed himself until he was red raw, then recalled the afternoon and evening, the way she had looked there, lying on the floor after he had positioned her. She had looked so perfect, just how he remembered her. He looked down and saw that his excitement had returned. He would have to be quick, after all, he had to go shopping before his family expected him home.

Moone told Butler to slow down when they approached the house in the back street in Mutley, only a hundred yards from the train station. The lights glowed orange, a nice cosy look to the place and he imagined a family getting ready for bed. Butler parked in a space, pulled on the handbrake, and killed the engine.

'Do you think they know?' Butler asked, nodding to the house in the middle of the street, wedged in between two bed-and-breakfast hotels.

'I don't know.' Moone sighed. 'Don't estate agents have to let you know if someone's been murdered in the house you're buying?'

'I doubt it. Twenty years ago, they reckon? Judy Ludlow was murdered in that house. This must be a copycat.'

Moone looked at her. 'Why must it be? It was only twenty years ago. Sounds like a long time ago, but it was only 2003.'

'Weird, isn't it? I wonder why they stopped. He kills two women by beating and strangling them, then bang, nothing more until now.'

'Maybe the killer was banged up for something else. That should be our first call. Look at local men who were locked up around that time who might have committed similar murders, burglaries, or rape.'

'Poor bloody cows.' Butler started the engine, then gave him a strange look.

'What?'

'So, going for coffee with Dr Jenkins?' she asked and huffed as she drove them away.

'To catch up.'

'Don't start discussing Parry and all that business.'

'I'm not intending to. Although if she brings it up, I can't just say nothing.'

Butler let out a deep pissed-off-sounding sigh. 'We did the right thing. We had no choice. Now we have to deal with *her*. And I mean *deal* with her. We have to find a way to get rid of her for once and for all.'

'It's not that easy though, is it? Carthew's cleverer than all of us.'

'Individually, maybe, but if we work together... We keep an eye on the cow and if she puts a foot wrong, we'll be waiting.'

Moone nodded, even though he had a

strange sense of doom rippling through him, invading his stomach and heart. It was the same feeling he'd had for the last few months since Parry had dived off the tor and they had lied about it all. The pressure of the lie was growing, filling him up, and sometimes he felt ready to explode. But if they got her, proved her guilty of some crime, and stopped her from living her sick dream of being their boss, then he had convinced himself he could live with the bad things they had done.

'Right then,' she said. 'I'll drop you home.'

'I can get a taxi.'

'You're in my car now, you wally. You still living in a caravan?'

'Yes. Mobile home. I like it.'

She made her usual unimpressed sound. 'One day I'll convince you to live in a real building with brick walls.'

Then she looked over at him, then away again, her mouth almost opening for a moment.

'What?' he asked.

'Nothing.'

'Go on. You were going to say something.'

He saw her face redden a little and he immediately felt uncomfortable.

'It was nothing really. I was just going to say that, well, my place is pretty big. I mean, it's just me…'

'Oh, right.'

'I mean, I'm not asking you to move in.' She laughed.

'No, of course not.'

'I meant, if you ever need somewhere to stay. Closer. Just for a night or something.'

'Thanks. I'll keep that in mind.'

She nodded. Then they were mostly silent on the drive out to the caravan park, a journey that seemed to last an eternity to Moone, her last words hanging in the air. When he was alone in his mobile home, he took out a bottle of beer from the fridge and put the TV on, trying to keep his mind on the murder, running everything through his brain, trying desperately to make sense of it all.

Without him realising it, his mind was back on Butler, wondering what she was really saying. His stomach started on a spin cycle like it always did these days when he tried to fathom what she was really trying to say. He drank more beer and pushed it all away and stared at the TV, trying to imagine the person who had waited twenty years to bludgeon and strangle another woman. They would have their work cut out trying to solve this one.

In the morning, Moone got the team to gather in the major incident room and nodded to them all as they came in and sat in front of him on the chairs DC Chambers had set up around the whiteboard. He opened the takeaway coffee he had grabbed on his way in and took a sip, going over what he was going to say to them all. Before he had gone to bed on a few bottles of beer, he had drafted a quick speech, basically an outline of what they knew so far, which was little.

He looked round when Butler strolled in and immediately felt his cheeks burn, recalling what she had kind of proposed last night. Somewhere during the night, he had started to pore over her words, trying to pick out the true meaning scattered among them. After a couple more beers, sleep had drifted in, saving him from any more brain ache.

She smiled at him, but it was a smile soaked in awkwardness, he noticed. He was glad to see that she felt just as ill at ease as him. Then she was coming over, a stack of murder books in her hands.

'About last night,' she said, hardly looking at him.

'Oh no, did I get drunk and dance to Taylor Swift again?' He smiled, then covered his mouth with his coffee.

'What is it with you blokes and Taylor Swift? Bunch of weirdos.'

'She's the only modern pop singer I could think of.'

She shook her head. 'Anyway, it's to do with what I said. Feel like you might've thought I was asking you to move in or something.'

He laughed. 'No, not at all. You were offering me somewhere to get my head down if I ever needed to be closer to here. I got it.'

'Good. Don't want you getting any funny ideas, Mr Moone.' She pointed at him, then started handing out the murder books to the team.

'Right,' Moone said.

When the team had stopped chatting and turned his way, he said, 'As you may have heard, yesterday there was a major incident. A murder. It's been a little while since we took on a major murder inquiry but here we are, back again.'

He turned and faced the whiteboard, where a photograph of Caroline Abbott had been stuck to the board, her name written in large red letters underneath.

'Caroline Abbott,' he said and looked them all over, feeling a little rush from being in front of them again, preparing for another difficult investigation. 'Forty-five. Previously married. Lived alone in King's Tamerton Road. That's where her body was found. She was beaten about the head, then strangled. The killer used her own tights to strangle her. Now, I'm not sure if any of you remember a case from almost twenty years ago, but this new murder bears an uncanny resemblance to that one. Twenty years ago, two women were found beaten and strangled in their homes. This happened a few months apart. Those two murders were never solved. Both women were found in their kitchens, and their bodies were arranged as if they were lying in a coffin already.'

The team started whispering among themselves, some of them staring down at the murder books and the crime scene images that looked back up at them.

'Now, we do know from a witness that she did have a boyfriend,' Moone said. 'So, the priority will be trying to track the boyfriend and the ex-husband down and eliminate them from the enquiry. Check with the neighbours, see if any of them know him, and can put a name to him. Also, there's a guy who cuts Abbott's lawn as well as the neighbour's lawn. We need to check him out too and see where he was. We'll be talking to the officers who originally investigated the murders…'

Moone was about to continue when he caught sight of Butler who had her eyebrows raised and was gesturing behind him. Moone turned round and saw the tall, lean and suited figure of DSU Boulton, who was adjusting his square spectacles as he stared at him.

'A word, DCI Moone?' Boulton said, then slipped back out of the incident room. Moone apologised and told Butler to carry on with the briefing.

'Mrs Abbott was found by her elderly neighbour,' he heard Butler say as he left the incident room and found Boulton standing at the top of the stairs, his back to the new office that had been set up over the last few days. Boulton's new office, Moone guessed as he faced his boss and said, 'Sir?'

'It's probably best that DI Butler takes over the briefing,' Boulton said and ran a hand through his thick, styled, slightly greying hair.

'Why's that, sir?'

'Well, you're a DCI, Moone. I don't know how things were run in the Met, but here a DCI has a very different role.'

'Do they?'

Boulton pointed a thumb towards the office. 'Read the name on the door.'

A little confused, Moone looked at the door and saw his name printed across it. He stared over at his boss. 'This is my office? But I usually...'

'Sit at a desk in the incident room? Those days are over, DCI Moone. Can I call you Peter?'

'Of course, sir.'

'Come in.'

Boulton held the door open, then shut it when Moone stepped in. Already his stomach was doing its usual job of tying itself in knots. He didn't like change and he knew neither would the troops, especially not Butler. He could see her face now.

'Peter,' Boulton said as he adjusted his tie and rested his backside on the desk. 'As I said, a DCI has other duties to attend to, meetings to be at and other boring stuff, I'm afraid. Your job is mostly a desk job. Do you think I get to run about with the rest of the team, knocking on doors, talking to witnesses?'

'No?'

'No. I don't. I go to budget meetings, I talk to Plymouth Council, I meet with the first responders, meet with the missing persons team.'

'Isn't the missing persons team just one person? Carol?'

Boulton held up a hand. 'My point is, you're not really in the field any more. You've got to dance the political dance.'

'I'm not much of a dancer, sir.' Moone smiled, but Boulton just stared back at him.

'Jake,' Boulton said. 'You can call me Jake when no one else is around. Do you go to the gym?'

'No. I don't really have time…'

Boulton stood up. 'You really should find the time. Really sorts your head out after a stressful day. You've got to have some kind of outlet. Feel my arms.'

Moone almost jumped back when Boulton flexed his right arm, making his shirt tighten around his bicep.

'Go on. Feel it.'

Moone hesitated, holding out his hand. He felt his tightened bicep then let go as quickly as he could.

'Rock hard,' Boulton said, nodding. Then he relaxed again, ran a hand through his hair and looked at Moone. 'Anyway, meeting in half an hour downstairs in the large conference room. We're liaising with the sexual assault team. Be there.'

Moone nodded and watched DSU Boulton about to stroll out, then turn on the spot and come back again. 'I just remembered something. DS Faith Carthew is returning tomorrow.'

'Yes, I know.'

Boulton folded his arms. 'I've heard that you two don't get along.'

'Well, it's more that she's rubbed a few people up the wrong way.' Moone saw his caravan on fire. Then he was hanging off the viaduct, staring down at the ground three hundred feet below. His stomach lurched and his heart started racing as he saw himself falling. *He didn't fall*, he told himself, tried to tell his body, but it didn't seem to want to listen. *He was alive.*

'Well, she's been cleared of any wrongdoing. She's been given a written warning and told to get on board and to take her orders from you. So, just try and play nice. Yeah?'

Moone felt his hand trembling, his middle finger wanting to rise. He nodded and smiled.

'Yes, sir.'

'Good.'

Boulton walked out and immediately started chatting to a uniform in the corridor. Moone went to shut the door of his new office but decided to leave it open as he stared round at his new surroundings. He put his face into his hands and shook his head, absorbing himself in the dark, trying to work out how exactly he was going to break all this to Butler and the rest of the team. He thought he heard something and took away his hands. He flinched and tried to catch his breath when he saw DS Carthew standing smiling in the doorway.

'Well, I never,' she said, looking round the room, shaking her head. 'How the meek have risen. How have you managed it, DCI Peter Moone?'

The beat of anger started in his chest, but he reminded himself that he was the boss.

'Come in, DS Carthew,' he said, putting a note of authority into his voice, or at least trying to. 'Sit down.'

She raised her eyebrows, then shut the door behind her and took a seat opposite his desk, smiling. He sat down, staring at her for a moment, thinking of how to continue. He thought he would start with the facts.

'You're not meant to be back until tomorrow,' he said and she nodded, losing her smile a little.

'I'm not really here, Peter,' she said, smiling again. 'Just popping in. Getting the lay of the land.'

'I'm your boss, DS Carthew,' he said, staring at her. 'You will call me sir or boss. Is that understood?'

She lost her smile and he thought he saw a tinge of the wounded lioness in her eyes. 'Yes... sir.'

'You'll be working with me, or rather under DI Butler, as it seems she'll be heading this investigation.'

Carthew raised her eyebrows. 'You won't be lead? Why not? I was hoping to be under you.'

He ignored the subtle wink she gave, and said, 'I'm a DCI and, apparently, I have other duties to attend to. Listen, I'm not going to lie. I don't want you on my team. In fact, I don't want you in this building or on the force at all.'

'I'm guessing you still think I had something to do with Armstrong's murder?' She raised her eyebrows and sighed.

'I don't think, I know.' He sat back. 'And not only his murder but the murders of Laptew and his wife. I just can't prove it.'

'That's because Laptew killed his wife then himself. It's sad, but no one really knows what's going on in someone's head. He must have been deeply troubled...'

'You also set fire to my caravan and tried to push me off Bickleigh viaduct.'

Her eyes widened, her hand pressing against her chest. 'You think I would do such terrible things? Set fire to your caravan? Push you off a viaduct?'

'Stop it.' He held up his hand. 'I don't want to hear this. I may not be able to prove you were involved in any of it, and I know I've got no choice but to let you back on my team, but I'm not going to put up with your games. You do as you're ordered or you're off the team.'

'Fine. What's the case we're working on?'

'A woman was found battered and strangled yesterday in her home. It seems to echo two murders that happened nearly twenty years ago but were never solved.'

She smiled, then leaned towards him. 'We'll definitely solve them. We make an excellent team.'

'No, we really don't.'

'But you and DI Butler do, I suppose?'

'I think we've proved that we do.'

'It won't be the same without Dr Parry helping us with his medical insights, will it?' She lost her smile and almost looked sad, he thought.

'No, it won't. I still can't believe he's gone.'

She shook her head. 'Like I said before, you just never know what's going on in someone's mind. I mean, what made him do it? Have you any idea?'

Moone stared at her. 'No, I don't. Anyway, back to the case...'

'Didn't I hear he was having family trouble?' She raised her eyebrows again.

Moone sat up, a strange sense of doom rippling up his spine, raising the hairs on the back of his neck. 'Where did you hear that?'

She shrugged. 'I'm not sure. Did he have a brother, or have I just made this up in my head?'

She was staring at him, the same old look in her eye, that knowing expression. Then she stood up, smiled and said, 'I probably just imagined the whole thing. Forget I said anything. Right, I'd better go home and get ready for my first day back tomorrow.'

'Bright and early.'

She nodded, went to open the door then looked back at him. 'Tell me, what's your secret?'

His stomach bit down on itself. 'My secret?'

'Secret to being such a good detective.'

'Just... paying attention.'

She nodded. 'Well, I definitely make sure I pay attention. That's how I learn people's secrets. See you tomorrow... boss.'

Moone watched her exit the room and then slowly disappear down the stairs. When she was gone, he put his head back in his hands.

No, he thought, she couldn't possibly know anything about what had happened with Parry that day. There was no way. It had only been him and Butler. But then he started to wonder, questioning exactly where Carthew had been that fateful day.

CHAPTER 3

'What's this fella's name again?' Butler asked as she flicked the indicator and turned into a narrow street lined with pastel-coloured terrace houses. A pub that looked like it had been done up lately sat on the corner. This was North Stonehouse, Butler had told him, an area troubled with burglaries and crimes of violence, especially on a Saturday night. These days the residents tried to keep the trouble to a minimum by making the place more attractive, filling it with bright street art and plants. It seemed to have worked for the most part, she told him, but there was always the bad minority.

'Gary King,' Moone said, looking down at his notebook. 'A former DI. He headed the first two murders. He was pushing forty at the time. Been retired quite a while.'

'Well, hopefully, he might be able to give us some clue as to who this nutter is. This is the house.' Butler pulled in and parked outside a terrace house on the right side of the street.

It had a white exterior and a black door. Unlike some of the houses, the paintwork looked like it needed updating and the front door was covered in scratch marks.

As Butler was about to climb out, he said, 'Wait, I need to talk to you.'

She looked at him strangely. 'Is this about what I said before?'

'No.' He looked ahead, staring down the street, seeing some seagulls starting to attack a bin. 'This is... listen, it doesn't look like I'll be part of this case, I mean, not doing the leg work.'

'*What*? What do you mean?'

'I mean that DSU Boulton has had a word with me and, apparently, a DCI doesn't get down in the trenches with the troops. So, I'm supposed to go to boring meetings, like the one I went to this morning.'

'Is that where you were? Jesus... so what, they're sticking you behind a desk?'

'I've even got my own office. Top of the stairs.' He looked at her and saw her look of disbelief and annoyance.

'This is rubbish. They can't do this.'

'Of course they can...'

Butler pointed at him, her eyes igniting. 'Hang on, is this her? Has she got her claws into Boulton already?'

'No, I don't think so. This is just him. He goes by the book, apparently. Listen, this is your chance to lead the team, to show them what you're capable of.'

She stared at him, no emotion for a moment. Then she pushed open the car door and climbed out. 'No, I'm not taking advantage of this...'

He climbed out and headed to the front door and pressed the doorbell. 'You're not taking advantage. This is your chance. Rise up the ranks. Piss her right off.'

'Carthew?'

He nodded as he saw the light change in the frosted glass of the door, someone coming to open up. 'Yes, Carthew.'

She seemed to be giving it some thought as she stared at him. 'OK, but only while you're out of action, and only to piss that psycho cow off. We're going to get you back where you belong.'

He gave a smile and nodded, but he felt no true sense of security in his reaction. Part of him felt a little relief too, knowing that he wouldn't be heading this one and would have less of a headache, even though he had several mind-numbingly boring meetings to attend.

The door opened and an elderly man, dressed in a white shirt and dark trousers looked out at them, his wrinkled brow furrowed. He had thinning grey hair, a hooked nose and a sharp chin. Moone recognised him from the police photograph he had seen at the station.

'Gary King?' Moone asked. 'Former DI Gary King?'

He looked between them, then straightened himself up as if he was about to stand to attention and salute. 'Once a copper, always a copper. At your service. What's with the accent, bey? Yous come all the way from the smoke?'

'No, I live here now,' Moone said. 'Can we come in and ask you a few questions about one of your old cases?'

He eyed them suspiciously but moved back to let them into the house. 'You'd better come in, then.'

Moone nodded and went in, moving down the narrow hallway, past the stairs on the right. The wallpaper was flowery, left over from the eighties. Family photos lined the wall over the stairs. He turned and went into a small living room with a high ceiling then faced Butler and King as they came in.

'Am I supposed to have done something wrong?' King asked.

'Nothing like that, Gary,' Butler said.

The old man looked at her, raising his eyebrows. 'Oh, so you're a proper Plymuff girl? Geddon, maid! Good to hear. What's this case you want to talk about?'

'The murders of Judy Ludlow and Teresa Burrows,' Butler said.

King sighed, then sat in a weathered armchair and picked up a pack of cigarettes from a coffee table. 'My last case. That one basically finished me off. So, I'm taking it some new evidence has come up?'

'Not exactly,' Moone said and sat down on an equally weathered sofa. 'There's been a murder. It seems to echo your last case. Primarily the way the bodies were laid out.'

King was about to poke a cigarette into his mouth but stopped. 'Where was this to?'

'King's Tamerton,' Butler said.

'King's Tamerton,' King repeated, nodding. 'Twenty years on? How was the body found?'

'Laid out like they were on the morgue table.' Moone stared at him, watching the old detective's brain fire up.

'We never made that part public.' He pointed his cigarette at Moone. 'Was this latest victim beaten about the head, then strangled?'

'Yes, beaten and strangled with her own tights.'

King let out a deep sigh. 'Blimey. He's back again. Why after twenty years?'

'Why did the bugger stop?' Butler asked.

'Prison?' King said. 'Or he was incapacitated for some other reason? Maybe he tried to change his ways...'

'But no one like this changes their ways, do they?' Moone asked. 'We'll look at anyone convicted of a similar crime. What about suspects?'

King sat back, rolling the cigarette between his fingers, staring off into space. 'Nothing really solid, no one who stood out. Robert Holman was the closest we came, but he had a pretty secure alibi.'

'What was his alibi?' Butler asked and sat by Moone.

'He was casing a house fifty miles away at the time,' King said. 'His car was picked up on CCTV in a street in Cornwall. Then he popped into a pub, and they remembered him being there about the time Judy Ludlow was murdered.'

'That was the first murder, wasn't it?' Butler asked.

He looked at her. 'That's right. So, he couldn't have done that one, or the other 'cause they were so similar. So we ruled him out.'

'What was his history?' Moone asked. 'Why did you look into him?'

'He'd been done for breaking and entering, general burglary, but he liked to take trophies.'

'What sort of trophies?' Butler asked.

There came a sigh from the old man. 'He liked to rifle through his victims' drawers. His victims were always single ladies, widows and the like. He took their underwear. Tights usually. From the dirty laundry if he could find any.'

'Lovely,' Butler said and huffed. 'Can't wait to meet him. Where's he to now?'

'Well, he was in prison but he's out now. I like to keep an eye on people like Holman. Anyway, apparently he's changed his ways. Got a family and everything. But people like Holman don't change their ways.'

'How old is he?' Butler asked.

'Forty-eight, I believe. He was twenty-eight when the murders happened. He went inside for a stretch not long after the murders, which would account for them stopping. But then he got a job as a handyman, then met his wife. She had a kid already. Not sure if she knows all about his past or not.'

Moone nodded. 'Chances are our killer will be in their late forties, or early fifties by now. A profile would tell us he would've been mid-twenties to somewhere in his thirties when the murders were committed.'

Butler stared at Moone. 'Why not younger? What if he was a teen back then?'

'Na, not likely,' King said, poking his cigarette between his lips. 'Your boss is right. He would've been in his mid-twenties, maybe older. Teens don't do this. Not crimes like this. Trust me, I've met all sorts.'

Butler made her old, I'm not impressed or convinced, sound in her throat, so Moone decided to change the subject.

'Where's your wife?' Moone asked.

'Passed away several years ago. Just me and my son now. But I don't see much of him. Too busy, and I think he was always a bit embarrassed to have an old man who was a copper.'

'Sorry to hear that.' Moone got up. 'Have you got an address for Holman?'

King pointed his cigarette over to a dark wood shelving unit stuffed full of books. 'Over there somewhere is my address book. It's in there, somewhere.'

Butler went over and looked through the books, which Moone could make out were mostly about true crime. She came back with a light green book that she handed to the old man.

'Cheers, my dear,' he said and thumbed the pages. 'Here we are. I knew he lived in Mannamead, but I just couldn't remember where.'

Moone got up and looked over King's shoulder, then took out his phone and took a snap of the address. 'Thank you, Mr King. We'll probably be back in touch with other questions as they raise themselves.'

'There's plenty of files to read through,' King said, pushing himself to his feet as Moone and Butler headed to the door. 'All on computer somewhere.'

'That's right,' Moone said, 'someone's putting it all together for us.'

Both of them headed back down the narrow corridor with King on their heels, still speaking, adding bits of information or commenting on the old days of the police force he knew. Moone suspected he was lonely and eager to shoot the breeze with people who understood what he had been through. He made a mental note to come back and see him, even if they had no official reason to. He imagined himself as an old man, wittering on about his old police days. Then he saw himself, sitting alone in his caravan. What if he passed away, who would even know or care? He thought of Alice and added another mental note to meet her for lunch that week.

'What he did to those poor ladies,' King started to say, then shook his head.

Moone looked at him. 'What did you make of it?'

'There was real anger in him, I always said. He must've been a really angry person. Something must've happened to him when he was young to make him like that, mustn't it?'

Moone nodded. 'More than likely. Thank you again, Mr King.'

When they were back in the car and getting ready to head to Mannamead, Moone turned to Butler and said, 'Can you imagine ending up like him?'

Butler flashed him a look. 'Is that what's

in your head now? You're a wally. You've got a family.'

'I don't see them much.'

'Whose fault is that?'

'I'm going to text Alice.'

'Good. We're dealing with a very twisted mind, aren't we? I mean, sounds like he doesn't like women much. Probably likes to knock his wife or girlfriend around.'

'We could end up arresting a lot of men.' Moone texted Alice as they drove, arranging a bite of lunch.

'True. Why beat them so much their heads are swollen, then strangle them with their tights? What's the significance of the tights?'

Moone shrugged. 'I don't know. There must be one, though.'

'Another weirdo.'

Moone suddenly saw the time. 'We better head to Derriford first. Jenkins will be finishing the post mortem.'

'I don't like going there now,' Butler said as she slowed, looking in the rearview mirror, then indicating. 'Not since...'

'Me neither.' Moone saw the old farmhouse burning, then Parry falling from the tor. He winced and shook his head. Then his heart pounded as he was reminded of what Carthew had alluded to when they had talked in his new office.

'I'm worried about Carthew,' he said.

She looked at him strangely. 'More than usual?'

'She came to my office today, for a chat.'

Butler let out a sigh, then slowed up and quickly found a parking space. She turned off the engine and faced him, her eyes burning into his. 'What has she said now?'

'She mentioned Parry's suicide. And the fact that he had a half-brother.'

Butler's eyes blazed, her mouth opening but no words coming out for a moment. 'You're bloody joking? How the hell does she… Oh, sweet Jesus, what else does she know?'

'I don't know. But what if she was following us that day?'

Butler's face turned scarlet as she slammed her fist on the steering wheel. 'That bloody bitch!'

'We don't know if she did. I mean, there was no one around, was there? Just us and him. In the middle of nowhere. I mean, she might've just found out he had a brother somehow, I don't know. She was probably gambling that I knew something and seeing what my reaction would be.'

Butler nodded, seeming to calm down. But then she looked at him. 'We can't take the chance though, in case that cow knows something. We need to find out if she does.'

'How?'

'You need to meet up with her. Privately.

Lay on the old Peter Moone charm.'

'No way.' He laughed, but he could tell Butler was determined.

'I've been thinking about what happened with Charlie Armstrong and Laptew and all the others she probably murdered...'

'What have you been thinking?'

'She must have had an accomplice. She can't have done it all on her own.'

Moone sighed, shaking his head. 'If she murdered them all. How could she? Maybe Armstrong, maybe his wife...'

'Come on, this is Carthew. She'd give the Yorkshire Ripper a run for his money. She killed them all, or she orchestrated it. But somebody helped her. I mean, she was being interviewed by us when some of the deaths occurred. She must have had help.'

'Who?'

Butler shrugged. 'I don't know. Maybe some lowlife scum she's blackmailed, an ex-con. Or even another copper, crazy like her. We need to go over everything again, sift through it all and find out who might have helped her pull it all off.'

Moone put his head back. 'What, right when we've got a serial offender to track down?'

'What do you think Carthew is?' Butler started the engine.

'Yep, she's certainly a serial offender. She

absolutely will not stop until she's our boss.'

Butler looked over at him, her eyes narrowed. 'What film is that from?'

Moone shrugged. 'Terminator.'

Butler shook her head. 'You're sad, Moone.'

'That's why you love me so much.' As soon as he said the words he felt his heart pound, the horde of moths released into his stomach.

She looked at him, her cheeks red. She huffed. 'In your dreams, Moone.'

He laughed, but his heart still hammered away. As they drove, he kept sneaking a look at her. Something had changed about her, he decided. Or was it he who had changed? What the hell was going on in his head? He shook it all away and stared towards the road.

He pulled on the handbrake of his van and looked across the quiet street. He wasn't far from Stuart Road, and Pennycomequick was only a few hundred yards away. The weather was quite warm, and his back was a little sticky and damp against the car seat. He turned and stared at the house. Number 36. He looked up and down the street, searching for any CCTV cameras. There were none. The woman had said she wanted some painting done. Sarah. Her name was Sarah. He had always liked the name Sarah. Then he recalled the girl he had a crush on at school, and immediately he felt his heart begin to race a little faster. He saw her, the young Sarah in the assembly hall, staring at him with that look of utter contempt in her eyes. She looked as if he had asked to see her knickers, and not what he had actually asked, which was for her to go to the cinema with him.

Even recalling that moment made his right hand tighten, his fist balling and trembling. He wondered where she was at that moment, and imagined she was now just an old slag with no husband and lots of ugly kids. He breathed deeply, controlling himself, reminding the darkness that had opened up inside him that the woman in the house was a different Sarah.

Probably a bitch just like her though.

He ignored the voice in his head and opened the van door and climbed out. He had his baseball cap on and a face mask already in place. He stepped up to the door and rang the bell.

Sarah was a bitch. Sarah was a tease. This Sarah must be a bitch, too.

Quiet, he said to the voice as the door opened. The woman, with light brown hair tied back, was quite attractive, probably in her late forties.

The same age that whore Sarah would be about now.

Shut up, shut up. It's not her. He smiled. 'I've come about the decorating. You messaged me.' He introduced himself, pushing his smile further, letting it light his eyes. She smiled too and opened the door wider as she said, 'Oh, yes, come in, come in. Sarah. That's me. Come in.'

She stood aside, letting him into the narrow hall, the walls painted an ugly light mint green. He saw the carpet had been pulled up.

'I'm going to get the floors sanded,' she said. 'I've only lived here about a year. Go through to the living room.'

He nodded, looking around the place, listening out for signs that anyone else was in the house. He stepped into a sizeable living room, a green corner sofa near the bay window, and a huge TV on the wall. Bare wood floors already sanded. The walls were magnolia, marked, grimy-looking.

'What colour were you thinking?' he asked, then turned and smiled.

She looked around the walls, putting a dark pink nail to her lips as she narrowed her eyes. 'I was thinking in here… sorry, do you want a coffee or tea?'

He shuddered, imagining her standing in her kitchen, the kettle in her hand, the cups before her, the light shimmering in from the garden. He felt the rumble in his chest, then the voice getting louder at the back of his skull.

The bitch is asking for it. Say yes, you want a drink, then she'll go to the kitchen.

'No, thank you,' he managed to utter. 'Do you live alone?'

That's it, find out if you might be interrupted. We don't want anyone walking in, do we?

Stop it. Stop it.

'Yes, just me. I was living in Bristol for a bit but came back here to be closer to my mum. She's not well...'

'Sorry to hear that,' he said and put on a look of sympathy.

Tell her you're glad the bitch is sick. Tell her you hope she dies.

'Sorry, I've got to go,' he said, and moved towards the doorway, sweat breaking out under his arms, along his back, his heart thudding. He had to get out before...

'Is everything all right?' she said, following him to the door.

He managed to turn, to smile apologetically as he muttered, 'Yeah, just remembered I've got another appointment. So sorry.'

He hurried up the path, past the gate, seeing his van parked not far away. Get to it, climb inside and start the engine. She's not Sarah, not that Sarah, he told himself, almost muttering it under his breath.

'Can you come back?' she called out from the doorway.

He stopped dead and then faced her. 'I'm

sorry...'

'It's just I haven't been able to get anyone to come round. It's like nobody wants the work.'

He stood there, staring at her, then forced a smile to his lips as he found himself nodding. 'Yeah, of course. I can come back tomorrow.'

She smiled, letting out a breath of relief. 'That would be great. I work from home now, so I'll be here, so just pop by.'

He nodded, then hurried back to his van, got in and pulled out his mobile to pretend to talk on it, half watching her as she retreated inside and shut the door. Then he dropped it and buried his head in his hands, trembling all over. He let out a whimper, shaking his head, then clutched his ears.

She wants you to come back. What does that tell you? She's asking for it, begging for it. Tomorrow, she'll be waiting for you, waiting to die.

He stopped whimpering and turned his eyes towards the house. He stared at the front door, picturing the woman inside. She did look a lot like Sarah, he thought and felt that first heat of rage, almost like the first dip into a hot bath. He would come back, he nodded to himself.

CHAPTER 4

It felt strange to be back in the autopsy room, staring round at the glistening white tiles, the metal instrument tables, the sinks. The scent of death and cleaning fluid burnt Moone's nostrils as always. All so familiar, but yet, he sensed everything was different. It was the guilt. The guilt of keeping the truth of what had happened to themselves, but how could they tell anyone what had really occurred? So many cases could go down the pan, and so many offenders set free. It was the right thing, Moone told himself for the millionth time, and he was almost beginning to believe it.

Butler sighed as she came in behind him, pulling on some surgical gloves.

'Well, this is wonderful,' she said as the squeak of wheels sounded from the doorway to their left, where the fridges were, where the dead rested. A technician, a middle-aged, balding guy pushed a metal table towards the centre of the room. The usual green sheet covered the body. Behind the table, came the figure of Dr Jenkins. She pulled on some purple gloves, smiling briefly at them both. Her hair was pulled tightly back, her face clear and pale.

'Caroline Abbott,' Dr Jenkins said. 'This poor woman suffered so badly at your killer's hands.'

'Injuries?'

'TBI,' Jenkins said as she stood at the head of the body. 'Traumatic brain injury. We gave her an MRI scan to allow us a better view of her injuries inside and around her skull. There were linear skull fractures as well as depressed skull fractures, this is where parts of the skull have actually sunk in.'

'Oh bloody hell,' Butler said, shaking her head. 'The sick bastard.'

'Exactly,' Jenkins said, then pulled down the sheet, revealing the misshapen head of the dead woman. 'She had contusions to the brain itself and intracerebral haematomas.'

'Did that kill her?' Moone asked, stepping closer, turning his eyes away from the woman's body.

'It's difficult to say. I'd say at some point she would have been unconscious, perhaps before the strangulation. But injuries to her brain were so severe that she could have died from those alone. I'm going to run more tests, but the strangulation could have finished the job.'

'So, basically, the bastard killed her?' Butler said with a deep sigh.

'Yes,' Jenkins said, nodding. 'He beat her and strangled her to death.'

'Any idea what he used to beat her with?' Moone asked.

'Hard to tell,' Jenkins said. 'But by some of the injuries inflicted on her skull, I'd say perhaps a claw hammer.'

'Jesus.'

'By the way, I've taken a look at the post mortem notes from the other two deaths you asked me to look at.'

'Same killer?' Moone asked, his shoulders and back muscles tightening.

'Similar. I'd say the second murder was definitely the same. A violent, aggressive attack. The first, I'm not so sure about. It's violent, I'll give you that, but not quite as wild and uncontrolled as the second. But that's my opinion. Also, I noticed something else...'

Jenkins went over to a file sitting near the sink. She took out a post mortem photograph from the file and held it up for Moone to see. It was an image of one of the dead women lying in her kitchen, laid out like the rest. Next to her was a piece of material, perhaps a dishcloth.

'What have you noticed?' Moone asked.

'The dishcloth,' Jenkins said. 'I'm wondering if she just happened to drop that, or whether the killer had placed that over her face. Maybe it got moved before the crime scene photos were taken?'

Moone looked closer. 'Is this the first murder? From twenty years ago?'

'It is.'

'But she could've easily dropped it,' Butler said. 'Doesn't mean anything.'

Moone looked back at her. 'It does if the killer placed it over her face. It means…'

'He might've known her,' Butler finished. 'I'm not daft, Moone. So he knew the first victim, kills her for whatever reason, then the sick bastard realises he likes doing what he did and wants to do it again. So he picks out some other random woman.'

Moone nodded. 'Could be. But what if the rest aren't random either? He must have found them somehow, picked them out. That's what we need to look at, the possible connection between the victims.'

'But why did he stop?' Jenkins said, dragging Moone and Butler's eyes back to her and the body. 'If he enjoys it so much?'

Moone sighed. 'There's still that question. Right, we better go and talk to the chief suspect at the time, unless there's anything else?'

Jenkins shook her head, then her eyes lit up for a moment. 'Oh, there was something I wanted to ask you, DCI Moone. In private.'

Moone looked at Butler and saw her eyes narrow before she let out a heavy breath, then left the autopsy room, banging the door behind her.

'Oh dear,' Jenkins said. 'I hope I haven't upset her.'

'She'll be fine.' He smiled. 'Eventually. Everything OK?'

'Yes, it's just we mentioned meeting for a coffee sometime.'

'Oh yeah, we did.'

'Well, what are you doing Saturday night in a couple of weeks?'

'On a Saturday? Nothing, why?'

'Well, I've been invited to this reunion thing. I went to Marjons, you see? Some of the girls and guys from my old dorm are getting together. I wondered if you'd come along?'

He looked towards the doors where Butler had just headed through. 'Saturday in a couple of weeks?'

'Don't worry if you're busy. I just didn't want to show up alone.'

He smiled. 'No, I'd love to. Shall I pick you up?'

'Yeah, I've got your number so I'll text you the address and time. Thanks.'

'No problem. Looking forward to it.' He smiled, then hurried through the doors, his head spinning a little, confused about what had just happened.

'What was that about?' Butler asked, appearing from nowhere and making him jump.

'Jesus.' He held his chest. 'Just wanted some advice.'

'On what?' She stared at him.

His mind scrambled. 'On whether to stay in Plymouth or head back to Wales.'

Butler started walking towards the exit. 'If I was her, I'd pack my bags. The way things are heading down here, she's liable to end up on that slab of hers.'

'It's not that bad.' Moone followed her. 'This is our first major murder inquiry in…'

'I know, Moone, I was joking. It's called humour.'

'Right, where's this suspect to?' Butler asked as she drove them away from Derriford, heading back in the direction of Mutley and coming to the large roundabout.

'King told us, remember? Mannamead.'

'All right, keep your knickers on, Moone,' she said, tutting. 'That's the way I'm heading. Nice area for an ex-con to live in.'

'That's what I was thinking. He must've landed on his feet.'

Butler soon took them into the heart of Mannamead, past the larger houses and their huge driveways, then went left into a quite wide road that was packed out with three-storey houses. Each one had steps up to large double front doors. She parked outside number

47, a cream-coloured house with a black front doors.

'Nice if you can afford it,' Butler said as she climbed out.

Moone followed her up the stone steps and to the front door, where he pressed the bell. He pressed it a couple of times before the muffled sound of someone calling out came from inside. Then the door opened onto a wide, tiled hallway, and an attractive blonde woman, perhaps in her early forties, looked out at them. She was dressed in a trouser suit, obviously ready to head out somewhere.

'Hello?' she said, looking between them, her dark and perfect eyebrows raised.

'Is Robert Holman here?' Moone asked and showed his ID. 'DCI Peter Moone. This DI Mandy Butler.'

The woman looked between them suspiciously as she said, 'He's upstairs. What's this to do with? He's put all that behind him.'

'We know,' Butler said. 'We just need to ask him a couple of questions. What's your name? Are you his wife?'

'Partner,' she said. 'Kelly Spears. I'll just call up.'

They stood outside, the door open, and watched as the woman tapped her high heels towards the wide staircase to the left. 'Robert! The police are here!'

'What?' the voice echoed down.

'The police. They want to talk to you.'

'Can we come in?' Moone asked. 'Feels cooler in there than out here.'

She stared at them with the same look of suspicion as Moone heard heavy footsteps somewhere upstairs.

'It's fine, come in,' a man's voice said above them, a hint of a Plymouth accent. The man came down the stairs, dressed in black jogging bottoms and a tight-fitting T-shirt. He was pushing fifty, with a thick head of greying hair and matching stubble.

'I've got to go,' the woman said to him, kissed his cheek, then headed past them and left the house.

'Robert Holman?' Moone asked and showed his ID again. 'DCI Peter Moone. DI Mandy Butler. We'd like to ask you a few questions.'

Holman nodded, let out a heavy sigh then turned to a door to his right and opened it. 'Come in and sit down, then.'

Moone looked at Butler, but she shrugged, so he followed Holman into a large living room and dining area. There were polished wood floors, a wall-mounted TV and shelves of books. Large canvases adorned the walls, mostly made up of modern art, with splashes of colours, the kind Moone never really understood.

Holman sat in a large black leather

armchair, then gestured to the sofa.

'Sit down, make yourself at home,' he said, then sat back and folded his arms over his chest. 'I take it this has got to do with my bad old days?'

Moone sat down, but Butler remained standing as usual as she got her notebook out.

'I'm afraid so,' Moone said. 'There's been a murder similar to the ones that happened twenty years ago. It's procedure to check up on any suspects.'

Holman's eyes widened a little as he sat forward.

'Hang on, this is to do with those murders? That was years ago. Anyway, I wasn't in Plymouth, I told the police back then.'

'No, you were scouting your next burglary,' Butler said and huffed.

The irritation was clear in Holman's eyes as he stared up at her. 'I know. I remember. That was a long time ago...'

'You don't break into women's houses any more and steal their underwear?' Butler raised her eyebrows.

'Butler,' Moone said.

Holman looked down, nodding. 'I'm not proud of that time in my life. I don't know what was wrong with me back then. I've been to see people about it, to try and understand...'

'We need to ask you where you were from three in the afternoon to about ten last night,'

Moone said.

Holman blew some air from his cheeks as he sat back. 'I was here. With Kelly. We went to bed about eleven, I think. I could hardly keep my eyes open, to tell the truth.'

Butler noted it down, then looked at him. 'We will be checking with your partner.'

'Good,' Holman said, clearly annoyed. 'Did you say there's been another murder?'

'Yes,' Moone said. 'But we can't really go into it. We just wanted to check with you. See if you had any information for us.'

Holman shook his head. 'I know nothing about it. Look, Kelly doesn't know about all that stuff back then. I mean, she knows I used to rob places, but not that I... you know.'

'Maybe you should come clean?' Butler said, staring at him. 'You know, about the underwear stuff.'

Holman looked down at his hands, his right leg beginning to jitter.

'We won't say anything.' Moone stood up.

'You won't?' Holman got up too, the relief clear in his eyes.

'Scout's honour.' Moone smiled. 'We won't take up any more of your time. But we might have to talk to you again, and we'll need to speak to Kelly to verify where you were last night.'

Holman managed a smile as he nodded. 'That's fine. I'll tell her to come and see you.'

Moone smiled, then started towards the doorway, his mind going over what had been said, and running through what they knew about their latest crime scene. Something occurred to him and he stopped as he was about to step into the hall and faced Holman. 'How did you used to gain entry to the homes you burgled?'

Holman looked awkward again, genuine regret seeming to fill his eyes. 'Well, there's usually a weak point in any home. People leave windows open, or there's a lock on a door that's not that secure. Some of the old locks just needed a good hard whack. You just needed to case the places. People are never as safe as they think they are.'

Butler huffed. 'You're telling us.'

Moone ignored her comment. 'But there would be some kind of indication of where you got in?'

'Yeah, where I broke a lock or jimmied a window.'

'You never knew of any burglars that could gain entry without showing signs of how they got in?'

Holman narrowed his eyes, then shrugged. 'No. I didn't really know any other burglars. We didn't have a club or anything. But no, I never heard of anyone like that. That would have to be Houdini.'

'Maybe that's who we're after.' Moone

laughed, then headed to the door.

As they arrived back at Charles Cross and watched the gate to the car park slowly opening, Butler said, 'What was the point of those questions you asked Holman?'

'Which ones?' Moone asked.

Butler drove them into the car park and found a spot close to the entrance. 'The whole how did you break in, thing.'

Moone shrugged. 'Just checking that we haven't missed anything. We're assuming these poor women let in their killer.'

'Well, there was no sign of forced entry.' Butler climbed out and started towards the station as she got out her swipe card.

Moone caught her up as he said, 'What if the previous detectives and SOCOs missed something? What if there was an entry point at the first murder scene?'

Butler swiped the door and pulled it open. 'Then we'll have to go through all the files and evidence when it arrives and double-check it all. We'll get a couple more of the civvies to help.'

'Then there's the dishcloth thing.'

Butler sighed, then turned to him. 'So, you're starting to think that this first murder was actually something else? An argument gone wrong?'

'Could be. If the killer covered her face.'

'But that would mean her boyfriend, husband, or whoever beat her almost to death, then decided to strangle her with her own tights, and lay her body out like he did.'

'Maybe she happened to be dating a nutter.' Moone shrugged.

'But if that's true, which I doubt, then how did the killer of the second woman know about the way the body was laid out?'

'I don't know.'

'But all right, let's examine the knots on the tights and the crime scene photos and see what we come up with.'

Moone nodded, then followed her up the stairwell and into the incident room. Before he had a chance to sit down, DC Chambers came hurrying over to him from her desk.

'Sorry, boss,' she said, her face a little red.

'Don't be. What have you got?'

Molly held up an evidence bag. 'The SOCOs passed this on to us. It's a receipt for a laptop Caroline Abbott purchased two weeks ago from PC World.'

Moone took it and examined the receipt. 'Where's the laptop? Has it been stolen?'

'No, it was there. Cost about a grand. Thing was, I had a word with her neighbour and she said Caroline wasn't very good with electronics. So, I'm thinking this other thing they sent over might be important.'

'What is it?' Moone felt his chest tighten

as Molly fetched another evidence bag and held it out to him. He took it and saw it was a small rectangular piece of paper with some words printed on it.

'Handyman,' Moone read out. 'No job too small. Repairs. Cleaning. Also handy with computers and the internet. There's a number listed. This isn't the lawn guy, is it?'

'No, we talked to him and he has an alibi. He was on a training course. This is someone else that she contacted.'

He looked up at Molly. 'You think she might have got this handyman in to sort her laptop out?'

'Maybe. The thing is, I tried the number and thought I could pretend to be a customer, but the number no longer works. It's a burner.'

Moone nodded, then stood up, and lifted the bag for everyone to see. 'Everyone, Molly has found our first solid lead. A leaflet was put through Caroline Abbott's door by a handyman. The number is no longer active, which tells us this could be our killer. We need to go door-to-door in the area and check if anyone else has used this person for any jobs. We also need to look at our first two victims' lives, especially the few weeks before they died and see if they had any jobs done around their house or if they found a similar leaflet. We also need to contact the former partners or boyfriends of all three victims. Have we checked out Caroline Abbott's ex-husband?'

'He's now living in Canada,' Butler said.

'OK, great. Check out the rest of their exes, the details will be in the old case files. Get on it, people.'

Moone lowered the leaflet and handed it to Molly, who was blushing. 'Good work, Molly. That's really great. Can you keep looking into Caroline's life and see if there's any connection between the victims at all? I know it's twenty years apart, but best to check.'

Molly nodded. 'Will do.'

'And when Harding comes in later, can you two go and talk to the staff at PC World and see if they remember Caroline? See if there's any CCTV from when she made the purchase. There might be something there.'

'OK,' Molly said and hurried back to her desk.

'Listen to you,' Butler said, almost smiling as she sat at her desk. 'You sounded like an actual detective.'

'Did I?'

'Almost.' Butler turned to her screen but looked back at him again and smiled.

His heart gave a sudden extra beat.

'They managed to find and unlock Caroline Abbott's phone,' Butler said.

'Really? Anything useful?'

Butler looked up. 'She had a smartphone but doesn't look like she knew how to use it very well. Facebook was set up, but there's not much there. But there are a few text messages to a man she calls Stu. Starts off all right, but about three months ago they stopped. I'm thinking it ended. I'm going to call him and arrange a little visit.'

'Good. Let's see what he has to say.'

'DCI Moone!' a voice said loudly from the doorway and Moone saw DSU Boulton standing there, arms folded.

'What have you been doing all morning?'

'Well, I've been...'

Boulton stepped closer, then looked at Butler. 'Hello, DI Butler. How's things?'

She looked at him with suspicion. 'Fine.'

'Hope you've been briefing the team, giving them their actions.'

'Of course.' She looked back at her screen.

He nodded, then looked at Moone and crooked his finger. 'Come on, DCI Moone, we've got a meeting to attend.'

'Have we, boss?' Moone dredged himself up from his desk and tried to force a smile on his face although the thought of another budget meeting made him want to yawn.

'We have. Come on.' Boulton turned and walked through the doors and out into the corridor.

'Is it in the conference room?' Moone asked as they headed down the stairwell.

Boulton stopped and looked back at him.

'It is, but it's not in this building. It's at Devonport station. I'll drive.'

'Excuse me, sir,' Butler's voice rang out, so Moone and Boulton turned and faced her. She looked between them for a moment, looking slightly bewildered.

'I need tomorrow off,' she said, seeming to decide to look at DSU Boulton.

Boulton sighed. 'But, Butler, you're leading this investigation. You're a DI...'

'Acting DI,' she said.

'No, I'm making it permanent,' Boulton said. 'The team needs a good leader and I think you've shown your worth, hasn't she, Moone?'

Moone nodded. 'You have.'

Butler's cheeks reddened a little, but she kept a straight face. 'Thanks. I appreciate that. But I still need tomorrow off. It's important.'

Boulton let out a breath, so Moone said, 'I can oversee things for tomorrow. It's no problem.'

The DSU sighed and ran a hand through his hair, then looked at Moone, then back at Butler. 'Fine. Take the day off if it's important. Come on, Moone, we've got to get to Devonport.'

Boulton turned and started down the stairs again, but Moone remained where he was, staring at Butler. Then he ran back up as he saw her shrug and turn away. When he caught her up, he said, 'Hang on.'

'What?' she said, raising her eyebrows.

'Is everything OK?'

'Yeah, of course.'

'Oh, right. Well, I hope tomorrow goes all right, whatever you're doing.'

She laughed, then sighed. 'You wally, Moone. I'm off to Bristol.'

'Bristol?'

'Yes. I'm going to do some digging round. I'm going to find out who's been helping that psycho cow, even if it kills me.'

CHAPTER 5

The former boyfriend of Caroline Abbott was called Stuart Courtier, and he was a painter and decorator. Butler had managed to find out quite a lot about him by researching him on Facebook. There weren't many photos, only blurry ones or shots taken from a distance of the man himself. There was plenty of anti-vaxxer stuff on his page, which seemed to be a growing trend with people these days. Butler decided to drag Harding along for the joyride once he arrived back at work and persuaded him to drive them both out to the estate where Courtier lived in Barne Barton.

'So, why were you late coming in today?' Butler asked as Harding drove them onto an untidy road lined by brightly coloured blocks of flats. 'Too much to drink over the weekend? By the way, it's the blue building.'

Harding indicated, then parked outside the blue block of flats. A couple strolled past arm in arm, walking a black collie. Harding seemed to stare out the window at them for a moment, his cheeks a little ruddy, a skin tone she recognised as an indication that he was worrying about something.

'You all right, Harding?' she asked, seeing him fidgeting a little. 'Your knickers giving you gyp?'

He laughed, but there was no lightness to his voice as he faced her. 'We had an appointment. Me and the missus.'

'I see.' Butler felt immediately uncomfortable, as her usual reaction to people wanting to discuss their marital lives was to sprint in the opposite direction. 'Everything all right at home?'

He sighed, then looked down. 'She's up the duff.'

Butler went to open her mouth, but her brain ran dry. She scrabbled around for something to say and found only, 'Your swimmers are working all right, then?'

Harding nodded. 'Yeah, must be.'

'Bit of a shock, eh?'

'That's putting it lightly. I'm getting too old to chase kids around. We always said we wouldn't bother, that we were happy... well, like we are.'

'Life never runs smoothly.'

'No, it doesn't. How did the party go the other night?'

'It wasn't a party, Keith. It was a serious meeting about what we're going to do about that psycho cow.'

'But you texted me and asked if I was coming to the party at your new place.'

Butler huffed. 'Yeah, well. Let's go and knock on Courtier's door and see what he's got to say for himself.'

Butler climbed out, glad to be out of the confines of the car and the weight of Harding's worries that seemed to be expanding with every passing second. She reached the entrance of the building and then watched Harding reach her as if he was giving an elephant a piggyback.

'Kids can be good for you,' Butler said and watched Harding nod slowly.

'I know.'

'They make you young again, they say.' Butler buzzed Courtier's flat. 'He said he was in today.'

'I've never changed a nappy in my life.' He looked at Butler, his eyes wide.

'You're not dismantling a nuclear bomb, Keith. It's a bleeding baby, you wally.'

'Hello, who's that?' a voice crackled from the intercom.

'Mr Courtier?' Butler asked. 'Stuart Courtier? It's the police. I called earlier.'

'Oh, right, you'd better come up,' the voice said, then the door buzzed.

'After you,' Harding said, opening the door and sweeping his arm towards the entrance.

'Such a gentleman, I don't think,' she said, then went up the cream-painted stairwell until she found Courtier's floor and headed to the penultimate red door near the end of the barren, dusty hallway. A baby was crying somewhere in the building, a TV was blaring out and a dog was barking out in the street. She pressed the doorbell as Harding joined her, moping along with his hands dug into his pockets.

'Come on, get your hands out of your pockets,' Butler said, giving him a prod. 'It's a baby, Keith, not a death sentence. I don't know, you bloody men.'

He sighed. 'I'm just not very... domesticated.'

'What's that supposed to mean?' She stared at him. 'You still piss and poop on the carpet? Jesus, Harding. Just buck your ideas up.'

The door opened and a man in his late forties, with a big square head and greying shaved hair, stared out at them. He was dressed in a Plymouth Argyle top and shorts. He opened the door wider and gestured for them to come in.

'Might as well make yourselves at home,' he said and nodded to Harding.

'Green army,' Harding said, making Courtier look down at his top and then say, 'Oh, yeah.'

'Terrible game the other night.'

'Did you go?' Courtier asked Harding as Butler went in and looked around the compact flat. She went into the living room, not sure what she was looking for. It was pretty tidy, apart from a collection of decorating equipment piled in one corner. There was a PlayStation, TV, sofa that was too large for the room and a coffee table that had an ashtray with cigarette butts piled up in it.

'Na, I can't be bothered these days,' Harding said as he followed Courtier and Butler inside. 'I haven't got any love for the game any more.'

'That's sad,' Courtier said, shaking his head. 'That's not about football. That's the state of this fucking country. You had that bloody vaccine?'

'Yeah, of course,' Harding said, which set off Courtier shaking his head as he sat down on the sofa and picked up a pack of cigarettes.

'Do you know how many people are dropping dead from that?' Courtier poked a cigarette into his mouth.

'A lot less than the ones sucking on those disgusting things,' Butler said with a huff. 'Please refrain from smoking while we're here.'

Courtier stared at her, then took the cigarette from his mouth. 'I ain't seen any ID.'

Butler took out her warrant card and held it in front of his face.

'What's this all about?' Courtier asked,

sitting back. Then he looked at Harding. 'Sit yourself down, mate. You're making me nervous.'

Harding sat at the other end of the sofa, but Butler decided to remain standing as she didn't want to stay too long. Her head was already halfway to Bristol, piling up with the questions she was ready to ask.

'Caroline Abbott,' Butler said. 'I'm afraid she's dead.'

Courtier stared at her for a moment, his eyes narrowed. 'She's dead? How? What happened?'

'Someone murdered her in her own home last night.' Butler folded her arms and watched the flicker of light going on in Courtier's eyes, the slow train of thoughts trundling along.

'Hang on,' he said, pointing his cigarette at Butler. 'What's this got to do with me? You ain't trying to make out like I had anything to do with it?'

'Where were you to last night?' Butler asked.

'The Brit,' Courtier said, looking smug.

'From when to when?'

'About six, I think, to closing. Anyway, ask Ray Schooling or Simon Jasper. They was there.'

'We will. When was the last time you saw Caroline?'

Still looking a little irritated, Courtier sat back and ran a hand over his hair. 'Don't know.

Couple of months ago, I reckon. You sure she's dead? I can't believe it.'

'I'm sorry, but we believe it's true. Although we are trying to contact her closest relatives to formally identify her.'

Courtier sat forward, fiddling with his cigarette. 'Far as I know, she didn't have any. She had a brother, but he died of cancer a few years ago, I think. Her dad died when she was quite young, and her mum died a few years back and left her that house.'

'You did pay attention, rare in a man.' Butler folded her arms.

'Yeah, well,' he said and shrugged. 'So you lot ain't got any idea who done this?'

'Not at the moment. Do you know of anyone who might've wanted to harm her?'

Courtier looked up, seeming a little surprised. 'Caroline? Harm her? No one would. She was... nice. Wouldn't hurt a fly. I can't believe it.' Then he sat back again, staring towards the floor until his eyes suddenly rose to Butler. 'You need someone to identify her, then? Make sure it's really her?'

'That's right.' Butler raised her eyebrows. 'You volunteering?'

He sighed, then looked at Harding before returning his stare to Butler. 'I suppose. Don't think there's anyone else.'

'Good. Now, why exactly did you two break up?'

He gave an empty laugh. 'What does it matter?'

'It matters right now. She's dead. Murdered.'

'Well, it was nothing to murder someone over. We disagreed on… let's say political ideologies.'

Butler huffed. 'You mean you were anti-vax, and probably anti a lot of things and she wasn't?'

'Something like that. Didn't want to hear what I had to say. Said I was always preaching. People don't want to hear the truth. They want to live in their little world made of lies.'

'Well, I don't know about that,' Butler said, 'but we'd appreciate it if you could identify her as soon as you can. In fact, we could take you now, if you like?'

Courtier blew out his cheeks, then looked at his cigarette and got to his feet. 'All right then. Let me have a smoke and I'll follow you wherever we're going.'

'Derriford Hospital,' Harding said.

Courtier nodded. 'Right. I'll have a smoke then.'

Moone had been stifling a yawn for the past half an hour as he was sitting in the conference room on the top floor of Devonport Police Station. He had his mug of coffee resting on the round table at the centre of the room which was surrounded by both uniformed and plain-clothed officers. There was an inspector giving a talk about the future of policing in Plymouth and Devon in general, a PowerPoint presentation showing on the screen behind him. Moone had lost track already, his mind drifting back to the death of Caroline Abbott and the other two women. He kept seeing flashes of the crime scene photos, their bodies laid out in an identical fashion. The cases had to be linked.

'Moone,' a voice whispered close to his ear.

He flickered out of his thoughts and turned to see DSU Boulton staring at him.

'Sorry?' Moone said.

'The Inspector asked you a question,' Boulton said, nodding to the front of the room.

Moone sat up. 'Sorry.'

'It's OK,' the Inspector said, smiling. 'I was sending myself to sleep too.'

'It's not that,' Moone said. 'It's all good stuff. No, it's just a case we've got on at the moment. A murder.'

'What case?' the Inspector asked.

'We'd better get on,' Boulton said, adjusting his tie and glaring at Moone.

'I'd like to hear about a murder investigation,' the Inspector said. 'Who's the victim?'

Moone looked around and saw all eyes were on him. He cleared his throat. 'Well, it's actually three victims. Two from twenty years ago, one last night.'

'A twenty-year gap?' the Inspector said, folding his arms. 'What makes you so sure that it's the same killer?'

'The injuries, the cause of death and the way the body was positioned. But the question is, why did he stop after the first two?'

'Maybe he didn't,' a plain-clothed officer said at the back of the room. 'What if he's been carrying on in a different city or even another country?'

'Possible, but I doubt it,' Moone said. 'More likely that he was locked up. We're going to check out people convicted of similar crimes.'

'Good start,' the Inspector said. 'Shall we break for some coffee?'

Moone nodded, glad to be having a break from more talks about new ways of policing Plymouth, and how working alongside the communities was the way forward. He didn't disagree, but his urge to be where the action was made his mind reel and the boredom set in.

'You need to let your team deal with it now,' Boulton said.

Moone nodded, then he looked towards the doorway, thinking about slipping out for a cheeky cigarette. Then his heart missed a beat. There she was. Carthew had walked past the conference room, on her way to somewhere.

'Is Carthew back today?' Moone asked

Boulton.

'No, tomorrow. Coffee?' Boulton got up and headed out of the room.

Moone followed, then stood in the corridor. He saw the back of her heading down the long corridor and towards the stairwell at the centre of the building. He looked round at the rest of the officers who had come out for a break. He wouldn't be missed for ten or fifteen minutes, he decided, so started hurrying after Carthew.

He saw her turn left and head into the stairwell, and stood back for a moment, listening to the heels of her shoes tapping all the way down. Then he followed again, half expecting Carthew to head for the car park, but instead she headed for the front entrance. She stepped out onto the front steps of the building and stopped for a moment as she took out her mobile phone. He kept back, and stood in the shadow of the foyer, watching her. After a minute or so, she was on the move again, this time heading across the road. He let her get a couple of hundred yards ahead, then started following again, watching out for signs that she knew she was being followed; he saw none as he kept behind her, observing her from a distance, and wondering where she was going. She had to be up to something, he decided, as it seemed to be her default setting. Something was telling him to keep going, to watch whatever she got up to, and he even reached for his phone in case he witnessed her commit a crime. He laughed at himself for even thinking that she would be foolish enough to do anything illegal in public.

Soon, Moone found himself being taken down a side street lined with takeaways and a couple of rough-looking pubs. Wherever Carthew was heading, he knew it wasn't going to be the most pleasant part of Plymouth. He was right, he realised, as she took another right turn and headed into an estate filled with low-rise blocks of flats that had seen better days. Young men in hoodies, some on bikes, guarded the buildings, probably getting ready to deal drugs, Moone thought. There were a few houses on the other side of the street, and old rusty cars sitting on the driveways. Another young man, dressed in a tight grey tracksuit came out of one of the buildings with a muscular dog on a lead. As Carthew passed him, the dog snarled and barked at her, but she just stared at it and went to move on.

'Oi, gorgeous!' one of the lads called out to her, but she kept on towards one of the blocks of flats further up the street.

Moone decided to walk the long way around and sneak up on her. Carthew slowed down at the second block of flats where Moone could see someone was already standing, smoking. Whoever it was, was short and slender with long, dirty yellow hair. For a moment, he couldn't tell if it was a man or a woman. It was only when he was half hidden by one of the buildings opposite, and took a snap with his phone, that he realised it was a young man in his late twenties. Carthew had stopped and seemed to be saying something as she looked around furtively at her surroundings. Moone ducked back out of sight as she swept her gaze towards his hiding place.

When he looked out again, he saw she was heading inside with the feminine-looking man. Then he looked at the photo again, which wasn't the best snap anyone had ever taken, but it would have to do. Someone at the station might be able to put a name to the face.

His phone started ringing in his hand and he answered it. 'DCI Peter Moone.'

'Moone?' Boulton's voice rang out. 'Where the bloody hell are you? We're all waiting for you.'

'Sorry, I thought I saw… a suspect in an old case.'

'Just get back here, now!'

'I'm coming.' Moone ended the call, then stared back at the building where Carthew had just headed inside. He had a sense of something, a deep-rooted feeling that Carthew was up to her neck in some plot as usual. But he would find out who the man was and, perhaps, just perhaps, he might get one step ahead of her. He turned and started walking away, keeping hidden behind the building opposite, laughing at himself and the notion that he might outwit the evil mind of Carthew. But it wasn't just him, it was all of them, the whole team he had ready to bring her down.

He opened the front door and stood there for a moment, hearing the TV talking away. It was a children's show, as usual, the saccharine rubbish that always seemed to be playing over and over, making his mind numb. He shut the door and looked up the hallway which was still half finished. One side had the old wallpaper scraped away, the other side still had the flowery paper covering it. He sighed, then stepped further along the hallway towards the kitchen.

'Oh, there you are!' his wife snapped, appearing out of the kitchen, her arms folded over her chest. 'You actually bothered to come home then?'

'Just for some late lunch,' he said and walked through to the lounge to see his daughter sitting on the sofa hugging her favourite toy, the fluffy elephant he bought her from Paignton Zoo. He stood there for a moment, watching her, the way her mouth fell open and she smiled at her favourite parts of the programme. She must have seen it a million times.

Her lying on the kitchen floor.

He shook the image away, put on a smile and walked to the sofa.

She needs to be taught a lesson.

No, no one needs to be taught anything.

'Hey, Daddy!' His daughter's eyes lit up, a big smile on her face and it reminded him of the way his wife used to smile at him, a hundred years ago.

Imagine her lying on the kitchen floor. That's where she needs to be. She's begging for it.

'Hey, sweetheart,' he said and ran his hand down the back of her long brown hair.

'You came home from work to see me!' She put her arms around him and squeezed.

'Of course I did. I had to get some time with my favourite little lady.'

She stared up at him, narrowing her eyes, wearing a look that meant she was about to tell him off. 'I'm not little any more, Daddy. I'm one of the tallest in my class.'

'Oh, yeah, of course you are.' He smiled.

'I suppose you want me to make your lunch?' His wife stood in the doorway, staring at him, her lips pursed.

It's her you want to do it to. The others are merely practice.

'No,' he said.

'No?' She stepped closer, her eyebrows

raised, the everlasting look of disappointment in her eyes. 'You don't want lunch?'

'No, I'll make my lunch.'

She let out a harsh breath, then turned and stormed off. He watched her, the tremor starting in his chest, having risen from that part of his stomach where the hate always seemed to form. Soon it was spreading through his whole body and making him tremble all over. He saw himself rushing to the kitchen, grabbing the hammer from his tool bag and raising it over her head. The look in her eyes would be worth it, the utter shock and horror at what he was going to do to her.

Do it. She deserves it.

'No.'

'What, Daddy?'

He looked down at her and ruffled her hair. 'Nothing, sweetheart. I've just got to go and talk to Mummy.'

He stood up, his legs almost failing him. He felt unsteady, the shaking spreading through him, the rage pumping out from his heart. He clenched his fists as he stepped into the kitchen and stared at her as she laid out some bread on a plate and buttered it. She looked at him briefly, then went back to making her sandwich. She stared at him again, her face changing, the look of annoyance making a return.

'What?' she asked, standing up straight,

staring at him. 'What's that look about?'

'Nothing.' He looked down, but the heat had flooded him.

'No, go on, you look like you want to say something.' She folded her arms again.

She always does that when she tells you off.

'It's nothing,' he said, then dug around in his head for something to say. 'I've got a job on.'

She let out a breath and shook her head. 'What? Mowing someone's lawn? Fixing their toilet? Anything that might bring some actual money in? I can't keep supporting us forever.'

'I know. It's a painting and decorating job.'

'Well, that's something I suppose.' She relaxed a little and went back to her sandwich-making. 'Your little angel will be back at school soon, and she'll need shoes.'

'I'll get her shoes.'

She finished the sandwich, then picked it up and went to walk past him. 'See that you do. Don't disappoint your daughter.'

He watched her walk off, then turned and looked at the sharp knife left on the work surface.

It would be so easy to take that and stick it in her.

'I can't,' he said and looked away.

If not her, then who? You know you have to release the pressure, the rage.

He took out his burner phone, his hand trembling and brought up the message from the woman called Sarah. He sent a text, telling her he could come by tomorrow to price the job.

A moment later, his phone beeped:

'That's great. I'll be here from nine in the morning.'

He put his phone away. He would paint her house, and get paid for it, and then he might not see so much disappointment in his wife's eyes.

No, you'll kill her and take her money anyway.

He nodded, knowing he couldn't fight it any more.

CHAPTER 6

After a brief telling-off from DSU Boulton, who reiterated the fact that Moone wasn't leading the search for the killer, and was only supervising, Moone headed back to Charles Cross.

When he stepped into the incident room, Butler sighed and said, 'Oh, here he is. How was the boring meeting?'

Moone looked around, making sure there wasn't anyone listening that shouldn't be. 'The meeting was boring, of course, but something occurred when I was there.'

'What?'

Moone looked past her. 'Harding, Chambers. Come over.'

They all came over to his desk and gathered around as he sat in his chair and put his phone on the table. He looked at their confused faces as he said, 'During one of the meetings, I happened to see Carthew in the building...'

'Where was this?' Harding asked.

'Devonport,' Moone said.

'What was she doing there?' Harding asked.

Butler punched his arm lightly. 'Let the man speak. It's bad enough that he's a faffer.'

'Thanks,' Moone said. 'I saw her leave the station, so I followed. She took me on a bit of a journey through the rough parts of Devonport, but she stopped at a block of flats. This bloke was waiting for her, and they talked, then she goes inside.'

'What bloke?' Butler asked, so Moone brought up the snap he'd taken.

'Couldn't have got a better photo, David Bailey?' Butler asked and sighed.

'Sorry, I was trying to hide at the time,' Moone said, enlarging the photo.

'I'm joking,' she said. 'Well, there is something familiar about him, but I don't think it'll come to me.'

'What if we run him through facial recognition?' Harding asked, looking pleased with himself.

'You wally,' Butler said. 'It's Carthew. We can't officially do anything involving her. I've got an idea though. We've got another excellent facial recognition system.'

'Have we?' Moone asked.

'Yeah, it's called Inspector Kevin Pinder. This was Devonport, right? If this bloke has done anything suspect, then Kev will know all about it. I'll give him a call.'

'Good,' Moone said and watched Butler sit at her desk and pick up her mobile.

'Courtier identified Caroline Abbott, by the way,' Butler said as she put her mobile to her ear.

'That's good.'

'What do you think she's up to now?' Harding asked, looking quite concerned. 'Carthew, I mean.'

Moone let out the air from his cheeks. 'I don't know, but I got the sense that she was definitely up to something. I mean, what was she even doing there?'

'Could be lots of reasons,' Molly said quietly, then shrugged when they all looked doubtfully at her. 'Oh, boss, we canvassed the length of King's Tamerton Road but no one else got one of those flyers we found.'

Moone sat back, a little surprised. 'No one?'

Molly shook her head. 'No one. I even tried a few houses on the next street, and no one got one there either.'

'So he targeted her specifically?' Moone stood up and went over to the whiteboard where there was now a photo of Caroline Abbott, which had been taken from her driver's licence. The first two victims were there too, staring back at him, almost pleading for him to find some rest for them. 'So, we need to find out if our first two victims received similar flyers. Have any of the old case files come through yet?'

'Some,' Harding said. 'They're coming from a police warehouse somewhere in Cornwall. They've sent quite a lot of the data files over, but so far nothing about a flyer.'

'We need to talk to the lead detective, King, again,' Moone said. 'See if we can jog his memory. None of the neighbours saw anyone enter her home that day?'

'No one so far,' Molly said. 'I was about to take Harding with me to PC World.'

Moone nodded. 'Yep, get their CCTV from that day. Go now.'

Moone sat down again, staring at the whiteboard, thinking through it all, half aware of Molly and Harding getting ready to leave. Then Butler was getting off her mobile and coming over to his desk. She stood there, her face not giving much away as usual, arms folded.

'He's going to pop in as soon as he can,' she said.

'Good.' Moone pointed to the whiteboard. 'Who does this? Who waits twenty years to do it again?'

'What if he hasn't waited? What if he's been doing it all over the country?'

Before Molly was about to go through the incident room door, she turned and said,

'I haven't found anything similar to this anywhere else in the country. Beatings and strangulation, but not with tights and not with the body placed how he positioned it.'

'Thanks, Molly,' Moone said, and she smiled, then walked out with Harding in tow. He looked up at Butler. 'He waited twenty years.'

'He was probably banged up for something else. A weirdo doesn't just stop being a weirdo.'

'True.' Moone stood up and let an awful thought enter his mind. 'What if this is it?'

'What do you mean?'

He looked at her. 'He kills two, then nothing for nearly twenty years. Then this one, and nothing again.'

Butler shrugged. 'Then no more women die, at least for twenty years.'

Moone sighed. 'But, if we want to catch him, we need more to go on.'

'We need him to strike again, you mean? Oh, the twisted irony.'

Moone put his face in his hands, enclosing his eyes in the deep pink darkness for a moment. Then he looked again at the victims. 'We need to find the boyfriend or partner of Judy Ludlow.'

'She had a fella,' Butler said. 'But he was nearly forty-two at the time. Can you see a man who'll soon be collecting his pension coming out of his murderous retirement to do this?'

'We need to talk to him anyway. Arrange for him to come in.'

'Yes, boss,' she said sarcastically.

'Anyone else we need to talk to who might know something about the first two murders? Any potential witnesses?'

Butler trudged over to her desk and started looking through her notes. 'There was a neighbour, a young lad who raised the alarm about the second victim, Teresa Burrows.'

'How young?'

'He was seventeen at the time. Apparently, Burrows' other neighbour couldn't get any answer at the door, so went to one of the doors down the street and the young lad was coming out of his house, so he went with her, and then they called the police.'

'I see. What's his name?'

Butler looked down at her notes again. 'Jon Michael Reagan, he gave his name as back then.'

'Do we know where he is now?'

'I'm trying to track him down. I'm trying to find him on Facebook. There's quite a few with that name around these parts, but I'm whittling them down.'

Moone was about to speak when he saw a dark-haired female uniform standing at the incident room doors.

'Did you want something?' Moone asked

as he went over to her.

'Sorry, sir,' she said, 'there's a Gary King here to see you. He said he's a former detective.'

'Where is he?'

'I've got him in the little waiting room next to the custody suite.'

Moone smiled. 'Thanks. I'll go down and talk to him.'

Former detective Gary King was rolling a cigarette on the small table he was sitting at, then tapping the end on the back of his hand as Moone came in.

'We meet again. Should I call you Mr King?' Moone said as he put out his hand.

King stood up briefly as he shook Moone's hand, then sat down again with a shake of his head. 'Na, just Gary will do.'

Moone leaned against a poster on the wall that warned about online fraud. 'So, Gary, what can I do for you?'

'Well, I remembered that we had this psychologist fella working with us when we were looking into those two murders. He was working at Plymouth University at the time. He had a lot of insight into the bastard we was after.'

'What was his name?' Moone took out his notebook and pen.

King scratched at the silver stubble that covered his jaw. 'Oh God. What was his name?

It was twenty years ago. I think it was Scott something… it must be in our old files somewhere. You should be able to look him up. He seemed to be very perceptive…'

Moone nodded, unable to stop himself from mentioning the obvious. 'But you weren't able to find him.'

King looked up from his cigarette, a flicker of annoyance and a little embarrassment in his eyes. 'Well, we didn't have a lot to go on. That's the thing, isn't it? To catch someone like this, someone who targets strangers, it takes you a few kills before you get a good grasp of them. Of course, you don't want that on your conscience…'

Moone pulled out a chair and sat down. 'You were convinced he was a stranger, then?'

King sat back, tapping the cigarette again. 'Yeah, we looked at the usual suspects. The boyfriends, the exes. Nothing. They had solid alibis.'

'What about the dishcloth?'

King's eyes narrowed. 'The what?'

'We took a look at the crime scene photos from the first murder. The photos show the deceased, Judy Ludlow, lying in her kitchen, placed how the killer left her. There was a dishcloth lying beside her, almost as if it could've fallen off her face.'

Gary shook his head, then gave a deep gravelly laugh. 'I know the photo you're referring to, bey. We questioned that too. We asked ourselves whether it could've been someone who knew her, and that they couldn't face looking at her, or as some kind of mark of regret... but no, it just happened to fall there. That's all.'

Moone sat back. 'Judy Ludlow had a boyfriend...'

'Yeah, and we looked into him. He was at work at the time. Worked in a pub. People vouched for him. Listen, are you sure these were done by the same killer?'

'The scenes are the same.'

'Yeah, but what if this bastard's been inside all this time? What if he's told some other nutter about what he did and they've decided to finish what he started? Or what if it's just a coincidence? Stranger things have happened.'

Moone nodded and let out a breath. 'Well, they're still unsolved cases. It's worth looking into them. Oh, I just remembered, you never had a suspect who was a handyman or anything? You didn't find a flyer posted through the door of either victim?'

'I don't remember anything like that.' King poked his cigarette between his lips and the sight of it made Moone's body itch. 'I think you're onto a loser, son. I'm telling yer, those two murders became an obsession with me. I went on to look into other cases, but none of them affected me like that one did. Two women, two poor women beaten like that and strangled. The mess he made of their faces.'

'I know.'

King took his cigarette from his mouth and pointed it at Moone. 'Don't you let it take over your brain too. This nutter decided to kill two women, then got locked up for some other crime, and he's probably still there now. I hope he is anyway.'

Moone sighed. 'Or he's out and he's looking to finish what he started.'

'You're barking up the wrong tree, I tell yer. This case cost me my marriage and my relationship with my son.'

'I'm sorry to hear that. Where is he now?'

The old man let out a deep sigh. 'Don't know. He wasn't very impressed with me the last time I saw him. I thought he might go into the police himself one day, he was pretty smart. I used to run ideas by him and he was pretty perceptive. But he wasn't interested. But there you go. He's got his life to live, I've got mine, what's left of it.'

'I'm sure you've got plenty of it left.'

King stood up and put the cigarette between his lips. 'Well, it is what it is, just don't end up like me.'

Moone smiled but thought of his empty box of a home in which he rattled around, and then pictured his estranged family. 'I'll try not to. Listen, I've got to get back to work. Let me know if you think of anything else.'

King stood up and poked the cigarette back between his lips again. 'I will. It's been sort of nice stepping back into it again. Like old times. Although, some of it isn't worth remembering, or you don't want to remember. It's funny, but it's all starting to come back now.'

Moone smiled. 'Well, don't let it affect you. Let us worry about it. I'll see you soon.'

After he got out of the small room, with a strange sense of loneliness hanging on his shoulders, Moone hurried back up the stairwell, checking his phone for a reply from Alice. The hope of meeting up with her had suddenly grown in urgency since his chat with the lonely old former detective. That wouldn't be him, he told himself, as he saw he had a message from Alice saying she could meet him for lunch tomorrow in their usual haunt, which meant the Gorge cafe on Royal Parade. He smiled to himself, only faintly hearing the sound of boots coming towards him.

'What did you want to talk to me about?' a voice said above him, and Moone almost dropped his phone as he jumped a little.

'Bloody hell, Kev,' he said, pressing a hand to his chest. 'You scared the shit out of me.'

'Sorry.' Inspector Pinder smiled. 'What was so urgent?'

Moone nodded to one of the corridors off the stairwell. He found an empty office, then stepped in and closed the door after Pinder had come in, looking suspicious.

'What's happened?' Pinder asked.

Moone took out his phone and brought up the photo of the mysterious long-haired man who Carthew had met up with. Pinder looked at him with deep curiosity stamped into his face before he leaned in to stare at the photo on his phone. Then he gave a dry laugh as he looked at Moone. 'Lloyd Redrobe? What's he done now?'

'I followed Carthew today and she met up with him, then went into his flat.'

Pinder nodded. 'Interesting. Lloyd Redrobe spends most of his time performing as Lola Rouge, a drag act. He does Madonna, Kylie Minogue and Taylor Swift tribute performances, and that kind of stuff, but he's also a nasty little bastard. Very violent.'

'What's he get up to these days?'

'You name it. Possession. GBH. Extortion. I even think he's got ties with the Tomahawks.'

'The Tomahawks? Who are they when they're at home?'

'They're a very dangerous, drug-dealing motorcycle gang. It's funny but Redrobe rides around on a little red scooter. God knows what the Tomahawks make of that. You know something else, Lloyd always seems to have a good solicitor waiting in the wings. He told me he had a wealthy sugar daddy once when I asked him how he paid for his legal defence. I've always assumed it's his drug dealing friends who pay for his expensive solicitors, but now I'm starting to wonder.'

Moone looked at the photo again. 'I'm starting to get suspicious, and putting two and two together and probably getting five, but he does look pretty feminine, doesn't he?'

'You should see him all dolled up when he's performing. What're you thinking?'

'Armstrong's murder. The so-called woman visiting his room that night.'

'They've put that down as DC Banerjee, haven't they?'

'They have, officially, but we know that's not right, don't we? No, there's something going on here. We need to talk to him somehow.'

Pinder huffed out a laugh. 'You're joking, aren't you? He won't talk to us about that if he was involved. He's not about to inform on Carthew, either.'

'Then what do we do?'

Kevin Pinder looked off, staring towards the window. 'Let me think about it. I'll come up with something.'

'Thanks, Kev. I better get back up there.'

'Hang on. How's Butler?'

Moone looked at him strangely. 'You

know, you saw her last night.'

'I know, but you know, she's a closed book. After her dad dying and everything…'

'She's OK. Same old Butler. She's off to Bristol tomorrow to dig into Armstrong's murder. We think there was someone else helping her.'

'Bloody hell. She better be careful, then. If Carthew gets wind of it and finds out we're onto her, then she'll kick up a stink.'

Moone nodded. 'I know. Get back to me on this Lloyd Redrobe as soon as you can.'

'I will. The thing is, like I say, if Carthew has some kind of involvement with Lloyd, then it can't be something good. I think we need to tread very carefully.'

'We will, and perhaps this time we can catch her in the act.'

His wife didn't like it, but he told her he had to go out again to price a job. She gave him that cold hard stare again, that look of disappointment, but he promised he would come straight back. She had said nothing more and turned away to continue cooking Bolognese for tea, so he took that as an 'OK, but you'd better be back very soon' and went out the back way. He stopped at the shed and looked back, making sure she wasn't watching him. Her back was still turned, so he unlocked the padlock on the shed, then stood in the warm light that came in, swirling and dancing with dust. Cobwebs covered the far corners. His wife didn't like being anywhere there could be spiders, which was just as well, he thought and reached for his tool bag. He was about to turn away, when he caught sight of the club hammer on the wall, right beside the two-inch bolster and his smaller hacksaw. He reached out, grabbed it and weighed it in his hand before he thumped it against his palm. He put it in the tool bag, then left and locked the shed.

He opened the back gates of the small yard where he kept his van parked, then got behind the wheel and started it up.

The drive out to Pennycomequick went by in a flash and he found himself parked up the road again, staring towards her house.

Sarah's house.

Not that Sarah, it's another Sarah.

They're all the same, all bitches, just with different faces.

She looked like her though, he thought, and she was the right age. Every time he had looked at her, he felt it, the tingle of desire that slowly gave way to the almost explosive fury that beat in his chest, making him tremble with the force of his anger.

Maybe it is her. Wouldn't it be wonderful if you could tell her and show her how much she hurt you?

He nodded, grabbed his tool bag and

climbed out. With every step, he felt as if he was growing, getting taller, expanding as he was filled up with hatred, the uncontrollable thud of his pulse. He saw her, so young and pretty, standing in the playground. Her words came back to him, her singsong voice ringing in his skull.

His hand was trembling so much he had trouble ringing the bell. He looked around the street, but no one was looking. The evening was soaking up the buildings, laying a thick and dark charcoal blanket of shadow over everything. On the second ring, he heard heels coming towards the door, that hard tapping sound echoing inside the house. She opened the door and his heart pounded at the sight of her. She now wore make-up, not a great deal, just a light covering. Her lips were a deep pink. Her hair was down, straightened and the scent of some fruity shampoo found his nostrils.

It's her, it's definitely her.

'Oh, hello,' she said, her brow furrowed with confusion. 'I didn't expect you until tomorrow.'

He smiled as brightly as he could. It was the smile his wife had said she had fallen for, the pleasant facade that fooled almost everyone into believing that beneath his flesh and bone beat the heart of an ordinary and good man. He was a good man. He was a kind father, and he tried to be a good husband.

You're bad inside, rotten to the core. She made you that way, you know she did and now is your chance to right that wrong.

'Sorry, but I was passing this way,' he said, turning up the smile a little. 'I just priced another job. Repairing a shed. I thought I'd come and have a quick look and give you a ballpark figure.'

She looked beyond him for a moment, then looked at her smartphone that she was holding in her hand. He noticed her nails were quite long and painted a light pink. Then she smiled, opening the door for him. 'OK, as long as you're quick.'

He looked down at the tool bag, his breath quickening a little, his hands trembling as he stepped into the hallway. The scent of her home seemed to race towards him, filling his chest with the distant rage, a storm a few miles away yet.

He saw her in the playground, staring at him, then her cruel face breaking into a grin, and eventually the echoing laugh. He could see her friends all joining in, calling him names.

She deserved to be punished back then, and she deserves it now.

'I was thinking just plain white in the hallway,' she said, looking round at the walls. 'Just to brighten it up a bit. It gets a bit dark otherwise. I'm thinking of putting in a larger window over the front door.'

'It's a lot of prep work,' he said, his voice just a harsh whisper.

'I'm sorry?' She stared at him.

'I said it's a lot of prep work.' He put down his tool bag.

'I know,' she said and turned towards the archway that led to the kitchen. 'I've been meaning to get started on it, but what with work, I haven't had the time.'

While her back was turned, he crouched down and reached inside the tool bag. His palm slipped around the handle of the club hammer, the coolness of it tingling against his skin. He stood up and hid it behind his leg.

'Can I see your kitchen?' he asked, and she looked at him, her eyebrows raised.

'I've had my kitchen revamped lately,' she said, smiling. 'It's through here.'

He followed her in, watching her move towards the window, the light streaming in. He stepped closer, gripping the handle of the hammer tighter.

This is it. It's time she was punished.

He flinched when the doorbell rang out. She looked over his shoulder, her eyes narrowing.

'I wonder who that is,' she said, moving around him. 'Unless it's Shena come round here first. She's meant to meet me at the pub.'

He turned as she moved past, hiding the hammer behind his back as she headed for the front door. He watched as she opened it, then listened to the sudden burst of laughter and chatter. He crouched down again, his heart pounding, the storm moving slowly away again. He put the hammer back into the tool bag and stood up quickly.

'I said I'd meet you there, you silly cow,' Sarah said, coming back from the door, followed by a slimmer, taller, and dark-skinned young woman. 'I'd better get going,' he said and picked up his tool bag, noticing the friend staring at him.

'This is the decorator,' Sarah said and looked at him. 'Sorry, I've forgotten your name.'

He hesitated. 'Dave.'

'Dave,' she said and looked at her friend.

'Nice to meet you, Dave,' Shena said, trying to hold back a laugh.

Even she's laughing at you now.

'Sorry, I had a couple of glasses of Sauvignon Blanc before I came here,' the friend said, coughing back her laugh.

'Maybe tomorrow would be better?' Sarah said to him, smiling.

He nodded, smiled and started towards the door, his hands still trembling as he carried the tool bag out into the darkening evening. He reached his van, climbed in and took out his keys. His hand trembled as he tried to push the key into the ignition.

Bitch. Bitch. I bet her friend's no better than

her.

He turned towards the house and saw the friend standing there, watching him, smiling. He looked away and managed to start the engine. He would come back tomorrow when the friend was gone, and he would make sure she was punished.

CHAPTER 7

Having had nothing better to do, Butler had decided to head to Bristol late the night before when the traffic would be quieter. She had managed to find a last-minute booking in a local Bed and Breakfast and had gone straight to sleep once she arrived. She was up and out of the Bed and Breakfast place before the day had truly got going. It was an old-looking pub just outside Bristol, but the room was nice, clean, and looked newly decorated. She had only booked one night, unsure whether she would stay longer. She headed for her car that was parked around the back of the place in a small private car park and drove towards the city centre and then towards Bishopsworth Police Station where she knew DI Crowne was based. As she drove, she remembered how much she had felt sorry for him when Moone had told her that Crowne had got it in the neck over the whole Armstrong murder case. In the eyes of the top brass, the whole affair had been a total fuck up, but Butler knew all too well that Carthew had orchestrated it that way. The bitch had it coming.

She pulled up at the station and buzzed the gate to the car park, then drove in when it opened up. As she was climbing out of her car, she heard Crowne's voice calling out to her. She looked round with a smile as she saw the detective, looking decidedly more dishevelled than the last time she had laid eyes on him. He was also taking out a cigarette and putting it between his lips as he reached her.

'If it isn't the South West's answer to Columbo,' she said, smiling.

'You look… different,' he said, looking her up and down. 'I hardly recognised you for a moment.'

She huffed. 'Lost a few pounds. That's what grief does to you.'

'Yeah, sorry about that.' He lit his cigarette and looked around him. 'So, what are you doing here, DS Butler? If this is to do with what I think it is, then it's over.'

'It's not over.' She sighed. 'We've got to work with her. She comes back today.'

He nodded and let out some smoke from his mouth as he lifted his cigarette. 'I was trying to give these up and was doing pretty well until she came along.'

'Yeah, she'll do that to you. So, you going to buy me a bad-tasting coffee or what?'

He smiled, then gestured to the station

as he dropped and stamped out his cigarette. 'After you, madam.'

They entered the station, stopping at the reception area where she signed in, then headed to the custody suite before climbing up the stairs at the far end of the building. As they climbed up, Crowne looked at her and said, 'What are you hoping to get from this visit exactly, Butler?'

'Some answers,' she said, breathing hard as they arrived at the top floor. She stopped and faced him, her eyes scanning the floor for prying ears. 'What she did, she couldn't have possibly done it on her own.'

Crowne let out a tired sigh. 'If she did anything at all. I mean, Banerjee had means and motive. They found the wig... she has a history of instability...'

Butler shook her head and let out a harsh breath. 'Who're you trying to convince? You've talked to her, right? Sat across from her in an interview room and witnessed that bloody smug look of hers? Yeah? Is that the face of someone who isn't taunting you, telling you she can do what she wants without anyone touching her for it?'

'I don't know any more. If she did it, she managed to off DSU Armstrong, Mrs Armstrong and her lover, and your Chief Super and his wife. I mean, who does that? And why? What did she gain by killing the Chief Super?'

Butler nodded, a bad feeling filling up her chest, and not wanting to admit that she hadn't a clue. 'She has her reasons. They were pretty cosy at one point, and there were rumours he'd had a few workplace flirtations... so maybe it was to do with that. I don't know.'

Crowne pointed at her. 'See, that's the thing, isn't it? Too many I don't knows. We have no idea why she does these things.'

'That's because her mind doesn't work like ours. She does things just for the attention and to see if she can get away with it. Trust me, that's how she works. We just need to figure out who the third person is.'

Crowne stared at her, his brow creasing up. 'Step into my office. Actually, it's not my office, but it'll do.'

Butler saw that he was gesturing to a small meeting room across from the stairwell, so went in and sat down on one of the chairs positioned around a large egg-shaped table. Crowne shut the door.

'What third person?' he asked.

'To do what she did, Carthew needed help. We think we might've found one person who helped her. There's this local scrote that she's been to visit.' Butler took out her phone and brought up the same blurry image Moone had taken and sent to her. She pushed her phone across the desk and watched Crowne stare at the image.

'Who is he?'

'Lloyd Redrobe,' she said. 'When he's not assaulting or robbing people, he's putting on dresses and performing as Taylor Swift and the like.'

Crowne stared at the photo again. 'He does look quite feminine, doesn't he? Are you thinking that he could be the woman on the CCTV, the one heading to Armstrong's room?'

Butler nodded and sat back. 'I think Lloyd was the one who killed him. Maybe Carthew went to his room earlier and incapacitated him somehow, then Redrobe comes along that night and kills him.'

'But they pinned it on Banerjee.' Crowne nodded. 'What about the deaths of Kate Armstrong and PC Wise? How was that miracle performed?'

Butler leaned forward. 'This is the tricky part. There were no signs of forced entry were there?'

'None.'

'So, what if they let in their killer?'

'Why would they? Unless they knew them?'

'Or...' Butler raised her eyebrows.

'Or what?' Crowne stared at her for a moment, but she waited for the penny to drop.

He shook his head. 'No, you're not thinking someone pretended to be a police officer and knocked on their door.'

'Maybe they didn't pretend. Whoever helped her, would need to know what we were thinking, and would be able to feed back insider knowledge to Carthew. I mean, she was a suspect, so she needed eyes and ears as well as practical help.'

Crowne shook his head again. 'You've been giving this a lot of thought.'

She stared at him. 'It's all I've thought about for the last few months.'

'Who though? Let's pretend you might be right. Who's this other police officer?'

Butler shrugged. 'I don't know. I was hoping you might have an idea.'

His eyes widened. 'What? You think one of my lot? No way. Not a chance. She's your problem, your crazy co-worker, not ours.'

'She managed to get Banerjee to do some of her dirty work, maybe she got into someone else's head too.'

Crowne gave an empty laugh, staring at her with disbelief and a subtle annoyance in his eyes. 'No. I'm telling you, you're barking up the wrong tree. She might have had this... Lloyd person wrapped around her finger, but not any of us. No way.'

'Fine. Well, someone helped her.'

'Look, I just want to forget all this and move on. It's already nearly wrecked my career, thank you very much. I keep getting pushed aside now when it comes to leading a team.

Even my detective sergeant is doing better than me. Although she does deserve it.'

'Who's that?'

'Rivers. She's now a DI.' Crowne stood up with an old man's grunt and stretched. 'She's doing well. Good luck to her. She's thinking of moving on to pastures new, and I don't blame her.'

'Is she?' Butler's mind started to rumble into gear, a strange feeling rising up her back. 'What does her boyfriend or husband think of that?'

'She's not that way inclined, if you know what I mean? Anyway, I've got to get back to work.' Crowne leaned over the table and pointed at her. 'You go back to Plymouth and tell Moone that this is over. She's your problem now. Leave us lot out of it. I still want to collect my pension one day.'

Butler stood up. 'OK, I'll head back up and pass on your lovely words. I'm sure he'll appreciate it.'

Crowne looked at her with a little regret then. 'Look, I appreciate all you lot did, and if there's anything I can do to help you all out, then don't hesitate to call or text, but as long as it doesn't involve Carthew.'

Butler laughed and nodded. 'I get it. Right, I'll leave you to it.'

She gave the detective one last look, smiled, and then headed out the way she had come. Already her mind had ignited and was travelling in all kinds of directions, but mainly towards DI Rivers. She could see Crowne would never have even questioned Rivers' loyalty, but she knew how Carthew worked and how charming she could be. It might have even been the case that she had something on Rivers, some blackmail material; but it was equally possible that Rivers was a rotten apple just like Carthew, and was just as good at pretending to be straight down the line when needs be. But Butler might also be wrong, there was that possibility too. As she headed back to her car and got in, she had that uncomfortable feeling in her stomach and the little voice whispering in her ear. She was onto something, she could sense it.

She sat in her car for a moment, staring at the station, thinking over her options, knowing it was all going to get dodgy if she pursued her line of enquiry. It would be safer to walk away, to not keep digging.

She huffed out a breath and took out her mobile. She sat for a moment, trying to remember the name of a pub, and then called it when the name came back to her. She talked to the landlord, who put her in touch with another dodgy character who might know what she wanted to know. Eventually, her mobile was answered by a thick Plymouth accent, and followed by a hacking cough.

'Paddy Fogg?' she said, smiling a little, knowing the confusion that would fill up his small brain.

'Who's this? How'd you get this number, lover?'

'It's DI Mandy Butler. Don't worry about how I got this number.'

'Fuck me. I ain't done what you're working on. I'm telling ya…'

'Shut up, Paddy. I ain't after you. Well, I'm not looking to arrest you or anything. I need your help.'

'Fuck off.'

'I've got a job for you. I need you to drop everything and meet me as soon as you can…'

'Where are you to?'

'Bristol.'

'Bristol? Fuck off.'

'I'll make it worth your while.'

There was a pause on the other end. 'Cash, you mean?'

'Yeah, plenty of cash.'

Another pause. 'Is this a set-up? 'Cause if it is…'

'It's not. You have my word. I just need your help. I need your particular skills. So, I'm going to send you an address and I want you to meet me there. All right?'

There was a longer pause. 'Fuck me. All right. You'll have to hang on a while, you knows what the bloody traffic's like down there.'

'Just hurry up.' She hung up, her heart pounding as she thought about what she was about to do. But she knew it was the only way to get ahead of Carthew in the game. It was time to play dirty.

Moone stood in the doorway of the incident room for a moment, blowing on his Americano that he'd bought on the way. Normally he would have something for Butler, but of course she was absent. Instead, he had bought a regular coffee for DC Molly Chambers. He didn't know if she drank coffee at all. He knew she liked a glass of prosecco, something he had gleaned from their parties that had evolved from their meetings.

He sat down and stared at the door, thinking about what Butler might have been up to, and whether she would actually succeed in finding out who might have aided and abetted Carthew in her murders. Butler was in his thoughts a lot these days, he realised, which was becoming problematic for him, as he didn't understand why she was on his mind so much. It's not like he had feelings for her. Did he? He pushed it all to the side with a heavy sigh, telling himself not to be so ridiculous.

'Hey, boss,' Molly said brightly as she stepped into the incident room.

'Morning, Chambers,' he said and stood up and held out the coffee he had bought. 'I got you a coffee.'

She looked a little taken aback for a moment, then hesitantly reached out and took it. 'Thanks. You didn't have to. But thank you.'

'It's my pleasure.' He smiled and sat down again.

Molly took the coffee to her desk as she started taking off her jacket and setting herself up for the day. 'My boyfriend doesn't even make me coffee in the morning.'

'I didn't even know you had a boyfriend,' he said and saw her face redden a little.

'Yeah. Been only a few months. He's a plumber. That's how we met, actually.'

'Handy. Having a plumber boyfriend.'

She nodded. 'Yeah. Sorry, did you want to hear about our visit to PC World?'

'Of course. Did you find out anything?'

Molly picked up her coffee and opened it up and blew on it. 'Not a lot, apart from that she told the sales guy that she was pretty much useless when it came to computers. She did tell the guy that she had someone who could help her set it up at home.'

'Someone?'

Molly nodded. 'Yeah. She didn't say who. We checked CCTV in the store and around the car park, but no one seemed to be following her.'

Moone nodded and sighed. 'So, we're back to our mysterious handyman. Has anyone been going through ANPR or CCTV footage?'

'Some of the civvies, but there aren't a lot of cameras in King's Tamerton. There is a camera at the tip on Weston Mill, but there are so many vehicles going back and forth. Plus, he could have taken a back route to her house.'

'Well, if he's a handyman, then he might have some kind of van. Go through the footage and try and identify the vans and their drivers. Focus on that afternoon at first.'

'OK, will do.' She smiled, then lost it as she looked around the room. 'Has DS Butler headed to Bristol?'

Moone gave a cursory look around too. 'She has, but keep it to yourself. We don't want...'

'You don't want what?'

Moone jumped a little when he recognised the voice and turned to see DS Carthew staring at him, a smile on her face.

'Nothing,' he said. 'Take a seat, DS Carthew. We've got plenty of actions to get through.'

Carthew nodded, losing her smile, and sat at a desk close to Molly. 'How's the investigation going? Any suspects yet?'

'It's early days,' Moone said and looked at the murder book on his desk, pretending to thumb through it, anything but to have to look at her.

'Well, how many hours has it been?'

Carthew asked, and he sensed her eyes on him. 'The new Chief Super will be breathing down your neck soon enough.'

He stared up at her and saw what he expected, the subtle smile of victory on her lips and in her cruel eyes. 'That's not your concern, Detective Sergeant. Just get on with what you've been assigned, please. You'll find them next to the whiteboard.'

Carthew stood up and went over to the whiteboard, but her eyes returned to him. 'I take it all the ex-boyfriends and husbands have been interviewed?'

Moone sighed. 'We're in the process of interviewing them. We're trying to locate some of them.'

'Like Judy Ludlow's secret boyfriend?' Carthew said, raising her eyebrows.

Moone sat back. 'Ludlow didn't have a boyfriend, or so the original files say.'

Carthew smiled. 'That's what the files say, but I know different.'

'How?'

'I'm a Cornish girl, but quite a lot of my family live in Plymouth. I chatted to my aunt, who lives near where Ludlow lived. She knew all the gossip.'

'Like what?'

Carthew folded her arms. 'Like the fella Ludlow was seeing was a married man. Hence why he never came forward back then when they were appealing for witnesses.'

'Didn't your aunt ever tell the police what she knew?' Moone stood up, feeling a slight irritation caused by Carthew being a few steps ahead once again.

'No one asked her,' Carthew said with a shrug. 'Sorry, but she can be a bit funny like that. I did tell her off.'

Moone nodded, watching her, observing the smug grin, and filling him full of a deep sense of unease. 'I bet you did. We'll need to talk to him. Does he have a name?'

'Of course. Nick Dann. At least that's who she thought it was. I believe he's still married, so might have to be a bit... delicate.'

'Nick Dann?' Chambers said, piping up.

Moone looked at her. 'Yes, have you heard of him?'

'Well, yeah, he's quite a big name in Plymouth. Local boy becomes successful businessman and all that. He part owns the Plymouth Raiders.'

Moone sighed, realising he was going to find himself in yet another complicated situation. He stood up and rubbed his neck. 'Then we'd better go and try and have a private word with him.'

Carthew nodded and went to grab her coat.

'Chambers, not you,' Moone said and watched the thunder rumble over Carthew's face as she turned and glared at him.

'I told you about him,' she said, the venom hardly hidden in her voice.

'I know. Thanks. But I've got other duties for you. Look at the action list.'

She kept glaring, not bothering to hide her contempt. 'Fine.'

Moone looked at Molly. 'Come on, let's go and find Nick Dann.'

The door of the incident room opened and a male uniform with short spiky blond hair poked his head in. 'Sorry, sir, but there's a young man here who says you're expecting him.'

'OK, what's his name?' Moone asked stepping towards the uniform.

'Jon Michael Reagan.'

Moone sighed. 'OK, we'd better talk to him first and see what he has to say. Molly, try and get hold of Nick Dann and arrange a private word with him. Carthew, come with me to interview Mr Reagan.'

As Moone headed to the door, he saw the smile of victory in Carthew's eyes. He only wanted to placate her for a moment, but he had underestimated the pleasure she would take from the minuscule olive branch he had offered. He only hoped Butler would turn up something and hopefully pretty soon.

CHAPTER 8

Butler spotted the old banged-up dark green Astra coming down the road as she sipped the takeaway tea she had grabbed before she nestled herself a couple of hundred yards from Rivers' building. Her flat was on the third floor, Butler had found out on the quiet, thanks to a friend who worked in the Intelligence department. The green Astra, which had a fed-up-looking Paddy Fogg at the wheel, slowed down and pulled in behind her. She watched the driver in the rearview mirror, noticing how much older and withered the man looked than he did the last time she'd seen him. The former housebreaker kept his nose clean these days. She had kept a careful eye on him over the years, knowing he now worked in the Tesco Express in town. The sixty-year-old climbed out of his car and slipped in beside her with an old man's heavy grunt.

'Who've you got the evil eye on now, Mand?' he asked, looking round the street as he rubbed his stubble-covered chin.

'Never you mind,' she said and turned to him. 'How's your house-breaking skills?'

He looked at her, his eyebrows rising, his mouth opening in shock. 'What? What the bloody hell is this? You know I'm straight now.'

'I know, but like I said on the phone, I need your skills.'

He looked at her strangely, then over towards the building across the street. 'You've got to be kidding. You expect me to break into one of those houses? Jesus bloody...'

'I know. Dodgy as you like, and I wouldn't normally be going about it like this, but this isn't a normal situation.'

He stared at her. 'Na, it can't be. Mandy Butler bending the rules? Jesus, never thought I'd see the day. Whose house is it? They must be real scum.'

'It's a flat, but yes, they are. Best you don't know the details. But you'd be helping me put away some real lowlifes, Paddy.'

Paddy shook his head and looked towards the building again. 'I'll need a look at the front door.'

She nodded. 'Got your equipment with you, then?'

He looked at her. 'Course. Let's hope they haven't got any newfangled locks. What about a dog? They got a dog?'

'No, don't worry, I don't think they've got

a dog.' Mandy laughed.

'I'm not worried if they've got a dog, Mand. If they have it's all the better. People with dogs think they're safer than people without dogs, so they drop their guard. And if the pooch barks, it doesn't make much difference, 'cause the neighbours are used to hearing them bark. Don't take much to win them over either.'

'Tell that to the posties.'

Paddy laughed, then climbed out and headed to the boot of his car. Butler watched him give the street the once over as he opened the boot, then took out some overalls that had the word Telecom written on them. He then grabbed a tool bag and closed the boot again. Mandy climbed out and cut him off.

'You really have come prepared,' she said, looking him over. 'Do you have all that gear in your car all the time?'

He looked at his equipment and his outfit. 'You can never be too careful, Mand. You never know when one of your mates might lock themselves out.'

She made an unimpressed sound in her throat then turned and pointed to the building. 'The middle building. Third floor. Number eight. How're you going to get inside?'

He looked at her as if she had gone mad. 'I'm going to buzz the other flats and tell them I've come to fix the internet. People love it when you've got to fix something.'

She shook her head and watched him head across the street, taking his sweet time about it. He was a faffer, just like Moone. She found herself smiling, thinking about the cockney wally. She caught herself and pushed him out of her head as she climbed back in her car and stared at the ageing burglar as he seemed to be buzzing the other flats. She found her hands clenching shut, her heart starting to pound a little, praying that none of the residents got suspicious. She breathed out when she saw Paddy opening the front door and slip inside.

Moone went into the interview room first and saw the man, who seemed to be in his late thirties, sitting at the desk staring at them as they came in. He was average height, with short dark hair brushed forward, and large watchful eyes behind square-rimmed glasses. He smiled at them with uncertainty. Moone sat down as Carthew did the same and folded her arms and kept her poker face on. An uneasiness sat heavy on top of his stomach as he watched her profile. She had killed, had murdered in cold blood and here he was bringing her in on an interview like nothing had happened. But if he didn't, if he showed any kind of prejudice against her, then she would just make a fuss to someone up the chain. Also, her suspicions could become aroused, and she might start to question what they were up to behind the scenes.

Moone turned back to Jon Michael Reagan. 'Thanks for coming in, Mr Reagan. We just have a few questions to ask you about an incident that happened twenty years ago.'

Reagan frowned as he pushed his glasses back up his nose. 'Twenty years ago? I don't know what you mean…'

'I don't want to bring back any bad memories, but…'

'The day you found Teresa Burrows dead in her kitchen,' Carthew said, coldly.

Moone turned to her, to give her a telling off with his eyes but she didn't look at him.

Reagan let out a ragged breath and sat back, staring at the desk for a moment before he nodded a little. 'I remember. I don't think I'll ever forget that day as long as I live.'

'You were only seventeen,' Moone said, putting a kind note in his voice. 'It must have hit you hard.'

Reagan looked up at him. 'It did. I've done my best to forget about it, but it always seems to come back around. It's like it's waiting for me, just around the corner.'

'I'm sorry we have to bring it up again.' Moone looked down at the file in front of him, the crime scene photographs placed inside. He decided to keep them away from his eyes. 'You were living in Ernesettle, in the same road as Miss Burrows, is that right?'

Reagan nodded, looking down again, a far away and troubled look in his eyes. 'I was living with my Auntie Carol. She's no longer with us...'

'I'm sorry,' Moone said.

'Someone knocked on your door,' Carthew said, leaning forward. 'One of your neighbours.'

Reagan looked up. 'Yeah, I can't remember who.'

'Mrs Harris,' Carthew said, still staring at Reagan. 'She went round to see the victim. There was no answer, but she knew she was in, she said, because her car was there. She always went out in her car, apparently. Then she ended up knocking on your door. Why your door?'

'My auntie had a key to her house, in case of an emergency.' Reagan looked down. 'I wish she hadn't. I really wish she hadn't. I wished she had called the police.'

'This key your aunt had,' Carthew said, staring at Reagan. 'You were aware she had it?'

'No, I didn't know anything about it, not until the lady knocked on the door.'

'Then what happened?' Moone asked. 'After you let yourself in?'

Reagan took another harsh breath, looking downwards again. 'I opened the door a little way. I didn't want to intrude. I called out, I think I remember. Yeah, I called out, asking if anyone was home, but obviously no one answered. Then I went in, and I looked around.

I went in the kitchen...'

Reagan shook his head and took another deep breath as he looked off towards the wall. 'I'll never get that image out of my head.'

'You didn't touch the body?' Moone asked. 'Didn't move her at all?'

Reagan looked a little surprised. 'No. I only stood there. I mean, maybe I should have done something, but I could see she wasn't breathing. And her... the way she looked... her head, I mean...'

'She could have been still alive,' Carthew said.

Moone turned to her, the anger rippling over him. 'That's enough of that, DS Carthew. Perhaps you could leave us for a moment.'

Carthew stared back at him, the glint of fury in her eyes before she stood up abruptly and left the room.

'I'm sorry, Mr Reagan,' Moone said. 'She can get a bit overzealous.'

'It's fine.'

Moone smiled. 'I hate to make you go through all this again, but I really need you to think about that evening. Can you recall seeing anyone hanging around her house or did you see anyone leaving her house?'

'It's a long time ago, and everything apart from what I saw when I went in... and, well, you know... I just can't remember.'

'I get it. I totally understand.' Moone

slipped a photo of the first victim, Judy Ludlow, out of the file and put it in front of Reagan. 'Do you recognise this lady?'

Reagan looked at the photograph briefly, then up at Moone with a confused look on his face. 'I don't recognise her. Who is she?'

'Judy Ludlow,' Moone said. 'She was murdered a couple of months before Teresa Burrows. You don't know her?'

Reagan shrugged. 'I don't know. I don't think so.'

Moone nodded and took back the photograph and replaced it with an image of their latest victim, Caroline Abbott. 'What about this lady? Caroline Abbott.'

He looked down at the photograph for a moment, then shook his head. 'No. Sorry, I don't think I know her. Who is she? Has she been...'

'I can't say too much at this point. We will want to know your movements on Thursday, the 31st of August.'

Reagan stared across at Moone. 'You want to know where I was? Because you think I had something to do with this?'

Moone raised a hand. 'It's merely procedure. I have to check everyone off on my list, I'm afraid. Do you remember where you were that afternoon?'

'What day was it?'

'Thursday, the 31st of August.'

Reagan squinted, looking past Moone. 'In the afternoon I would have been working. I work from home.'

'I wish I could do that. Who do you work for?' Moone smiled.

'I work for myself. I design websites and do a bit of graphic design.'

'I see.' Moone noted it all down. 'Can anyone verify where you were?'

The man sat back, looking up at the ceiling for a moment. 'I'm trying to think. I've had a few meetings with some potential clients over the last few days, trying to drum up some more business. I'll have to check, but I'm sure I was probably in a meeting most of that afternoon.'

'Well, if you can check and let us know.'

Reagan nodded, but Moone could see he looked a little concerned as he sat forward. 'Do you think this... person who did that to that woman all those years ago is doing it again?'

'I can't discuss the case, I'm afraid. Please just let us know where you were. And if there's anything else you can think of that might help us, let us know. Right, you're free to go.'

The man stood up, nodding a little and then started towards the door. Then he turned to Moone again. 'You know, there was somebody I saw outside her house a few times. He looked like he might be about to go in. I don't know if it's relevant.'

Moone opened his notebook. 'Who were

they?'

Reagan shrugged. 'I don't know who they were, but it was a man. He wore a suit. Quite tall, I think.'

'Skin colour, hair?'

'They were white. I think… yeah, I think dark hair. Maybe a beard? A goatee beard, maybe?'

Moone noted it down. 'Did this person turn up in a car?'

'Yeah, actually he did. I think it was something flashy. Can't remember what sort of car. I'm not very good with cars.'

'Anything else?'

Reagan shook his head. 'Sorry, that's all I can remember. I only remember him because he looked… you know, important or something. He kind of stood out.'

'Well, thanks very much.'

DS Butler walked across the quiet street and towards Maxine Rivers' building, her eyes jumping to the houses on the other side of the street. The occasional car came down the road, but no one seemed to pay her much attention. She walked around the back of the building and into the small private car park, then up to the back door of the building. She looked at the time on her phone. Rivers would be at work and wouldn't be home before the evening, which meant Butler had plenty of time to snoop around.

Paddy opened the back door and let her in. Butler shook her head when she saw he had a baseball cap pulled down over his face. She slipped past him and headed up the stairs and into Rivers' flat. When Paddy had joined her, she shut the front door and stared round at the quite small place. There was a double bedroom, a box room, a bathroom and a living room. Everything was neat and tidy, all in its place, so she started snapping photos of everything with her mobile phone.

'You didn't tell me this place belongs to a copper,' Paddy whispered as he took a framed photograph off the mantelpiece and held it out for her to see. Butler glanced at the photo of Rivers in uniform at some kind of ceremony and shrugged.

'Don't worry, Paddy,' she said and started examining the books on a set of shelves near the dining area. 'This won't come back on you. You were never here.'

'Jesus Christ, Mand, I bloody well hope not. What is this all about?' Paddy came over and watched her as she opened drawers in a sideboard.

'I told you. Someone's been up to no good and I'm checking them out.' She straightened herself and stared at the old burglar. 'If you want to go, just go.'

He stood there for a moment looking at

her, narrowing his eyes and shaking his head. 'Bloody hurry up and find what you're after.'

Butler sighed. 'That's the bleeding thing, Paddy, I don't know what I'm after. I don't even know if she's the person I think she is.'

'You're not even sure?' Paddy paced the room, rubbing his hands over his stubble.

'Where would you hide something you didn't want anyone to find?'

Paddy shrugged, looked around the room, and then turned his eyes towards the hallway. 'The bathroom's always a safe bet. I've found plenty hidden under baths.'

'Come on then, let's have a look.' Butler headed out of the living room and along to the small bathroom where she stood staring at the bath. Paddy joined her and looked over her shoulder.

'How're we going to get the panel off without her realising what we've done?' Butler asked. 'By the way, Paddy, you stink of fags.'

'Thanks, subtle as always, Mand.' Paddy went and fetched his tool bag and placed it by the bath. He looked back at her and managed to form a thin smile. 'These things take skill.'

'Well, hurry up about it.' She folded her arms across her chest and let out a deep breath.

Paddy rolled his eyes, then went to work, taking some tools out and carefully removing the panel in front of the bath. He sat back after a moment and allowed Butler to see the dark and grungy underside of the bath.

'Looks like there's something back there,' Paddy said and went to reach in.

'Stop!' she snapped. 'Keep your filthy hands off it.'

'Charming.' Paddy stood up with a loud grunt and got out of her way as she took some photos of the underside of the bath and the polythene bag stuffed at the back. Then she pulled some gloves on, crouched down and reached in and grabbed the bag.

She smiled to herself when she pulled out the bag that seemed to have a cheap-looking mobile inside and a few SIM cards.

'Someone's been up to no good,' Paddy said as he watched her slipping the mobile from out of the bag and carefully turning it on.

'Of course they have, you fool, that's why we're here. Looks like there's some charge left.' Butler examined the phone that had only a small percentage of battery power left. First of all, she looked in the contacts and saw there was only one number programmed in. Next, she looked at the texts.

'Jesus…' Butler said, staring down at the messages that she started scrolling through.

'What is it?' Paddy tried to take a look, but she stepped away from him.

'Messages from the person who lives here to a person who I really hope is the person I think it is. The problem is, there's no names being used. Just dates and times and arrangements. Hang on, there's photos on here.'

'What of?' Paddy tried to look again, but Butler glared at him before looking at the photos. She let out a harsh breath. For a moment, she found it hard to gather her thoughts, her mind spiralling, shocked at what she had found. There on the phone, were images of a battered and stabbed DSU Charlie Armstrong.

CHAPTER 9

As soon as he arrived back at his house, he knew he had to go out again. He managed to slip out of the house mid-morning, telling his wife he had another job to price up. He could tell from her dark expression that she didn't believe him. She seemed to be growing suspicious of what he was doing, and the thought that terrified him the most was that she might find out the truth about him and what he liked to do. If she knew, she might tell his daughter and he just couldn't face that.

There is one way you could stop her from telling anyone the truth.

No, don't say things like that. I could never do that to her.

But you might have to if she ever finds out.

She'll never find out the truth, I won't let that happen.

He headed to his van and then drove all the way to the allotments at the top of Peverell Park Road. He unlocked the gate, then slipped in and nodded to the other gardeners. None of them ever made much conversation with him and now he was glad of it. It was safer being a loner. He passed the hen house of chickens that quietly clucked away, then went to the small shed the previous owner had constructed on the far side of the allotments before he died. It was close to the iron gates that cut the area off from the rest of the park. He went in, stepping into the gloom and turned on the light. The bulb flickered on, bathing the room in a bright glow. The dead man's tools lined the walls, each of them clean and gleaming, looking proud. Nothing was out of place. In the corner was the small electronic safe he had purchased online. He crouched down and punched in the code. The door clicked open, revealing the wallet of photos sitting on the top shelf, and the pay-as-you-go mobile beneath it. He took out the wallet of photos and looked at them as he backed up to the camping chair and sat down. He trembled as he took out the photos and put them on the small garden table. He spread them out and stared at them, the fire in his chest, the beat of his blood pounding around his skull. He moved the images delicately, slipping the newer photos behind so he could see the two older sets. He sighed when he saw the two shapes lying on their kitchen floor. The older photos were grainy, taken by an old mobile he'd had back then. It made him sad that the beauty of that first triumphant moment had been captured in such an amateurish fashion. Nonetheless, he had something to remind him of that exquisite moment. It was at that moment when he first saw her lying there, battered and so peaceful, that he realised his true calling. All the anger and frustration he had felt through the years, seemed to rise up and talk to him, to whisper in his ear that this was what he was made for.

You must do it again soon, must be filled with the same feeling of power.

He balled his fists and then opened his hands again, feeling the tremor of his excitement that seemed to push the rage away, or at least muffle it for a while. He remembered what had happened when he made his visit to Sarah's house, how he had got so close to feeling the power flood him once again. The anger of disappointment bubbled in his chest, while his stomach churned. But she would expect him back again, and he knew where she lived in case she didn't.

No, not like that. She has to invite you in. You know the rules.

His eyes jumped over to the phone still sitting in the safe as it beeped out at him. He was frozen for a moment, praying it was from her, beckoning him back. He pushed himself up and stared at the lit-up phone, barely able to bring himself to look at it, fearing it would only bring disappointment.

It's her. She wants you to come back and finish what you started. The bitch, the slag wants you back.

It might not be. It could be a misdialled number. It has happened before.

It's her, and this is your chance to make her pay all over again.

He hesitated, still staring at the phone, almost fearful that it was her, calling him back to her to finish what he had started. He cleared his throat, ignored the palpitations of his heart and stood up. His legs felt weak as he stepped towards the safe and grabbed hold of the mobile and pulled it out. His hand was trembling as he brought up the message that had arrived.

It was from her.

Of course it's from her, what did you expect? The bitch wants to die, wants you to punish her.

'Hi, it's Sarah,' the message read. 'Sorry about the other day. I was hoping u could come and finish pricing the job. Perhaps tomorrow?'

He stared at the words, his mind spinning, the far off beat of fury somewhere in the distance, getting louder by the second. He got ready to reply, but he couldn't stop his hand from shaking.

Pull yourself together and text the bitch back and arrange for the day she's going to die!

He took a breath and calmed himself a little, feeling the twitch of excitement in his gut.

'Yes, I can make tomorrow morning,' he texted back. '9 a.m. OK?'

'Ten would be better,' the reply came. 'See u then xx.'

He let out a ragged breath when his eyes jumped to the kisses at the end of the message and he almost stumbled backwards. What was happening?

I told you, she wants this to happen, wants you to punish her.

'See you then.' He didn't put any kisses, even though something told him it would be permitted to do so. He put the phone down on the table and stared at it, confounded by what had just occurred. It must be true, he thought and clasped his face. She wanted this to happen, she was welcoming her punishment.

'He's pretty influential, isn't he?' Chambers asked as she drove them over to the industrial estate close to Lee Mill. They had headed along Embankment Road, then towards Marsh Mills and onto the A38.

'Sorry?' Moone looked up blankly from his phone, wondering why he hadn't got an update from Butler yet.

'Nick Dann,' Chambers said and flicked the indicator when she saw the turning for Lee Mill. 'He's a well-respected businessman in Plymouth. Raises a lot of money for charity.'

Moone nodded and put away his phone. Butler was probably busy investigating or rubbing someone up the wrong way. He just hoped she had come up with something useful. 'Apparently, he does, but we can't let that get in the way of our investigation.'

'No, of course not.' She blushed. 'I mean, I can just imagine him knowing one of the top brass.'

Moone sighed and looked up to see Chambers was turning into a large section of the business park. In the distance were huge, newly built warehouses with several trucks parked in front of the buildings. Warehouse staff were busy loading up the trucks from pallets filled with boxed goods of some kind. Chambers parked the car close to an office near the warehouse.

Moone climbed out and watched all the staff working hard, laughing and chatting as they delivered pallets of goods to the lorries. Then he turned his attention to the two-storey office building and saw more bodies moving around inside.

'Let's go and start some trouble,' Moone said as DC Chambers climbed out and joined him.

Moone stepped through a pair of sliding doors and found himself facing a crescent moon-shaped desk that had a dark-haired, attractive young woman sitting behind it. Her thick, obviously inflated lips were stuck in a pout as she looked up at them both with her thick, dark eyebrows raised.

'Welcome to Dann Deliveries International,' she said in a voice that Moone could tell was trying to hide her Plymouth accent.

Moone took out his ID and held it out towards the young woman. 'We're from the police. I'm DCI Peter Moone and this is DC Molly Chambers. Is Nick Dann here?'

'Oh right,' she said, tapping her long red nails on the desk and looking towards the stairs on her left. 'Well, he might be in. I'd better check.'

Moone watched her get up in a hurry and tap her high-heeled sandals to the stairs and up to a door she disappeared through.

'She looked a bit worried,' Chambers said.

'We have that effect sometimes. I just hope he comes down and talks to us.'

As soon as Moone stopped talking, the door at the top of the staircase opened and a tall, dark-haired man stood there dressed in a blue suit that was stretched against his muscular frame. When Moone had looked him up, it said he was in his early fifties, but Dann looked at least ten years younger. Moone hated him already.

The young woman stood whispering up at the much taller man before he waved away whatever she was saying and stepped down towards them. He held a large hand out to Moone.

'Nick Dann,' the man said, smiling. 'What brings you fine, hard-working officers down here? All my trucks and financial affairs are in order...'

'It's in connection with a murder,' Moone said and saw the seemingly genuine look of surprise cross Nick Dann's face.

'Someone's been murdered?' Dann asked, narrowing his eyes at Moone. 'Who?'

'Maybe we should do this in your office?' Moone pointed behind him.

The businessman looked back towards his office, then gestured for Chambers and Moone to go up. As he was going up, Moone looked back to see Dann saying something in his PA's ear before his hand slipped down the young woman's body and patted her rear. She smiled, nodded, and went back to her desk.

When they were both standing inside the open-plan office, facing his desk and the huge floor-to-ceiling windows, Dann stood in front of them, arms folded.

'So who's been murdered?' Dann asked, looking between them.

Moone brought out his phone and showed him athe photo of their latest victim, Caroline Abbott. The businessman stared at the image for a few seconds before he shrugged.

'I don't think I know her,' he said. 'Who is she?'

'Her name is Caroline Abbott,' Chambers said.

'No, I don't know her,' Dann said. 'I don't get what this has to do with me.'

'We're getting to that,' Moone said and brought up the photo of Judy Ludlow and held it out for Dann to look at. He observed the businessman's face as he glanced at the photo momentarily before looking up and shaking his head. Moone had seen it, or at least he thought he had, that minute flicker of recognition.

'I don't know her either,' Dann said, adjusting his tie and turning and walking to his desk and sitting down.

'Are you sure?' Moone asked.

There seemed to be a little annoyance in Dann's voice as he said, 'Of course I am. What the hell is this about? I've got a business to run.'

'We appreciate that.' Moone nodded, taking his time. 'The woman in that photo was called Judy Ludlow.'

'Is that name familiar to you?' Chambers asked, her voice a little shaky.

Nick Dann looked away from them as he shook his head. 'I don't think so. Should it be?'

'You've never met her?' Moone asked.

'I don't think so.' Dann sat up. 'Listen, I know this is what you do, ask questions like this, but I'm sorry, I've got things to do, clients to call.'

'You never had an affair with Judy Ludlow?' Moone asked. 'We were told you did. Twenty years ago. Not long before she was murdered.'

Moone saw the change in him, the little pretence of being hospitable starting to crumble away as he stood up again. 'Who told you that rubbish?'

'It's not true, then?'

'Of course it's not. But I'd like to know who's been telling lies about me.'

'We can't discuss that,' Molly said, seeming to find more of her voice.

Dann stared at her, then back at Moone. 'Well, then I'd better inform you that I know a lot of influential people. Solicitors, judges, police officers. Higher ranking police officers than you two.'

'We're just here to carry out an investigation.' Moone knew he wouldn't get anything else from the businessman, but he thought he'd give it just one more shot and brought up the image of their second victim, Teresa Burrows. He held up the image of her as he stepped towards Nick Dann. 'What about this woman? Have you ever met her?'

Dann looked away. 'I'm not looking at that. Now, I think it's time you left.'

'Her name is Teresa Burrows.' Moone

watched his face. He thought he saw something, perhaps a slight twitch at the sound of the name but he couldn't be sure.

'I think you'd better leave.' Dann pointed to the door. 'I'll be having words with my police friends about this.'

Moone made to leave, signalling for Chambers to start heading out too, but then he stopped and faced the businessman. 'Be sure to tell them what a sterling job I did, won't you?'

'Oh, I'll tell them all about you.' Nick Dann's teeth seemed to grind as he stared at Moone. 'You're going to be in a lot of trouble.'

Moone turned and walked out, following a quite flustered-looking DC Chambers who hurried on before him and climbed in the car. Moone joined her and let out a heavy sigh.

'Can he get us into trouble?' Molly asked, starting the engine.

Moone looked at her. 'Don't worry, Molly, it's me who'll get into trouble, not you.'

She nodded, but the worry was still clear in her eyes as she drove them away from the industrial park and headed for the A38. 'Do you think he really knew our first victim?'

Moone nodded. 'I think so. He got very jumpy when she was mentioned. And I thought I saw something in his eyes when I mentioned Judy Ludlow. What do you think?'

'He did get pretty upset.'

'Yes, he did. I think he knows something.

What if he was seeing Judy Ludlow and they had an argument or something? He's a married man and was twenty years ago. Maybe Judy was threatening to say something to his wife or something...'

'So he kills her?' Molly nodded. 'Takes off her tights to make it look like she was killed by some deranged killer.'

'But he can't bear seeing her staring up at him, so he puts the dishcloth over her face.'

'Why did he kill Teresa Burrows, then?'

Moone thought for a moment. 'I don't know. Maybe he wanted to stretch out the crazy killer scenario, or he realised he enjoyed the act itself. He wanted to do it again.' Moone shook his head and let out a harsh breath. 'But why wait all these years to do it again? Shit.'

'Maybe he committed the first murder, but not the second or our latest one.' Chambers signalled and started heading onto the A38, the cars tearing past.

'It's possible.'

'It won't be long before it's lunchtime, but I don't think I'm very hungry now.'

'Shit.' Moone took out his phone and stared at it.

'What's wrong, boss?'

'I'm going to be late for lunch with Alice.'

Molly looked at him, full of concern. 'Where are you meeting her?'

'The Gorge Cafe in town. I don't think we'll

make it.'

Molly put her foot down, the engine roaring. 'We'll make it.'

The car stopped on the opposite side of the road to the Gorge Cafe on Royal Parade. Moone's heart was still thumping, his feet still pressed hard to the floor as if to apply the brake. Molly smiled at him, seeming not to notice his pale face and flustered appearance.

'We're here, just in time,' she said.

'Thanks,' he said. 'I won't be too long.'

Moone pulled himself out of the car and resisted the urge to get on his knees and kiss the pavement. He turned and poked his head back in the car. 'Check up on Nick Dann. See if there's any other connection between him and the other victims. Especially Caroline Abbott.'

'Will do. Go and enjoy your lunch with your daughter.'

He nodded, then shut the car door and watched her drive off before he hurried across the road. The Gorge cafe was a hive of noise as always, the racket of scraping chair legs, cutlery, and chattering filling the air. He pushed past the queue, looking around to see where Alice was sitting. Then he found her, sitting at a table at the back. He stopped for a moment, staring at her as she sat smiling, giggling a little at whatever the young man was saying who was sitting next to her. He gave a surprised laugh, then told himself to pull himself together and headed to the table.

'Dad!' Alice jumped up and hugged him. For a moment he hardly reacted, surprised by this sudden show of affection. Over her shoulder he found himself exchanging awkward looks with the young man. He was slender, pale, with dark floppy hair that nearly covered his eyes.

'I only saw you the other week, Alice,' he said and laughed. 'Come on, sit down.'

Alice sat down, and Moone did the same, his eyes jumping to the young man.

'This is Lewis,' Alice said, smiling and blushing a little. 'This is my dad, DCI Peter Moone.'

Moone put out his hand and saw the young lad go red in the face before putting out his and giving a gentle shake.

'It's nice to meet you,' Lewis said, nodding. 'Alice talks about you a lot.'

'Does she?' Moone raised his eyebrows at his daughter.

'Hardly ever.' Alice made a face at him.

'So...' Moone sat back, nodding, trying to pull up some conversation from the depths. 'Are you two... friends?'

'Of course.' Alice looked at him like he'd dropped his trousers. 'Actually, no, he's my arch-enemy. I like to take my enemies for lunch.'

'I'd better go,' Lewis announced and got to his feet.

'You don't have to go,' Moone said, feeling a little guilty under all the surprise and confusion.

'I do, actually.' Lewis smiled. 'I work round the corner and my lunch break is almost over. Was nice to meet you though.'

'And you, Lewis.' Moone got up and shook the young man's hand again.

'Text you later?' Lewis said to Alice, then ambled out of the Gorge.

When they were alone, Moone raised his eyebrows and sat back as he said, 'So, Lewis seems like a nice boy.'

She narrowed her eyes at him. 'Don't start.'

'Don't start what?'

'You know.'

'Is Lewis…?'

'Yes. Lewis is my boyfriend. OK? Happy?'

'I am if you are. Sorry, it was just a bit of a shock, that's all.'

'Sorry, I probably should have given you some warning.'

'A text might have helped,' he said, but smiled. 'Just to help your old man avoid a heart attack or stroke.'

She laughed. 'Sorry. But you like him?'

'He seems… nice. But, I always say, never trust boys.'

'Come on, they're not all bad...'

'I was a boy once you know. A million years ago, but I still remember what used to go on in my head.'

Alice grimaced. 'Please, Dad, yuck, let's change the subject. How's work?'

'It's OK. Think they're trying to keep me on a short leash.'

'Why do you think that?' Alice leaned closer.

'Nothing really. Just trying to stick me to a desk. They've even given me my own office.'

Alice's eyes widened as she smiled. 'That sounds great. I'd love my own office.'

'Anyway, are you going to buy your old man a coffee?'

Alice laughed, then joined the queue for food and drinks. It wasn't long before she put a large Americano in front of him, so he put a couple of sugars in it and stirred it well. He smiled at her as he asked, 'How's everything at home?'

Alice let out a sigh.

'Oh, dear, that was a heavy sigh, Alice. What's wrong?'

She looked at him a little sadly. 'Mum keeps talking about going back to London...'

Moone was about to sip his coffee but put it down again. 'You're joking. She's only just got here. Why?'

Alice shrugged. 'I don't know.'

'I thought she had this new fella. What was his name? Carl or something?'

'Charles. The Cornish bloke? No, it didn't work out. Which I'm glad of because he was a bit hectic. Always dragging us off cycling or walking or something…'

'Sounds horrendous. She's not seriously considering dragging you back to London? Really?'

Alice shrugged and stared at him. 'Do you ever think about going back?'

Moone sipped his coffee as he gave it some honest thought. 'I used to. I honestly used to think that this was just a stopgap or something, or just some time out…'

'But not now?'

He raised his shoulders. 'I suppose it feels like home now. I feel like I'm doing some good. Back in London, I just felt like… like I was being swept along, carried out to sea.'

'And here you've got your trousers rolled up and dipping your toes in?' She smiled cheekily.

'Well, anyway, I like it here. I like the place, the people.'

'How's your love life?'

He laughed. 'In the morgue.'

'Really, Dad? Isn't there someone?'

Dr Jenkins came to mind, along with the gentle stirring of desire that arose when he pictured her. 'I have kind of got a date in a couple of weeks with a lady...'

'Mandy Butler?'

Moone almost spat out his coffee. 'No. Why would you think that?'

'Well, it's just...you know.'

'What?'

'I don't know. I know I've only seen you together a couple of times, like when she came to see me in hospital... and last month... but I like her and I see the way you look at her.'

'What? I don't look at her any way.'

'Yes, you do. I've seen you. It's this strange look you get...'

'Right, enough of that. Anyway, it's not with my colleague, it's with Dr Jenkins, the pathologist. I think it's a date. She's invited me to this do she's going to.'

'Nice one.' Alice looked up then and seemed to stare at someone behind him.

'You OK?'

'I think someone's here to see you.'

Moone turned to look past the other customers, expecting to see a uniform or even Butler herself, but his heart thumped in panic. There she was, staring at him. Then came a smile that looked almost genuine as DS Carthew walked towards the table.

'So, this is the famous Alice?' Carthew said, smiling gently down at her.

'What's wrong?' Moone asked, hearing the coldness in his own voice. 'What's happened?'

'Nothing. I just needed a word, boss.' The gentle smile came again, followed by the promise in her eyes that she wasn't capable of harming another person. But it was in those eyes, though, the lie, the desire to set all she saw on fire.

He saw his mobile home burning.

'Well, I better be going,' Alice said and got up. 'Nice to meet you. I'll see you soon, Dad.'

'Be safe,' Moone said, forcing a smile to his lips as she headed off.

Carthew slipped into the booth opposite and faced him. She smiled. 'She seems lovely.'

'Don't even think about going anywhere near her. I mean it.'

Carthew put on a shocked face and placed a hand over her heart. 'Me? Who do you think I am? I would never...'

'How many have died now, Faith?'

'In the world in general? I don't know... millions?'

He let out a deep huff. 'This can't go on. Yes, I accept you're back, and I've got to work with you, but I will not have you...'

'Dr Parry.' Carthew smiled and sat back.

'What about him?' Moone felt his stomach turn into black spiders and scuttle off into the shadows.

'His last moments on this earth.' She sat forward. 'His apparent suicide. Let's talk about that.'

'He committed suicide. The inquest…'

'I don't doubt he did. In fact, I know he did.'

'Do you?' Moone's blood started pulsing at speed through his heart. A heart attack seemed only moments away.

'I do.' She lost her smile. 'I followed you and the lovely DI Mandy Butler that tragic day. I wondered what you were up to when you went to that old farmhouse. A house owned by Dr Parry. Imagine my surprise when I saw you go in, then later Parry sets fire to the house. All very strange.'

Moone couldn't speak. He was frozen, his heart now hammering, the beat of it in his ears as a headache arrived like a mallet to the top of his skull.

'Lost for words?' Carthew's smile returned. 'I even took some video footage.'

'Say I believe you…' His voice came out low, brittle, hardly like him at all.

'You know it's true. Anyway, the point is, I have the upper hand.'

'What do you want?'

'Carte blanche to do as I please.'

'You know I have to police you…'

'I know. But this investigation isn't going very well, and I want to make sure the killer of those women gets proper justice.'

Moone had a bad feeling arrive in his gut, worse than the one already sitting down there.

'What sort of justice?'

'You know. The sort of justice I would have given to Colin Samson if you would have given me the chance.'

'It's a good job I stopped you, or you would be in prison now.'

She laughed. 'I wouldn't. They would have seen that I did what I needed to do to protect my colleagues.'

'With a hammer?'

She shrugged.

'You were out of control.'

'This killer, who beats these women almost to death and then strangles them with their own tights... I'm going to find him.'

'We all are. That's our job.'

Her eyes twisted, became somehow darker as she clenched her fist and thumped it on the table. 'No, I'm going to find him and stop him.'

'You mean you're going to kill him?'

She sat back, seeming to drag herself back towards a sort of sanity. 'Let's just say I'm going to find him.'

'Why? Why're you so obsessed with this killer?'

'Because of what he did to those women.'

Moone couldn't help laughing. 'Really? You remember Charlie Armstrong? Jason Wise? Kate Armstrong, Charlie Armstrong's widow? Laptew and his wife? DC Banerjee?'

'Are you suggesting I had something to do with their deaths? How could I possibly? I was in custody when some of them were killed.'

'You're very clever...'

'Thank you.' She smiled. 'You're not so stupid yourself, and you're quite sexy in your own way.'

He stared at her.

Then she leaned forward, narrowing her eyes. 'But the problem with you is, my darling Peter, that you're too good. You're too nice. You have to play by the rule book, putting aside your involvement in the Parry affair, of course. But I suspect Butler was really behind all that, pushing you to cover all that up. But you, yourself, you haven't got what it takes to catch this kind of killer and dispense some real justice.'

He sighed, ignoring the sickness filling him up, and shook his head. 'Just let us get on and find this killer...'

'Have you got any suspects?'

Moone let out an empty laugh. 'No one substantial yet.'

'I'm building a profile. Something I'm going to use to catch him.'

'Then share it with us.'

'No way. There's so much you've missed already.'

'Carthew. Faith.' He softened his voice, scrabbling around in his brain for some words that might placate her. 'Please, don't…'

'If you want to stop me, then you'll have to raise your game and find him first.' Carthew got up and straightened her clothes and tidied her hair. 'That's the game, you see. The first one to find him gets to dispense some justice. Let's see who wins.'

Moone tried to find something to say, but she was already walking out, leaving him to stare at the empty seat opposite. His mind returned to Butler and prayed to whoever might be listening, if a higher being existed, that she had found something useful or incriminating.

CHAPTER 10

For some reason, Butler was drawn to the same glass and steel hotel where DSU Armstrong had been found murdered. It was somehow fitting, she felt as she walked into the large, tiled lobby and headed for the reception desk at the far end. It would be touch and go if she managed to get a room seeing as the kids were still off school for another week. She had decided to stay another night in Bristol and head back to work in the early hours before the network of slow-moving traffic formed. If she left now, she would probably get caught up in a traffic jam.

There was one room available, a cancellation, so she took it and headed up to the fourth floor. She slipped the key card into the lock and then went in. The room lights blazed on and she stood there for a moment, listening to the distant traffic of the city, and examining the smart, plain room. Then she carefully took out the evidence bag with the phone and SIM cards and placed it on the bedside table. She stared at it, still amazed that DS Rivers had kept something so incriminating. But it was insurance, she guessed. There were messages on the phone that must have been sent by Carthew, little snippets of text that mentioned the other people on the course, and hinted at the arrangements. There was a subtle code used between them, but it was there, in between the lines. They were arranging Armstrong's death, but it wasn't anything substantial, not enough for a jury to convict them both. There were photos taken by the killer in Armstrong's room, snaps of his lifeless body on the floor. It made her feel sick to even think of them, let alone look at them again. But there was nothing substantial linking Carthew to the murder, she had been too careful as always.

She had been tempted to text Moone and let him know what she had found, but she didn't want to risk it, didn't want her words out there for some tech genius to steal. It was also the fact that she wanted to face him when she gave him the possible good news, the little step closer they were to arresting Carthew. If they used the evidence on the phone to force Rivers into confessing her and Carthew's involvement in Armstrong's murder, then they were almost home, almost free of the bitch.

She opened the drawer of the bedside table and slipped the evidence bag and phone inside.

A celebration seemed in order, she thought and looked around the room for a mini bar, but there wasn't one, only room service, but she'd be stuffed if she was going to pay those prices, and there was no way anyone was going to swallow it as expenses. She was on leave, not working.

She sat on the bed and put the TV on and found the BBC news channel. Then she changed the channel and found something funny to watch. She stared at the screen, wondering what Moone's reaction would be, looking forward to seeing the smile on his face. She liked it when he smiled. Then she caught herself and told herself off for being soft.

Her head spun towards the door when she heard the knock. She stared at the door, her heart skipping into a faster beat. No one knew where she was. She stood up, still looking towards the door, blindly searching in her bag for her Casco baton. She found it and flicked it to full length as she started towards the door, her heart now thumping hard.

'Hello?' she called through the door, then put her eye to the peephole.

'I've got fresh towels for your room,' a voice said. Whoever they were, they spoke good English with some kind of Eastern European accent. Butler could see a young woman standing outside her door. Dark hair with blonde highlights. Polish, perhaps.

'It's OK,' Butler said. 'I'm all good for towels.'

The woman held up a large towel. 'I forgot the larger towel. I need to put it in there or I get in trouble.'

Butler sighed and kept watching her, then looked beyond her at the corridor. No one else was about. 'Just leave it outside, I'll put it in the bathroom, don't worry.'

'Sorry, but I have to put in there myself,' the woman said. 'I have to use my key card, so they know I've been here. I don't get paid otherwise.'

Butler sighed and looked through the peephole again. She could only see the young woman. 'Is there anyone else with you?'

She saw the young woman look around her, then face the door again with a shrug. 'No, is only me. I work by myself. I'm sorry for the trouble.'

Butler gripped her Casco baton tighter, unlocked the door, opened it a fraction and stepped back. 'Come in but be quick.'

'Thank you,' the woman said through the gap Butler had opened up. The door swung open, knocking Butler backwards, sending her stumbling down the short hallway of the room. She gained her balance and stared up at the open door in time to see a bottle being held in front of her face. Spray exploded into her eyes, burning them. She let out a grunt of pain, her eyes blurring as she started swinging the baton. Something smacked into her wrist, knocking the baton to the carpet. A blow to her knee sent her sprawling.

Moone's heart was still thumping when he reached the station and headed back to the incident room. He kept seeing Carthew staring back at him across the table, that same old look of victory dug into her face. Her words kept playing over, making him want to run to the men's room and throw up. She knew about Dr Parry and she had proof of what they had done. Of course, she had. Moone got his phone out as he stood outside the incident room, determined to call Butler and give her the god-awful news. He tried to think of some good news that might help the very bitter-tasting medicine go down, but his brain ran dry.

'Moone?'

His heart thumped even more as he heard DSU Boulton's voice echoing up the stairwell. He put his phone away and faced the annoyed-looking detective as he came up towards him.

Boulton reached him and put his hands into his pockets. 'Tell me why I've just had a very pissed-off Nick Dann on the phone?'

Moone let out a tired breath. 'We had to talk to him, sir. Intelligence came to light...'

'You heard a rumour about him having an affair with one of the victims and decided that was enough to go bothering a businessman who has helped raise a lot of money for charity and brought a lot more jobs to this city? Jesus, man, are you trying to fuck up your career?'

'No, I just...'

'Leave Nick Dann out of this.'

'I think he might have had an affair with Judy Ludlow, our first victim twenty years ago, and I think I saw a response when I showed him a photo of the second victim...'

'You think? Jesus. I've talked to him and he says he's never met these women. Have you got anyone who saw him at their homes around the time of the murders?'

Moone shook his head. 'No.'

'Then leave it alone. If anything else does come up involving Mr Dann, run it by me first. OK?'

'Sir.'

Boulton looked at him for a moment, the disappointment clear in his eyes as he let out a sharp breath. 'Thing is, I don't know why you were even there, Peter. I told you, you need to be here supervising, not off here and there.'

'Well, I'm covering for Butler.'

He nodded. 'OK. But she's back tomorrow, so no more gallivanting about. Understood?'

'Sir.'

'Get back to work and find Caroline

Abbott's murderer. Look at her friends and family. You'll find her killer there, I'm sure. Put out an appeal too. Right, I've got a meeting to attend to.'

When DSU Boulton had sauntered off, Moone hurried back into the incident room to find DC Chambers. As he headed to her desk, he couldn't help but notice Carthew was absent.

'Molly,' he said, standing at her desk. 'Where's Carthew?'

'She went out just after you left. Said she had a lead. Is everything OK, boss?'

'Not really.' Moone ran a hand down his face, wanting desperately to confide in someone about Carthew and what she had witnessed. But he couldn't. No one else, apart from Butler and himself could know the truth about what had happened to Parry. 'I've just been told by DSU Boulton to stay away from Nick Dann.'

Chambers nodded. 'Oh, yeah, I thought that might happen. He knows a lot of influential people.'

'Thing is, I'm sure he reacted when I showed him the photo of Teresa Burrows. And Jon Michael Reagan said he remembers seeing a smartly dressed man hanging around Teresa's house close to the day she was killed. What if it was Nick Dann?'

'Do you want to get Reagan in again, maybe show him some photos and see if he can identify Dann?'

Moone nodded. 'Yep, arrange it. What if Nick Dann was seeing these women and decided they needed to be kept quiet?'

'But does he know Caroline Abbott?' Chambers asked, her eyebrows raised.

'We'll have to find out *if* Reagan identifies him.'

'Oh, sorry, I just remembered, I managed to find a number for Scott Eason, the criminal psychologist... well, former criminal psychologist. He's some kind of life coach now. He comes from North London originally but now lives in Cornwall. Anyway, he said he was heading here to see you.'

Moone stared at her, the name still ringing in his head. 'Did you say Scott Eason?'

'Yes, why's that, sir?'

Moone laughed a little. 'I was at school with a guy called Scott Eason. Well, I didn't really know him very well, but I saw him around. He was always a bit of a ladies' man. I had no idea he was a criminal psychologist, if he is even the same Scott I knew.'

'Well, if he is, maybe you can catch up with him.'

'Thanks, Chambers. Might be interesting to hear what he says.'

Butler's hands were grasped, forced behind her back and zip-tied.

'What're you going to do with her?' the maid's voice said, sounding panicked.

'Don't worry,' another woman said – it was Rivers, sounding out of breath. 'She's under arrest. She's been up to no good this one...'

'Don't listen to her,' Butler gasped, her eyes still streaming. 'She's the one who should be under arrest.'

'Go on!' Rivers snapped at the young woman. 'Get out. Go back to work.'

There seemed to be hesitation, then the sound of the door to the room opening and closing again. Butler was pulled to her feet and helped back to a chair.

The next thing she knew a wet towel was being pressed into her face, the water running down her cheeks along with her tears. Rivers cleaned her eyes for her, and soon she could see a little again, at least enough to see the blurry shape of DI Rivers looking down at her, a Casco baton in her hand.

'Where is it?' Rivers asked, a dark edge to her voice. 'You've got two minutes.'

'What's your plan?' Butler laughed. 'Get it back, then kill me? In a hotel room?'

'You'll find out if I don't get it back.' Rivers moved, becoming a blurry shape that started to open drawers and then the wardrobe. 'Ha. Here it is.'

'Wouldn't be the first time you killed someone in a hotel room, would it?' Butler said, pissed off that she had left it in such an obvious place.

'It would actually.' Rivers faced her again. 'I saw you break into my flat, with your friend. I have cameras hidden all round my place, you see. Can't be too careful.'

'I should've known you'd be sneaky like her.' Butler looked down, shaking her head, trying to figure a way out of this. She wondered where her phone was and then looked up to see the less blurry shape of Rivers holding two things in her hands. One seemed to be the phone Butler had taken from her flat, the other was her own mobile. Shit.

'Let's see who you've been messaging about this,' Rivers said, then was silent for a moment before she looked up and gave an empty laugh. 'No one, I see. So you haven't told DCI Moone about your discovery. That was stupid of you. Good for us though.'

'Meaning you and Carthew? Do you really think you can trust that cow?'

'As far as I need to.'

'And what happens when she's done with you? Do you think she'll hesitate to...'

'Shut up. I know what I'm doing.'

'What is it between you two? As far as I know, she was having a thing with DC Banerjee...'

'That was a convenient little arrangement.'

'So, you and Carthew sitting in a tree, is that it? Not kissing but planning murder and mayhem. Nice. Well, she'll be planning your murder pretty soon.'

'You can't get in my head. Anyway, let me think. I need to decide what to do with you.'

'Well, you can't get rid of me like you have the others, can you?'

Rivers stepped closer, lowering the phones. 'Why not? What's one more suicide or misadventure?'

'Sooner or later people will start asking a lot of questions.'

'No, they won't. Haven't you noticed? They like it all neat and tidy. A murder-suicide is easier for them to take, is much neater and means less paperwork. All we have to do is deliver it all to them in a nicely wrapped parcel and they don't ask questions.'

'Well, if I disappear after coming down here to look into all this, then Moone will ask questions. Don't forget my friend who helped me to gain entry to your place. I told him to contact Moone if I should disappear. I knew there might be a risk of it…'

'Bollocks.'

'OK, take your chances. Keep me here then. But sooner or later…'

Even though her face was a little blurry, Butler could see the doubt flickering in Rivers' eyes.

'Faith will know what to do with you.'

'Oh, I see. Haven't got a brain yourself, so you need to go running off to find Carthew.'

'Shut your mouth. You can't get in my head like that. I just need time to think.'

'Well, you can't leave me here. And you can't go running to Carthew, can you?'

'Why not?'

'Well, you call her and she realises you kept that phone as evidence, she'll know that you're not to be trusted. She'll have me and you to worry about. She won't like that. But, of course, she's a psychopath, so she won't bat an eyelid when she realises she's got to get rid of you. What do you think?'

Butler watched Rivers' face, seeing the calculations going on behind her troubled eyes, praying her words would get into her brain and convince her not to go calling Carthew. If she did go running to her, Butler knew she would be finished for sure. Then her brain kicked into gear, the fear having faded a little and allowing her a few unhindered thoughts.

'There is a way out of this,' Butler said, staring up at Rivers as her face came into view, clearer now.

'Yeah, I know. I go with you and make a statement about what I know and did.'

Butler shook her head. 'No. That's doing it by the book, and I think we're way beyond that now, aren't we?'

Rivers narrowed her eyes. 'I'd say we are. Then what do you mean?'

'You help me bring down Carthew. If she doesn't know this all went on, that we're talking, then we've got the upper hand.'

'She's smart, always one step ahead...'

'True. But we're going to be several steps ahead. But what we need is incriminating evidence on her. There's nothing on that phone that substantially links to her. A good lawyer could destroy it. Even if you testified against her...'

'I'm not doing that,' Rivers snapped. 'That would be me finished, my career and life down the plughole. No way.'

'I know. That's why we need her to admit to what she did.'

Rivers let out a harsh breath, then turned away. 'That'll never happen. She's careful about what she says. If I start up a conversation... I mean, she'll know something's up.'

'Then we have to be very subtle. What about you contact her, tell her you need to meet up with her because I've been digging around. Arrange a place and time, and we get her on tape?'

'She'll never go for it.'

'You have to convince her. Go to Plymouth, contact her there. Make her believe you.'

Rivers sighed. 'Say I agree to this, what

about DCI Moone? Is he going to go along with this?'

Butler shook her head. 'No, but he doesn't need to know. This will be just me and you. We can get her. We can get her on tape and then we'll have her. We can get her to move on, get out of our lives. You get to carry on being a police officer.'

Rivers examined her for a moment, then looked at the evidence bag with her burner phone inside it.

'You've got that,' Butler said. 'You can destroy it. There's nothing tying Carthew to the murder of Armstrong. Only you. Destroy that and then we get her.'

Rivers made a noise, a strained and frustrated sound as she turned away and paced the room. Then she came back and pointed at Butler.

'If I do go along with this, then I'm trusting you more than I've trusted anybody.'

'We haven't got much choice but to trust each other, have we?'

'I suppose not.'

'Are you going to untie me now or what?' Butler turned her body and moved her wrists.

Rivers took out a small knife and stepped around the back of Butler. She felt the straps tighten, her heart beginning to race a little, not completely convinced she could trust the bent officer behind her who had hold of a sharp knife. Then the straps fell away and her hands were loose once more. She got up and rubbed her wrists, watching her new ally for a moment, thinking things over as her curiosity grew.

'How did you do it?' Butler said. 'I have to ask.'

Rivers looked up at her. 'Armstrong?'

'All of it.'

'It wasn't me. I didn't actually murder anyone.' Rivers put the knife away and straightened her clothes.

'But you must have helped.'

Rivers sighed. 'Someone else pretended to be Armstrong's widow. Well, actually Carthew said this person she knew, who she trusted more than anyone, would do it, would dress up to look like a mysterious blonde woman and then kill Armstrong.'

'She said she trusts them more than anyone? She actually said that?'

Rivers nodded. 'I know. I thought I was the only person she trusted. But that's not true. I didn't know what she was going to do to Laptew. She never said. Kept it to herself.'

'Who murdered them?'

'Same person who killed Armstrong.' Rivers looked down, her face tight.

'You know who they are, don't you? You must have met them.'

Rivers looked up. 'If I admit that, then I'm

admitting to some pretty incriminating stuff.'

Butler held up her hands. 'Listen, we're not after you. We're after that psycho. She wants to be our boss...'

'If she's set her mind on that, then there's not much anyone can do about it.'

'What about Kate Armstrong and DC Jason Wise? One person couldn't have taken care of that. So who helped there?'

Rivers turned and faced the window, her right-hand fidgeting, tapping erratically at her leg.

'You?' Butler asked.

'I helped. I didn't do it.' The police officer turned and faced her, a look of remorse in her eyes, maybe even tears. 'Listen, by that point, I'd gone too far. There was no going back. When she gets into your head...'

'I know. Just tell me. Was it this mysterious person again?'

Rivers nodded. 'It's a man. Although it's hard to tell when he's dressed up... I get the feeling he's her cousin or something. I mean, who do you trust more than family?'

Butler nodded. 'Makes sense. So he killed them? What was your part?'

'I went to Armstrong's house when they were out. Wise had been sleeping there off and on, so I knew they'd be together. My job was to put some drugs into their food. We knew their routine, what they might eat or drink. When we knew they'd be out of it, then he went in and... he... well, you know.'

'And you helped with making it look like Wise hanged himself?'

When Rivers looked up and stared up at her, Butler could see pain in her eyes. 'Yes, I helped. I didn't kill him. Either of them.'

'You could've stopped it happening.'

Her eyes widened, Rivers' thumb pressing into her own chest. 'She would have killed me if I hadn't helped. You know what she's like.'

'You keep telling yourself that.' Butler huffed. 'How did this begin with you two? How did you find each other?'

'When she came to Bristol for work. It happened fast. She asked me to go for a drink... then, it just happened. We talked. She told me about her plans. Before I knew it... I don't know... I hate myself for going along with her, but it's like I couldn't stop myself.'

'Jesus. I don't want to hear any more. Just come to Plymouth, go and see her. Then tell me when it's going to happen and we'll get her on tape. Here, take my card, my mobile number's on it. Get a burner phone and use that to call me.'

'She'll never fall for it. She's too clever.'

Butler stepped up to her, pointing a finger in her face. 'She better had, darling, because if she doesn't, then you're fucked.'

CHAPTER 11

Moone had introduced himself and then had Professor Scott Eason delivered to one of the more pleasant interview rooms, but not before offering to make him a coffee. Milk, two sugars, Eason had said, with a big smile. He was tall, at least taller than Moone, and quite slender. He wore a smart suit and tie and glasses. He looked neat, his slightly wavy dark hair short and oiled back. Moone couldn't be sure that he was the same Scott Eason he had been to school with, but there was definitely something familiar about him, even though he had a quite well-spoken voice and none of the old Enfield twang.

Moone took the coffees into the interview room where Eason was waiting, looking perfectly relaxed.

'Thank you,' Eason said as Moone put a coffee in front of him. 'It's been a while since I was in a police station. Must be about twelve years, give or take.'

'Nothing much changes,' Moone said and

sat down and sipped his coffee.

'Your colleague said you wanted to talk about those two murders I helped with a few years back,' Eason said, then stopped talking, his eyes narrowing at Moone, his right index finger rising. 'I'm sorry, but you look really familiar.'

'You do too,' Moone said, smiling. 'Did you used to go to Albany School a million years ago?'

The professor laughed, then nodded. 'That's it. Peter Moone. I thought I knew the name. And now you're a detective chief inspector. You've done well.'

'I don't know about that.' Moone laughed. 'But sounds like you have. Police psychologist and everything.'

'That's right, I was a criminal psychologist, but not any more.' Eason sat back and took off his glasses and gave them a clean with his tie. 'It wasn't for me. I wanted more from my job.'

'More money?' Moone laughed.

'I suppose. I certainly have a better lifestyle. But it was more than that. Seems a hundred years since we were at school, doesn't it? What a rough place that was.'

'Certainly was. There was some kind of massive fight every day, I remember.'

Eason nodded, then pointed at Moone. 'Not you though. You always managed to stay out of trouble. You were always one of the good guys.'

Moone laughed. 'Still am, I hope.'

'Oh, have you heard from Deep?'

'Deep? Deep Bhogal? No, how's he doing?'

'He's a millionaire businessman now. Got some export business. It's funny seeing you after all this time, because the other day, when I popped back to London, I bumped into that lad who used to follow you round everywhere.'

'What lad?'

'Big lad. Not very bright. I've forgotten his name again. Terry... was it?'

Moone sat back, a flurry of memories flooding his brain. 'Terry Hankin. Jesus, I'd forgotten all about him. How is he?'

'Still the same. Massive. Does kickboxing and weights and all that rubbish. He didn't say, but I did hear that he's been involved in some dodgy goings on too, some violent stuff. It's funny isn't it, but he asked after you. Wonder what he would say if he knew you were a police officer. Anyway, I said I hadn't seen you in years, and now here we are. Synchronicity.'

'Maybe. Anyway, back to this investigation. How come you ended up working on that case twenty years back?'

Eason put his glasses back on and adjusted his tie. 'They approached me. I guess they needed an expert criminologist and there I was. I had a couple of books out by then. A few theories about sexual murders, and serial rapists.'

'But they never caught him.'

For a moment, Moone thought he saw a flicker of annoyance cross the psychologist's face, but it was soon replaced by a slight smile as he nodded and said, 'True. But that's more to do with the fact that they didn't take on board what I was saying about their killer. I mean, I put together a pretty comprehensive profile on him, but they ended up disregarding most of it and that's where they went wrong.'

'Interesting.' Moone sat back, the word profile ringing in his ears, recalling how many of his colleagues no longer believed in that kind of psychological process any more. So many killers had been caught or uncovered by DNA years later and had been found not to match the profile that had been built around their despicable crimes. But nonetheless, he was curious. 'So, do you remember what sort of killer you thought they were after?'

'It's not what I thought,' Eason said with a smile as he sat forward. 'It's what I knew. You're looking for a man who would have been between the ages of twenty-five and thirty-five back then. He'll be living a double life. He'll be quite successful in his work life, but he desires something else, something animalistic that money can't afford him. He despises women, I mean he really hates them. He wants to punish them. He takes their tights off and uses them to strangle them, which is symbolic...'

'Symbolic of what?' Moone remembered his coffee and took a sip.

'Symbolic of the pretence that women hide behind, hiding their bare selves, pretending to be something they're not. He considers them to be a subspecies.'

Moone nodded, hearing the theories and wanting to disregard most of them straight away, but he kept his look of interest. 'You said he would've been between twenty-five and thirty-five. So, he could be fifty-five now?'

'Indeed. I know what you're thinking.' Eason put his hands on the desk, smiling, giving a knowing look.

'Do you? What's that?'

'Why wait until now? Why did he stop the killing after two?'

'I am thinking that. What do you make of it?'

The psychologist sat back. 'Well, there's the obvious reasons. He could have been in prison for a similar offence, or he was somehow incapacitated. But more likely is that life got in the way.'

Moone laughed. 'You make it sound like killing was only a hobby for him.'

Eason shrugged. 'Maybe it was. Perhaps he could turn his rage off and on. My theory is, he tried to settle into a normal life and probably entered into a relationship.'

It was certainly an interesting theory, Moone decided, and there was something about it that intrigued him. 'So, if you're right about this, then why start again now, nearly twenty years later?'

Eason pointed at him. 'Well, that's the million-dollar question, isn't it?'

'Yep. What's the answer?'

'I don't know. But it could be he got bored. Or maybe the life he's formed to keep him from committing these murders has fallen apart. Or there might have even been some sudden trauma in his life that's brought it all back, that desire to strike out at the world.'

Moone sat back, nodding. 'Sounds like you might be onto something.'

'I think so. Have you got any suspects, by the way?'

'No one that stands out. There is one suspect. Obviously, I can't mention his name, but he is quite successful.'

Eason looked suitably pleased with himself as he smiled and sat back. 'There you go. What's his personal life like?'

'He's married, but we think he might be a serial adulterer.'

'I'd take a look at his marriage now. You might find he's going through a rocky patch. Well, more than a rocky patch really. I mean, it's got to be something pretty messed up within his marriage, this perfect cover life he's built, to screw it all up and get him thinking about what he used to enjoy.'

Moone nodded, sitting back, deciding he liked the way Eason was thinking. 'It's always there, isn't it? The desire in him, that desperate need to relive what he did back then?'

'Always. It never goes away. I mean, I'm surprised he's managed twenty years. His fantasies would have still been there, going around in his head, practically begging him to go back to his old ways. The man you're after must have a strong will. At least, stronger than most of us. You'll hear a lot about how killers will never stop killing, at least until they're stopped… but that doesn't mean they're not strong enough to pause things for a while. I think your killer is stronger-willed than most.'

'Could you do me a favour, then?'

Eason smiled, already nodding his agreement. 'You want me to update my profile based on the latest murder.'

Eason was quiet for a moment, staring at Moone, seeming to contemplate the favour. 'OK, as long as you and your colleagues take it seriously this time.'

'You have my word.'

Eason stood up and stretched a little, then finished his coffee. 'Then I'll need to see the latest crime scene photos, the files, and I should probably visit the scene itself.'

'I can arrange that, but we'll have to keep it on the quiet. Come by in the morning and I'll take you there.'

'Eight?'

Moone smiled. 'Perfect.'

'It's good seeing you again,' the former criminologist said and turned to face the door. A thought occurred to Moone, a question that had been revolving in his head all this time.

'What's his motivation for all this?' Moone asked, making Eason turn to face him again.

'His motivation?' Eason put a finger to his lips. 'Well, I'd say that it's not really sexual, even though there might be a degree of pleasure he gets from the act itself. No, I would say this is more about anger and revenge for something. Yes, I'd say this is all born out of rage.'

'I think I have to agree. Well, with your help, hopefully, we can stop him before he does it again.'

Jim Nair stood back for a moment as he took out a cigarette and searched for a lighter in his denim jacket. He found his lighter and lit his cigarette and took a long lungful as he looked over the bodywork of his gleaming Harley. Then he spotted a smudged fingerprint on the 3.6-gallon petrol tank that he had recently replaced and wiped it over. He had rebuilt the Sportster from a cracked and rusty skeleton, giving her new life. He looked around at the garage, still smoking, his ears picking out the deep thud of base coming from the stereo in the clubhouse out the back. He was thirsty for a drink, but it was too early. He'd promised his missus that he wouldn't put away any more pints until after six. He sighed, then headed out of the garage and across the concrete yard and into the clubhouse. It wasn't much of a place, just a few old pub tables he'd got hold of and a couple of worn sofas, and of course the bar he'd had built in the corner, but it was somewhere they could all hang out away from prying eyes. He turned off the loud rock music that was playing to no one and surveyed the empty place, remembering how far they had come after the last few years, and how they would be further up the ladder if it wasn't for the Tomahawks.

As Nair went over to the coffee machine behind the bar to make an espresso, he saw the back door open and the thuggish, tattoo-covered frame of Jason come in. Steve came in behind him and collapsed onto the sofa.

'How was last night?' Nair asked, pouring sugar into his coffee.

Jason sat on one of the stools at the bar and tapped his fingers on its surface. 'Went OK. Got half the money. Said they'd have the other half by next week.'

Nair let out a harsh breath.

'What?' Jason shrugged. 'They're good for

it.'

'They take fucking liberties, these people. They better have it, or you and Steve'll be over there smashing their place up.'

'I know. Listen...'

Before they could finish their conversation, there was a knock on the side door, and they both stared towards it. No one ever knocked on that door. Everyone in the gang knew to use the back door. Jason looked at Nair with a question in his eyes.

Nair raised a finger to his lips, then crept towards the door, picking up a baseball bat on the way. He stood beside the door as he called out, 'Who's there? This is private property.'

'I want to talk to Jim Nair,' a woman's voice called back.

Jim turned and exchanged surprised glances with Jason before he said, 'Who are you?'

'A police officer.'

'Shit!' Jason grunted.

Jim hushed him. 'You can get lost. We ain't done nothing.'

'This isn't official. I just need a friendly chat.'

'Who else you got with you?'

'No one. Open the door and you'll see.'

Nair stood back, thinking it over, wondering why some woman police officer would be visiting their clubhouse. Then he started to wonder if it was a police officer at all. It could be the Tomahawks, he thought, sending over some bitch to try and trick them. 'Let's see some ID. Push it under the door.'

A moment later there was a scraping sound as a black wallet was pushed under the door. Nair crouched down and retrieved it, then opened up the warrant card. It looked genuine.

'Detective Sergeant Faith Carthew,' he read quietly as Jason came over.

'What the fuck does she want?' Jason asked, then stepped towards the door. 'What the fuck do you want?'

'I have a proposition for you, Mr Nair,' she said. 'But I don't really want to shout it through a door.'

Nair sighed, shaking his head and looked at Steve, then Jason. 'What the hell is this?'

'Some kind of sting operation or something?' Jason shrugged.

'Nah, she wouldn't announce she's a pig if that's what it was. They wouldn't have a leg to stand on in court. Let's let her in. Open the door.'

Nair went over to one of the tables, sat down and lit a cigarette as he saw Steve sitting on the sofa looking gormless. 'Get lost, Steve. Go and clean my bike or something.'

When Steve had gone, Jason opened the door. She was stood there, a strange kind of smile on her face. He was pleasantly surprised to find she was not bad looking, actually quite a sort, he decided. Strawberry blonde, in shape, not too skinny like they got these days. He watched her as he smoked, looking her over, noticing how she clocked everything around her. He thought of himself as a good judge of character and had always been excellent at sizing someone up in just a few observations. She was devious, he got that sense from her, and clever, and probably extremely ambitious.

'Nice place,' she said, but he couldn't tell if she was being sarcastic or not.

'It's a shit hole, but we like it,' he said and pushed out a chair with his boot. 'Take the weight off, darling.'

She looked at the chair for a moment as if she suspected it might be booby-trapped, then sat down. She stared at him, looked deep into his eyes and he forced himself to hold her gaze, even though there was something in her eyes that made him uncomfortable.

'You said you had a proposition,' Nair said. 'Come on then, let's hear it.'

'You make quite a bit from your drug dealing operation,' she said and sat back. 'But you could be making a lot more.'

'Drug dealing? Us? I don't know what you're talking about.'

She sighed, then took out her phone and slid it across the table before she took off her coat and lifted her shirt, revealing her black bra and bare skin.

'See, no wire and my phone's not recording,' she said and sat down again. 'Your problem is, you're afraid of us. We've constantly got operations set up to catch you in the act. We've put away five of your club members over the last two years.'

'They didn't end up with long stretches though because I can afford good lawyers.'

She nodded. 'And you'd be able to afford even better ones if you had me on the inside to feed you information.'

Nair huffed out a laugh. 'But you're forgetting our rivals.'

'The Tomahawks?'

'They're a bunch of tossers,' Jason said but closed his mouth when Nair glared at him.

'He's right,' Nair said. 'They murdered one of ours last year. Kicked the poor lad to death, but no one's been pinched for it. How can I trust you when you're one of them who can't do their job?'

'Heard of Lloyd Redrobe?'

Nair looked at Jason for a moment, seeing if he returned his look of surprise. 'I know him, does some of the leg work for the Tomahawks. What of that little tranny?'

'He's my brother, half-brother, actually.' She stared at Nair, her eyes not giving anything away.

'That's even worse. You're that little psycho's sister? And you're a fucking copper? What a fucking family, Jason.'

Jason laughed, but the police detective didn't look amused as she seemed to examine them both closely. 'He'll do anything I say, so you don't have to worry about him doing anything sneaky for your rivals any more.'

Nair laughed. 'It's not just him though, darling, is it? He didn't kick our lad to death. That was one of the other bastards in their moronic club.'

She stared at him for a moment, then leaned forward. 'Give me a name.'

Nair huffed. 'We don't grass. We never grass.'

'You're not grassing to them, you're telling me who you think murdered the lad. But I can probably work it out. Stuart McAllister is the muscle of the Tomahawks. He's been done for ABH and GBH. My money's on him. If I'm wrong, tap the desk.'

Nair didn't move, knowing of course she was right on the money. There was something about this woman, something deep inside of her and it scared him a little. She was wrong somehow, and there was a coldness in her eyes. What sort of woman walks in here and starts making deals like this? he asked himself. He got the sense she would do anything to get what she wanted, which made her dangerous, but that could be a good thing if she was on their side.

'I'll take that as I'm correct,' she said and stood up. 'I'll take care of McAllister.'

'What do you mean, take care of him?' Jason asked.

'Shut up,' Nair ordered and stood up, then pointed at Carthew. 'If you take care of him, get him out of the way, then maybe we can do business.'

She smiled. 'Don't worry, it'll be taken care of. Give me two days.'

Before Moone could reach awkwardly for the door to the interview room, balancing the photographs he had in a file under his arm, DC Chambers appeared and opened it for him.

'Thanks, Molly,' he said, smiling before he went in and saw Jon Michael Reagan sat at the interview desk, his hands round the steaming hot drink one of the uniforms had fetched for him. Moone seated himself with a smile as he sorted through the photographs in the file. Molly sat next to him and he looked over to see her smile and blush at Reagan.

'Thank you for coming in, Mr Reagan,' Moone said.

'It's OK,' Reagan said, smiling briefly before his eyes became fixed on the file on the desk. 'I don't mind. Anything to help.'

'That makes a refreshing change,' Moone

said and gave a short laugh.

'You said you wanted me to try and identify the man I saw?' Reagan asked, staring at the file.

Moone sat back. 'That's right. We're going to show you some photographs. The man you saw outside Teresa Burrows' house might be amongst them, he might not. Just take your time...'

'Thing is, it's nearly twenty years ago,' Reagan said, his eyes lifting, looking full of despair.

Moone nodded. 'I know. We're asking a lot, but just take your time and have a look.'

Moone took out the photographs they had gathered together, which as always were a mixture of images of police staff and offenders of various other similar crimes. In there somewhere was the photograph they had found of Nick Dann from roughly twenty years earlier. Moone placed them on the desk, his heart starting to thump in his chest as he sat back and prepared to wait. His heart raced for two very good reasons. One being that he was excited that Reagan might pick out Nick Dann, which would prove he probably knew both the original victims and they might be one big step closer to finding their killer, and the second reason was that if he did pick out Nick Dann, Moone would then be in a very awkward position with his bosses. He held his breath as

Jon Michael Reagan leaned forward, his eyes scanning each image. He looked up briefly at Moone and Chambers, but they both kept their poker faces on.

Then Reagan's hand lifted, his forefinger wavering. Then he tapped the photograph as Moone's heart began to thump a little faster, his stomach unknotting and knotting again as he realised the ramifications of what the man had just done.

'You recognise that man?' Moone asked as he slipped the photo of a younger Nick Dann back towards himself.

'I think so,' Reagan said.

'Where from?' Chambers asked.

'I'm pretty sure I saw him outside her house, the woman who was murdered. I think I saw him there a couple of times, now I think about it. He was sitting in his car... it was a flash car...'

'Do you remember the make, the colour?' Moone asked.

'I think... it was a Mercedes? Dark. Maybe black.'

Moone nodded to Chambers and she took out her notebook and wrote down the information.

'Thanks,' Moone said. 'Did you ever see this man enter her home?'

'No. Just that time outside, as if he was waiting or... I don't know. Then I think he was in his car. Yeah, he was in his car, just sitting there. Maybe he was waiting for her or something.'

Moone sat back, forcing a smile to his face, a look of gratitude even though inside he was all mixed up. Now he had an eyewitness identifying Nick Dann, a businessman of influence, a man probably used to socialising with Plymouth's high and mighty. People like his bosses. There was trouble ahead, and Moone didn't have any dancing shoes.

CHAPTER 12

Moone waited with bated breath out in the corridor for Butler's return, a takeaway coffee in his hand. He kept moving the position of his palm on the cup as he had neglected to take one of those cardboard protectors and the heat of it was starting to burn through the cup. He looked up when he heard footsteps coming from the stairwell. He knew her step, could feel her coming towards him before he even saw her. His heart started to beat a little faster, but he lied to himself and pretended it was merely the much-anticipated news on the Carthew situation that raised the excitement in his heart.

She saw him and there was a brief smile before her gruff exterior was back in place and she eyed the coffee in his hand.

'That for me?' she asked, not sounding impressed at all.

'I thought you'd appreciate a morning coffee.'

'Yeah, I would, but I wouldn't appreciate

getting my hand burnt off. Put it on my desk.' She went to move on.

'So?' he asked, and she faced him with a heavy sigh.

'What?'

'What happened? Did you find out who might've been aiding her?'

'No.'

'No? You didn't find anything?'

She let out a deeper sigh. 'Look, I'm working on it.'

'You're working on it?' Moone shook his head, then looked at her again, realising now had to be the time to inform Butler how imperative it had become that they take Carthew down.

'Yes, I'm working on it. Trust me.'

Moone nodded and rubbed his eyes. 'Thing is, we need to get it all sorted like, well, yesterday. The state of play has changed a little.'

Butler's face tightened, her head starting to shake side to side. 'What the hell have you done? Or what's she done?'

Moone took a look around to make sure no one was earwigging their conversation, then stepped closer to Butler and lowered his voice. 'She knows.'

Butler's brow creased. 'She knows? What does she know?'

'About Parry.'

Butler's skin lost all colour, her eyes widening. 'You're bleeding well joking?'

'I wish I was.'

Butler buried her face in her hands for a moment, then looked up at him, her eyes digging into him. 'When did she tell you this?'

'She ambushed me right after I met Alice for lunch. She says she's got film of us at Parry's place.'

She closed her eyes, her teeth gritted. 'Jesus… that bloody…'

Then her eyes opened and they narrowed as she took in Moone. 'Did she say she followed us or something?'

'Yep. And saw us head to his place.'

'I didn't see anyone else on the road that day. I was checking. No cars following us. And there was no one hanging round his house that day. Just me, you and Parry.'

'Then how does she know?'

Butler looked away, staring off into space. 'She's trying it on. She's got wind of something and put two and two together and was seeing how you reacted. Knowing you, it probably put the wind up you and now she knows something went on.'

'Maybe.'

Then Butler pointed at him. 'What did she say she saw exactly?'

He shrugged. 'Us going to Parry's house and then said about him setting it on fire.

Why?'

'The girl we rescued. Did she mention the girl?'

Moone laughed. 'No, she didn't.'

'Because she wasn't there.' Butler nodded. 'Yeah, crafty cow. Somehow, she knew we went to his house not long before Parry killed himself, but she was just guessing at the rest.'

'But what if she's not? What if she has got film?'

'Next time she mentions it, you bluff it out. It didn't happen, you say, so she can't have film. She'd have to show it to you, wouldn't she?'

Moone nodded. 'OK. I hope you're right.'

'Where are we with our three murders?' Butler asked, obviously wanting to change the subject. He let it ride and pointed to the incident room.

'I was about to brief the team,' he said, handed Butler her coffee and walked into the incident room with her right behind him. He clapped his hands together as he said, 'Morning people. Listen up. Let's see where we are with our three murders. Come on, everyone gather round.'

Moone stood there, arms folded, eyeing his small team as they all pulled seats to where he was standing in front of the whiteboard. The gathering team included DS Carthew, and she caught his eye with a knowing smile that he pretended not to notice.

'Right, let's sum up where we are,' Moone said and looked over at the crime scene photos. 'Let's face facts. We're not very far along, with not that many leads. But we do have an eyewitness, Jon Michael Reagan, who has identified Nick Dann as possibly being the suited individual he saw hanging around outside Teresa Burrows' house on a couple of occasions.'

'How reliable is Reagan?' Butler interjected with a slight huff. 'It's twenty years ago. It could've been any man in a suit.'

Moone nodded. 'True. But he also said that the suited man he saw was driving a dark, maybe black, Mercedes. Nick Dann did own a dark blue Mercedes at that time. Look, this is one of the few leads we've got. I've talked to Dann and I got the feeling he was hiding something.'

'Yeah, the affairs he's had,' Butler said. 'He's scared his missus will find out and divorce him and take half of his fortune.'

Moone sighed, knowing she was mostly right, that the one lead they had was pretty flimsy. 'I know. It's not much, but it's all we've got at the moment. What if he did murder Judy Ludlow? Maybe she wanted to make it all public, wanted more from him…'

'Sir,' Molly said, her voice wavering as she slightly raised her hand. 'Sorry, boss…'

'Yes, Molly?'

She cleared her throat, looking round the room nervously. 'I've been looking into Nick Dann's background, and I've found that he didn't have... well, much of anything twenty years ago.'

'You mean he didn't have a pot to piss in?' Harding said and laughed.

Chambers blushed. 'It was his wife's money that he was living on. She's got plenty of it herself. It wasn't until a few years back that he started having any success.'

Moone smiled. 'So, if Ludlow had made a fuss or told his wife about their affair, then he could have lost it all. Thanks, Chambers. That gives us a motive. Nice work. What about CCTV?'

'We've started checking round Caroline Abbott's house, and further out, but there's not much around,' Harding said. 'Same with the first two victims.'

'What about this handyman?' Butler asked, stepping forward. 'Caroline Abbott had that leaflet through the door, didn't she? Has anyone seen any vans parked nearby or anything?'

'None of the neighbours have mentioned a van,' Harding said with a shrug. 'And no leaflet either. Could be a dead end.'

'Well, we need to bloody well find him still,' Butler huffed.

'We will,' Moone said. 'I've been talking to the criminal psychologist who helped on the first two murders. He's going to put a new profile together...'

'A profile?' Butler shook her head.

'What?'

'Well, profiles are based on the kinds of murderers we've caught, the ones who fit a pattern of behaviour. What if this bleeder doesn't fit that?'

Moone sighed. 'I know. They're never perfect, but Scott Eason, the profiler, says this guy would be very successful in his chosen career. That sounds like Dann, doesn't it? Let's at least give it a try. Of course, we're going to keep trying to find this handyman. But now we've got an eyewitness who's identified Nick Dann, I think we should talk to him again. Right, team, you've got your action lists, so let's get to work.'

When the team had dispersed, Moone went over to Butler's desk where she seemed to be filling out some paperwork.

'You all right?' he asked.

She let out a breath as she sat back. 'Yeah, fine. I didn't mean to give you a hard time, but this whole Nick Dann thing is a bit thin.'

'Don't tell me you know him too.'

She made a sarcastic face. 'No, I don't know everyone in Plymouth. Just a lot of people.'

'The six degrees of Mandy Butler.' He smiled.

'Thing is, Nick Dann has a lot of influence. No one's going to like us knocking on his door.'

'I know. Boulton's already told me to stay away.'

'See?' She let out another heavy breath.

'But we can't ignore what we know. What if he is our man? Anyway, the last time we dealt with a successful man, you thought he was our killer straight away. Remember Marino Black?'

'How could I forget? It wasn't him, I was wrong. But I don't think it's Nick Dann either. My money's on the handyman.'

'OK, we'll see who's right eventually.'

'Excuse me.'

Moone heard Carthew's voice behind him and turned to see her not looking too happy.

'What's wrong?' He knew exactly what her complaint was going to be, but he kept his face full of ignorance.

'I'm on CCTV duty?' She folded her arms, her cheeks reddening.

'Someone's got to do it.'

She raised her eyebrows. 'I know. But the reason we've got Nick Dann as a suspect is because of me. I deserve some kind of credit.'

'Thank you,' Moone said, the words almost choking him. 'But we all need to pull our weight.'

She stepped closer to him, moving herself

round so Butler could also hear what she was about to say. She looked between them as she lowered her voice.

'Don't forget,' she said, her eyes finding Butler's. 'I'm privy to certain events that happened a few months back. We wouldn't want that to get out, would we?'

Butler gave an empty laugh. 'Go on, you, get back to your CCTV duty. We're not going to be blackmailed. Jog on.'

Carthew returned her icy stare to Moone, her eyebrows raising. 'What would DSU Boulton and the new Chief Super make of it all?'

'They wouldn't believe you.' Moone stared back at her, keeping his face blank.

'Wouldn't they? What about when they saw the footage?'

'Show them and we'll find out.' He put on a smile, even though he could feel himself trembling with anger.

She stared at him, her cheeks still red, the flames in her eyes. He thought of his caravan, then hanging off Bickleigh Viaduct. His stomach rolled over and over, his hands shaking.

'Maybe I will,' she said, then walked away and returned to her desk.

Moone let out a harsh breath and faced Butler, his heart pounding. 'Jesus…'

'Well done,' Butler said, actually sounding

pleased for once. 'You've managed to enter puberty and grown some balls.'

'Thanks, but seriously, what if she does have a film of us?'

Butler looked over at Carthew, her eyes narrowed, full of contempt. 'She doesn't. She's bluffing.'

'I hope you're right, because if you're not then we're up shit creek without a boat, let alone a paddle.'

'Trust me. We're close to bringing her down.'

His hands were trembling as he turned the steering wheel, edging over the road, the indicator making its clicking noise as he prepared to turn into her road. Sarah's road. She would be home and alone, waiting for him to finally price the job.

This is it. This is the perfect moment to punish her.

What if she's not alone?

She will be. She's waiting for her punishment, ready to be finally disciplined for what she did to you all those years ago.

But this isn't her, this is a different Sarah. She hasn't done anything to me.

It doesn't matter.

He took the turning, the wheel moving through his hands that trembled, feeling the burning wave of fury building inside of him.

As he parked, his mind took him back all those years, the moments in between disintegrating as he found himself walking down the corridor, the same old stench of the polished floors, marked with a million scuffs from all the shoes that had marched along there. The summer sun glistened through the windows of the classrooms; muffled music came from one of the rooms along the corridor; the smell of food from the home economics class. He trembled as he saw her in the small hall, where all the kids were, getting ready for the assembly. There she was. Sarah. Her golden blonde hair shone, glowing almost as the sunlight beamed through the thin rectangular windows that lined the hall. For a moment she stepped away from her friends. He took a deep breath and tried to ignore the pounding of his heart in his chest as he forced his legs to carry him across the polished floor, past the scattering of other kids. She turned and looked at him before he even got within a couple of feet of her. Her eyes said it all, the disdain clear in them, but somehow he fooled himself into thinking that it might work, that she might say yes. Then he uttered the words in a hurried breath, half mumbled as he burned all over with horror. A crowd had gathered, the other kids in the hall, swooping in, smelling the scent of carcass in the air.

'You'd think I'd actually go out with you?'

she said, her voice sharp with venom. She started laughing then and everyone seemed to join in until the whole school was pointing and laughing at him. He looked round him, the hall seeming to spin, his spirit lifting out of his body so he could watch the whole spectacle, the horror of it unfolding from across the room. His face burned as he started to back away. He would have run out, but some kid stood in his way, and he backed into them.

'Watch it, you little shit,' the boy said, staring down at him with dead eyes. 'Oh, you going to cry? Go crying to your mummy 'cause she didn't want to go out with you?'

Then the laughter grew. He was laughing, the taller boy, looking round at his mates as they all laughed.

He didn't realise he had moved for a moment, but he was tearing towards him, his hands claw-like, cutting the air. The larger boy fell to the floor and he jumped on top of him, pummelling his fists into his face. The boy was screaming, crying, begging for help. Then hands grasped at him and dragged him away from the boy whose face was now covered in blood.

He didn't care what happened to him when he was sitting outside the head teacher's office, his face burning still, his heart thumping as the laughter kept playing over and over in his head. Other pupils passed him in the corridor, all of them whispering things, saying he was crazy. He didn't look at them, just stared straight ahead.

He almost hadn't noticed the man with the broom who was sweeping the corridor.

'You gave him a right seeing to, didn't you, bey?' the man said, but he didn't look at him. He was just a blurry dark shape in his peripheral vision.

'If you was being bullied before, I don't think anyone will bully you from now on,' the man said, leaning against his broom. 'At least that kid won't.'

He looked down, feeling tears rising to his eyes, a sob vibrating its way up towards his mouth. He kept it down, even though his hands and legs were trembling.

The man came over and sat down next to him. There was a pause before he said, 'She's not worth it.'

He hung his head, feeling the tears threatening to pour out again.

'Girls like that,' the man said, his voice growing deeper and lower as he leaned towards him. 'They're little bitches. Every one of them. Think they're God's little fucking angels or something. They're just bitches. Girls like that...'

He almost looked at the man, waiting to hear what he was going to say next.

'Well, they need to be taught a thing or

two,' he said, his voice lower, more a deep growl than an actual voice. 'They need to be punished. Don't they, bey?'

He was right. You know he was right about all those little bitches.

He blinked himself out of his dream, his heart still pounding at the memory of it all. The laughter of all those kids resounded in his skull. The voice of the man, the man dressed in dark clothing, remained deep within his chest and hands long after that moment.

He stood at the front door, staring at it for a moment, trying to see it without the shadows of his past playing across his vision. The hate was there in his chest, moving to his hands, the surge of hot blood. He had decided already, he would do it as soon as the front door closed behind him. He would drag her to the kitchen and do what he was meant to do.

That's right, it's time to make that little bitch pay, along with all the other bitches.

He pressed the bell, everything around him stopping, no noise reaching his ears apart from the pounding of blood.

The door opened and he flinched, almost shaking his head with confusion as he took in the face of the person looking out at him who wore a pleasant smile. It wasn't Sarah.

'Hi,' she said, still smiling. 'Sorry, Sarah had to go out. Some kind of emergency, so I'm here instead.'

The friend, he said to himself, desperately trying to put a name to her face.

Another bitch, whatever she's called.

'Is it still all right to come in?' he asked, pulling himself out of his frozen state of shock. He forced a smile to his lips even though his hands were trembling.

'Yeah, of course,' she said, stepping back to let him into the hallway. 'Sorry, she's not here. You'll have to put up with me.'

He forced himself to laugh as he moved towards the kitchen, the disappointment and frustration filling him full of sickness.

'Do you want tea or coffee?' she asked and moved past him, smiling as she went.

The bitch. She would have laughed at you. She's a bitch like all the others, just like Sarah.

He watched her enter the kitchen, the warm sunlight pouring in through the windows, covering her outline in a sparking glowing light. Angelic, he thought. But it was a lie. He knew she was anything but.

'Did you want a tea?' she asked again, and he shook himself out of his dream.

'No, thank you.'

'So,' she said, filling up the kettle. 'Are you married?'

'No.'

'Girlfriend?'

He shook his head and put down his tool bag. He looked down at it and saw the handle of the hammer sticking out.

Pick it up. Pick it up and punish her.

'Hello?' she said and laughed. 'You're not married, you said. So do you have a girlfriend?'

He stared at her, then bent down as his heart started pounding again, that flood of rage pouring out of it. He gripped the handle with his trembling fingers and lifted it.

She looked at what he was doing, frozen, frowning.

'What's that for?' she asked, a strange note in her voice.

'For you,' he said, watching the fear start up in her eyes. 'Do you or Sarah have any tights?'

CHAPTER 13

Nothing could have prepared Moone for what awaited him inside the house. The sun was going down, lending the evening air a little bit of coolness but not much. The neighbours were gathering outside and he'd given orders for the uniforms to keep them back. The cordon had been set up by the on-duty inspector, traffic through the scene kept to a minimum. SOCOs were already at work, taking photos, prints, and anything they could get their latex-gloved hands on. Moone was decked out in a light blue forensic outfit, a face mask covering his jaw, beating his breath back at him. He was standing on the cusp of the kitchen, staring down at the body that was lying there. He had a sudden ball of vomit try and rise to his throat, but he swallowed it back down. He looked away, but the image of the victim's head, a swollen, red and black mess, remained in his vision. He had seen the black tights tied around her neck. His eyes jumped to a letter on the kitchen table, and he read the name. Sarah.

Sarah Launce. They had a name for the victim.

'Same knot,' a female voice said behind him.

He turned, glad to have a reason not to be looking at the body any longer.

Dr Jenkin's eyes were fixed on him, barely visible through the hood of her forensic outfit and her face mask.

'You're sure?' Moone asked.

'Pretty sure,' she said and looked past him at the body. 'Obviously, we'll know more once she's on the table. But looks like the same killer, doesn't it? The beating and the tights.'

Moone nodded, tasting the bile at the back of his throat. 'It does. It's him. We need to search the place, see if there's a leaflet or flyer advertising…'

'Boss,' Chambers called from the front door which had been encased in a forensic tent.

'Excuse me,' he said and went to move past Dr Jenkins.

'This probably isn't the time,' Jenkins said as he got parallel with her. 'But don't forget about the party next Saturday.'

He looked at her blankly for a moment, then he recalled the conversation from their last crime scene. He nodded, although the thought of attending a party seemed like the last thing he wanted to do. 'Of course. Can't wait.'

'You don't have to.' He could see she

smiled through her eyes.

'I'm looking forward to it. I'll need a few drinks after this week. I'll talk to you later.'

He moved on, desperate to get out of the confines of the house and the SOCO outfit, his body temperature seeming to rise quickly. He needed air, fast. He rushed through the tent and found Molly standing at the end of the short front garden. Behind her was a couple of uniforms trying to console a distressed and crying young woman.

'Who is she?' Moone asked after pulling off his mask, his heart being gripped and squeezed.

'She found the victim.' Chambers looked back at the woman who was panting and still sobbing. 'I'm going to take her to the hospital.'

'Good idea. What's her name?'

Chambers took out her notebook. 'Sarah Launce.'

Moone turned and faced the house that was being lit up by the flicker of the incident response cars' blue lights. He took down his hood and looked at the distressed young woman. 'There was a letter inside addressed to a Sarah Launce. This is her house.'

Chambers raised her eyebrows. 'So maybe she was the intended victim?'

Moone walked over, watching the woman wiping her eyes, trying to swallow down her sobs. He stood in front of her and held up his ID.

'Hello. I'm DCI Peter Moone. I'm so sorry for all this. It's Sarah, isn't it?'

She nodded, blinking back her tears. 'I can't... Shena...'

'Is that Shena?' Moone gestured towards the house.

'I... I think so. I just... she was so... oh God...'

The crying started again, her body trembling. There seemed to be no colour in her face except the blue light that lit up her skin every few seconds. She could be in shock, Moone told himself. It was no good asking her a lot of questions right then, her mind would be all over the place, but they would need answers pretty soon. He looked at one of the uniforms, a slender, male uniform with a goatee beard. 'Get her to Derriford, would you?'

'I'm fine,' Sarah said, taking a shaky breath.

'We need to get you checked out before we ask you any more questions.'

Sarah nodded before she was escorted to an incident response car.

Moone was waiting close to the turning to Derriford Hospital, having a crafty cigarette when he saw Butler's work car pass by. He quickly dropped his cigarette and moved away from the rest of the smokers and hurried towards the Emergency Department where

Sarah Launce had been taken. The dead woman was Shena Caballero, a fact they had gleaned from her ID in her purse found in the kitchen. He assumed the dead woman must be Sarah's friend. A case of mistaken identity, he wondered as he reached the doors of the hospital. Butler met him by the cafe and they started walking towards the Emergency Department.

'Had a cheeky fag, have we?' Butler asked, shooting him a look as they sidestepped a hospital bed that was being pushed by two porters.

'What makes you say that?' He didn't look at her and instead stared at the large man at the centre of the bed whose skin was quite yellow.

'You stink of it.'

'Thanks.'

'You're welcome.' Butler hurried on, and he followed her into the emergency triage area that echoed with the cacophony of cries, orders being barked and general chatter. Machinery beeped while people lined the corridors on beds.

'So our killer struck again?' Butler asked, stifling a yawn.

'Looks like it,' Moone said, then approached an Indian-looking doctor and showed his ID. 'Sarah Launce. She was brought in a few minutes ago.'

The doctor looked round and then

checked a whiteboard on the wall. He pointed towards some curtained-off bays as he said, distractedly, 'Bay four.'

Moone hurried on down with Butler close behind him, mentally preparing himself to face a woman for the second time who had come home to discover her friend beaten and strangled to death. He took a deep breath and then gingerly pulled back the curtain. He saw Sarah lying on a bed, while a dark-haired, caramel-skinned nurse was sitting beside her.

As soon as the nurse spotted Moone she was up and chasing him out.

'You can't come in here,' the nurse said, her face full of venom as she ushered him back out.

'I'm DCI Peter Moone,' he said, showing the nurse his ID. 'This is DI Mandy Butler. It's imperative that we talk to Sarah.'

'Well, I don't care,' the nurse said, shooting them both stern looks. 'She's under our care. That poor woman's in a state of shock.'

'We know, but we need to ask her some questions,' Moone said.

'I understand that,' the nurse said, seeming to soften a little. 'But I have a duty of care. I have to consider her right now.'

Butler pushed Moone aside and stared at the nurse. 'We understand what you're saying, and we appreciate what she's been through, but right now there's a psycho out there looking for another poor woman to murder. It could be anyone's daughter, sister, mother... have you got kids?'

The nurse sighed, then nodded. 'Listen, if it was me who had been...'

'It's OK,' a quiet voice said from within the cubicle.

They all looked round at the young woman with the red, wet eyes, who had a blanket wrapped around her. Even from there Moone could see she was trembling and for a moment he felt as if he should walk away and leave the young woman to rest, but then his police brain kicked in. When the nurse stepped aside, Moone and Butler went in and stood looking down at her while the nurse stood guard.

'I'm so sorry,' Moone said and leaned against a cupboard close to the bed. 'I can't imagine what you're feeling right now...'

'I want you to catch him,' the woman said, staring up at Moone, the determination clear in her eyes. 'Please, go and get this bastard.'

Moone nodded. 'We will. Sarah, do you have any idea who might want to hurt you or your friend? I mean, he was in your home...'

'She was there to house sit for me,' Sarah said, closing her eyes, and swallowing down another sob.

'I see. You were at work?'

'No. I had to get some stuff for work. Thing is, I had someone coming round to price a job... Shena said she'd wait in for him... Oh God, do you think it was him?'

Moone looked to Butler and saw she wore the same wide-eyed expression as he probably did. He turned back to Sarah. 'Who was this man?'

'He calls himself Dave. He's like a...'

'A handyman?' Butler said.

Sarah nodded. 'Yeah. He's cheap and... but why would he do that? I don't understand.'

'We think he targets women, puts leaflets through their doors in the hope they contact him...'

Sarah shook her head as she sniffed back some tears. 'I didn't get a leaflet.'

'You didn't?' Moone straightened up. 'Then how did you find him?'

'A friend recommended him,' Sarah said, then more tears came. The nurse brought out a pack of tissues and gave the young woman one.

'Who was this friend?' Butler asked, stepping closer.

Sarah looked at her. 'Jane Mitchell. She said he does all kinds of jobs for her. Why would she recommend him?'

'Where does she live?' Moone asked and took out his notebook.

'I don't know.' Sarah raised her shoulders. 'I only know her from Facebook. She's a friend of a friend. I ended up befriending her. Oh God, so Shena... because she was...'

Then she looked up, and her eyes widened. 'He meant to, he was planning on...'

'Don't think about that, love,' the nurse said, patting her on the shoulder. Then she looked at Moone. 'I think you'd better leave it there. She's been through enough, don't you think?'

'I understand,' Moone said. 'But before we go, Sarah, we'll need you to describe him, so we can put together an image of him. Can you do that, do you think?'

She nodded. 'I'll try.'

'OK, thanks. We'll get someone to come and talk to you about it. And do you have a phone number for this Dave, and can we have permission to access your Facebook so we can find this friend of yours?'

Sarah managed to nod, so Moone, feeling awkward, said, 'Sorry, but we'll need your username and password.'

The nurse shook her head while she tutted, but Moone ignored her as he watched Sarah take out her mobile and bring up the details, including the mobile number she had for the mysterious Dave. He noted them down then thanked her again and gestured for Butler to follow him outside. There was a dark-skinned uniform outside when they came out of the cubicle, so Moone told him to stand guard. Then he and Butler walked outside where the setting sun was trying to blaze through the thick cloud that had gathered over the hospital.

'Are you thinking what I'm thinking?' Butler asked, so Moone stopped and faced her.

'What are you thinking?'

Butler pointed a thumb back at the Emergency Department's entrance. 'That this friend of hers, Jane Mitchell, doesn't really exist. It's what they do now, isn't it?'

'Who?'

'Scammers, stalkers, killers. Take your pick. They befriend one of your contacts online, then actually befriend you after a while. Interact normally, stalk you, observe your life, looking for a way in.'

Moone looked away, feeling the burn of the sun on his forehead. 'So, you think he's out there somewhere making flyers and stalking women online? And he waits until they need work done or something and then pretends to be this online friend and suggests this handyman, who is in fact him?'

'Yes, that's exactly it.'

Moone nodded. 'So what about Nick Dann?'

She sighed and shrugged. 'Doesn't sound like him, does it? I mean, so he happened to know both of the first victims. If we arrested everyone in Plymouth who happened to know those poor women or even Caroline Abbott, then we'd be arresting people all over the place. This isn't London, Moone, here people know people, their neighbours.'

'OK, well, when Sarah helps put together an image of this handyman, then we can also slip in an image of Dann and see what she says, can't we?'

'We can, but it won't be him. Nick Dann, businessman, swanning along to these women's houses and murdering them? He's too high profile in Plymouth.'

Moone nodded again, knowing she was making sense, but there was also a niggling feeling at the base of his skull, a sense that Nick Dann did have a part to play in all this, and it was to do with his reaction to the photos of the dead women. But he decided to put it all aside and follow Butler's lead for once. 'OK, let's forget Nick Dann for the moment. So where do we go now? We've got a mobile number for this Dave, but what's the chance it's untraceable?'

Butler looked surprised for a moment, then nodded. 'Yeah, probably a burner, but we'll soon find out. Well, let's get into Sarah Launce's Facebook account and see what's what. Maybe Barry's the best man for the job. Like I said, my feeling is this friend of hers, Jane Mitchell, doesn't exist, but we'll know for sure soon.'

DS Rivers was sitting at the back of Jake's

takeaway, nursing a cappuccino, pretending to look through her phone and not eyeing the door and waiting for Faith Carthew to step inside. She hated herself for watching the door, staring at it every now and again, hoping to see her standing there. It had been quite a while since they had met up, but she had promised that eventually they could be together properly when the dust had settled. She had sounded like she had meant it, and Rivers had truly believed her, at least she had until she had met DI Butler. Something about what the grumpy cow had said rang true, and a little amount of doubt had started to expand inside her bit by bit until all she could think was that Carthew was only out for herself. What did she expect? She knew what she had planned, and what she was capable of, so of course she shouldn't be surprised that her colleague and lover was duplicitous. But when they were alone together, she saw nothing in her eyes or felt nothing in her touch that told her she couldn't trust her.

She had sent her a text asking to meet up. The reply had been a simple, '*No. It's too dangerous, what if people saw us together?*'

'I have to see you, it's important.' Then there were several minutes of nothing. 'Please,' she had messaged.

'*Jake's,*' the reply came. '*Ten minutes.*'

She knew Carthew suggested Jake's

because it was close to the police station, right under their noses. There was also little CCTV coverage as long as you didn't park too close to the Charles Cross Police Station and didn't go anywhere near the cashpoints outside the Co-op up the street. All you had to do was park a few streets away in one of the residential areas, careful not to get a parking ticket, and then walk the back streets and head into the cafe. Jake's had one CCTV camera pointing at the counter, and as long as you kept your back to it, you had deniability. Anyway, why would anyone arrange a conspiratorial meeting in a place so close to a police station?

She heard the bell of the cafe door, then stared towards the entrance that was masked by the counter. A shadow fell, then she watched it stretch out towards her. Carthew appeared, decked out in a hoodie, the hood pulled up over her head as she hurried through the dining area and sat down opposite Rivers. She looked blank, emotionless as she lowered the hood and adjusted her ponytail. Rivers couldn't help but smile at the sight of her, despite knowing that behind her eyes lay a plot to get rid of her at the next opportunity.

'It's good to see you,' Rivers said, leaning forward.

'Put down your phone,' Carthew said, coldly. 'Flat on the table.'

Rivers sighed and shook her head. 'You

really think I'd try and record you?'

'Phone.'

Rivers put down the phone and pushed it towards her where Carthew examined it for a moment, then pushed it back.

'This is a bad idea,' Carthew said.

'It's the best place for us to meet, you know that. Anyway, we're just two colleagues meeting up for a coffee.'

'Then you'd better buy me a coffee,' Carthew said, her eyes blank. 'For appearance's sake.'

Rivers smiled, although her heart was starting to sink a little, a dark sensation invading her nervous system. She stood up and went and ordered a cappuccino for Carthew and brought it back.

She hadn't moved and seemed to watch her like a hawk as she sat down and pushed the drink towards her.

'Why are we here?' Carthew asked, lifting the coffee.

'They've been poking round.'

Carthew sipped the coffee, no sign of shock in her eyes. 'So? I told you they would. They're not as stupid as they look. At least, Moone isn't. Butler is just an unthinking, ignorant cow.'

'It's her that's been nosing round. She came to Bristol…'

'I know.' Carthew put down her drink.

'You knew?'

'Of course. I knew one of them would. They're trying to find whoever helped me. But they'll never find them.'

'They think it's me.'

'But you were elsewhere, so you haven't got anything to worry about, and I'm sure Crowne will vouch for you.'

'He would. They've got nothing. Everything you said has worked out.'

Carthew leaned forward. 'Then why am I here?'

'You know.' Rivers leaned forward, smiling.

'You're an idiot.'

'I need you.'

'No, you don't.'

'I do. Please, let me come to yours tonight. No one will see me.'

'It's tempting, but I'm busy tonight.'

'Doing what?'

Carthew sat back, her eyes moving away from Rivers to the rest of the cafe. 'It's not important, I'm just busy.'

Rivers felt her chest tighten, and despite herself, she felt a pang of jealousy. 'Busy with someone else, you mean?'

Carthew looked at her again, but this time there seemed to be a look of disappointment in her eyes. 'Oh, dear, I didn't expect to hear that come from you. Jealousy, really? Come on, you're better than that. No, it's not a romantic thing, it's just some other engagement. A work thing.'

Rivers' chest relaxed and she was left feeling a little foolish. 'Then when can we meet up? We need to talk things through.'

Carthew stared at her, seeming to size things up, before she said, 'OK, if you really are that worried...'

'I'm not worried. I just think we need to discuss the situation.'

'OK then. Tomorrow night. About eight. My place. I'll text the address.' Carthew stood up and pulled her hood back over her head. 'Don't contact me until then. And don't worry, I've got everything in hand. Moone and Butler won't be bothering us for long.'

CHAPTER 14

Barry was stifling a yawn as Moone and Butler walked into the long narrow room he used for his one-man IT department. As usual, Moone could see the remnants of takeaway boxes, chocolate bar wrappers and the discarded cans of energy drinks. Butler tutted, grabbed a nearby bin and started to tidy up. Barry watched her blankly as he turned in his chair to face them both.

'What's she doing?' Barry asked, rubbing his dark eyes that had two pillow-sized bags beneath them. To Moone, the lad looked even more tired and strung out than the last time he saw him, and part of him wanted to walk out and not trouble him. Then he felt the surge of desperation inside him override his misgivings. There were more potential victims out there and the thought of facing another battered, strangled woman was more than he could bear.

'Tidying up, by the looks,' Moone said,

then forced a friendly smile to his face. 'How are you?'

The IT lad nodded. 'Good. Not too much on, if you've got something for me. At least it'll get me away from this other godawful stuff.'

'What stuff?' Moone looked over at his monitor but whatever he had been working on had been minimised.

'Children,' he said and shook his head as he looked down. 'Online predators. Sick bastards.'

'You all right, Barry?' Butler said as she put the bin down. 'You look like you could do with a break.'

'I'm fine.' He looked at Moone. 'What've you got?'

Moone sighed inwardly. He saw flashes of the dead women, their battered heads almost twice their normal size. He lifted his notebook and showed Barry the details he had taken from Sarah Launce. 'We need you to take a look at the Facebook account of a woman who was targeted by our killer. We need to find a friend she knows on there. We think it might be a fake account.'

Barry took the notebook with a nod, then turned around faced his monitor and started to go to work, typing away at his keyboard. 'Jane Mitchell?'

'That's the friend,' Butler said, standing over his shoulder. 'I reckon she doesn't exist.

She's supposed to live in Plymouth, but we don't know where to.'

'I'll soon tell you if she's real or not.' Barry brought up Facebook and logged in as Sarah Launce. He was moving through her contacts and information at lightning speed. Soon Jane Mitchell's profile appeared. Barry let out a huff.

'What is it?' Moone asked, stepping closer.

'She hasn't posted anything for a couple of weeks. The stuff she has posted over the last year has been a lot of shares, or really obviously fake stuff. I can see the comment she posted on your witness' page, suggesting this Dave, the handyman, but there's not much else after that. Everything stops.'

'So she isn't real?' Butler asked. 'I bloody knew it.'

Barry sat back. 'Her account started about a year ago. She became friends with your Sarah Launce about that time. I'll have to contact Facebook to see if I can get an IP address and go through the rigmarole of trying to track this person but might take a while. Chances are it won't lead us anywhere.'

'So he set this up a year ago?' Moone stared at the screen. 'Just to try and trap Sarah Launce?'

'Probably not only her,' Barry said and pulled out a can of energy drink from under the desk and opened it. 'I'll check for anyone else this Jane Mitchell has contacted.'

'How many other potential victims has he been stalking like this?' Moone asked out loud.

Moone and Butler looked at each other as they both sighed. Moone shrugged, then patted Barry's shoulder. 'Thanks. We also sent you a mobile number to check out.'

Barry nodded, then took out a sheet of paper and read it. 'Pay-As-You-Go phone. A burner. I'm trying to find out where it was bought. Your killer might have made a mistake and got himself caught on CCTV when he purchased it.'

'I'm not holding my breath,' Butler said. 'At least we can see where it was used, can't we, and track it?'

'Yeah, I'll let you know what comes up.' Barry smiled briefly and sipped his drink, staring at them.

Moone sensed it was time to go and leave the sickly-looking lad to his job, so he gestured to the door. 'Come on, Butler, we've got Professor Scott Eason coming in.'

'Oh, bloody hell, we haven't, have we?' Butler sighed and elbowed past him to head up the stairs to the incident room.

'What have you got against him?' Moone asked, hurrying after her.

She stopped and faced him. 'A profiler. I've already told you what I think. He'll be getting us chasing geese all over the shop.'

'What can it hurt? He might actually have

some useful information.'

Butler stared at him for a moment, then said, 'I hear he's from your neck of the woods, isn't he?'

'Yes,' Moone said, hesitantly. 'We went to the same school. Why?'

'That's all we need, two Enfield boys leading us astray.' She shook her head and carried on up the stairs towards the incident room. They both stopped abruptly when they came face to face with the sight of Professor Scott Eason standing chatting with a female uniform outside the incident room.

'There he is,' Eason said, stepping away from the uniform and putting out a hand to Moone. 'Good to see you again, Pete.'

Moone shook his hand, feeling the professor's hard grip, one eye on an unimpressed Butler. 'And you, Professor.'

'Call me Scott,' Eason said, his smiling dark eyes taking in Butler. 'We went to the same school.'

Butler nodded. 'So I hear. What happened to you?'

Eason frowned. 'I'm sorry?'

'Your voice? You don't sound like him, all wheelbarrows and cockles.'

Eason laughed. 'No. I've travelled about and managed to lose the old Enfield twang. But I miss being one of the common people.'

Butler exchanged a strange glance with

Moone, but he stepped in and said, 'Let's get this show on the road. In here, Scott.'

'DCI Moone!'

It was DSU Boulton's voice that echoed up the stairwell, so Moone smiled an apology and told them to go in without him as he prepared to face another telling-off.

Boulton was adjusting his tie as he reached the top of the stairs, his face emotionless. He stared at Moone as he stepped closer and put his hands into his trouser pockets. 'Was that Professor Eason?'

Moone nodded. 'It was. I'm thinking he might...'

Boulton held up a hand. 'Save it, Moone. I want to hear what he's got to say before I add his wages to the budget. It's an interesting idea, getting a profiler in. Not often done these days. But you realise, if he gets it wrong and you end up chasing a wild goose, then it's your career that goes down the toilet?'

Moone pushed a smile to his lips. 'I know. We've got other leads too and a surviving female victim who should be able to give us a description of our killer.'

'Good. I hope she does. By the way, I have noticed you seem to be leading the investigation, and not Butler...'

'I know, but I feel...'

'It's OK. I want to see how you get on.' Boulton started towards the doors.

'Thanks, boss.'

Boulton paused and looked back at him. 'Give you enough rope, I meant.'

Moone stood for a moment, watching the back of Boulton entering the room, then listened as he greeted the team. They had all started to gather around the whiteboard, encouraged by Butler. Moone went in, nodding to Eason as he stepped up to the whiteboard, then looking over the team, but avoiding the eyes of Carthew.

'Right, you lovely people,' Butler said, rubbing her hands together. 'It's briefing time. As you know, there's been a fourth victim. Shena Caballero was found late last night beaten and strangled. Everything points to the same killer. We know she was in Sarah Launce's house to let in a handyman who calls himself Dave. We've got a number for him but looks like it's a burner phone. Sarah Launce, who we believe was the killer's intended victim, found this handyman through one of her so-called Facebook friends…'

'Don't tell me,' Harding piped up. 'This friend doesn't exist.'

Butler huffed and narrowed her eyes at him before she said, 'Annoyingly, Harding's right. We think this killer puts leaflets through the doors of his intended victims or stalks them online.'

'So that's how he gets in,' Carthew said,

nodding.

'Yes, that's how he gets in,' Butler said, sounding annoyed. 'But Sarah Launce has met the handyman who came round to visit her, the man who we believe murdered her best friend, and hopefully she'll give us a face.'

A few fists punched the air in celebration.

'But right now, we have with us today, a guest. Professor Scott Eason. He worked on the original investigation, which obviously failed to find the original two victims' murderer. Professor?'

Eason looked a little put out as Butler moved past him and allowed him to take the floor. He smiled over the room, then adjusted his tie as he looked back at the victims' photos on the whiteboard. 'These women all have something in common. Yes, they're all dead, all targeted by the same deranged killer, but there's something else. They're all single, they live alone. They're strong, independent and attractive women.'

Eason looked them all over again, no smile this time. 'That's part of what drives him. He doesn't like that these women are independent, that they don't need a man in their lives to complete them. That makes him angry because he is driven to be that man. But it infuriates him that he can't be that man, that he isn't that man...'

'Is he single?' Carthew asked.

Eason looked over at her. 'Interesting question. Now, with a lot of cases like this one, we might be looking for a killer who hasn't been able to keep a relationship going like a lot of psychopaths fail to do, but not this one. I believe he's in a relationship, he might even have kids. But his wife, I think she's the dominant force in this relationship, and therefore he's come to resent that, her power and his lack of strength. Think about what we know about this man, how he earns a living, and how he uses that living to pick out his victims. He offers his services, his help. He wants to help them with jobs around the house that only, in the way he sees it, that a good strong man can provide. He wants them to look at him almost as a hero...'

'Right before he batters them to death?' Butler interrupted, letting out an exasperated breath.

Eason turned to face her, nodding a little. 'I know, it's hard to reconcile the two versions of this man, and that's probably because he's having trouble reconciling the two sides of himself and his two lives. Family man on one side...'

'Psycho on the other.' Butler folded her arms. 'The wife has to know.'

'Not necessarily,' Eason said. 'Not if her life is busy, which it probably is. In fact, she's probably pretty successful...'

Butler pointed at him. 'Didn't your previous profile on this killer, the one you did for our predecessors, say that you thought the killer would be a successful man himself?'

Eason lost his superior look and subtle smile. He looked awkwardly around the room for a moment, and Moone thought he saw a little anger flicker in his eyes. 'Profiles... they're never easy to put together, especially when the killer stops murdering for nearly twenty years. Now he's started again, and you've got more information to help me with... well, it sheds more light on the case, the killings and the man we're tracking down.'

Eason smiled again.

'That *we're* tracking down, you mean?' Butler raised her eyebrows and huffed out a short laugh.

Moone decided it was time to step in. 'Thank you, Professor Eason. We look forward to reading your profile, now you have more information. We won't detain you any longer.'

The professor shook Moone's hand, but he saw the man's dark eyes jump over to Butler with the same flicker of anger. Then he was all smiles again as he waved at the team and bid them farewell until next time.

'He was full of himself,' Butler said as she and the rest of the team returned to their desks and their duties.

'Well, I know he didn't add much that we

didn't already know,' Moone started to say.

'You're right about that.' She let out a breath and faced her monitor.

'Well, Moone,' Boulton said, nodding a little. 'He seems to know what he's talking about. Well done.'

Moone caught sight of Butler's smirk but ignored it as he smiled politely at his boss. 'Thanks, sir. We've got plenty of other leads too.'

'You said before.' Boulton looked around the room for a moment, then stared at Moone again. 'I take it they don't involve interviewing Nick Dann again?'

Moone opened his mouth to speak, but it was Butler who said, 'We still haven't properly eliminated him from our enquiry, sir.'

Moone watched on helplessly as Boulton looked over at her, then faced her, arms folded. 'Is that right, DI Butler? And why is that? As far as I know, all he's guilty of is knowing a couple of the victims. Isn't that right, Pete?'

Butler stared at him intently.

'Well, yes, but…'

'Well then,' Boulton interrupted, 'I don't want him bothered again. Not unless something incriminating turns up, which I'm sure it won't. Anyway, carry on the good work.'

Moone watched Boulton stride out of the room, then stop dead when Carthew called out to and hurried over to him. They seemed to be talking as they left together, and much to his annoyance and suspicion, he recognised the flirtatious way Carthew was acting as they disappeared down the stairs.

'She doesn't waste any time,' Butler said, still facing her monitor. 'Thanks for backing me up, by the way.'

'I tried to but he just doesn't want to listen.'

'Doesn't want one of his fellow masons arrested for murder more like.'

'You don't even know if either of them are masons.'

Butler looked at him and raised her eyebrows. 'A young copper quickly rising up the ranks and a successful businessman who seems untouchable even though four women have been murdered. Give me a break.'

Moone sighed, unable to find an argument, while his mind went back to Carthew, remembering the blackmail material she said she had on them. Then he remembered her threat, her promise to find the killer first. He laughed to himself, sure that she wasn't suddenly going to have more luck than them. *Where the hell was the killer?*

It was late afternoon by the time he managed to get back to the house. Not the one he lived in with his family, but the one that had been left to his wife in her father's will. It was pretty much gutted, with layers of dust lying over everything. His steps echoed as he entered, carrying the rucksack on his back. His hands were trembling as he carried on through to the back of the house and found the room with the laptop and monitor he had set up. It was a safe place, a place where he could think clearly. He sat down at the desk and breathed out as he booted up the laptop, listening to it hum as it came to life. He then logged into Facebook under one of his many new identities. He had a VPN in place, so he didn't have to worry about them tracking him through his IP address. This time he was called Tara. Tara Kirkland. She worked in a clothes shop in the city centre and usually had her lunch at Subway because it was healthier, supposedly. He bent closer to look at the profile picture had stolen online, taken from another social media site. Some other poor woman whose life was going nowhere, going through the same drudgery as all the other sad ones, punctuating her life with selfies that always masked her true face with a filter. He found a few other profiles of women in their forties, lonely ladies posting about how empty their lives were.

Don't feel sorry for the bitches. Don't make that mistake. They bring it on themselves, lording their beauty over all those pathetic young men when they were at school, rejecting any poor lad who might work up the courage to talk to them.

Young men. The same pathetic kind of boy he was at school, covered in acne, so ugly that no one could bear to look at him.

They laughed at you. They always laughed at you.

My wife didn't laugh at me, he told himself as he sat back, recalling those days so many years ago, long after he had learned to behave like everyone else and the acne had cleared up. He had also started to work out and dress a little better. There she was one night, sitting in the downstairs bar, ready, like him, to do the speed dating thing. All the women he had talked to as he was sent around the room, along with a carousel of desperate men doused in aftershave and booze, had seemed just as desperate, just as nervous. Of course, there were a couple of stuck-up women who felt they were too good to be there.

They were all bitches, every last one of them.

Not of all of them, not her. She listened, smiled, and somehow it seemed easy to be himself around her. Not completely himself, but that facsimile of a real person, of an actual human male that he had carefully crafted. He used to be good at copying pictures when he was a kid, amazing his parents and teachers with his ability to take a brief look at a drawing in a book and then reproduce it almost exactly. Now he did it with people, observing other men and trying to behave like they did.

It didn't stop her from growing to hate you, did it? To look down on you every chance she gets.

He swallowed it all down, the hate that started to pulsate through him, making his heart feel like it would explode at any moment. He breathed deeply as his hands trembled over the keyboard. Just find the next one, he told himself and tried to concentrate.

Find the next bitch, so she can be punished.

His head sprang up, his body freezing and his heart thumping as he heard a sound echo through the old house. He listened out, slowly getting up. There it was again, the sound like a key in a lock.

No, it couldn't be anyone coming in. Unless...

He raced out of the back room and closed the door behind him and hurried along the hall to the front door. Just as he reached the porch, he could see her shape through the frosted glass. It was her. His chest tightened, his fists clenching.

The inner door opened and her eyes sprang to him. Immediately the look of annoyance and disappointment was there before those dark brown dots started to examine the rest of the place.

'Jesus, what have you been doing?' she said, the venom thick in her voice as she stepped in. 'Haven't you managed to do anything to this place?'

His head started to pound in time with the pulse deep in his ears. 'I've been busy.'

Her eyes jumped to him, wide now and full of a look close to disgust. 'Busy? You? Give me a break. Jesus Christ, look at this place. You said you were going to do it up...'

'I'm working on it.'

She looked around again and started moving through the house, heading towards the kitchen. That would mean she might see the back room.

The bitch can't see the back room. You can't let her see the back room.

He rushed after her, watching her as her eyes jumped to every wall, every skirting board.

'What're you doing here?' he asked as she got closer to the back room.

She turned and looked at him, stared with that same old look of contempt. 'Riding a bike. What do you think? I'm looking the place over. My dad did leave it to me, you know?'

'I know. I will get it looking nice soon.'

She moved on towards the kitchen and stopped, seeming to stare into the room that was probably the worst of the house. Then she turned and looked at him, her face almost blank, except for the flicker of annoyance in her eyes. 'You'd better pull your finger out. I mean it. I want to see some progress here and I want to see you bringing home more money.

There's plenty more jobs for you out there, but you're not trying to find them...'

'I will, I'm trying...'

'I mean, I wonder what you do all day?'

He looked down, feeling the thud of fury in his chest.

You could do it now, find your tools, pick up the hammer and finish the bitch.

He looked up at her, shaking his head. No.

'Why are you shaking your head?' she asked, the same look of disgust on her face.

'I'll do my best, I promise. I was just about to organise some jobs to look at and price up.'

She released a deep, heavy breath, then moved past him, moving away from the back room. He let out a breath as she kept on going, not stopping to say any more. She opened the front door and went out, shutting it hard as she left. He breathed out all the flames and let his hands tremble. He looked towards the room that he could never have let her enter or leave. He still had work to do. His hand shook as he opened the door to the room and stepped in. He breathed out the fear and terror she had instilled in him in that bitter moment, then tucked it away as he thought of the greater game. He went over to the small secure unit he had bought several months before. It sat in the corner, looking like a tiny shed, the kind of unit people usually kept in their gardens to keep a small amount of tools in. He undid the padlock and opened the doors. There it was, the large piece of card he had bought. His heart beat wildly again, staring at the images, the photos he had taken of them, each of the women he had picked out.

Bitches.

He ran his hand over the few photos he had taken as he stood in their kitchens, staring down at their bodies, so still but transformed. The hate and rage had still bubbled in his system as he raised his mobile phone to take the shots. His hands had trembled as he took the photos, making them a little blurred. But that didn't matter. He moved the collage aside and took out the calendar he had marked with the specific dates. He placed his finger towards the end of the month and dragged it towards the bottom of the calendar. He nodded, seeing the date he had marked off in red. It was coming, that perfect moment.

Stuart McAllister climbed out of the taxi and immediately almost fell face-first onto the pavement. He managed to grab hold of a lamppost at the last second and steady himself. He laughed as he straightened up, his eyes trying to focus on the bright exterior of the club. The word Revolutions became illuminated in his pickled vision for a moment, then seemed to darken again as a crowd of young women, far too young for him, came screaming and singing along the pavement, their high heels tapping along, their breasts almost tumbling out of their low-cut dresses. Too young, he told himself and watched them go noisily into the same place he was heading.

'He ain't puked back there, has he?' the cab driver shouted as Webby paid him and climbed out.

McAllister leant in the passenger window and pointed a finger at the driver. 'I never puke. Never. I can hold my drink.'

The driver shook his head and started up the taxi, mumbling under his breath. He obviously didn't know who he was, who he had insulted. He was lucky he hadn't cut the bastard.

'Come on, Stu,' Webby said and pushed him towards the club's entrance. 'Let's get some shots and see if there're any tasty women in there.'

McAllister let himself be guided towards the door where two stocky and suited bouncers were standing ready to bar his way. But then they clocked him, and they knew who he was, knew the reputation of the gang he belonged to. They nodded with respect and stepped aside.

'Have a nice night, Mr McAllister,' one of them said.

The beat of music vibrated through the walls and travelled up his legs as he stumbled inside. They headed towards the ground floor bar that was already thick with bodies, made up of mostly young women with not much clothing on and a cloud of perfume following them. There were a few groups of young lads too, all stood back, eyeing the young women with a look of drunken awe and lust on their faces.

'Shot?' Webby shouted in his ear as he tried to push through the crowd at the bar.

'Tequila,' McAllister said and looked around him, listening to the tune playing, bobbing his head in time with the beat, still trying to focus on the environment. He could just make out more women coming down from upstairs in the club, and crowds of men necking drinks. Suddenly he felt himself sniff involuntarily, and his body tremble. He was coming down a little, he realised and started patting his shirt, searching for the little bag of coke he had. He looked around, and then moved towards the bar, stumbling into a group of lads, spilling one of their drinks. They started to make a fuss, but McAllister stared them all down, moving his head in close to all of theirs one by one until they all looked ready to go crying to their mummies. He pushed past them and made for Webby who was still holding out his cash card towards a barman who was too busy ogling the young women to serve anyone. He was going to tell him that he was going to head to the bogs to do a line, but then he realised he couldn't be bothered and started staggering off towards the stairs.

The thump of the music clouded his brain as he pushed past more crowds, heading for the toilets, one hand digging into his pocket and gripping the little bag of coke. He went in and saw a couple of guys waiting for the one toilet cubicle that was working. When the door opened and some young lad came sliding out, McAllister barged everyone out of the way and went in and shut the door. He told them all to fuck off, shouting up at the dividing wall. Then he poured out a line of coke, cut it up a little with his credit card and then snorted it up with a rolled-up fiver. He felt the burn in his nostril, then tilted his head back and laughed for no real reason. He felt a pound of excitement in his chest, the thump of his pulse that seemed to fall in time with the beat of the music.

Then he was outside again, the lights spinning over his eyes, the thump, thump of the music vibrating through his whole body, his heart racing. He stumbled down the stairs trying to find Webby, but not being able to see him anywhere. Where the fuck had the useless wanker gone? He didn't care.

Then someone bumped into him, nearly knocking him sideways. He was about to give them a mouthful when he spun round and saw a beautiful, stunning face staring back at him.

She had dark hair, a tanned face, and bright red-painted lips.

'Watch where you're going,' she said, then started moving through the crowd again. He flickered out of his dream and looked her over, noting the very short dark dress she wore, her bare, sexy legs and high-heeled black boots. He started to push through the packed club, following her as she headed through the crowds. She looked back at him, a frown forming, a look of disgust almost. He smiled and followed her to the bar on the other side of the club.

'I'll buy you a drink, beautiful,' he said, pushing in beside her.

'I don't think so,' she said, not looking his way.

'Stu,' he said, looking her up and down. 'What's your name?'

'That's for me to know.' She flashed her eyes at him, giving him the once-over.

He smiled. 'I can't keep my eyes off you.'

'I noticed.' She let out a huff, but he saw the flicker of a smile.

'Go on, let me get you a drink.' He signalled the barman. 'Oi, mate, get her a drink. Whatever she wants.'

'Thanks,' she said and said something in the barman's ear when he bent in close.

Soon she had a large glass of white wine in her hand, while he had a shot and a beer. He smiled at her but she hardly looked at him.

'Think you're a hard man, do you?' she said, sipping her wine. 'Big man, thinking he can get what he wants?'

'I usually do get what I want.' He necked the shot. 'Stuart McAllister. That's my name. You heard of me?'

'Should I have done?' She raised her eyebrows.

He moved closer. 'Most people in Plymouth have. I'm a legend. You heard of the Tomahawks?'

She nodded. 'Are you one of them?'

'One of them? I'm practically the fucking leader.'

'Practically?' She laughed and looked away.

'I am the leader.' He moved closer, pressing himself against her a little, noticing she didn't move away.

'I've got to meet my friend outside,' she said, after taking a gulp of her drink.

'You're going?' He had to at least get her number.

'She's waiting for me.' She looked up at him. 'You'd like my friend. Blonde. Pretty. Killer legs.'

'I like you.' He stared at her.

She smiled. 'Then come outside and meet my friend. We do everything together.'

'Everything?' He raised an eyebrow. *What*

a fucking night this was turning out to be.

'Everything. Come on, let's go outside.' She finished her drink, then started through the crowd, only occasionally looking back to make sure he was following. When she found that he was, she would give a little smile. Every time she smiled like that, he felt a deep stirring. *This was it. A fucking threesome was on the cards. Wait until the lads hear about this.*

Then they were outside, passing the drunken lads and young women laughing and stumbling about, trying to hail taxis. She kept going, leading him away from the club and into a back street. He couldn't keep his eyes off her, and she knew it.

'There she is,' she said and pointed towards an alleyway that ran behind the club.

He looked and saw the back of a blonde bird, resting against the wall as she smoked. Short black sparkly dress, fishnets on. High heels.

'Come and say hello,' the dark-haired one said and led him along towards her friend.

'Hey, I've found a friend for us to play with,' she said to her friend.

Stuart watched the friend throw down her cigarette then start to turn. He smiled as she faced him.

'What the fuck?' He stared at the friend. 'Hang on, I'm not...'

Then he saw it, the flash of silver as the

knife was raised. The burn tore through him. He tried to raise his arms, but the blade went in again. And again. He grasped at his body as he stumbled backwards, feeling the warm blood coating his hands. He slumped to his knees, trying to open his mouth to call out. The blade went in again, spearing his chest. Then the wave of icy darkness came rising up.

CHAPTER 15

Moone stopped and stifled a yawn at the top of the stairwell when he saw Kevin Pinder standing near the incident room waiting for him, holding two takeaway coffees. He smiled apologetically and stepped towards him.

'Morning, Inspector Pinder,' Moone said and looked at the coffees. 'Don't suppose one of those is for me?'

Pinder held out the takeaway cup in his left hand. 'Americano, just for you.'

'Thanks. I don't think you've ever bought me a coffee before. What're you after?' Moone removed the lid and then carried on into the empty incident room.

'Nothing,' Pinder said, following. 'Just following up on our conversation. You know about Lloyd Redrobe?'

Moone put his coffee on his desk. 'Did you find anything out?'

Pinder stared at his desk. 'Don't you have your own office now?'

Moone sighed. 'Yep, I do, but I feel a bit cut

off when I'm in there.'

Pinder nodded and rested on Butler's desk. 'I get it. Makes sense.'

'So, Redrobe?'

'Yeah, I've been talking to some of the people who live near him and hang out at the same sort of places.'

Moone stared at him. 'What people? Criminals?'

'Some. Don't worry, I've been very careful. Anyway, they tell me that Redrobe isn't up to much these days, apart from the drag act. Apparently, he's been making a big deal out of the fact that he's bored and nothing much is happening with him at the moment. Can't stop telling people how bored he is.'

Moone nodded and smiled. 'Meaning he's up to something?'

'Sounds like it. I've heard it all before. Not only that, but I found out he was supposed to do a gig a few months back, a quite well-paying one, but he ended up pulling out, saying he was ill. Guess what night the gig was?'

Moone laughed a little. 'Not when DSU Armstrong was murdered?'

Pinder nodded. 'That very night. So, sounds like your theory is correct. It was Lloyd Redrobe she got to dress up and go to Armstrong's room and kill him.'

'But we can't prove it.' Moone sighed and shook his head. 'We can't put him in Bristol that night, can we?'

'No. Not so far.'

'And no one wants to reopen the murder of Armstrong, so it's not like we can do anything officially. Do you think Redrobe might talk to us?'

Pinder gave a heavy sigh.

'What?' Moone asked, sensing something ominous was coming.

'Redrobe grew up in a little fishing village in Cornwall. Brought up by a single mum. Guess who else grew up in that fishing village?'

'Carthew?'

'The very same. Rumour is that Redrobe didn't know his dad. But I've got a theory that Carthew knows who his dad is.'

'Who?'

'I'm thinking it's her dad. He's no longer with us, but I've been doing some digging and I get the feeling he liked to stray. I think they're related. Family.'

'Carthew's dad and Lloyd's mum?' Moone rubbed his eyes. 'So they're bonded by blood? Perfect. Chances are he won't grass on her then?'

'I don't know. I mean, he's a little psycho anyway, and now he's a little psycho who's recently learned he has a half-sister. I think he'd do anything for her.'

Moone leaned over the desk, shaking his head, thinking over it all, trying to find a way to entrap her, but not finding anything. 'Shit. So where does that leave us?'

'He'd do anything for her. But he's also a survivalist, and terrified of going to prison. I know that much about him.'

Moone nodded. 'I see. So, we'd need something incriminating on him and then he might start telling tales on his sister?'

Pinder shrugged. 'Honestly, I don't know. Maybe. But there's something else that came to my attention this morning when I went through my overnight incident reports. There was a fatality last night. A stabbing near the Revolutions club.'

'Jesus. I hadn't heard. Who was stabbed?'

'Stuart McAllister.' Pinder raised his eyebrows.

Moone shrugged, feeling a little lost as was usually the case when they discussed local and usually infamous individuals.

'We talked about the Tomahawks and the Dark Horses a while back, remember?' Pinder said.

'The motorcycle clubs. I remember.'

'McAllister was a leader of the Tomahawks. Now he's dead.'

'Gang-related, then?'

'Stabbing outside a club? Would look like it, but they said he left with a woman. Dark hair, attractive, average height.'

'Is this to do with Redrobe?'

'I don't know. But it's a coincidence, isn't it? He's on our radar, he's got dealings with these gangs and suddenly one of the leaders of the Tomahawks is murdered. It'll put things into chaos. The Dark Horses stand to gain a lot from this chaos, like the Tomahawks' territory.'

'Jesus. I wonder...'

'What?' Pinder said, but Moone was watching the female figure that had appeared up the stairs and was about to pull open the incident room door.

Pinder turned and joined him in watching DS Carthew breezing into the incident room, a smile on her lips. She looked at them both, still smiling and then headed to her desk.

Pinder stepped closer to Moone and lowered his voice. 'She seems very cheerful this morning. Do you think she got laid last night?'

Moone still had his eyes on her. 'Or she got her kicks some other way.'

'I don't think I want to even contemplate that.'

The incident room door opened and DC Molly Chambers stepped halfway through, her coat still on her shoulders as her eyes jumped to Moone.

'Boss,' she said, keeping her voice low. 'I just checked in with Barry about the burner phone. He found out where it was bought. Turns out it was purchased at a place called House of Fone, in Liskeard.'

Moone felt the old tingle of excitement along the back of his neck. 'How far is Liskeard?'

'About half an hour,' Pinder said. 'Allow for traffic though at this time of day.'

Moone nodded and looked at Molly with a smile. 'Fancy a nice drive to Liskeard, Chambers?'

Butler was parked on a side street, close to North Prospect Road. She could see the library and the shops and the new build houses that weren't so new any more, now the beige exteriors had rainwater stains down them. She sighed and watched the traffic coming and going, checking the time and seeing she was going to be late for work, but this couldn't wait. She still felt a little guilty not telling Moone the full story, but she had convinced herself it was best he was kept in the dark, and therefore if it did all go wrong then he would have deniability. It would be her job, not his. She told herself off for being so soft and pushed aside that stupid feeling she got when she thought about him. *What the hell was she playing at?*

Butler jumped when there was a tap on the passenger window. DS Rivers waved a hand, her eyes jumping to the street furtively. The poor bitch was scared, and she had every right to be, but she wasn't about to drive that fact home.

Butler unlocked the car and watched Rivers get in and seat herself, her eyes facing the street.

'So?' Butler asked.

'She's being very cagey,' Rivers said and let out a harsh breath.

'Of course she is. She's a cunning cow.'

Rivers nodded a little and looked down at her hands. 'I don't like any of this...'

'You feel like you're betraying her?'

'I am.' She looked at Butler. 'It's not often I meet someone who understands me...'

Butler couldn't help but laugh and shake her head.

Rivers' eyes widened. 'What? Is that funny to you?'

'Oh no. Well, sort of. Listen, I know how you feel. You meet someone, you work with them and you kid yourself that you're getting feelings for them or something... but it's just a...'

'Just a what?'

Butler shrugged. 'I don't know. A workplace crush or something.'

Rivers examined her for a moment, adjusting her position so she could get a better look at Butler. 'I don't work with her. That doesn't sound like you're talking about me. Sounds like you're talking about yourself.'

Butler huffed and looked towards the street, watching an old man pulling an equally old dog along the pavement. 'Chance would be a fine thing.'

'You work with Moone, don't you? You're partners, buddies, aren't you?'

Butler looked at her. 'This is real life, Rivers, not a Hollywood cop movie. Yes, we work together. What of it?'

Rivers smiled. 'Nothing.'

'No, go on.'

'Sounds like you like him.'

Butler found another huff escaping her, and that no words seemed to come to her lips.

'Life's too short not to tell him. You never know what's around the corner.'

'Are you a copper or a life coach? Listen, just tell me what's going on with Carthew. Are you meeting up or what?'

Rivers nodded and looked through the windscreen. 'We met yesterday…'

'Yesterday? Why didn't…'

'Hang on, let me finish. It's fine. We met up in Jake's, the takeaway place behind Charles Cross. But we're meeting up tonight at her place. I tried to arrange it for last night but she had something on.'

Butler let out a sigh. 'Where's her place? I'll park close by.'

'I don't know. She messaged and said she'd tell me at the last minute. You don't have to worry, I'll be fine, I don't need you looking out for me.'

'Right, OK, then you need to be wired for sound, though.'

'What, you want me going in there wearing a wire?'

'No, don't be ridiculous.' Butler opened the glovebox and brought out a small, black digital recorder and handed it to Rivers. 'Take this with you. Conceal it somewhere, then make sure you get a moment alone to hide it somewhere and record her.'

Rivers gave an exasperated laugh as she held up the recorder. 'Conceal this? Where?'

'You've got a good imagination. Where do the junkie prostitutes hide their drugs?'

Rivers raised her eyebrows. 'Jesus. There's something wrong with you.'

'Yeah, they keep telling me. Just get that recorder into her place and record her talking about all the fucked-up stuff she's done.'

'Oh, yeah, I'll just get her admitting to murder... easy.'

'I know you have doubts, that maybe she's got a good heart under it all, but trust me, she hasn't, and she'll get rid of you in a heartbeat.'

Rivers let out the air from her cheeks and put the phone away. 'I know. I know what she is. Doesn't make it any easier.'

'And don't go thinking I've somehow forgotten that you were all too willing to go along with her shenanigans. I haven't. Do this and I might not dob you in.'

Rivers' bottom lip seemed to quiver as if tears might be on the way, but she sniffed and looked at Butler. 'I will. I'll record her. But that's it. Then it's over for me. I'm finished after this.'

'Fine. Call me right after.'

'I'll try if it's not too late. If not, I'll call you in the morning.'

Butler huffed. 'Where are you staying, by the way?'

'Jury's Inn, room 68, under the name Holly Varjak.'

'Interesting name.' Butler shook her head and let out a breath.

'Thanks. It's an identity I used when I was undercover for a couple of years. I thought it might come in handy one day.'

'Well, it has. Right, best I get on then.' Butler started the engine.

'OK, short and not so sweet.' Rivers watched for the traffic in the wing mirror then opened the door.

Butler had a pang of uneasiness suddenly that reached her mouth before she could think twice about it. 'Rivers?'

She stopped as she was about to climb out. 'What?'

'Be careful. Remember, you might have feelings for her, but she's still a psycho. Don't trust her. First sign of trouble, you get out of there. Got it?'

'Yes, Mum.' Rivers laughed, then climbed

out and crossed the street.

Butler started to drive, her stomach churned up, half a mind to call it off. But it was their only chance to catch the psycho bitch out.

Chambers was driving, taking them deep into Cornwall after travelling over the Tamar Bridge, heading to Liskeard. Moone was silent for most of it, thinking over everything that had happened, the two most recent murders as well as the motorcycle gang-related death. A stabbing. The victim was last seen with an attractive woman. He sighed, trying to attach significance to it somehow, but as Pinder had said before he headed out, the Tomahawks and Dark Horses had been at each other's throats for a long time and there had been more than a few causalities in the past. He mentally shrugged and returned his tired brain to the matter in hand.

'I wonder if they keep their CCTV footage or wipe it,' Moone said out loud.

Chambers looked at him briefly. 'Most places wipe it unless there's some kind of incident. Unfortunately.'

He nodded. 'Could be a wild goose chase, then.'

'But he was here, actually here, buying a phone. There has to be something.'

Moone nodded, hoping she was right and that they weren't up against some kind of genius.

As if she had read his mind, Chambers said, 'He's going to make a mistake. He probably already has. He's got some kind of compulsion driving him to do all this and that'll trip him up at some point. Plus, Sarah Launce has given us a description, so we've now got an image of him.'

Moone sighed. 'Have you seen it? Baseball cap, dark hair, average-looking guy. Nothing that stands out.'

'It's a start. But like I said, he's obsessed. He'll make a mistake.'

Moone sat up. 'What is this all about, do you think? I mean, he kills two women, then stops for all this time then decides to start again. Why? What happened?'

'Could be a lot of things...'

Moone looked at her. 'But this is about rage? Real fits of furious violence. What can keep that in check for twenty years? I mean, take Carthew for example. She's driven by the desire to show how clever she is, and to get what she ultimately wants...'

'To be top dog.' Chambers hit the indicator and took them towards Liskeard.

'That's right, and there's no way she would just stop unless...'

'She died.'

'But our killer is alive and he's even more furious than ever. He's going to kill again and soon.'

'And we have no idea who he's targeting.'

'Unless Barry turns up something. We're getting nowhere fast.'

'We'll get there in the end. But what about Carthew? What are we going to do?'

Moone gave her a smile that tried to hide his absolute lack of a plan. 'I'm working on it.'

She nodded, then indicated when they reached the town centre. There was a car park close to the station, so Chambers took them there, then they walked in the early morning sun that was already starting to sizzle everything in sight. Moone loosened his tie as the sweat started to seep down his sides, hoping he remembered to put on his deodorant. He didn't want Chambers thinking he stank of B.O.

'I'm a bit worried about Keith,' Chambers suddenly said.

'Keith?' Moone was lost for a moment. 'Oh, you mean Harding?'

She nodded. 'Yeah, Harding. He's not been his usual jokey self lately.'

'People have off days.' Moone saw the phone shop and pointed it out. 'Just up there.'

'I know. I heard a rumour that his wife, well… she's in the family way.'

Moone stopped dead. 'Really? He's not said anything to me… but I don't suppose he would. Oh well, it's a lot to deal with, I guess. Being a dad.'

She smiled, but there was no real conviction behind it, so he said, 'I'll have a word with him soon.'

'That would be good. Shall we go in?'

They headed into the interior of The House Of Fone and moved towards the counter, past the shelves full of mobile phones and cables and endless accessories.

'Quite clever that name,' Moone said, watching a youngish, long-haired assistant talking to a middle-aged man at the counter.

'What name?' Chambers said.

'The shop name. House Of Fone. House Of Fun. Madness.'

Chambers looked at him blankly. Then he remembered the age difference and he suddenly felt a million years old as he said, 'They were a band in the eighties. Had a song called House Of Fun.'

Chambers broke into a bright smile. 'Oh, right, yeah, I get it. I hope they keep their CCTV footage.'

It was only a few seconds later that the middle-aged customer had gone and Moone and Chambers moved up to the counter. Moone produced his warrant card and held it up. 'DCI Peter Moone. This is my colleague, Detective Constable Molly Chambers. Don't worry, we're not here to buy any party poppers or coloured balloons.'

Moone laughed, but the shop assistant

just stared at him blankly.

'Tough crowd. Anyway, we're here because a pay-as-you-go phone was purchased here several months ago and has had some involvement in a very serious crime.'

The young man raised his eyebrows and looked between them as he swept some of his hair from his eyes. 'Well, we just sell people phones, so we can't be held accountable for what they use them for, can we?'

'That's not why we're here.' Moone smiled. 'The phone was purchased in April this year, on the fifteenth to be precise. That was a Saturday.'

'We're always really busy on Saturdays,' he said, giving an awkward smile. 'It's a madhouse in here on Saturdays.'

'Well, do you keep your CCTV footage?' Moone asked, gesturing to the small camera pointed towards the counter.

The young man looked round and stared up towards the camera briefly before he faced Moone and shrugged. 'No, sorry, that gets wiped every month unless there's some incident, and I can't think of anything happening for a long time. People come in wanting a new phone, or they're having problems with their phone... it's pretty dull stuff.'

Moone looked at Chambers and she seemed to be wearing the same look of disappointment as he knew must be on his face. 'Right, OK, that's not very helpful…'

The shop assistant shrugged. 'Sorry, wish I could help. What happened, I mean what crime was committed?'

'Sorry, we can't discuss that,' Chambers said as Moone turned away for the moment, thinking about it all, trying to come up with something useful. Only one thing came to mind. He turned back to the assistant and said, 'Were you working that day?'

The assistant shrugged. 'Can't remember.'

'It was a Saturday,' Moone said, and let out a tired breath. 'You said it's a madhouse on Saturdays.'

He nodded. 'Yeah, but I have some Saturdays off. I have a life.'

Moone rubbed his eyes. 'OK. Sorry, what's your name?'

'Gareth.'

'OK, Gareth, can you find out if you were working that day or who was? Please?'

Gareth closed his eyes briefly, shook his head and started to turn towards the door marked "private" behind him. 'I'll try and find the rota.'

'Thanks.' Moone looked at Chambers, putting on a look that said he might cry like a baby. 'Why is nothing straightforward? Why are we never chasing a moronic killer who makes mistakes left, right and centre?'

Chambers smiled. 'Don't worry, boss, he's

going to make a mistake. I've been thinking, if this is about rage like you said, then we know people are impulsive when they're angry. That's when they mess up.'

Moone nodded. 'It's good. Thanks. Yep, you're right, he's bound to do something stupid sooner or later.'

The door to the back room opened and Gareth came ambling out with a sheet of tatty A4 paper in his hand which he placed on the counter.

'I was right,' Gareth said, seeming to smirk a little as he tapped the paper. 'I was on holiday. Went camping.'

'Nice,' Moone said. 'So, who was working?'

'We had the boss in then,' Gareth said. 'Don't tell her I said so, but she can be a bit of a cow.'

'We won't let on. What's her name?'

'Rachel Yeo,' Gareth said. 'Doesn't live far from here. Just a couple of miles out.'

'Can you write down the address?' Moone put on a smile, but it didn't seem to help the young man move any faster.

'Sure.'

'Oh and can you check for payments that day and see if anyone paid for any pay-as-you-go phones with cash or card?'

Gareth looked up at him with a tired expression. 'Sure.'

Moone turned and smiled at Molly. 'We're

getting somewhere.'

The drive took them about three miles from Liskeard town centre and out into the countryside and the narrower lanes. Moone looked up and saw the sunlight breaking through the canopy of trees that almost made a tunnel of the road. There was a tractor ahead, but Chambers soon overtook it and then the SatNav told them to take the next right, which took them down a private road which led to a huge, paved driveway and the large, quite imposing house that stood beyond it. To Moone, it looked as if at one time the building could have been a large stable or something similar and quite recently converted into a red brick affair.

Chambers parked on the driveway, close behind a dark red Range Rover, and then they both climbed out and stared up at the house and the grounds.

'What do you reckon this goes for?' Moone asked.

'No idea. Got to be something like half a million or something like that.'

'Half a million?' Moone stared at her. 'It's got to be double that surely? And to think I live in a bloody caravan.'

'You said it was a mobile home.' Chambers laughed.

'Well, in an instance like this, it's a

caravan. I tell you what though, this Rachel Yeo is security conscious.' Moone pointed to the gable end of the house where there was a cluster of security cameras pointed towards the road.

The front door opened then and a woman dressed in a short-sleeved white shirt and dark grey skirt came out, tapping along the driveway in her high heels. She had quite long, light brown hair styled a little like Rachel from Friends, Moone thought.

'Can I help you?' the woman said, her perfectly plucked eyebrows raised.

Moone took out his warrant card and showed it to her. 'DCI Peter Moone. This is DC Molly Chambers. Are you Rachel Yeo?'

She folded her arms over her chest, her eyes narrowing a little. 'Yes, I am she. What's this about? It's not my daughter, is it?'

'No, don't worry.' Moone smiled. 'It's to do with your shop, the one in Liskeard. We were told you were working there one Saturday a few months back.'

'Come inside,' she said and turned and started walking towards the house, her heels tapping loudly over the driveway. Moone shrugged at Chambers and gestured for her to go first, which she did.

Moone followed them both in and found himself in a long and beautifully designed kitchen that was sprinkled with sunlight from four skylights above. The woman directed them to a large round dining table where she sat and crossed her legs, waiting with her eyebrows raised.

Moone sat down at the same time as Chambers and smiled at Rachel Yeo. 'Do you live alone, Mrs Yeo? Apart from your daughter, I mean?'

'It's Miss Yeo,' she said, with a flicker of a polite smile. 'I'm divorced. And my daughter doesn't live here any more. She abandoned me to go and live with her boyfriend. But what I really want to know is what this is all about.'

'Of course.' Moone nodded. 'We believe a suspect of ours bought a phone from your shop. A burner phone. And seeing as your CCTV footage is wiped regularly, we need to see if anyone remembers this man.'

She sighed. 'Then you need to talk to my staff...'

'We did and they said you were working that day. It was on the 15th of April of this year. That was a Saturday.'

'You expect me to remember some random customer who came in to buy a cheap, pay-as-you-go phone? You're wasting your time.' She stood up, obviously ready to show them out, but Moone remained seated, as did Chambers.

'He wouldn't have wanted to be recognised,' Moone said. 'He might've worn sunglasses, a hat or even a face mask.'

Rachel Yeo looked between them with disbelief in her eyes. 'You're kidding, aren't you? You've just described half the men who come into my shop. This is a waste of my time.'

'So you don't recall,' Chambers started to say until the woman stared at her.

'No, I don't recall.' Yeo folded her arms. 'Every now and then I like to go into my shop, the first one I set up, and work behind the counter. I used to love doing it, but now I hardly have the time.' Then she took a smartphone from a pocket somewhere and stared at it. 'And I have a Teams meeting soon. So, if you don't mind...'

Moone nodded and got to his feet, then gestured for Chambers to follow him to the door. He started heading for the same door they came in by, the beams of sunlight swirling in his vision, trying to imagine what might have happened the day their killer bought his phone. Then as he reached the door, a thought flickered into his brain. He turned and faced Chambers and lowered his voice, noticing Yeo was standing watching them leave.

'He targets single, attractive women,' Moone said. 'Doesn't he?'

Chambers looked confused. 'Yes, why?'

'Women that live alone.' Moone looked round the room. 'She lives alone.'

Moone didn't wait for Chambers' reply

and headed back over to Rachel Yeo who was now looking at him with a mix of annoyance and surprise in her eyes.

'This man we're after targets single women,' Moone said. 'I'm not trying to scare you, I'm just wondering if after that day you've noticed anything unusual or anyone hanging around?'

The woman lost her look of annoyance and Moone could see something had occurred to her.

'There was something,' she said, and walked to the door and opened it.

Moone joined her as she looked out across the drive.

'There was a van,' she said. 'I've seen it a few times, parked over there. I assumed it was some delivery person stopping to eat their lunch or something, and I went out there one day to tell him off, but he suddenly drove away.'

'What make of van?' Moone asked and took out his notebook.

Rachel Yeo shrugged. 'I have no idea. It was just a white van. In good nick, clean.'

'You didn't happen to catch the registration number?' Moone raised his eyebrows doubtfully.

'Sorry, no.' She stepped out onto the driveway, staring towards the spot where she said the van had been parked, then turned round, and faced the house. 'But one of my cameras might have. I'm pretty security-conscious, as you can see. My ex... well, let's just say he didn't make life very comfortable for me after the divorce, and so I ended up installing some cameras.'

'It couldn't have been your ex-husband in the van?' Chambers asked.

Yeo looked at her and smirked. 'No, thankfully he's locked up. He ended up assaulting someone and they caught it all on camera, ironically.'

Something else occurred to Moone as his eyes took in the extensive property. 'I don't suppose you remember having a flyer put through your door? An advert for a handyman?'

Miss Yeo looked thoughtful for a moment. 'No, I don't remember anything like that, but then I have someone who comes and cuts my grass and does little jobs for me. Is this what this... person does? Pretends to be a handyman and stalks single women?'

'We're not sure at the moment, but please contact us if you see the van again, or you get a flyer through the door. Here...' Moone took out his card with his number on it. 'Call that bottom number if anything occurs, OK?'

She nodded, now looking a little alarmed. 'I will. Thanks.'

'I'm sorry, but can we see the footage?' Moone asked.

'Sure,' she said and walked back into the house. 'I'll download it for you.'

'Thanks,' Moone called out as she disappeared. He then turned to Chambers and smiled. 'One of those cameras is pointing right at that lay-by she reckons he stopped in. This is it, Molly, we're getting close to catching this bastard.'

CHAPTER 16

Jim Nair opened up the throttle and picked up speed as he headed towards Prince Town. The afternoon sun danced over his visor as he let rip, hearing the deep roar of his Harley's engine, the rumble travelling up his body. The seemingly endless moorland rushed past. He looked into his wing mirror and saw Jason was just about keeping up on his Yamaha. Then Nair saw the turning for the car park and took a quick look to make sure no cars or trucks were sneaking up on him, then roared over the road and skidded round into the makeshift car park, spitting up stones into the air before he slowed down. He stopped the bike, kicked down the stand and sat there for a moment after taking off his helmet, feeling the sun beat down on the back of his neck. He was staring towards the only two cars parked nearby. One looked like it had been dumped, all weather-beaten and covered in rust. The other was a nondescript dark Ford something. Someone was sitting at the wheel, but the glare of the sun prevented a good view of whoever it was.

Jason came roaring into the car park, came to a stop beside him and took off his helmet.

'Is she here?' Jason asked and followed Jim's nod towards the car.

'Can we trust her?' Jason said. 'She's fucking filth.'

Jim turned and glared at him. 'I know what she fucking is. Don't fucking tell me what I already know.'

Jason nodded and looked down. 'Sorry, I didn't mean...'

Jim climbed off his bike and headed across the dusty car park, staring at the figure behind the steering wheel. Then he reached the passenger door and looked in and saw her sitting in the driver's seat, staring ahead, as cool as a fucking cucumber and sipping some kind of iced coffee. She lowered the window and told him to climb in. He did and looked at her.

'I'm taking it that was you the other night?' Nair said and watched her suck her drink through a straw.

'Where's your phone?' she said, still not looking at him.

'My phone? Not here. Somewhere else. I'm not stupid.'

She nodded and looked at him. 'I guess I've paved the way for you now.'

He gave a slight laugh. 'True, you have.'

He reached into his leather jacket and pulled out the envelope of cash and put it on the dashboard.

She looked at it. 'What's that?'

'Payment, for a job well done. Twenty grand.'

She let out a breath. 'Take it with you. I didn't do it for payment.'

'Then was it out of the kindness of your heart? Come off it, love, you don't have a heart, do you? I've met some interesting sorts in my time, all kinds of ruthless bastards and bitches, and I can tell that there isn't much going on in that chest of yours. In your head, yeah... but nothing else.'

'You're making me blush,' the crazy bitch said.

'Why're you doing this then?' He turned and put out his arm, resting it on her seat.

'Because other people like the peace, like their relaxation time... I enjoy and take great pleasure in the chaos.'

'That doesn't come as a surprise. If you don't want money, what do you want?'

She sucked on her drink for a moment, then looked at him again, staring him in the eye. 'First of all, I want to be cut in on your operation. I've got to make a little nest egg for myself, haven't I?'

'Makes sense. What else?'

She looked away, seeming to think for a

moment. 'I have someone in my life that I no longer need in my life.'

'I see. So, you want me to deal with them like you dealt with my problem person? It's a scratching each other's back situation, is it?'

She nodded. 'It is. Do you have a problem with that?'

'No. No problem. Who are they?'

'Just someone who I can't have around any more. He's served his purpose and now he must go.'

'Then consider him dealt with. Just let us know his movements and all that and we'll take care of it.'

She smiled. 'Oh, don't worry, I will.'

'We've got it!' Moone said as he burst into the incident room, holding Rachel Yeo's pink memory stick that held the downloaded CCTV footage.

Butler turned round in her chair as he headed for a laptop. 'Is that your new lipstick, Moone? Suits you.'

'Funny,' he said as he plugged in the memory stick and waited for the drive to appear on the desktop. By the time he had pulled over a chair to the desk, everyone had gathered round. He looked up at them, seeing the light in their collective eyes, the excitement he was carrying now infecting them. It was all good, and he could see them now as greyhounds waiting for the hare to be released. They were getting close, he could feel it. This wasn't some genius serial killer with some ultimate plan, it was just a broken individual that life had seriously messed up. He wondered, as the footage loaded up, what had happened to this man as a child to make him so deranged, so full of rage and intent on destroying the lives of these women he chanced upon.

'Here it is,' Moone said, then turned to Molly who had appeared on his right. 'Chambers, can you do the honours?'

'Yes, boss.'

He stood up to give her his seat then went over to Butler who was standing at the back of the crowd.

'What's new?' Moone asked.

'Only my underwear,' she said, with a fleeting smile that quickly faded as her eyes jumped to the action in the room. 'You think you've caught this nutter on camera?'

Moone joined Butler in her vigil over the team and stood shoulder-to-shoulder with her. 'I hope. I'm thinking he pops into the phone shop which he thinks is far enough away from Plymouth, goes to buy his burner phones, and pays with cash... we checked that day for any payments made for burners, and someone paid cash for two... anyway, he buys his phones and who serves him? An attractive woman of the right age, the type he seems to target. Then I think he follows her right back to her nice expensive home in the countryside. He even parks up in his white van...'

'White van man?' Butler huffed. 'Handyman? Is this guy a walking cliche?'

'Maybe. But anyway, he stops a few times and watches her, thinking he might target her next.'

'Or it was just some builder or labourer who happened to stop there a couple of times for a piss on his way home.'

Moone sighed, shaking his head. 'Come on, I'm trying to be mister positive for once.'

'Well, that's good. Well done. Have your great detective and observational skills let you notice who's missing from the incident room?'

Moone took a quick sweep of the room and saw that the delightful Carthew was missing, which seemed a relief for a moment before the slow panic started to rise within him. 'Jesus, where the hell is she now?'

'She's meant to be on CCTV and ANPR duty, but she's not doing that. God knows where she is.'

Moone rubbed his tired eyes and lowered his voice. 'I keep thinking about what she said, about you know, Parry and all that. What if she did follow us? I mean, how does she know so much?'

'Guesswork? I don't know. But she's only

tried it on once and hasn't given us any proof that she knows what we know. No, the bitch is lying.'

'What do we do about her?'

Butler let out a breath, then looked at him with a determined look in her eye. 'I told you last time. We've got to play as low and dirty as she does. I'm working on something.'

He stared at her, a strange ominous feeling cloaking his back. 'Working on what?'

'I'll tell you when the time's right. Trust me.' She looked away, then suddenly looked at him with a question in her eyes. 'You do trust me, don't you?'

He was blindsided for a moment, then found himself wearing a smile, the words automatically rising to his lips. 'More than I trust anyone.'

Her face softened. 'Good to hear. I feel the same.'

He nodded, his heart beating rapidly. 'Apart from Alice and the kids, that is.'

'You have to spoil it, don't you?' she said, but he saw the smile that flickered onto her lips.

'I've found it,' Chambers said as a cheer and a few claps came rising from the crowd of officers as Moone and Butler pushed through them.

On the screen was a paused colour image of the driveway at Rachel Yeo's impressive home. Beyond house was the lane, the stone wall, the trees and bushes. As Chambers started the footage again, but slowly, a white van came into shot and parked. Moone leaned in, but it was hard to see the driver. He was just a dark blur. Moone sighed, then looked at Molly. 'Well done. Do we get any clear shots of the van? The make, or registration number?'

'Well, it's there for about half an hour on this occasion, then drives off. As it passes by the entrance to her drive, the licence plate can be partly seen, but it's pretty far away and blurry. Maybe Barry can help with it?'

Harding came forward and said, 'Get some images of the van and I'll find the make, and maybe we can track it down if it was bought round here.'

'Going to be thousands to check,' Butler said and sighed.

Moone looked round at her. 'You're right, but that's what we do. Come on, people, let's get on this and find this van and our potential first real suspect. Harding, identify the make, then get hold of the DVLA. Molly, check the rest of the footage for any more sightings of the van. Let's spread our net wide and see what we can catch. So we want to cover from Devon and Cornwall up to Somerset.'

There came a collective groan from his team. He held up his hands. 'I know, it's a wide net, but if Barry gets us any of the digits on that van's registration number, then we'll be able to search the DVLA records, the highway agency and all CCTV and ANPR. I'm sure the net will get smaller very quickly. Anyway, let's get to work.'

Moone stood back as everyone dispersed and headed back to their desks. Butler came and stood next to him, arms folded, also seeming to observe a hungry team.

'They've got the scent now,' he said.

'This is going to be painstaking work.' She sighed heavily. 'And it could still be just some builder on his way home...'

He looked at her. 'We'll soon have the times he was there, and so we'll be able to check CCTV and ANPR around then. We're getting close.'

'Good. Let's hope it goes somewhere.'

'It will. I can feel it in the pit of my stomach.'

'You sure you didn't have a dodgy curry last night?'

'Funny,' he said, then watched as she headed to her desk and started making phone calls. He kept staring at her, unable to take his eyes away, even though with every panicked beat of his heart, he feared she might look up and see him. What the hell was this? An answer came rising in him, but he didn't listen to the voice, refused to. No. This wasn't happening. He shook his head, refusing to accept what his body, his heart mainly, was trying to tell him. Forget it, he told himself as a thought occurred to him and a sudden memory speared into his brain. He looked at the date on his phone. Jesus. It was Friday. That meant tomorrow was his date with Dr Jenkins. He sighed, feeling strange all of a sudden, and not at all as if he was looking forward to it. She was an intelligent, attractive woman and he should have felt excited to be going out with her, but he kept looking up at Butler and wondering what she would make of it. Would she be bothered? No, of course not.

She looked up and stared right into his eyes.

'What?' she asked.

'What?' His heart pounded.

'Why're you looking at me funny?' She glared at him.

'I wasn't. I was just looking your way, thinking about the... case...' Then his phone started ringing and he thanked God for it. It was Inspector Pinder calling.

'Kevin?' Moone said, turning away from the still glaring Butler. 'What is it?'

'I've been called to an altercation,' Pinder said. 'I'm stood in the yard at Nick Dann's depot.'

'What's happened?'

'There's some young man here and he's accusing... look, I think you should come down and see this.'

Moone decided to leave everyone to get on with the jobs he'd given them while he headed to meet Pinder at Nick Dann's depot. He parked up outside the yard and immediately heard shouting coming from within. He hurried out of the car as he started to hear Pinder's voice coming over everything else, talking in his usual, calm and polite manner.

Moone entered the yard and immediately saw Pinder and a blonde female uniform he didn't recognise, trying to calm down a man. As Moone got closer, he realised that the man was Jon Michael Reagan, and he looked quite upset.

'Mr Reagan?' Moone said to the young man who turned away from Pinder and looked at him.

'Maybe you can help,' Reagan said and stepped towards Moone.

'I'll try,' Moone said. 'What's going on here?'

Reagan jabbed a finger towards the main building. 'It's him. He's in there. The one who murdered those women. He's just walking round, thinking he's gotten away with it...'

'No one's got away with anything at the moment,' Moone said, trying to wear a reassuring smile. 'Look, we don't know for sure if he's involved in these murders...'

'I saw him! He was there.'

Moone took a breath, feeling a little sorry for a young man carrying around quite a lot of guilt. 'Listen... Jon... I know you saw someone that day outside Judy Ludlow's house, but that could be just a coincidence. In fact, I don't think he's the man we're looking for. We've got another lead, another possible suspect.'

Reagan lowered his arm that he was still half pointing towards the building, a look of confusion on his face. 'Who? You can't have... Who?'

'I can't discuss that. But I'm pretty sure Mr Dann isn't the man who murdered Judy Ludlow or any of the other women.'

'But he knew them.' Reagan stared at him.

'What do you mean? He knew them all?'

Reagan nodded, determination glinting in his eyes. 'All of them. The woman who died a little while ago, Caroline Abbott...'

'How do you know about her?'

'I know people who live there. They know her house, know you lot were there and a woman was killed. It has to be Caroline Abbott. Anyway, I know he knew her.'

Moone looked towards the main building as his stomach twisted, and his eyes jumped to the suited figure standing at the glass wall of the office. Nick Dann was watching them. 'How do you know?'

'He was seen there. One of the neighbours

had seen him turning up at her house. That can't be a coincidence, can it? He knows all three and then they're murdered?'

Moone looked back at Reagan, trying to make sense of it all. 'What about Teresa Burrows?'

Reagan nodded. 'Her too.'

'How do you know that?'

Reagan looked down to the ground. 'I've been looking into it. Asking around.'

'This isn't your job, Jon. This is for us to do. Look, I know that what happened back then must have affected you, but you've got to try and get past it. We've got people you can talk to...'

He looked up, staring at Moone. 'I don't need to talk to anyone like that. I'm not crazy. It's him. I'm telling you. Ask him if he knew them.'

'I already did.' Moone recalled asking him about all three of the initial victims and sensing that Dann was holding something back. He would need to find out where he was when Sarah Launce's best friend was brutally murdered, and that was going to be tricky. Moone looked over at Pinder and signalled him to come over.

'Everything OK?' Pinder asked, his hands resting on his stab vest.

'Can you get Mr Reagan out of here, please?' Moone then looked at Reagan, making sure the disturbed young man was looking him in the eye. 'Listen, Jon, I promise you that I'm going to look into this and find out if he was involved or not. OK?'

Jon looked down. 'You promise?'

'Scout's honour.'

Then they collectively spun their heads around when the sound of a roaring engine came from the entrance to the depot. A silver Lexus RS came swinging into the yard and came to a sudden stop.

'Oh, Jesus,' Pinder said and leant his head back, looking skywards as he let out a heavy breath.

'What is it?' Moone asked, trying to see who was behind the wheel. Then his stomach folded in on itself when the driver's door opened and the suited, unimpressed figure of DSU Boulton stepped out.

'DCI Peter Moone,' Boulton called out, his face tight as he adjusted his tie and shirt collars. 'A word, if you don't mind?'

Moone made eye contact with Pinder and got a returned look of sympathy as he turned and headed in the direction of Boulton.

'Sir,' Moone said, feeling his shoulder muscles locking into position, probably never to move again.

'What the hell are you doing, Moone?'

Moone looked round and saw Pinder directing Jon Michael Reagan away from the scene. 'I was called out because there was a disturbance...'

'No, that's incorrect.' Boulton folded his arms. 'Inspector Pinder was called out, you just came to stick your nose in.'

'Thing is, sir, Nick Dann...'

'Is an influential Plymouth businessman who does a lot for charity, we've been through this...'

'There's a good chance he knew three of the initial victims. We need to ask him about that...'

'Where did you get this from?' Boulton looked past Moone, then pointed at Reagan as he was being frogmarched away. 'From him? The disturbed young man who just turned up at his company, shouting and hollering? Oh, he sounds like a credible witness, doesn't he, Moone?'

'He says there are witnesses who saw Dann turning up at Caroline Abbott's home. We need to check them out at least.'

Boulton stared at him, shaking his head slightly. 'I was told you'd be trouble, Peter Moone. Fine, talk to these so-called witnesses, if they even exist, and see what they say. I'm sure it'll come to nothing.'

'I will, sir. Thank you.'

Boulton stared at him for a moment, as if he was going to say something more but seemed to decide against it as he walked around Moone and headed to the office building where Nick Dann was waiting.

Some of DSU Boulton's words started replaying in his head, so he said, 'Sir…'

Boulton stopped and faced him, looking tired. 'Yes, Moone?'

'If you don't mind me asking, but who said I would be trouble?'

Boulton lost any sign of his former friendliness, at least the little that there was. 'It doesn't matter, Moone, just leave this to me, and I'll try and smooth things over.'

'It matters to me.' Moone felt a sudden stab of courage, so he found himself asking, 'It wasn't DS Carthew, was it?'

More of the kindness dissipated from Boulton's eyes and his whole face seemed to tighten. 'Moone, just go and get on with finding this killer. Now.'

Moone didn't go back to his car straight away, deciding to watch for a moment. He saw Nick Dann opening the door to the building, getting ready to greet DSU Boulton like an old friend. How far did they go back, he wondered? Then he caught the eye of the smug-looking businessman himself. He stared at Moone, smirking, knowing he had put one over him. He was now determined to find out exactly what Dann's involvement was in the case. If Reagan was right, and Dann did know all the victims, then the stuck-up suit was up to his neck in something bad.

CHAPTER 17

'What exactly are we doing here?' Butler asked as she parked up halfway along King's Tamerton Road and pulled on the handbrake. Moone ignored her question for a moment and looked over to the little bit of puddle-shaped lawn and the houses behind it, all huddled together. One of those houses had a witness in it who had allegedly witnessed Nick Dann visiting Caroline Abbott.

'Are you... what do they call it up your way?' Butler said. 'Mutton?'

Moone looked at her as he half laughed. 'Mutton. Yep, Mutt and Jeff. No, I was just thinking about it all. The fact that one of the people in those houses over there might have seen Dann visit Caroline Abbott.'

'And the fact that Boulton just told you off for looking into this hasn't put you off?'

Moone shrugged. 'He knows we have to look into it. I just think he doesn't want us to look too deeply if you know what I mean?'

'I do. Let's face it, they probably go to the same lodge, and roll up each other's trouser legs or whatever they do there. But do you think he's our man?' Butler sighed. 'He's not even a handyman, is he? He's a successful businessman. Which pretty much makes him a tosser but not necessarily a murderer.'

Moone nodded, agreeing with her in his head in principle, but there was that old nagging feeling at the back of his mind telling him the man had something to do with it all. He looked at her. 'Successful businessmen are usually pretty ruthless... in fact, a high proportion of business people are on the psychopathy scale.'

Butler huffed and climbed out of the car, so he joined her as she said, 'Still doesn't make him our killer.'

'You've changed your tune,' Moone said as they headed over the road and crossed the strip of grass. 'You usually go for the business people when it comes to picking a likely murder suspect.'

'Yeah, well. I've changed my mind.' She stopped and looked over the first lot of houses. 'Saturday tomorrow.'

'It is.' Moone nodded and started heading for the front door of the first house and noticed a kid's bike left in the front garden that he stepped over.

'What are you doing tomorrow night?'

Butler asked as she headed to the front path of the next house.

He stopped and looked at her, his finger about to press the bell. 'Well, I...'

'Want to have a drink at my place?' She didn't look at him, just reached the front door and pressed the bell, then rattled the letterbox.

'Thing is,' he said and pressed the doorbell. 'I promised someone I would do something with them...'

'Who?' Butler looked at him, her eyes fixing him with her usual interrogative stare. 'Alice?'

Shit? What could he say? He didn't want to tell her about Dr Jenkins. 'Yep. Alice. There's lots going on at home. Apparently, my ex-wife is thinking of starting a new job away from Plymouth. Obviously, that means my family would go with her.'

Butler was about to say something, her face taking on a look of shock, but then both doors they had knocked on opened up simultaneously.

It was a middle-aged woman with short, greying hair and a tanned and wrinkled face who greeted Moone. He brought out his warrant card and held it up as he heard Butler introducing herself to the neighbour.

'Afternoon, I'm DCI Peter Moone,' he said, putting on the pleasant but plastic smile he wore for the public. 'I'm not sure you're aware, but across the road...'

'What happened to that poor dear?' the woman said, her eyes jumping over to the house. 'I know, I was here that night. Your lot already came round asking 'bout it. Can't tell you nothing else. You any closer to finding the evil bastard?'

'We hope so. We're doing our best. It's why we're here. Do you know if Mrs Abbott was seeing anyone? I mean, did you see any men or anyone paying her a visit?'

'See, I didn't know her really. I remember her mum, bless her soul. She was a lovely lady, had a heart of gold and did anything for anyone.'

'Moone!'

He spun his head around to see Butler had managed to get a few doors down already and was waving for him to join her. He turned to the woman at the door apologetically and took out one of the crime reporting leaflets that had been put together by Chambers, with the major incident room's number on it. 'I'm sorry. Got to go. Here's our number in case you think of anything.'

Moone hurried on down to the house Butler was outside. At the door stood a short man with dark, thinning hair and a large moustache who was probably in his late thirties.

'Hello,' Moone said, nodding to him.

'This is Dom,' Butler said. 'He says he saw a flash motor turning up here a few times and a fella go into Caroline's house.'

Moone took out his notebook. 'Could you describe this man?'

Dom scratched at his moustache and shrugged. 'I suppose. He was just some geezer she was seeing, I think. Nice motor it was, though.'

'Do you know what make it was?'

He shrugged again. 'Range Rover, I think. Black.'

'You didn't get the registration number, I suppose?' Moone asked.

'Na. But definitely a Range Rover. Can't mistake those great big things, can ya?'

'What did he look like, this flash so and so?' Butler asked.

Dom raised his shoulders again. 'Dark hair, quite tall. Big fella, I suppose.'

'Clothes?' Moone asked, writing it all down.

'Think he was wearing...' Dom scratched his moustache, looking down at the grass. 'A shirt and tie, maybe?'

'He was smartly dressed?' Moone asked, that bite of excitement trying to take a chunk out of his stomach as he ignored the ominous sensation that snuck in with it.

'Yeah, like I said, he was a bit of a flash sod. Could tell he loved himself.'

'You should be a copper,' Butler said, and Moone heard the thick layer of sarcasm in her voice.

Dom's eyes jumped to her, full of disgust. 'You must be fucking joking, love... I mean, I couldn't do your job. That's what I mean. Hours are long, ain't they?'

Butler pointed at him. 'You're very familiar, Dom. Have we met before?'

Dom shook his head, suddenly looking a little nervous. 'Na, don't think so. Anyway, is that all? I got things to do, people to see.'

'You got a job?' Butler asked.

'I keep busy.' Dom looked at Moone, putting on a plastic smile. 'That all, officer?'

'Yep. We will have to ask you to make a full statement and take a look at a few photos, to see if you recognise anyone. If you could come to Charles Cross station tomorrow at about nine and ask for me, DCI Peter Moone. That OK?'

'Yeah, whatever.' Dom sighed and shut the door, leaving them staring at the paintwork, then at each other.

'There's something shifty about him,' Butler said and started walking back towards their car.

'You think he's lying?' Moone said, striding to catch up with her.

Butler shrugged. 'I don't know. Why would he make up something like this? Unless he's our killer and he's trying to put the blame on someone else.'

Moone looked back. 'We'd better find out where he was.'

'Dominic Sullivan,' she said. 'I knew it would come to me. Petty theft. Waste of space. Wouldn't hurt a fly though, trust me. But I'll find out where he was, I have my sources.'

When they reached the car, Moone said, 'So, does this put Nick Dann back in the frame? He's got possible links to nearly all the victims.'

'What about Shena?' Butler raised her eyebrows. 'Did he know her?'

Moone climbed in once Butler unlocked the car. 'Sarah Launce was the intended victim, I'm pretty sure of that. She fits the profile of our victims. All single, strong, independent and attractive women.'

'Isn't that a song by Beyoncé?' Butler asked and started the engine.

'Quite possibly.' Then Moone heard his phone ringing and saw Chambers was calling. 'Hello, Molly. Got something for us?'

'Yes, boss. Rachel Yeo called a little while ago. She talked to her cleaner, who says she remembers finding a leaflet or flyer advertising the services of a handyman called Dave, she thinks. She threw it away, apparently.'

Moone nodded. 'Of course, she did. But that means he did target her. He saw her on the off chance and she took his fancy. It was impulsive, and now we have him on camera. Has Barry come up with anything yet?'

'No, not yet, but it's early days.'

'OK. Thanks, Molly. See you in a while.' Moone looked at Butler. 'Looks like Rachel Yeo, owner of the phone shop, did have a leaflet put through her door. Which means, he was targeting her.'

'So we put eyes on her house, see if he comes back?'

'If he's clocked all those cameras, I doubt he'll come back. Anyway, we've already got eyes on Sarah Launce, so I doubt they'll agree to budget for more bodies keeping an eye on Rachel Yeo as well. Best we can do is find a fast response team close to Liskeard and alert them to the risk of her being targeted.'

Butler drove them away, taking them down the far end of King's Tamerton Road and out onto Trevithick Road where she turned left. 'So, is our killer Nick Dann, arsehole businessman or some deranged handyman?'

'Why not both?' Moone looked at her.

'So, you think Dann moonlights as a handyman when he's not running his multimillion-quid business?'

'I don't know, but we need to find a way to get him in so we can interview him and find out where he was when the women were murdered.'

'I can't wait to see you try.'

Jason Harris was standing at the back of his house, looking across the garden that was overgrown with weeds. It used to be nice, with flowers and shit like that, when his gran was still alive. He took out his packet of cigarettes and lit one, took a lungful of smoke and watched two magpies landing on the fence at the end of the garden. He started to think about Nair and all that was happening with the dodgy copper woman. There was something decidedly suspect about her, he thought, and couldn't understand why Nair was trusting her so much. He was greedy, that was his trouble, all he saw was pound notes, and now they could move in on the Tomahawks' territory without any trouble from their number one enforcer, Stuart McAllister. He laughed as he blew out some smoke, thinking of the wanker now lying in the morgue. He got what he deserved, he nodded and turned to pick up the coffee he'd made before he'd come out the back.

He jumped as his eyes caught sight of the person standing by the alley on the side of the house, nearly knocking over his coffee. Instinctively, he had dug his hand into his pocket to bring out his folding knife.

'You won't need that,' Carthew said and stepped towards him, her hands behind her back. She was wearing a flowery summer dress, her hair piled up on her head. She was made up as if she was off on a night out, he thought and realised that she looked pretty hot when she made the effort.

'What the fuck are you doing here?' he asked, his heart still thumping from the shock. He picked up his coffee, turned away from her and took a sip.

She stood next to him and joined him in his vigil over the overgrown garden.

'You need someone to come and see to all this,' Carthew said. 'Tidy it up a bit.'

Jason took a drag on his cigarette. 'I'm selling it sometime soon. Got to clear it out first. Was me nan's house.'

'I know.'

He looked at her. 'What do you mean, *you know*?'

She smiled. 'That it was your nan's. I've been doing a little research.'

He laughed. 'What? On me nan?'

'Funny. No, on you mostly.'

He looked at her. 'What the fuck is it with you? You're a fucking... pig, and you're doing all this dodgy fucking stuff.'

She shrugged. 'What can I say? I like to do things a little differently. Anyway, I came here because I need your help.'

'My help? You've already got Jim under your thumb, can't he help you?'

She smiled. 'Do you know why he's so willing to help me?'

Jason shrugged. 'I dunno. Cause you've got nice tits?'

'Could be that. But no, I think it's because he's scared of me. He'd rather have me on his side than go up against me.'

Jason took another drag of his fag as he stared her in the eyes, wondering if she was having him on or not. 'So, what do you want my help with?'

'I'm on the hunt for someone.'

'I feel fucking sorry for them, then.'

She laughed. 'They're a killer. A murderer.'

'A murderer? Like you, you mean?'

'This is a very different animal. He likes to beat and strangle women.'

He stared at her, feeling a little curious, wondering exactly what the hell was going on in her head, and then wondering what it would take to get her upstairs. He huffed out a laugh and looked away again. 'You want me to help the filth catch some killer? Yeah, right, do I look like some grass or something?'

'I'm not asking you to grass someone up. And this isn't to do with my job, not really.' Carthew reached over and took his cigarette as he was about to poke it into his mouth. She took a drag, still staring at him then said, 'I want to catch him myself.'

'Then do what?'

She lost her look of mirth, and moved closer, looking up into his eyes. 'I'm going to kill him, then dispose of his body so nobody ever finds it.'

He laughed, took back his cigarette as he waited for the punchline, but she just kept looking up into his eyes and he realised that beyond those eyes, which certainly had some playfulness in them, there was a darkness that disturbed him. But then there was the other feeling too, the excitement he felt in her presence, the strong pull of her, the almost overwhelming urge to grab her and kiss her. No, he told himself to stop thinking like that. She was dangerous. Was trouble. More trouble than she was worth.

'You're not joking?' he said.

'No, why would I joke about it?' She raised her eyebrows.

'I don't know. Then why kill him? Have you got something against him? Oh, shit, wait... did he kill someone you know?'

'No.'

'All right.' He took a drag of his fag. 'So why?'

She smiled. 'Because it'll drive everyone crazy. Imagine it, they're looking for this brutal, women-hating killer and then... bang... he just disappears, just stops killing, never to be heard of again. Plus, justice is served.'

He could only stare at her, still caught between the fear of her, of the darkness beyond her eyes, and the desire for her. Then he found his voice again. 'Why're you telling me all this?'

'Because we can help each other.'

'Can we?'

She nodded. 'I want to rent out your house from you. You'll get a nice wad of money, and I get to use your house for a couple of weeks.'

'You want to use my house? Why?'

'Because it's in the geographical area where the killer has targeted his victims.'

He stared at her, the penny suddenly dropping. 'Hang on, you want to use my house, my nan's old place, to knock off some psycho killer?'

'That's right. I'm going to find a way to lure him in. Probably through the internet. Is that a problem?'

'Is that a problem? Yeah, it's a fucking problem. You're planning on offing someone in my nan's house. Course it's a problem.'

'I'll pay you well.'

He huffed out a laugh, then took a drag, looking away from her, his mind starting to travel down a different path. He glanced at her. 'It'll take more than money.'

'Why doesn't that surprise me? You men are all alike. Only after one thing.'

He nodded. 'Yeah, sounds about right. I take it that's a no?'

'I didn't say no, did I?' She took his cigarette and puffed on it again, smiling a little. 'We'll have to see how things go. Like I said, I want you to help me as much as I help you.'

'Help me how?'

'You could do with rising up the ranks in your gang, couldn't you?'

He turned to her. 'That's dangerous talk.'

'But it's true, isn't it? How long can Jim Nair really be in charge? He's getting on now. They need new blood.'

'Do they?'

She nodded. 'Yes. So do I. But first, how's the other arrangements going?'

'Oh, the other person you need help knocking off? Yeah, it's all in hand, don't worry. Jim's made all the arrangements. He won't see it coming.'

He parked the van up the road, a few turnings away. There were no cameras around here, no CCTV apart from the cameras the locals attached to their doorbells, and he'd learnt by now which ones had them and which didn't. He couldn't risk the van being caught on camera, so he took the back streets and avoided the main roads. People thought that the cities were overrun by cameras and that they were being watched twenty-four-seven, but the truth was there was little in the way of surveillance outside the city centre apart from the traffic cameras. You had to be careful of cash machines and buses, but apart from that if you knew the right routes to take, you could go pretty well unseen for the most part.

He walked back to the house, feeling tired from working all morning painting the fences of an old dear in Ernesettle, and then pricing a couple of jobs in Crownhill. They were families, both young couples with little kids. None of them stirred his rage and desire. He kept thinking of her, still out there, walking round, having escaped her punishment.

You could go back and get her.

The police will be keeping an eye on her. I can never go back.

Yes, you can, just wait a while and then go back and finish what you started.

His hands trembled as he opened the front door and stepped in, feeling the dust beneath his feet, the coolness rushing towards him. Outside it was warm, the temperature rising along with the angry, furious thud that seemed to pound in his chest more and more. Inside was cool, and he could think straight. He heard something then, as if someone had said something, a man's voice speaking somewhere in the house. His pulse began to pound in his ears as he took a step along the hallway.

'Who's there?' he called out.

'It's me,' the deep, gravelly voice came back. He knew that voice, recognised it from so long ago. No, it couldn't be. There was no way, he told himself as he stepped into the bare living room where there was nothing but an old, battered armchair covered in cigarette burns.

Usually, it would be empty.

Now there was an old man sitting in it, staring at him. His face was in darkness, a shadow across it. He was dressed in dark clothing too, a lit roll-up cigarette in his wrinkled fingers.

'Didn't expect to see me, did you, bey?' the old man said.

'How did you find me?' He stepped closer, trying to fathom how he could be here.

'It was easy. You can't hide from me. I know you, bey. Once you know someone, once you get in their head, then they can't escape you. And I know you, so I always know where you're to.'

He thought about it, rewound his past, right back to his school days when he had met the old man when he was younger and swept the school with a broom. 'The school records? I lived near here with my aunt who practically raised me. All you had to do was find her house and ask around. That's it, isn't it?'

The old man gave a rattling cough. 'You think you're clever, don't yer, bey?'

He ignored the question and the mocking look in the old man's dark eyes. 'Why? Why now?'

The former caretaker sat forward as he took a puff from his roll-up and then pointed a thin finger at him. 'Cause I knows what you been up to, don't I, bey? You've been naughty, ain't you? Just like you was all those years ago.'

He looked away, away from the dark eyes that always seemed to look deep into his soul. He could never hide anything from the old man. 'It's none of your business what I've been up to.'

'Ain't none of my business?' The old man gave an empty laugh. 'I'm involved, ain't I? I know all about it. I'm as guilty as you.'

'I won't tell no one about you. Just go. Clear out and no one will know you were here.'

The old man stared at him, smoking away, those cold dark eyes taking him in until he pulled himself to his feet with a deep grunt. Then he stepped closer until he was barely a foot from him. He was so close now, too close, and he could smell the pungent odour that almost made him gag. He stunk of fags and stale piss and God knows what else. He didn't want to know what else.

He was looking down, too scared to stare into those black eyes that he knew held so many dark secrets. He was terrified of what he would see.

'Look at me, bey.'

He dared to look up. And there it was, what he knew he would see, the cavernous grey and hollow darkness of the underground car park. Her crying voice echoed until he held his hand over her mouth. The old man was there, watching on as he put his own hands over Sarah's mouth, hushing her, trying to keep her quiet. Then she was breaking free, crying and running out of the car park. He never laid eyes on her again.

'We were both there, bey,' he said, nodding and taking another drag of his cigarette. 'This is you and me.'

'I don't know if I can stop. I know I should...' His hands trembled and tears sprang to his eyes.

'I'm not here to stop you, bey. I'm here to help.'

CHAPTER 18

It was late into the afternoon and the heat of the day had cooled down a little when Moone hurried into the incident room after grabbing a quick bite of a sandwich from Jake's, the takeaway place. He also fetched Butler a coffee and put it on her desk. She wasn't anywhere to be seen. He'd hardly sat down when the tall, tired and strung-out frame of Barry came into the room. He looked about nervously, fidgeting with a sheet of A4 paper.

'Barry?' Moone said and stood up. 'Have you got something for us?'

Barry nodded and came into the room, holding out the sheet. 'The van.'

'You've got the registration?' Moone's heart kicked into gear as he took the sheet, which showed a grainy, colour still of the white van as it seemed to be driving away. There was the plate too, a small blurry image. His heart sank.

'Only two letters,' Barry said. 'WN.'

'That's West of England,' Harding said,

his head appearing over his monitor. 'DVLA's memory tag for Bristol is WN, or one of them anyway.'

'So the van's from Bristol,' Moone said, nodding. 'That's a pretty wide net.'

Harding stood up. 'Not necessarily, boss. It's a van, so we could check for businesses, see if any companies bought vans, see if the memory tag comes up.'

Moone sighed. 'Worth a shot, I suppose, although this man operates as a handyman and probably works alone. Run it through the DVLA anyway and see what the tags come up with. Thanks, Keith. And thanks Barry for this.'

'Boss,' DC Molly Chambers said, getting up from her desk. 'I've been going through the statements that were taken the night Caroline Abbott died.'

'Anything?' Moone asked, walking over.

'Well, once we spread the net further, we found a lady who lives a couple of streets away and she said she saw a white van parking up there that day. Her description of the van matches the Transit we're looking for. Could be our killer.'

Moone nodded. 'He parks the van a couple of streets away so the neighbours won't see it. Thanks, Molly. Right everyone, let's get looking for any more sightings of this van. Well done.'

Then Moone noticed Barry was still in the room, yawning and rubbing his tired eyes. As

Barry went to turn away, he could see the IT man was trembling a little.

'Barry?' Moone said, going over to him. 'You OK?'

'I'm fine.' Barry looked around furtively, one of his eyes twitching a little.

'You look tired.'

'Was up late.'

'Have you been to bed at all lately?'

Barry shrugged. 'I've got a lot on. Paedophiles don't catch themselves.'

'Jesus. Look, I'm going to get you some time off, OK?'

Barry had the flicker of a smile on his face for a moment. 'I wouldn't mind.'

Moone told him he'd sort it and then the still trembling IT man walked out and disappeared back down the stairs. He felt sorry for the poor sod, hardly able to imagine the things he saw or had to read about. Moone's heart and stomach took a nosedive as his mind rebelled at the notion of doing his job.

'You're not going to believe this,' Harding said, doing a good impression of a frightened meerkat over his monitor.

'What won't I believe?' Moone hurried over.

'There were four vans sold almost a year ago. Four white Ford Transits and they all have Bristol tags. You'll never guess who bought them.'

Moone shook his head as he said, 'You're not going to say Nick Dann's firm? You're not, are you?'

Harding grinned. 'I am. He bought four Ford Transits a year ago. It can't be a coincidence, can it?'

Moone gave an incredulous laugh. 'I don't know, but that would mean he's been using one of his own vans to stalk and kill these women. That's risky, isn't it?'

'What's risky?' Butler said, appearing in the incident room and finding the coffee he had placed on her desk. 'Your love life, you mean? Or your fashion sense?'

'Ha ha,' Moone said, pretending to be a little offended, although he couldn't help but feel happy to hear her making jokes, even if it was at his expense. 'No, not my love life. Nick Dann bought four Ford Transits a year ago. Same tag numbers as the van that parked up by Rachel Yeo's place. Plus, looks like a similar van was spotted a couple of streets away the night Caroline Abbott was murdered.'

Butler took a sip of her coffee and then sighed. 'Do I have to be the voice of reason again?'

'Let's hear it.'

Butler folded her arms. 'We don't know if this van driver, whoever it was that stopped by her house, was our killer for one. Could've been any builder as I've said before. Secondly, so Nick

Dann purchases four vans for his business? So what? That's what he does. He has a fleet of vans and trucks. You've got tag numbers, not a full licence plate. The van spotted the night Abbott was murdered could have been anyone's van. Boulton isn't going to let you drag Dann in here on that. Sorry to be the bearer of bad news, but there it is.'

Moone nodded, feeling deflated knowing she was perfectly correct, and sat down at his desk.

'What now, then?' Harding asked, looking just as sad as Moone.

Moone shrugged. 'We need more.'

'You need the van on camera,' Butler said, and sat down, sipping her coffee. 'You need footage from around the time of at least one of the murders.'

Moone put his face in his hands, thinking, then looked up. 'But we haven't managed to go through all the CCTV footage yet.'

'Who's supposed to be doing that?' Butler asked, but her eyes sprang over to Carthew's corner desk.

Moone's eyes followed hers. 'Where the hell is she?'

'Off doing God knows what. She needs to be brought in line.'

'She needs to be convicted of something,' Harding said and dawdled back to his desk.

Moone sighed and was about to say

something else when he heard his phone beep in his pocket. He took it out, his mind still reeling as he realised he had a message from Alice.

'Hi, Dad. Can we meet up for a coffee tomorrow? I need to talk to you about something x.'

'What's wrong?' he sent back.

'Nothing. Just need a chat. I'm okay.'

'OK. One-ish? Usual place? Xx.'

'I'll see you then x.'

Moone put his phone away and looked up to see Butler glancing at him. 'That was Alice.'

'She OK?' Butler asked.

Moone stepped closer and lowered his voice. 'I think so. She's got a boyfriend now. I've forgotten his name.'

'Oh dear. It's started.' Butler shook her head, a smirk on her lips. 'She'll be getting married next.'

'Don't even joke about it. She's still a kid.'

'How old is she again? Twenty-one?'

'Nearly.'

'She's not a kid, Moone. She and her bloke...'

Moone held up a hand and grimaced. 'Please, I don't want to go there. I'm still contending with the fact that my ex-wife might take my kids away from Plymouth.'

'Where to?'

'Her mum has been threatening to get a

job in London.'

Butler had looked away but stared at him again. 'Really? What would you do if they did?'

He shrugged. 'I really don't know. I mean, I can't spend my life following them around, can I?'

'Not really. Depends if you've got anything keeping you here.' She looked away and started working on her computer.

He watched her for a moment, something building in his chest, a slow thud, a bundle of words clambering up to his mouth. He searched around in his brain for the right words but nothing came up. 'I like it here. I like Plymouth.'

She stared at him, her eyebrows raised. 'That's it? You *like* Plymouth? I mean, I love Plymouth, I'm a proper Plymouth maid, but when your family leaves, you need more than just *liking* the place. You've got to make up your mind, Moone. And don't faff.'

Moone was about to say something, but Harding fist-pumped the air and stood up as he shouted, 'Geddon! Boss, I think I've got it.'

Moone went over to his desk, still searching for the appropriate words to say to Butler, the perfect sentence that he could utter and make her realise how he was feeling, at least how he thought he was feeling. The truth was, he was confused. Tomorrow night was his date with Dr Jenkins and he was starting to feel guilty about that.

'I checked CCTV and ANPR on the route from Rachel Yeo's house to Dann's firm. On the same day she got the van on film, I've got a Ford Transit arriving at Dann's firm...'

'But vans must come and go there all the time,' Butler said and huffed.

'Yeah, of course,' Harding said. 'But look at the side of the van in the footage from Yeo's house. I can see a rectangle just around the back of the van as if something has been put on the side to cover something up. Dann's vans have the company name on the side, so I think he put something on there to cover it.'

'But that still doesn't tell us if it's the same van,' Moone said.

'True. But I noticed on the clearest image a couple of marks on the side of the van where it must have scraped along a wall or something. Look at the image of the van heading for Dann's firm.'

Moone looked, staring at the van that had Nick Dann's company logo on the side, and noticed Harding was right, there were scrape marks on the bodywork. Two of them. He looked over to the image of the van caught on film outside Rachel Yeo's home. Yes, there they were, identical marks.

'He's right,' Moone said, looking over at Butler. 'They look the same to me. We need to examine his vehicles to find that exact one.

And we need to look at all the CCTV footage from the night Caroline Abbott died and see if the van parked nearby that night has the same tag numbers and the scrape marks.'

Butler groaned. 'We'll need a search warrant to examine his vehicles. Which means we need a magistrate to sign off on it, which means you've got to go and see DSU Boulton so he can give the go-ahead. Have fun.'

Moone's initial excitement was dampened a little as the reality kicked in. 'He's not going to like this, is he?'

'No,' Butler said, 'but looks like our handyman might work for Dann, so go and show him the footage and see what he says. Go on, London boy, sweet talk him.'

Moone groaned as he stood up. He looked up and saw his team was looking at him with expectation in their eyes. Shit, he thought and went to find Boulton.

Jason found himself sitting at a laptop in his kitchen. Faith had supplied it, saying it was bought second-hand with cash so there was nothing linking her to it. She also had a VPN in place so the IP address wouldn't be traced to his house. He sighed, shaking his head, wondering what exactly he had got himself caught up with. He looked up and saw her opening his fridge and bringing out two bottles of beer. She opened them and put one beside him.

'Cheers,' he said and took a swig.

She drank from hers as she leaned against the kitchen work surface, watching him all the time with a subtle, self-satisfied smile on her lips. She was trouble, serious trouble, but he couldn't stop looking at her, and fantasising. He kept getting flashes of them together, her bent over the kitchen table, her dress pulled up. He pulled himself back to reality and stared at the Facebook profile in front of him.

'So, what do you want me to do?' he asked.

'Just post a few things,' Carthew said. 'You know, the usual mundane shit people usually do. Find a few photos of home-cooked dinners and post them. Anything normal. But we need to make it clear that she's single. Lives alone. Join some local home improvement groups or something. We need this to be seen.'

'Bit of a stab in the dark, isn't it?' He shook his head and took another sip of his beer.

She stared at him, her face now blank.

'What?' he said.

'Do you think I haven't thought all this through? Do you think I haven't planned this all out? Do you think I'm stupid?'

He saw the dark look in her eyes, the way they changed from playful to terrifying in a heartbeat. She scared him. He wouldn't admit his fear to anyone, but there it was, mixed in with the strange desire he felt for her too. The moth and flame came to mind.

'No, I know you're not stupid,' he said. 'I think you're very clever. If you want something, I think you always get it.'

The playfulness returned and he breathed out a sigh of relief as she said, 'Then you're smarter than most men I've met. Anyway, there are only roughly two hundred and fifty thousand people living in Plymouth. This killer hunts mainly in Plymouth. He probably belongs to some of the groups we've joined. Plus, I know some things that my colleagues don't know or haven't realised yet.'

He looked at her. 'Really? Like what?'

'The name Sarah is significant to him.' She took a swig of her drink.

'How do you know that?'

'The last woman he murdered wasn't his intended victim. He meant to kill a woman called Sarah Launce, but when he found himself confronted with her friend instead his rage took over and he killed her in an even more brutal manner. He was disappointed.'

'But how do you know that's to do with her name?'

'The first victim all those years ago. Her middle name was Sarah. I checked it out and she used to go by the name Sarah a lot when she was younger. Preferred it to her real name.'

'Fuck me, you are clever.'

'Yes, I am. It means he must have known her when she was younger. The second victim, who was also murdered nearly twenty years ago, had a sister called Sarah, but she died when she was a teenager. It can't just be a coincidence. I haven't figured out Caroline Abbott yet, but there must be a Sarah connection.'

'So that's why you've made this fake profile in the name Sarah Farmer? Clever. But this profile we're using is old, I mean there are posts going back at least three years.'

Carthew nodded and stood next to him. 'That's because I set it up three years ago to… well, keep an eye on someone, but I didn't need it. But it's come in handy anyway.'

'Well, I've joined just about every group you wanted me to, and every group these other victims joined. Now what?'

'We wait, of course. Tell me, is Nair going to get done what I need to be done?'

Jason sat back and swigged his beer. 'He's a man of his word. Just needs to find someone to take this man out for you. It's not easy…'

'Why don't you do it?'

He stared up at her, ready to laugh out loud, but she had fixed him with those penetrating eyes of hers. 'Me? You're joking?'

'No. Why not? I trust you more than I trust the rest of your lot.'

'But there needs to be no connection between the person who does the job and the target. No motive. If I do it, they'll put two and two together straight away. No, no way.'

'That's only a problem if you get caught. You're not going to get caught.'

'How do you know?'

She smiled. 'Because I'm a police officer. A detective. The last thing I want is for you to get caught. If they do happen to find any evidence linking the crime to you, then I can make it disappear.'

He kept staring up at her, thinking it all through, mainly thinking of the money that Nair was going to pay whoever had the balls to pull it off. 'It is a lot of money.'

'It is. Plus there are other rewards to have.' She raised an eyebrow.

'Is there?'

He flinched a little when she reached out her hand and touched his cheek and caressed it. Her playful smile was back again.

'I'm very attracted to you, Jason,' she said and ran her thumb over his lips.

'And I fancy you.'

'Of course you do. So, why don't we go upstairs and I'll give you a taster of what else you can enjoy after you've done this little job for me?'

He stood up, half expecting her to laugh and say she was pulling his leg, but she took his hand in hers and led him up the stairs to the master bedroom where she helped him out of his clothes. Then, naked and sitting on the bed, he watched her strip off and realised at that moment he was probably the luckiest man on earth. And all he had to do to keep enjoying it, was to kill a man, a man he had never met. *How difficult could it be?*

On his way to find DSU Boulton, Moone found himself on the floor beneath the major incident room, where he knew there was a smaller incident room set aside for other important investigations. The investigation into Stuart McAllister's murder was being conducted out of that very room, so he wandered along to it, listening to the sound of music that was coming from somewhere on that floor. It was when he reached the smaller incident room, that he realised the music was coming from it. He looked in and saw a slender blonde woman wearing a trouser suit and sitting at a desk, typing something up in an office that was quite bare. A male detective was sitting at the other end also working on his computer.

'Hi,' Moone said and knocked on the open door.

The female detective looked round, staring at him blankly for a moment, then smiled as she stood up. She was quite tall Moone noticed, towering over him as she approached.

'Can I help you?' she asked, folding her

arms over her chest.

'DCI Peter Moone,' he said. 'Are you looking into the McAllister murder?'

'We are, sir,' she said, nodding and smiling. 'I'm DI Anna Jones, sir. Sorry, about the music. I'm a bit of a Celine Dion fan.'

'You don't have to call me sir.' He smiled. 'The music's fine. I don't think I know much of her music, apart from the Titanic song she did.'

She laughed. 'Well, this is my favourite song. I'm Alive, it's called.'

'Is that her?' Moone pointed to a life-size cutout of Celine Dion that was standing at the end of the room near the whiteboard.

Jones laughed. 'It is the legend herself. Sorry, that was a joke birthday present from my colleagues. Anyway, you wanted to know how our investigation is going, yeah? Come in.'

DI Jones went and stood by her desk, smiling a little as Moone came in and nodded to the other plain-clothed detective. 'Yes, I was wondering if you were any closer to finding out who killed him or if you had any theories.'

'Well, it's very early days.' Jones sat down. 'But it's looking more and more likely that he was killed by one of his rivals from the Dark Horses. McAllister was the Tomahawks' enforcer, and he'd messed with the Dark Horses a lot and taken a lot of their drug dealing territory in Plymouth.'

'I see. And what about this woman he was

seen with?'

'Yeah, that's interesting.' DI Jones looked down at her files and then put a finger under one of the lines she had written. 'Dark hair, attractive. He was seen drinking with her, then they must have gone outside. Chances are she was sent there as the honey trap. He was a notorious womaniser and they used his weakness against him. Anyway, why are you so interested? Aren't you investigating a serial murder case at the moment?'

'I am, but your case has got me curious. Did you find the murder weapon?'

'No, not so far but we're still looking. He was stabbed fifteen times. The final wound to his heart finished him off.'

'You don't think the woman who took him outside could be his murderer?'

'Well, thing is, I've got witnesses that put her back in the club not long after he was killed, but no sign of blood, and whoever killed him would have had quite a bit of blood on them. So, I'm pretty certain she tempted him outside to meet his killer. I'm going to be dragging Jim Nair in this afternoon. He's the leader of the Dark Horse gang, but I expect he'll keep his mouth shut. He's got a pretty expensive solicitor. You're not thinking there's a link between your murders and mine, are you?'

'No, nothing like that,' Moone said and shook his head. Then he started to weigh up something in his mind, and that was whether it might be best to tell DI Anna Jones about the possible involvement of Lloyd Redrobe in the gang-related crimes of the Dark Horses and the Tomahawks. Redrobe had more than likely killed before, even though they had no physical evidence he murdered DSU Armstrong. It was all guesswork, but he saw no harm in mentioning his name in case he had come up in their investigation. If they did have something on him, then perhaps it could be used as leverage to bring down Carthew.

'I don't suppose,' Moone started saying, but then his phone started ringing in his pocket and he saw it was Pinder calling. He smiled apologetically at DI Jones. 'Sorry, I better take this.'

Moone stepped out into the corridor and walked down to the end. 'Hello, Kevin.'

'Hi. Got some information,' he said, no sign of the usual mirth in his voice.

'What is it?'

'I've been keeping an eye on Redrobe,' he said. 'Well, today, he went on his scooter down to the ferry. Guess who else was there, waiting for him?'

'Carthew?' Moone felt the muscles in his neck and shoulders knot.

'No. I'll give you another... actually, I'll just tell you. Jason Harris, a member of the Dark Horses. They put his scooter in the boot of the car and then drove off. Unfortunately, we lost them. But what do you make of it?'

'Jesus. It's him, isn't it? He knocked off McAllister, didn't he?'

'More than likely, but we've still got no hard evidence. Nothing useful has come back from the crime scene. Not sure if they've collected CCTV footage from the whole area or not. But say it was Redrobe, chances are he'd be dressed up as a woman. They wouldn't be looking for a woman among a horde of other pissed women on a night out. Would they?'

'No, they're looking in the wrong place.'

'They are. What's this got to do with Carthew? Is she even involved in this, do you think?'

Moone sighed. 'Well, it's clever. It's almost a perfect murder. Sounds like the sort of thing she'd come up with, doesn't it?'

'Shit. So she's hiring herself and her half-brother out as contact killers?'

'Could be. I wouldn't put it past her. It's funny, but I was just talking to the detective in charge of the biker gang murder, DI Anna Jones...'

'She's good. Are you going to tell her what we know? Because if you do, they'll go after Redrobe and that'll frighten Carthew off. Then we'll never get her. If we can catch Redrobe in the act, then we might get him to dob her in.'

Moone closed his eyes for a moment, then

turned and looked at the small incident room, trying to decide what was for the best. They were getting close to nailing Carthew, he could feel it. 'No, I'm not going to mention him. We'll keep an eye on him. I think I'm going to send the team home for the day, give them some rest before I ask Boulton to give permission for us to talk to Nick Dann.'

'Oh, Jesus. Good luck.'

'Thanks. I'll talk to you tomorrow, Kev.'

Moone ended the call, feeling disconcerted and a little guilty as if he was doing something terrible. He slipped back up the stairs to the major incident room, ready to call it a night, holding the terrible truth in his heavy heart.

CHAPTER 19

Moone was just about to make his escape from the incident room when he bumped into DSU Boulton coming towards the glass doors. He sighed, then quickly put on a smile as he stepped into the corridor to greet him.

'DCI Moone,' Boulton said, nodding and looking past his shoulder towards the incident room. 'Off home, are we?'

'Yes, sir,' he said, straightening his tie. 'Not much else to do at the moment. We've still got a lot of CCTV to go through.'

'Any new suspects?'

'Well, that's something I needed to talk to you about.'

Boulton looked at him and folded his arms as he leaned on the wall. 'Go on.'

'Well, we've been looking into the driver of a van who we know parked outside a witness' house. We think the driver might be our handyman, scouting out his next victim…'

'You think?' Boulton sighed heavily. 'None

of this sounds substantial, Pete.'

'Well, we managed to get the tag ID from the number plate and a couple of extra numbers. We also managed to locate a good match for the van, and it was heading to Nick Dann's depot...'

Boulton gave an empty laugh and shook his head. 'You never give up do you, Moone? What is it you've got against Nick Dann?'

'Nothing, sir. Honestly. This is probably nothing to do with him, but what if one of his drivers is moonlighting as a handyman... and a killer? The van seen outside the witness' house had scrape marks on the side, the same van was seen heading to Dann's depot. There was also a very similar van parked near Caroline Abbott's street the night she was murdered.'

Boulton gave another heavy sigh. 'It's still nothing substantial, is it?'

'Well, it won't be until we take a look at his vans. This is what we do. Follow leads. We can't ignore what we've got, even if it might be just a coincidence. One of his drivers might be our killer.'

Boulton seemed to chew his lip for a moment, before pointing a finger in Moone's face. 'OK, Moone, fine. I'm going to get in touch with him, ask politely if we can check out his vehicles for this mysterious van.'

'What if he says no?'

'He won't. Not if I explain he's not a

suspect. I'll try and arrange it for the morning.' Then Boulton stared at him and pointed at him again. 'But, Moone, I warn you if you find nothing but you still keep chasing him, then I'll personally make a complaint of harassment for him. Have you got that?'

'Yes, sir.' Moone nodded, looking as grave as he could, although inside he felt he was getting closer to catching his killer.

DS Rivers was sitting in her car parked just round the corner from the flats where Carthew had told her that her new place was situated. It was getting darker now dusk was settling in and the sky was painted a dark hue of blood red.

There was no CCTV anywhere close to her building, but she told her to be careful where she parked so she wouldn't get a ticket. Carthew wasn't taking any chances, Rivers told herself and adjusted her sitting position again as she grimaced. She didn't know how junkie prostitutes put up with the discomfort of having something shoved up their front bottom, but then she guessed they were probably too high to even feel it. She hadn't known if Butler had been joking about hiding a recording device inside herself, but after she had given it plenty of thought she couldn't come up with a better hiding place. Carthew was bound to search her, even though she had given orders for her to leave her phone on and at home. She had tested the digital recorder Butler had given her at home, and found it picked up her voice pretty well, even across a room. All she would have to do was go to the toilet when she got there, retrieve it and find somewhere to hide it. That all seemed pretty straightforward, compared with getting her to talk about the crimes she had committed and incriminate herself. She couldn't make it too obvious, it had to be brought up in casual conversation. Nerves started to kick in. She took a few calming breaths, then reached down and picked up the carrier bag which contained the bottle of Prosecco she'd picked up from the nearby Co-op. Then she climbed out into the slightly cooler summer evening and headed slowly to the corner block of flats halfway along Greenbank Road. She stopped and looked round for a moment and realised how quiet the area was and the fact that the building was set back from the street a little way and was quite hidden from the main road. Carthew had picked somewhere she could enter and leave without being observed. She was always one step ahead, and that had been a large part of the reason why she had admired her and ultimately came to fall for her. But now the blinkers were mostly off and she recognised the dangerous situation she was in. She had to cut herself off from Faith before she went down or risk sinking with her.

She stepped under the shelter of the red brick building and buzzed flat Number Six. Another buzz came and the outer door clicked open so she went into the bare hallway and up the stone steps on her left, the tap of her shoes echoing all around while she could hear quite loud music coming from one of the flats. Carthew's floor was quiet, but the closer she got, the more she could smell food cooking. It smelt good and when she stood in front of the door, she realised it must be Faith cooking a meal for them.

She knocked and after a few seconds, Carthew opened the door, wearing a dark red off-the-shoulder summery dress. She smiled, then stepped back and allowed Rivers to enter.

'You're a little early,' she said, still smiling.

'Am I?' Rivers went in, looking round the place, noting all the framed artwork on the wall, mainly of the impressionists. It was the kind of artwork someone might put up to look normal, she thought. Carthew was anything but normal, and again it had been one of the things about her that made her more attractive. It was a small, compact flat, with a medium-sized living area and a small but modern white kitchen separated by a small archway. Rivers could see that pans were bubbling away on the stove.

'Something smells nice,' she said and held

up the carrier bag with the bottle of wine in it.

'Oh, for me?' Carthew put on a look of mock surprise and took the bag. 'A moving-in gift? How lovely.'

Carthew came over, staring into her eyes for a moment, losing the smile. Then she kissed her passionately, making a warm flow of emotions rise up in her which made her question what exactly she was doing there.

Carthew stood back, the smile returning.

'I'm sorry if I was cold the last time I saw you,' she said.

'It's fine,' Rivers said, smiling.

'No, it's not. I shouldn't be like that with you. You're just about the only person I can trust.'

'But not the only one.'

Carthew nodded. 'No. Not the only one. But that's different. He's family. Look, I know how you feel about me, the depth of your feelings...'

Rivers felt a tightness in her chest as butterflies escaped from somewhere and entered her stomach. 'It's OK...'

'Listen, if I could feel about anyone like that... I would feel it about you.'

'Why do you think that you can't feel like that?'

Carthew looked down. 'Because of what I am. I know people think I'm a monster...'

'I don't...'

'But everyone else does.' Carthew looked up and there was a strange look in her eyes, almost as if she was going to cry. 'It's because of what I've had to do to try and survive. For a long, long time, I tried to fit in, I really did. I pretended to be a good little girl, but I just couldn't.'

'I know. I understand...'

Carthew smiled. 'I know. I'm glad you're here. Right, I'd better get this meal finished. I'll open the wine and pour us both a glass.'

Rivers smiled and watched her head off in the kitchen with the bag with the wine in it. Carthew's words kept playing over in her head, wrapping around the warmth of feeling that was now thudding in her chest. Guilt was rising too, aware of what she was meant to be doing. Had to do, in fact as she didn't have a choice. She knew they would bring Carthew down and with her, she would go too. She had to be one step ahead to survive. It was her or Carthew. She took a breath, then called out, 'Where's your toilet?'

'Just in front of you, turn left.'

Rivers hurried on, taking the turning and finding a small shower room with a toilet. She shut and locked the door, then stood there for a moment, her heart racing, her stomach flipping over and over. She had no choice. She didn't want to betray her, but what could she do now? The honest truth, which she found deep inside herself once she dug around for it, was that she couldn't trust her. Even though she had seen a different side to her tonight, she couldn't risk her own survival.

She made her decision, then lowered her trousers and her underwear, and took a deep breath before retrieving the small recording device. She gritted her teeth and then pulled it out. It was wrapped in a small clear plastic food bag, which she washed and hid in her pocket. She dressed, then pulled the chain and headed back to the living area. Carthew came out of the kitchen, holding two glasses of white wine and held one out to her. Rivers took it with a smile even though her heart was pounding, feeling the recorder she had now stuffed in her back pocket.

'Thanks,' she said and took a sip.

'Are you OK?' Carthew asked. 'You look a little flushed.'

'I'm fine. I'm starving though. It smells delicious.'

Carthew looked back to the kitchen as she took a sip of wine. 'Only bolognese, I'm afraid. I'm not much of a cook.'

'I love bolognese.' Rivers took another gulp of wine, trying to calm her nerves.

'Then I'd better get ready to serve it up.' Carthew hurried into the kitchen again.

Rivers swept round, searching the room for the perfect place to hide the recorder, the blood pounding around her body, crashing in her ears. Her eyes jumped to the bookshelf near the door. There were all kinds of factual books and classical CDs. She saw a gap at one end, where she could see that if she moved one of the books slightly, then she could hide the recorder behind it. It would still be able to record any conversations they had while they ate. She checked Carthew was busy in the kitchen then took out the recorder, switched it on and started recording. She hid it, her chest-thumping, then picked up her wine and tried to act normal and calm.

'I'd better go to the loo before we eat,' Carthew said, gave an apologetic smile and then ran off down the hallway.

When she was alone, Rivers let out a breath and turned to stare at where she had hidden the recorder. She stepped back, then moved round the room, checking it couldn't be seen easily. It couldn't. Then she could hear noises in the bathroom, the sound of the tap running, and the door opening.

Carthew came back into the room and picked up her wine then stepped closer to Rivers. She smiled a little as she raised her drink as if to make a toast.

'Isn't this nice?' she asked and sipped her wine.

Rivers nodded and drank some more of her wine. 'It is. Really nice.'

Carthew seemed to stare at her for a while before she said, 'Can I ask you something?'

'Of course.'

There was another shorter pause. 'When did they approach you?'

'Who?'

'Butler and Moone. When did they talk to you?' Carthew's eyes were digging into her, her face calm, blank almost.

Rivers' heart started pounding again. 'What do you mean? They haven't... I don't...'

'I have cameras in this place,' Carthew said, smiling a little. 'They see everything. So I see everything. Including you putting that little device, whatever it is, on the bookshelf. So, my question still is, when did they approach you? I'm guessing they have something on you that they used to get you to betray me. Yes?'

Rivers couldn't find the words as the panic pounded in her chest and ears. She clasped at any half-reasonable thought in her head. 'It's not like you think. They don't know anything. We can use them...'

'What were you going to do? Get me into conversation? Get me to spill my guts?'

'Listen, Faith...' Then she felt it, a strange sensation coming over her, a kind of dizziness. The room seemed to move or the ceiling came closer. No, the walls were coming in closer, then falling back, like they were breathing. She shook her head, trying to rid herself of the fog that had enveloped her brain.

'It's the wine,' Carthew said, lifting her glass. 'The wine you're drinking. Not mine. In a moment, you won't be able to move...'

Her legs became wobbly, the panic now flooding her entire body. 'Faith, no, please, listen to me...'

But she found herself falling backwards, stumbling against the bookshelf, trying to put out her hands to right herself, but they hardly moved. Nothing seemed to move properly or work. No. Oh God, no, please.

'Faith, please... let me...' But then she found her mouth opening and no words able to form. She heard a mumbling sound as she fell backwards and slipped to the ground. She was still sitting upright, resting against the bottom of the bookshelf.

Carthew crouched down, staring blankly at her. 'Don't worry, darling, in a moment you won't feel anything. You should have trusted me. Now I have to make you disappear. You only have yourself to blame.'

She could only watch as Carthew stood up. Her heart was pounding but her body wouldn't move. A tear crept out of her eye as she realised that this was it, no one knew where she was. Then the darkness crept closer, crawling in from the corners of the room. Soon, there was nothing.

CHAPTER 20

It was early in the morning and he was sitting at the small kitchen table, staring through the back window that was spotted with bird mess. He looked around the old-fashioned kitchen and then took another spoonful of cornflakes and started munching them. The house would take a lot of work, a lot of man hours he could hardly afford, but his wife wouldn't stop going on about it. He had got up early and left, telling her he was going to get a start on prepping the place for decoration. Then she started moaning again, telling him what he already knew, which was he was behind and needed to work faster so they could have a nicer home. She was always going on at him, nagging him, reminding him he wasn't worthy of her.

'Does your missus know anything about what you really get up to, bey?'

He froze, the spoon almost touching his mouth. He could smell the deep pungent burn of the roll-up cigarette the man was smoking.

What the hell was he doing here anyway?

'I want to help you,' he said and stepped around the kitchen table and sat down. He took a deep drag of his fag and fixed those deep dark eyes on him.

'I need to work on getting this place ready.' He started eating again, taking his eyes from the old man's that burned out to him through the wisps of smoke.

'That's not what I mean. What you do, that's your real work, isn't it, bey?'

'I'm not going to do that any more.' He stood up and put the bowl and spoon in the sink.

The old man laughed and it was a deep rattling sound that echoed around the room. 'You think you can just stop? I thought you had some brains in your head...'

'I stopped for all those years, didn't I?'

'Did you?'

He could feel his eyes on him.

'Yes. Almost twenty years... then I ended up in her house. I tried to walk away...'

'Oh, I'm sorry, was that just bad luck? You happen to walk into her house?' Another deep rattling laugh. 'You was looking for her.'

'I wasn't looking for her. It was just a job. She needed someone to set up her laptop with...'

'You might not have been looking for her, but you found her. Deep down you knew you'd found her. You put the leaflet through her door, didn't you?'

He stared at the old man, his pulse thumping in his neck. 'How did you...?'

'I know you. I know what you did twenty years ago. I know what you've been doing since.'

'I don't know what you're talking about.'

The old man took a deep drag of his cigarette. 'You can't put a pause on what you are...'

'I got married, and we had a child... so I knew I had to stop...'

The old man stood up and stepped closer, pointing the bent, stained cigarette at him. 'You told yourself you'd stop, but you didn't, did you? You just changed what you did, where you did it, didn't you, bey? You were working away for a few years off and on. Oil rigs, then off doing building jobs in London and up North, all while your missus set up her business. That gave you plenty of time to play, didn't it? There must be plenty of girls they're looking for, but they'll never find them. Will they?'

'I was working, trying to earn a living... she was pregnant...'

'Then when she became the breadwinner, the one who wears the trousers, well, you didn't need to work away, did you? You had to come back home, didn't you, bey? Had to come home and play happy families. But now her business isn't doing so well, is it? You've got to help bring in the bread. The pressure's on, and when the pressure and stress is up, that's when you need an outlet for all that anger inside you, don't you?'

He hung his head. 'No. That's not true.'

'You can't hide the truth from me, bey. I've known you too long. Right from when you were that snivelling, weakling little shit that the girls used to laugh at. Remember her? What was her name?'

'You know her name.'

He nodded and took another drag of his fag. 'I do. I'll never forget her name. Sarah. They're all Sarah, aren't they? When you go to work on them, you see her, don't you? You see her pretty face. You want it to be her, don't you?'

He shook his head, feeling the tears leaking from his eyes. 'No. I don't think about... I've forgotten about all that.'

The old man laughed for a moment. 'Yeah, right, you've forgotten about how she made your life a misery, made you the laughing stock of that school and for years after. Even when you saw one of those fucking kids on the street years after, they'd point at you and call you names, wouldn't they, bey?'

He went to walk past him, telling him he had to do some work on the house, but the old man grabbed his arm and moved his wrinkled face close to his ear.

'I meant what I said,' the old man said. 'I want to help. Just like I helped you all those years ago. Or have you forgotten?'

He shook his head. 'I haven't. You were the only one that listened...'

'I didn't just listen. I helped you. I showed you the way. Don't turn your back on me. Without my help, you'll just get yourself caught. Now, tell me who's next. You fucked up the last one, didn't you? Killed the wrong bitch.'

His head sprung up and he stared at the old man. 'You've been following me.'

'I have to keep an eye on you, don't I? Aren't you going to go back for the bitch you were meant to kill?'

He shook his head. 'Too dangerous.'

'But that's part of the fun, isn't it, bey?'

'There's others.' He lifted his hand and pointed towards the locked room where the computer was sitting, waiting.

The old man followed his hand. 'There always is. Then let's find them together. Like old times.'

Moone was sitting in their car, parked outside the gates to Dann International Deliveries, watching the drivers coming in, getting ready for another day's work. He picked up one of the takeaway coffees they had grabbed up on the way and saw DSU Boulton heading to the main office where he was greeted by Nick Dann himself. The businessman wore a gruff look but then broke into a smile as he shook his buddy's hand. Then they were talking, chatting away, their eyes jumping back to Moone every so often, which gave him a deep sense of unease. Then he looked into the rearview mirror and saw Butler still on her phone, trying to get through to whoever she was trying to get through to, without much success. She hadn't said who she was trying to get hold of, but Moone got a sense that it wasn't something serious.

The gates started grinding their way open, so Moone lowered the passenger window and stuck his head out. 'Butler! We're going in.'

He watched her in the mirror put her phone away, then tramp back to the car and climb in behind the wheel where she put it into first and took them slowly into the yard. Behind them came a response car with three uniforms sat inside, ready to assist them in trying to identify the killer's van.

'Everything OK?' Moone asked, taking another sip of his coffee.

'Yeah, good.'

'Did you get hold of them yet, whoever they are?'

She stared at him as she parked and yanked up the handbrake. 'Oi, nosey, keep your snout out. I can't believe you got Dann to agree to this.'

'I didn't. This is all Boulton.'

Butler huffed. 'Probably gave him one of those handshakes they give, you know the ones they do with one trouser leg rolled up.'

Moone climbed out. 'Probably. But let's see where this gets us.'

Butler climbed out as Boulton and Nick Dann started walking towards them.

'Mr Dann, you've met DCI Moone,' Boulton said, his face not giving away his mood. 'This is DI Mandy Butler.'

Dann nodded as he folded his arms, staring them both down for a moment before he said, 'I hope this isn't going to take long, as I do have a business to run.'

'It won't take long,' Moone said, putting on a polite smile. 'As soon as our people have checked the vans then your drivers can get them out of here.'

'Good.' Nick Dann nodded again. 'Get on with it, then.'

'Have you got a list of the registration numbers of all your vehicles?' Butler asked, causing him to stare at her for a moment before he turned around and looked over to a collection of drivers who were standing around chatting.

'Gary!' Dann shouted. A stocky, grey-haired driver hurried over, taking out some papers from his pocket.

'Here, these are all of them, Mr Dann,' Gary said and handed the printed sheets to his boss.

Dann took them and gave them a brief examination before holding them out to Moone, who turned around and saw the uniforms all standing waiting for their orders.

'Right,' Moone said, 'examine the vans, take their registration numbers and a photo of their bodywork. You know what we're looking for.'

As the uniforms started spreading out with their clipboards, Moone turned back to face Dann and his boss and gave them both a polite smile. 'This won't take too long.'

'What is this about exactly?' Dann asked, his face tight with annoyance. 'First of all, you come here asking questions about some women I'm supposed to have known, and now you're searching for a van? Do you think I'm involved somehow?'

Boulton turned to him, shaking his head. 'No, Mr Dann, no one thinks you're involved. We just have a lead to follow up, you know, forms to fill, procedure...'

'Should I contact my solicitor?' Dann asked, staring at Moone.

'Only if you've been up to no good,' Butler said, smirking.

'DI Butler!' Boulton snapped. 'Please apologise to Mr Dann.'

Moone turned to see Butler lose her smirk

and her cheeks redden as she said, 'What for, exactly?'

Boulton stepped up to her. 'For implying that Mr Dann has been up to no good.'

Butler folded her arms. 'I merely informed him that he should only get a solicitor if he's committed a crime. Apparently, he hasn't, have you, Mr Dann?'

Everyone looked at the businessman, who glared back at Butler, his eyes flaming. 'No, I haven't committed any crimes at all. Not even a parking ticket, so if you could move this along and let my people get back to work, I would be very grateful.'

'It'll be all over pretty soon, I assure you,' Boulton said.

'Sir, there is that other thing,' Gary said, approaching again.

Dann turned to him, a little distractedly. 'What other thing?'

'The break-in?' Gary said, seeming to avoid the gaze of everyone apart from his boss.

'Oh, yeah, that.' Dann nodded and looked at Boulton. 'I meant to mention this earlier, but we had a break in a while back. One of the vans was stolen.'

Moone turned and stared at Butler and saw she was looking back at him with the same expression of disbelief.

'When was this exactly?' Boulton asked, a look of annoyance in his eyes.

Dann shrugged. 'Months back. They only took the van.'

'You didn't think to report it?' Moone asked.

Dann stared at him, smirking a little. 'No, it was just one van. It didn't work that well, and I could easily afford to replace it, so there was no real point.'

'Where were your security people when this was going on?' Butler asked with a deep huff.

'I gave them the night off.' Dann smiled. 'They'd been working hard, so I thought they'd earned a break.'

'And this van thief just happened to choose that night to break in?' Butler laughed. 'Convenient.'

Boulton held up his hands. 'Right, let's not...'

'You know what isn't convenient?' Dann started to say. 'It's –'

'Let's just settle down,' Boulton said, raising his voice. 'Nick, if you could provide any information on the stolen van, that would be great.'

'I've got the registration number here,' Gary said, taking out a small page of a notepad.

'You couldn't have produced that earlier?' Butler went over and snatched the note from him and read it, then handed it to Moone. 'This matches the first few digits of the van we're looking for.'

Moone took it and examined it, then sighed, realising she was right. Conveniently, the van they were chasing had been stolen months before. Dann was looking at him, a smirk still dug into his face. 'CCTV?'

'We had a look, but you couldn't see their face,' Dann said, 'so I had it wiped.'

'Right then,' Boulton said, turning to Moone. 'Looks like we've got all we need from here. Let's wrap this up and let Mr Dann get back to work.'

'Can you believe that self-important stuck up… prick,' Moone said as Butler drove them away, the incident response car not far behind.

'Yeah, I can,' Butler said.

'So, is he the killer after all?' Moone asked, trying to work it all out in his head. 'He uses one of his vans to pretend to be a handyman and then kills these women? Which doesn't make sense, because we know he's already met and wined and dined some of them and turned up in his flash motor. And why would you use a van linked to your own company?'

'None of it makes sense.'

'No. I don't think it's him, but why did he give the security staff the night off and wipe the CCTV footage so quickly?'

'Because he was up to something that night that he shouldn't have. Knowing him, it probably involves a woman.'

Moone nodded. 'I think you're right, and he didn't want anyone around to see it. But the killer chose that night to break in. Why?'

Butler shrugged. 'I don't know. But there is something I need to talk to you about.'

She indicated and parked up in a wide lane, close to the hedges that lined one side. The response car went on past, leaving them both sitting in silence.

'What is it?' Moone asked, his stomach tightening a little. 'Everything all right?'

'Not really.' Butler stared ahead. 'I think I've made a mistake.'

'Go on.'

Butler looked at him. 'When I went to Bristol, I did find something out. Turns out it was DS Rivers who was aiding and abetting Carthew…'

'You're joking? How did you find that out?'

'I followed her. Anyway, to cut a long story short, I ended up confronting her. I told her if she didn't help us nail Carthew, then she'd go down too.'

Moone turned to her, a thought blazing into his mind. 'Hang on, if she's in on it, then she can go on record that she helped Carthew commit murder. She could be our star witness…'

'Yes, but her and the bitch are lovers, and there's no actual physical evidence of Carthew's involvement. It would be Rivers' word against hers. Plus, they've already tied a neat bleeding bow around it, so they're not going to listen to us or Rivers and our new theory.'

'So, we need to get something concrete on Carthew, using Rivers...'

Butler sighed and looked down.

'What? What's happened?'

'Rivers was meant to go to Carthew's last night. The plan was, she got her on tape admitting to her part in Armstrong's murder or something criminal at least...'

'But?'

Butler looked at him. 'She was meant to call me after, but she never did. I've tried to call her today, but there's no answer on the burner I gave her.'

Moone looked forward, then buried his face in his hands and let out a groan. 'She's got wise to it, hasn't she? She somehow knew something was up, then she...'

'Oh fuck, if Rivers is dead, it's all my fault. That bloody bitch.'

'I'm guessing we don't know where Carthew is living. I know she did have a house in Plympton.'

'No, she's living in the city somewhere. Rivers was waiting for Carthew to tell her where just before they met up. She never told me. Oh shit...'

'What about Rivers? Where's she staying?'

'The Jury's Inn. Room 68. She booked herself in under a different name. Holly Varjak. I've tried to contact her there, but there's no answer.'

'Holly Varjak?' Moone said, a flicker of memory igniting somewhere in his mind. 'I know that name somehow. Why do I know that name?'

'You don't. She used it when she was undercover years back. Forget it.'

'OK. Then let's go there and see if she turns up or see if we can find out where Carthew is.'

Butler nodded and took a deep breath before she started the engine. 'Right then, Jury's Inn it is.'

They went into the wide reception area of the Jury's Inn Hotel. Butler inquired at the reception desk after Holly Varjak, while Moone headed for the lifts near the hotel bar. He felt a strange sensation coat his back, a film of cold sweat appearing over his skin and under his armpits. It was the place he was in, and the memories it held. In one of the rooms people had died right in front of him. He called the lift when he saw Butler strolling over, then stepped in when the doors pinged and opened.

'You alright?' she asked, watching him with an intense stare.

'Yep. Fine.'

'Try not to dwell on it,' she said, her voice

sounding a little softer than he was used to.

'Did you find anything out?'

'Not much. They haven't seen her since last night.' Butler moved to the back of the lift and tapped her head on the wall. 'Shit. Shit. This is my fault. That psycho bitch has done something to her, and it's all my bleeding fault.'

Moone turned to her. 'You don't know that. Let's look around and see what we find.'

The lift doors opened, and Butler moved past him and headed left, down the neat, red corridor that was lined with cream-coloured doors. She was standing by room sixty-eight by the time Moone caught up with her. She knocked, then knocked again.

'She's not here,' Butler said, the guilt ringing in her voice.

'Hang on,' he said and walked back down the corridors where he thought he had seen the cart of a house cleaner. He was right, it was parked outside the open door of one of the rooms, so he took out his ID and knocked on the door frame.

'Hello? It's the police.'

A woman, maybe in her mid-forties, with caramel-coloured skin and tied-back glossy black hair came out of the bathroom and stared at him wide-eyed. 'Police? Am I in trouble?'

'No,' he said and smiled. 'There's a room along the corridor. We need to get inside. It's important.'

The woman stepped closer to him, staring at his warrant card as if she didn't quite believe him. 'You're police?'

'That's right. If you let us in that room, it could save someone's life. It's pretty urgent.'

'I should call my supervisor,' she said, looking nervous. 'I could get in trouble.'

'Trust me, you're not going to get in trouble. Please, this is urgent.'

The cleaner seemed to think for a moment, staring off towards the door, then took out a card from her pocket and headed out of the room. 'I won't get in trouble?'

'No, you won't,' Moone said again and nodded to Butler as he and the cleaner approached the room. The woman put the key card into the lock, stopping only to give Butler a suspicious once-over. When the door to the room was open, Moone watched Butler take out a couple of twenty-pound notes and hold them out to the cleaner.

'We were never here, understand?' Butler said as the woman took the cash.

'OK, I never saw you,' the cleaner said, then turned around and left the corridor.

Moone took out some latex gloves and pulled them on as he stepped across the threshold, giving the place the once-over. The hotel room was pretty much identical to all the others he'd ever been in. Identical to the one he'd seen people die in. He shuddered, his head pounding. He took a deep, harsh breath as Butler followed him in and passed him.

There were clothes on the bed, some on the chair by the TV. A half-drunk bottle of prosecco and an empty glass were stood on the bedside table.

'Untidy cow, isn't she?' Butler said, then seemed to drop the look of mirth she had been wearing. 'Sorry.'

'You're not speaking ill of the dead,' Moone said, heading to the desk by the window.

'Aren't I? This is Carthew we're talking about.'

Moone nodded as he searched the clothes left draped over the chair. 'I know, but for all we know Rivers and Carthew could be shacked up in bed.'

'I hope so.' Butler pulled open the drawer of the bedside table. 'Hang on.'

'What is it?'

Butler put her gloved hand into the drawer and took out a smartphone. 'Rivers' phone. She left it here because Carthew probably wanted her to, so we couldn't track it. She knew what she was doing.'

'Turn it on.'

'No. Best we leave it. Anyway, she's bound to have a passcode or facial recognition. What the hell're we going to tell Crowne?'

Moone enclosed his face in his hands for a moment, trying to think, to fathom what

Carthew might do next. There was nothing, no answer, and he knew he wasn't clever enough to catch her out. 'I don't know. I honestly don't know. Perhaps nothing. We take the phone because it might come in useful. Bag it up and we'll put it somewhere safe.'

'Then what? Wait calmly for her to become our boss with our fingers stuck up our arses?'

'No. We're going to stop her. This time she doesn't get away with it.'

'But how? Have you got a plan?'

Moone shook his head. 'No, but I promise you this is where it ends.'

CHAPTER 21

The sun was burning the back of Jason's neck, so he turned up the collar of his thin leather jacket then took out his cigarettes and poked one between his lips. He lit it as he watched the road. All he could see was the wild and rugged land, the tors in the distance and the white blurry shapes of the sheep that surrounded them. He took a puff, then turned and looked over at her car, where she was sitting, looking down at her phone. He stared for a moment, digging his eyes into her, wondering if she might look up. Could people really sense you looking at them? Then she did look up and he flinched a little. He turned away, thinking about the afternoon they had spent in bed. They hadn't done everything, not all that he had wanted to do, but what they had done, all the sweaty, crazy things, were still hanging around in his head, clouding his thoughts. *She* clouded his thoughts. She was dangerous, that much he understood and, of course, she scared him a little. He'd hardly slept after the act, as there was the fear she might cut his throat, remove his testicles, or boil his rabbit if he had one. But she was clever and determined to go places, to rise up the ranks, she had told him as they lay there smoking. She would rule Plymouth and he could sit on the throne next to her once Nair was out of the way. One day he, Jason, could be King of the Dark Horses and so much more. She scared him, but he found himself being drawn into her world.

The deep rattling and familiar roar of Nair's hog came thundering down the road. The bike and the leather-clad figure riding it came swerving into the car park and came to a stop. Nair took off his helmet and sat there for a moment after he kicked down the stand. He nodded to Jason, then looked past him and at her car. He climbed off and rested the helmet on the back of the bike, then walked over to Jason.

'What's this then, Jay?' Nair asked, nodding towards the car. 'You said it was urgent.'

'It is.' Jason took a long drag of his cigarette, chewing it all over, recalling her proposition, taking his time because he knew it would annoy the old geezer.

'Fuck sake, Jay, you gonna get on with it or not?'

'I'll do it.'

Nair narrowed his eyes. 'Do what?'

'What she wants done.' Jason pointed his thumb behind him.

'You're going to do it? You're going to... you're going see to him, are you?'

'Why not?'

Nair gave an empty, tired-sounding laugh. 'She's calling the shots now, is she, lad?'

'No. But this needs to be done right. We don't want any fuck ups.'

Nair stared at him for a moment, then leaned closer, lowering his voice. 'What's it with you two, then?'

He shrugged, not wanting to go into too much detail. 'We see eye to eye on things. I think she can help us.'

'She's filth, you remember that, don't you? You can't trust her, can't trust any of the bastards.'

'You're trusting her.' Jason laughed, then looked away as he blew out some smoke.

The blow pounded into his gut, knocking him forward, the air bursting from his mouth along with his cigarette. He doubled over then slipped to his knees. When he looked up, he saw Nair standing over him, his face tight with rage.

'You don't talk to me like that, bey, you got that?'

Jason caught his breath, then nodded.

'Yeah... I got it.'

Then there was the sound of a car door opening behind him and then the tap of Carthew's heels on the hard ground.

'Is there a problem?' she asked as Jason pulled himself from the ground with a grunt.

'No problem,' Nair said. 'Just telling Jason something he needs to realise.'

'You were having trouble finding someone who would do the job,' she said, putting her arm through Jason's when he straightened himself. 'Now you've got him.'

'So I heard.' Nair let out a harsh breath. 'Fine. You do the job, Jason. But if you get caught, that's down to you. You don't talk, you do your time. You got that, lad?'

Jason looked at her, his stomach still burning, his hands balling into fists. He wanted nothing more than to take out his knife and gut the old man, but he knew better of it. He looked at him, stared into his eyes and nodded.

'Yeah, I've got it.'

Nair shook his head. 'Right then, I'll let you know when it's happening. I'll be in touch. Best you stay away from the clubhouse for a while.'

Jason watched the old man climb back onto his hog and start her up, then roar out of the car park, leaving them alone.

'Fucking old wanker,' Jason said, taking out another cigarette and lighting it. 'I could've cut him up.'

'I know, but we need to be patient. Soon you'll get your chance. Then you'll get it all.'

'What about you? Do I get you?'

She smiled, then stroked his cheek. 'You know you will. I'll be all yours.'

'Are we going to do the next obvious step here or not?' Butler asked, almost announcing it to the whole incident room as Moone came walking in.

'And what's that?' Moone asked.

'Setting up a fake Facebook profile, and trying to catch this nutter like that?' She straightened up. 'I mean, he seems to target within Plymouth, so we set up a fake profile of a single woman, aged in her thirties, maybe early forties. We can get Barry to set it up.'

'Barry's got a lot on his plate,' Moone sighed.

'This is what he does. Get him to set it up, and then me and Molly can run it.'

'Run what?'

They all looked round as Carthew came strolling in and sat at her desk.

Butler turned and faced her, the thunder clouds darkening her skin. 'We're talking about doing some work, you know police work?'

Carthew laughed. 'I think I recall that. In

fact, that's what I've just been doing, going through CCTV and finding this van now we have the full plate.'

'Did you find anything?' Moone strolled over, feeling sick to his stomach to even be breathing the same air as her. It was stale with a hint of sweet perfume. Despite himself, a memory of them together, lying in his bed, long before he realised that she was a monster, unfolded in his mind.

'Actually, I did,' she said and looked at Butler. 'I was just about to say before DI Butler interrupted me. Anyway, a camera picked up the van heading towards a small village in Cornwall. Shrewtin, it's called.'

'Shrewtin?' DC Molly Chambers had stood up and was staring over at Carthew.

'That's right,' she said, smiling as if she had never killed a soul.

'What is it, Chambers?' Moone asked.

'Well, it's just…' She looked down at her desk. 'I came across that village a little while ago.'

Moone went over to her desk. 'Where did you see it?'

'Sorry, boss, but I don't think you're going to like this,' she said, lifting a piece of paper. 'But it's the village where Professor Scott Eason lives.'

'You're joking?' Butler said and hurried over and took the piece of paper.

'Just because the van passed through there, doesn't mean he's our killer,' Moone said, finding it hard to believe that his old school friend could be a psychopath who strangles women in their own homes.

'I checked another camera that was put at the end of the village to stop vehicles speeding through there,' Carthew started saying.

'And the van doesn't appear again?' Butler said, nodding. 'Can you believe it, he's actually been in this room, lecturing us on the type of psycho we're looking for? Cheeky...'

Moone sighed. 'We still don't know anything. This could be a coincidence. What about the van coming back out of the village later, the next day?'

'Nothing,' Carthew said. 'I'll keep checking...'

'So we go and see him,' Butler said, staring at Moone. 'Find out where he was when these women were beaten and strangled.'

Moone knew he wasn't going to win this, especially when he saw most of the team waiting on his word. 'OK, let's go and pay him a visit. Can you send me his address, Molly?'

'Sure, I'll send it now.'

Moone smiled, then headed towards Butler who was already getting set to follow him out. Then his eyes jumped to Carthew who was standing up, her eyes narrowed, full of anger, her mouth poised to say something. He stopped and faced her, thinking that diplomacy might be a better approach. 'Thanks, DS Carthew, keep up the excellent work.'

The anger faded away from her eyes, leaving a blank expression, so he hurried on and followed Butler out.

He was sitting at the computer, staring at it, looking at the new friends he had made. No, not him, but her, the woman he had invented. He scrolled through them, checking their names, his heart beginning to thump. He could smell the deep burn of the roll-ups the old man was smoking behind him as he stood looking towards the window as if on guard. He still couldn't believe he was here after all these years. It made him scared, terrified that if the old man managed to find him, then it wasn't beyond the realm of possibilities that the law might find him too. But he calmed himself by telling the voice in his head that the old caretaker knew his darkest secrets, knew exactly how his mind worked because his mind worked the same way. The law couldn't know his thoughts.

'The filth can't find you,' the old man said. 'Not with my help, bey. I'll keep you safe.'

'I don't need your help,' he said, turning to look at him. 'They haven't got me so far, have they?'

'But it's different now, bey, isn't it? You didn't do it back here for all those years, not on your front doorstep, did you? But now you've given in to the rage and brought all the punishment back home.'

He turned away and decided to ignore him and the foul stench that drifted from his stinking cigarettes. He started looking through the photos again, bringing up the names and faces of the women the fake woman had befriended.

'What about that one?' The old man stood over him, his odour flooding the air. 'Her name's Sarah. You're always after another Sarah, ain't you, lad?'

'But it's not her, not her face.'

'No, it never is. It'll never be her. Not again.'

'Because of what you did to her.'

The old man laughed. 'Not just me, bey. You was there too. If they ever found out what we did, then you'd go down. Life, you'd get. They'd stick you somewhere like Broadmoor.'

He shook his head, trembling all over, vomit rising to his mouth. Suddenly all he could see was the darkness of the car park, the stench of dank concrete filling his nostrils. He could hear screams, muffled at first, then loud, echoing around in the half-darkness. Then she was quiet, the old man's dirty hand over her face. He could hardly see him in the shadows, hidden away, but he could smell him, that same acrid, pungent stench that he could smell now.

'I can't go to prison,' he said, grasping his face. 'No. I couldn't. I couldn't have them knowing either. They can't find out.'

The old man laughed. 'No, you couldn't have your little girl knowing what you are, could you?'

'No, never...'

'Of course, there's one way to make sure they never find out.'

He let go of his head and turned slowly to see that the caretaker was standing smoking, staring down at him with those dark, fathomless eyes as he nodded.

'You know what I mean, bey,' he said, his eyes widening.

'Fuck off!' he said, jumping to his feet. 'I couldn't ever. You evil fucking...'

'Me?' The old man started laughing until he started coughing. 'I'm not evil, lad. Nor are you. You're just giving out the punishment they deserve.'

He stared at the old man for a moment, trembling still and then turned away to face the screen. His eyes fixed on one of the profiles. He bent in, seeing her face clearer. He felt a shudder deep inside him, an echo of something long ago.

'She could be her,' the old man said behind him, reading his thoughts. 'Older, of course, but just like her. A bitch just like her too, I bet.'

He nodded, then looked at her name. Sarah. She was perfect.

'What the bloody hell was that?' Butler huffed as she drove them over the Tamar Bridge. Moone had been watching the hot sun glinting off the dark green waters of the river and the boats that bobbed, pushed and pulled by its current when he heard the question. He'd been expecting it since they set off, but surprisingly Butler had managed to keep it together for a while.

'Diplomacy,' he said, and kept the smile from his face.

'Diplomacy?' She gave a laugh as dry as a Jacob's cracker. 'That's what you call it? Well done? Jesus. That's the only police work she's done for God knows how long. I don't know how she expects to become our... no, strike that, I know exactly how she plans to do it. Have you seen her cosying up to Boulton?'

'He's got a wife, and a young kid, hasn't he?'

Butler looked at him and then let out another cracker laugh. 'That never stops them. I haven't heard anything from bloody Rivers, have you?'

'No.' Moone looked down. 'But we can't raise the alarm. And we've got no proof Carthew's done anything to her.'

'But we know she has. She's either got her somewhere, or she's done her in! Jesus Christ and she's just sitting there like butter wouldn't melt between her arse cheeks. We've got to do something, Moone, and bloody soon.'

He nodded. 'I know. But we can't alert anyone because we've got nothing on Carthew, nothing substantial, and we don't even know where Rivers met up with her that night. We're stuffed for the moment. We've just got to wait it out. We've got no choice.'

'That bloody bitch.' Butler let out a quick and deep scream as she gripped the wheel tight.

Moone looked at her, feeling her pain and frustration. It was digging into him too, even more so he felt as part of him, the illogical part of his brain, assumed he was guilty of starting it all. Right from the moment he had made the error of getting involved with her, he felt as if he had set events in motion and she was his responsibility. He shook his head, then looked over and saw the sign for the village where the road narrowed and the houses, mostly small cottages, started to crowd in along it. There was the pub, the Fox and Hound that Molly had mentioned in the directions she had sent by text.

'I think it's the next turning on the right,' he said, pointing.

Butler sighed, then indicated and started to slow. 'We need to plant that mobile at her place.'

Moone stared at her. 'Carthew's place?'

'Yeah, I know we need to find it first.'

'We can't do that.'

She spun the wheel and turned into a narrow road that seemed to lead to a distant and quite large house. 'Why not? She would.'

'We're not her. We're not going to start planting evidence. Anyway, we don't even know where her new place is.'

'We'll find it, and we'll plant the phone and she'll have a lot of difficult questions to answer.' Butler pulled up close to the driveway of a sizeable new build house. There was a dark blue BMW sitting on the driveway, which Butler parked close behind. As soon as she had turned the engine off, the large black front door opened and a dark-haired, attractive woman, dressed in a grey skirt and white blouse, came hurrying out towards them looking annoyed.

'You can't park there!' the woman snapped as Butler climbed out. 'You're boxing me in!'

Butler climbed out and took out her ID. 'I'm so very sorry, but we're investigating a few murders.'

The woman lost her look of annoyance and it was quickly replaced by a little confusion. 'Murders? What murders?'

Moone came over, putting on a smile as he scanned the house and noticed it had a rather large garage attached. 'There's been a few in

Plymouth...'

'What's it got to do with us?' the woman said, the look of anger flickering back into her eyes. 'I've got a meeting to get to and I'm already late.'

'Is your husband here?' Butler asked, stepping towards the house.

'My husband?' She looked at Moone. 'Why do you want to see him?'

'He's been helping us, giving us advice,' Moone said.

The woman nodded, a little relief seeming to shine through. 'Oh, right, I see. He did mention helping with something... actually, I was glad to hear that he might be getting back to his former work.'

Butler turned round and looked at her. 'Former work? What does he do now?'

'This and that,' she said, with a deep sigh. 'He was doing quite well for a time, helping the police, and writing a few books, and then he got into the life coaching business... but then the books stopped selling so well, and, well, Covid hit and it was like no one wanted his advice any more...'

'So what does he do now?' Butler stepped closer, her eyes digging into the woman.

'He does work for people round here. Odd jobs, nothing substantial, I'm afraid.'

Butler was staring at Moone, her eyebrows almost leaping off her forehead, the look of triumph shining brightly in her eyes. Moone felt his world slide to one side for the moment.

'Does he own a van?' Moone asked, bracing himself.

She looked at him curiously. 'Yes, he does. Why?'

'No reason. Just curious. Will he be back soon?'

'I hope so. He's got to take our daughter to her friend's house. I texted him a little while ago. Look, I've got to go into the house, I'm sure he'll be here soon. Sorry.'

Moone and Butler watched her hurry back into the house and then looked at each other, Butler wearing a big smile. Part of him was glad to see her so happy, but the rest of him wanted to throw up.

'Looks like we've got him,' Butler said.

'It can't be him.'

'He worked on the case last time.' She widened her eyes.

'Yes, because they asked him to.'

'You better call King and find out more about what went on.'

Moone could only stare at her and see the determination in her eyes. She believed Eason was guilty and nothing was going to change her mind. He shook his head and took out his phone as he stepped away, walking a little way back up the lane. He brought up the number they had for the former detective and rang it.

It was only a few seconds before the old man answered with a deep cough.

'Sorry,' King said, his voice hoarse. 'This is Gary King.'

'Hi, it's DCI Peter Moone,' he said, hearing Butler walking up behind him, getting ready to earwig his conversation.

'How're you?' the old man said, his voice brightening. 'Any closer to finding the sick bastard?'

'We're not sure. But out of curiosity, how did you find Professor Scott Eason?'

'The profiler bloke? Well, we didn't find him.'

'I'm sorry?'

'He found us. He got in touch when he read about the murders and said he could help...'

Moone closed his eyes for a moment, unable to find any words as he turned and looked at Butler. 'So, he offered his services?'

Butler let out a huff of a laugh and shook her head.

'Yeah, why did you want to know?' King asked. 'Has something happened?'

'No. Just making sure of his qualifications. Thanks. I've got to go.'

Moone ended the call and put his phone away, still looking at Butler. 'Don't say a word.'

'It's him, isn't it?'

'I don't know. But he volunteered his

services after the two murders. No, it can't be him. I mean, I went to school with him...'

'You said you didn't know him that well.'

He saw Butler's eyes jump to his side, looking at something at the end of the lane, at the same time as he heard a diesel engine rumbling its way closer. Moone turned and saw a grey van getting nearer with Scott Eason at the wheel. The van slowed as it reached the house and then stopped. The engine rumbled to a stop, then the driver's door squeaked open and Eason stepped out, dressed in a grubby blue polo shirt and black jeans. He was staring at them both, his face tight, looking at Moone like someone who had been caught out.

'Didn't expect to see you, Pete,' he said, pulling himself together and walking towards them. 'Has there been a development?'

'Is that the only van you own?' Butler asked, nodding at it.

Eason looked suspicious and confused for a moment, then looked back at the van. 'Yes, that's my only van. Why?'

'You don't own a white Transit?' Butler asked, stepping closer, and Moone heard the victory already clear in her voice.

'No,' Eason said, then looked at Moone. 'What's going on, Pete?'

Moone sighed. 'I'm afraid, we're going to have to ask you to answer a few questions at the station.'

Eason laughed. 'Really? What if I say no?'

Butler stepped closer to him. 'Then we'd have to arrest you on the suspicion of murder.'

CHAPTER 22

Moone paused outside the interview room for a moment, thinking, assessing the whole situation, trying to put the puzzle pieces together and finding they were probably the wrong pieces for the right puzzle. How could Scott Eason be their killer? It was true, Moone hadn't known him that well at school, but his sense of him back then was that he was OK, he was a good kid. He wasn't one of the popular ones, just like Moone wasn't, but he was not one of the bullied kids either, at least not as far as he knew. Now he seemed to have a good life, with a wife that seemed to be doing well for herself.

'Are we going in?' Butler said, appearing out of nowhere and making him flinch.

'Yep. Just collecting my thoughts.'

'Still don't think it's him?' Butler sighed.

Moone faced her. 'The truth is I don't know what to think. The uniforms we sent haven't found the van, have they?'

'No. Probably got rid of it after his latest

kill.'

'We haven't got enough to arrest him or charge him. He's helping us with our enquiries.'

Butler glared at him. 'I know, Moone, I'm quite aware of how this works. Come on, let's get on with it.'

Butler went in first and sat down at the desk, adjusting her clothing for a moment and not looking at Eason, who looked worried to Moone. His face looked paler, and he was tapping his fingers on the desk.

Moone sat down and smiled a little. 'Thanks for coming in.'

Eason let out a deep breath. 'I didn't seem to have much choice. I still can't believe you think I've got something to do with these women... being murdered. You know me, Pete...'

'Does he?' Butler raised her eyebrows, now staring at him.

'We were at school together.' Eason looked at Moone. 'Yes, we weren't like best friends but, you know...'

'So, you're a handyman?' Butler asked, her eyebrows going even higher.

Eason tapped the desk. 'I wouldn't call myself a handyman...'

'Then what?'

Eason shrugged. 'I just help people out, doing jobs here and there...'

'Sounds like a handyman to me.' Butler

folded her arms and leaned back in her chair. 'I hear your other work isn't going so well. No one's buying your books, no one wants their life coached any more. Well, not by you anyway.'

Eason stared at her for a moment, seeming to examine her closely. 'Have I done something to upset you, DI Butler? Is it because I know more about the criminal mind than you? Does that threaten you in some way?'

Butler huffed out a short-lived laugh. 'Oh, I know you know the criminal mind better than us, and there's a reason...'

'Because you think I killed those women?' Eason laughed and shook his head. 'My wife is on her way down here, once she sends our daughter to her friend's place. It's a good job she is because she's my solicitor...'

Moone leaned forward. 'You're not under arrest. In fact, you're free to go at any time, but it would help us greatly if you could tell us your movements on the 31st of August this year, between five in the evening and ten p.m., and the 3rd of September, between 3 p.m. and eleven p.m.'

Eason sighed, then looked over to his left, the cogs starting to turn. 'The 31st? What day was that?'

'Thursday,' Butler said. 'Sunday, for the second date.'

Eason nodded. 'Well, I think on the

Thursday I was pricing a job. Out In Ernesettle.'

Butler took out a pen. 'We'll need their name and address.'

'Fine. I'll have to look them up on my phone.'

'And the Sunday?' Moone leaned forward.

Eason looked down, tapping the desk again. 'I don't usually work on Sundays... unless it's on the book I'm writing. I was probably at home. My wife will verify it.'

'We'll ask her when she gets here,' Butler said. 'There's something else that interests me...'

'Go on,' Eason said, narrowing his eyes at her.

'You said you were approached by the police all those years ago, but apparently that's not true. You approached them after you read about the second murder, or so we've been told.'

'It's a long time ago,' Eason said, shrugging, but Moone noticed his face tightening.

'You lied to us,' Butler said. 'Why?'

'Because it sounds better.' Eason folded his arms and sat back. 'OK? It just sounded more impressive. Believe it or not, I didn't murder anyone.'

'You never owned, or saw a white Ford Transit in your village?' Moone asked, feeling in his gut that he'd been right, that Eason had nothing to do with the murders.

'No,' Eason said, his eyes imploring Moone to believe him. 'I've got my van, and it's the only van I have. You can check...'

'It was stolen from Nick Dann's company,' Butler said. 'It was driven into your village and it wasn't seen coming out again. A stolen van connected to a murder.'

He looked at her. 'Nick who? I don't know who that is. And I've never stolen a thing in my life... no, tell a lie, I stole a bag of sweets from a shop up the road from my junior school... and I still feel bad about it now.'

Butler sat back again, letting out one of her deepest sighs. 'We'll be checking your alibis. Thoroughly.'

'Please do.' Eason rolled his eyes, shaking his head, then looked at Moone. 'I had nothing to do with this. The person who murdered these women is full of rage, and hatred. I've been looking into it, doing some reading, and I came across a theory, and it's to do with childhood...'

'It always is,' Butler said and tutted.

'Go on,' Moone said.

Eason leaned forward. 'Do you remember when you were a kid, that feeling deep inside you, a kind of overwhelming urge to be bad?'

Moone sat back. 'I think so. You mean like having tantrums?'

'Sort of. I mean, before you really get

to understand right and wrong, children have this surge of a kind of primaeval rage, but eventually it goes away...'

'What's this theory, then?' Moone asked, his curiosity ignited.

Eason stared at him. 'Your killer, his childhood compulsion, his rage, it never went away. It grew and grew until he had to do something, something very bad indeed.'

'This is your theory, is it?' Butler tutted.

'It's not my theory, it's just one I happen to agree with.' Eason then turned his eyes on Moone. 'What if this killer, this same psychopath from twenty years ago, learned that I was back on the case? What if he decided to mess with us both by driving his stolen van into my village to make it look like I was involved?'

'Where did it magically disappear to?' Butler sat back, arms folded.

'Well, have you found it on my land?' Eason asked. 'In my garage? Anywhere?'

'No,' Moone said.

Eason leaned back, seeming to relax a little more. 'No. There's another way out of there, a path that leads towards the woods, then a private road for a little way which is just about wide enough for a van. That's probably how he got out.'

Moone took in Butler and the expression she was wearing that clearly said she didn't believe a word of it. Moone looked back at his old school friend and his eyes that implored him to believe his story.

'Let's talk outside,' Moone said to Butler and got to his feet.

Jason parked the car in the far corner of Devil's Point car park and looked out towards the sea and the hazy dark shape of Drake's Island, where a huge white ferry was just emerging from behind it. Then he looked in the rearview mirror and saw Carthew on the back seat, her head turning with a smile to her half-brother, who was dressed as a woman. He adjusted the mirror to get a better look, to examine his face that was covered in thick make-up, a straight blonde wig finishing the look. If he hadn't known it was her half-brother, then he probably would have been fooled. It was only his voice that gave him away; he tried to talk in a feminine manner, but there was a harshness to his voice, a deepness that gave away the lie.

'Is this it now?' Jason said, breaking them out of the strange smiling stare they were sharing. 'Am I the fucking chauffeur now?'

Carthew's eyes engaged his reflection. 'For now, you are, but soon you'll be so much more.'

Then her eyes turned back to her brother's. 'How are you, darling?'

'I'm good,' he said in the same strange hybrid voice. 'Where is Nair?'

Jason was about to answer when there was a rumbling sound as Jim Nair appeared on his Harley, heading into the car park. He came to a stop at the other end of the car park, closer to the pleasant view of the sea and the boats coming and going. Jason watched him and observed the old man clamber off his bike with a grunt after taking his helmet off. He shaded his eyes as he stared around the car park, then spotted Jason and came slowly over. Jason lit a cigarette and wound down the window, the screech of seagulls and the sounds of the sea coming flooding into the car. The passenger door opened and Nair climbed in and looked everyone over.

'This him?' Nair asked, looking at Carthew in the rearview mirror.

'This is my brother,' she said and Jason noticed her hand moved to hold Lloyd's again. 'Lloyd, darling, this is Jim Nair.'

'I've seen him around,' Lloyd said and looked out of his window.

'Of course you have,' Nair said. 'You did a lot of work for the Tomahawks, didn't you? Ran a lot of errands for them. You had your feet firmly under the table there, didn't you?'

'Well, he removed a key player for you,' Carthew said. 'Without McAllister, things are going to be easier.'

Nair nodded. 'True. But I'm still not sure I can trust your brother. Jumping from one side to the other pretty quick like this. What's to say he won't go running to the law next?'

'He would never,' Carthew snapped. 'He'd rather die.'

Jason found his eyes jumping to hers in the mirror. She looked calm, cold even. He wondered if he could trust her, tried to move past what they had done to each other that morning in bed, to remove the cotton wool she had so obviously wanted to fill his mind with. She was cold as Arctic ice and ruthless and it scared him. But it excited him too.

'He needs to prove himself,' Nair said and turned his head to look at the young man.

'He doesn't need to prove anything to anyone,' Carthew said. 'He's my family. The only family I have left.'

'That may be, but I don't know him from Adam. I don't know you either, bird.'

Carthew stared at him. 'But you need me to clear the way for you, make your life a lot easier.'

Nair pointed at Lloyd. 'But what do I need him for? To stab me in the back one day? Fuck that. But don't get your knickers in a twist, detective… or yours, Lloyd.'

Nair laughed, looking round the car for confirmation of how funny his joke was before he quietened down. 'Alright, boys and girls, I've got an idea. We've got a big stash to move soon. I don't trust any of our usual places to store our gear, not with the filth eyeing our every move. So we're going to move it all. Usually, we'd use a taxi service we've got a stake in, they'd take calls from us, telling them where to pick up customers. But they're not picking up customers, they're our people delivering our packages here and there, ready to distribute. But I don't want to risk any of my people carrying such a large consignment, as I said before, the law has its eyes on us. So I think we should use a different courier service, something they won't be expecting.'

'What are you suggesting?' Carthew asked.

Nair's eyes jumped to Redrobe. 'What say your brother here does it on his bike? It's a lot of pills and packets that need moving from A to B, so if the law has got wise to our taxi service and they stop any of them, then they won't find nothing. It'll mean him going back and forth a few times...'

'That's too risky,' Carthew said, gripping her brother's hand. 'What if they pull him over? He'll be fucked.'

Nair nodded. 'True. But they're not likely to stop him, are they? Not if you make sure they don't, or are you full of shit?'

Carthew stared at him for a moment. 'You're missing something, a detail that will make this easier.'

'Am I?' Nair asked. 'Enlighten me.'

She sat up. 'In about a week and a half, there's a big political conference happening in Cornwall. Most of our uniforms will be there protecting the political elite. It's the perfect time to move your drugs.'

Nair smiled. 'Good thinking. He can move them then. I love it when fate plays a part.'

Jason watched her and saw a flicker of something in her eyes he didn't recognise before she turned back to her brother. 'What do you think, Lloyd? There'll be hardly anyone around to interfere and I'd make sure they don't pull you over and do a stop and search. If they did, I'd protect you and straighten it out.'

Lloyd looked at her, then at the old man. 'It would have to be worth my while. It's still risky. A pretty thing like me won't last five minutes inside.'

The old man looked at Jason and rolled his eyes before he said, 'Twenty grand. That'll buy you a lot of frocks.'

'Twenty grand?' Carthew sat forward, glaring at Nair. 'This is my brother...'

'Half-brother,' Lloyd said and looked out the window.

Carthew stared at her half-brother for a moment. 'He's worth more than a measly twenty grand.'

'What do you suggest?' Nair asked with a tired breath.

'Fifty,' Carthew said. 'That's the end of the

negotiations.'

Nair pinched his nose. 'Fine. Fifty grand. But if he gets pinched, he don't say nothing about us.'

'I'd rather die,' Lloyd said, then he looked at his half-sister. 'Can we go and get something to eat now? Maybe a burger?'

Carthew smiled and patted his leg. 'Of course, sweetheart. I'll treat you.'

Nair pushed open the door. 'Right. I'm out of here. I'll let Jason know the date and time for the drop-off. See you lot sometime. Nice to have met you, Lloyd.'

Lloyd nodded but didn't look at him, so Nair climbed out and went back to his bike and rode off. It was quiet in the car for a while, so Jason kept his eyes on Carthew, seeing how she kept staring at her brother in a way that put him on edge. She was cold most of the time, barren of any true feeling. But then when she took him to bed, there came an explosion, a wild and ravenous attack. How long could that last, he wondered, but felt the pull of her, the icy heart of a black hole dragging him inside. He felt powerless to fight against it. When would he ever be with someone like her again? he asked himself and decided life was too short not to give it a chance.

'What do you think?' Moone asked when they stepped out of the interview room.

Butler leaned her back against the wall and folded her arms. 'It doesn't matter what I think.'

He stared at her, seeing the slight shrug of her shoulders. 'What do you mean? Of course it matters.'

'You know what I think. He's guilty as sin. He offered his services the first time round, which he lied about. The van goes into his village and disappears. He knows a secret way out. And let's not forget he now works as a handyman.'

Moone nodded, then looked towards the interview room, knowing that all she said was true. But still, he couldn't swallow it, couldn't see his old school friend as a psycho who bludgeoned and strangled his victims. But right now, he didn't want to ignore Butler; he wanted her to feel valued.

'OK,' he said.

'OK?' Butler straightened up, her eyes widening. 'You're agreeing with me?'

'Yep. Like you said, there's a few pieces of circumstantial evidence pointing at him which we can't ignore.'

'Circumstantial.' Butler nodded and let out a sigh.

'What?'

'You don't agree with me. You don't think he's our killer.'

'Honestly, I don't know what to think, but

he's one of the few suspects we've got. Let's look into him, take a closer look at his past, let's find out where he was when the murders happened.'

'Right then, let's get on it. I'll get a photo of him and put it together with some others and show them to Sarah Launce.'

'Good idea. What's happening about the fake Facebook profile?'

'Barry's set it up, but we haven't had a bite yet.'

Moone sighed. 'Shame. OK, let's get back to work.'

Moone was about to walk on when Butler said, 'Are you still busy tonight?'

'Tonight? What day is it?'

Butler rolled her eyes. 'It's Saturday. You need to take your head out of your arse.'

'Saturday?' Moone recalled the date he had made with Dr Jenkins and his stomach sank at the thought, but it seemed too late to pull out now. His eyes met Butler's and for a moment he didn't know what to say. 'Still busy. I think I'm letting this case get to me.'

'King warned you, didn't he?' Butler raised her eyebrows. 'Well, just relax tonight and try not to think about the case too much.'

He nodded. 'I'll try. What are you going to do?'

'Get a bottle of plonk, watch whatever crap's on the TV and slowly get drunk.' She smiled sadly, and the guilt rose over him.

'Well, maybe next Saturday we can do that together?' He smiled.

'OK, but I won't hold my breath. So, I better go and check out these alibis.'

Moone watched her walk off as a strange sensation washed over him, making his heart race and cold sweat drip from under his arms. He had the urge to run after her and tell her he was going to cancel his plans and join her. But he didn't move, scared of what her reaction might be.

The van was grumbling, the diesel engine rattling his body as he watched the house. Number thirteen. He wasn't superstitious, but something about it didn't sit right with him. She was a single woman, aged about forty. Her name was Sarah, and it all sounded perfect. But his gut tied itself in knots.

'What's the problem, bey?'

He looked at the reflection of the old caretaker in the rearview mirror, just a dark shape smiling in the back of his van.

'I don't know,' he said, his hands tight on the wheel to stop himself trembling.

'Go on, lad,' the voice said. 'Go and put a flyer through her door. Better still, pick up this claw hammer here and go in there and see to her.'

'I can't.'

'Why not? You gone all soft, bey? That's it, ain't it? Can't get yourself hard these days, can you, bey? That's why her indoors don't like you no more, cause you can't get it up.'

'Shut the fuck up!' he snapped, spinning round to stare at the old man. But there was just that deep, pungent smell and the laugh. 'Why don't you fuck off, old man?'

'Fuck off? Where to?' He laughed. 'You need me, bey. Trust me, go and put a flyer through her door. If the police get you, you won't get another chance.'

He swung round again, staring through the windscreen at the house. Even though his heart beat madly with hate for the old man, he couldn't deny that what he said was true; the police were getting closer, he could sense it. They were still hunting him and he was running out of time. It was the moon. The blood-red moon that was near and the tides would turn back and he knew the blood lust would rise in him.

'Go on, bey,' the old man said, his voice a whisper now. 'Be a good lad and put that flyer through her door.'

He looked at the flyer on the passenger seat, then reached for it with his trembling hand, feeling the flood of fire consume his chest. He snatched it up and climbed out of the van and jumped down onto the pavement.

'That's it, bey!' the old man called out

before he shut the van door and turned to face the house.

For a moment it was as if he was caught in a nightmare, his shoes rooted to the spot. And all he could do was listen to the tweet of birds in the trees beside him that lined the road, and the moan of a lawnmower just up the way. He pulled his baseball cap down and forced himself on, gripping the flyer in his hand and almost crushing it. Number thirteen. He stopped dead. A coldness took him over, a sickness burrowing deep into his insides, making him want to find somewhere and crawl into a ball. Even though the afternoon sun burned down, roasting the back of his neck, he felt the icy coldness gripping him, making his teeth begin to chatter. What was wrong with him? He moved towards the front gate and the small, tidy garden beyond. No. He spun round and started to hurry away.

'Can I help you?'

He froze, staring back towards his own van, wondering if he should run for it and drive off. He turned and saw a woman standing near the front porch of the house, gloves on her hands, staring at him with eyebrows raised. She looked quite different from her online photograph, but there she was. She looked older than her photo, but that's what people did these days, lie to everyone and themselves most of all.

'Sorry,' was all he uttered, forcing a smile to his face. 'I was about to put a flyer through your door.'

'Oh, OK,' she said, smiling a little. 'What's it for?'

He could almost hear the old man whispering to him, urging him on, telling him to do what needed to be done.

'I'm a handyman,' he said, lifting the flyer. 'No job too small. Cheap, too.'

She came towards him, holding out a gloved hand over the low fence. 'Let's see it then.'

He held out the slightly crumpled flyer and she took it and held it up to her face. After a second, she looked at him, nodding a little.

'Well, I do have a shed out the back that needs painting,' she said. 'Oh, I've been planning on painting my kitchen too. Do you decorate?'

He nodded and swallowed, the tremble, the rise in excitement beginning to pump out of his heart. 'Yeah, anything like that. I can come by any time and price it up.'

'OK,' she said, folding up the flyer. 'I've got to pop out soon, but you could come back this afternoon and kill me, beat me to death.'

He flinched. She was staring at him, sweat pouring down his sides. 'Sorry?'

'I said, I'll be in this afternoon. What time?'

'About two?'

'Don't forget your hammer. You'll need it to smash my skull in before you rifle through my underwear drawer and find my tights.'

'So you want me to come over this afternoon? About two?' His heart was pounding, not knowing if she had said those words or not. No, of course she hadn't. He was hearing things.

'That's right. Don't be late.'

He smiled. 'I'll be here.'

He turned as he heard her say, 'I'll be waiting to die!'

He hurried back to the van and climbed in and sat there shaking his head, trying to stop his chest from exploding.

'How did it go, lad?' the old man asked.

'She wants me to come back this afternoon and price a job.'

'Good, good. Then we'll have plenty of time with her.'

He turned and looked at the old man. 'We?'

'I'm not letting you do this alone, bey. You need me.'

He faced the front again, then started the engine, staring at the house, watching the woman who was still in her front garden, doing something to her flowers. 'She said... I mean, I thought she said...'

'What did she say?'

'That she wanted me to come round and… smash her skull in. But she couldn't have, could she?'

'Course she could. Maybe not with her words, but it's how she says it. You just pick up on that, bey. You can hear their true feelings. It's a gift.'

He nodded, then put the van into gear and started to drive away from the pavement, his mind whirring and spinning. Then the darkness took over, bringing with it the pounding beat in his head and the whispered voice that told him what he would do.

CHAPTER 23

When Moone realised what time it was, he headed out of the station at speed, half jogging over the crossing outside Drake Circus Shopping Centre, and then entered the building itself. His mind wasn't on his lunch with his daughter at all, and if he could have rescheduled, he would have, even if seeing Alice, one of his most favourite people in his life, was always a stabilising force, a way to find his balance. His mind was rushing back and forth between the puzzle pieces, trying to make sense of the mess and devastation. Eason wasn't their killer, he was pretty sure of that, but they had to make sure and he'd left Butler to follow up on it all. Butler.

He sighed as he passed the coffee shops and cafes and turned right onto Royal Parade, regretting that he had made the date with Dr Jenkins. In a few hours he would be going to the do with her, but he knew the whole time he would be thinking about Butler, who would be drinking by herself.

Alice waved at him from a table near the back of the busy cafe, so he squeezed through the crowd, the usual chatter and clatter of cutlery filling his ears.

'All right, Alice?' he asked and stood over the table.

'Yeah, you OK, Dad?' she said and smiled, but he saw the tell-tale signs of emotional strain there.

'Where's what's his face, today?' Moone sat down.

'His name is Lewis,' she said, rolling her eyes. 'You'd think a detective would remember a detail like that.'

He laughed. 'But you see, I have a lot of information to keep up in my old noggin. Not a lot of room for names of boyfriends and stuff.'

She smiled and then sipped her drink, but the smile faded as she looked down at the table.

'Something's wrong, Alice,' he said, leaning forward. 'What's happened?'

She looked up, her face tight. 'It's Mum. She's determined to drag us back to London. I don't want to go back there… not now.'

'What about her job here?'

'She's applied for another in London. Deputy head position, more money. Which would make sense here, but a bit more money up there doesn't count for much, does it?'

Moone sat back, nodding. 'No, it doesn't,

but that's not what it's about for your mum. She's been after a deputy head position for a while.'

'Great, so I get to go back to that place, with all the stabbings every five minutes?'

'London isn't as bad as all that,' he said, but the argument lost ground in his mouth as he spoke. The dead bodies, the murders and unexplained deaths piled up in his head. He saw the pale, lifeless shapes of young children and teenagers. His chest thumped, screamed out for mercy at even the thought of being back there.

'You can't even finish that sentence, can you?' She burrowed her eyes into him.

'Not really. Sorry. Maybe your mum won't get the position...'

'She knows someone who knows someone and they've practically said that if she applies then she's bound to get it.'

Moone covered his face in his hands for a moment, then looked at Alice again, one solution coming to mind. 'Can't you stay in Plymouth? You are twenty-one now.'

Alice shrugged. 'Mum says I have to come with her, that she doesn't trust me to live on my own.'

'She knows you're twenty-one, doesn't she?'

'But she worries.' Alice's eyes were filled with pleading and he knew what was being asked.

'Well, I haven't got that much room in my caravan,' he said, quietly, almost to himself.

'I know.' Alice looked down.

'So, I guess it's about time I looked for a proper place to live, a flat or a house.'

Alice looked up again, a smile appearing. 'Really, Dad? I'd only need a small room... and it wouldn't be for long, just so Mum wouldn't worry...'

He held up his hand. 'It's OK. You can have a nice big room. The biggest bedroom in the house. Just need to find a house.'

'You're sure you don't mind?' she asked, grinning.

For a brief moment, he watched his freedom fading away, his bachelor lifestyle running for the hills and him unable to catch up with it. He put on a smile, a little relief coming to him that at least he would know where she was. But then there were the other children to think of, the fact that he and Alice would hardly see them.

'You OK?' Alice asked. 'You don't have to...'

He shook his head. 'It's not that. It's your brothers and sisters. When am I going to see them? When will you see them?'

Alice nodded and moved her cup around in the saucer. 'I know. I'm going to have to go with them, aren't I?'

Moone let out a sigh. 'I don't know. Your

bloody mother. Can't she stay in one place for more than five minutes?'

'Well, it has been nearly three years...'

'Three years? Has it? It's gone helluva quick.'

Alice laughed.

'What?' Moone asked, smiling.

'Helluva? That's a real Devon, Cornwall thing to say. You're becoming a proper Plymouth bey.'

Moone laughed. 'I'd miss it here.'

Alice nodded. 'Me too.'

Then Moone made up his mind and sat forward. 'I'm going to talk to your mum.'

'And say what? You know what she's like when her mind's made up.'

'I know. But she's running off and taking you lot with her again. It's not fair, what about their schools and friendships? She's selfish.'

'She is that.' Alice let out a harsh breath. 'She won't listen.'

'She has to. This time she has to.'

'Maybe I could move in with you for a bit if she'd let me stay? We could go up to London and see them every chance we got.' There was that pleading look in her eyes again.

'I'll talk to her and see what she says.'

Alice smiled, but he could see she wasn't convinced. Then her eyes jumped beyond him. A coldness ran down his back as he asked, 'What? Is someone there?'

'No. Who was that woman last time? The one who turned up?'

'A detective colleague.' He looked down, trying not to think about Carthew.

'You don't like her, do you?'

Moone looked up at her and shook his head. 'No. I certainly don't. If you ever see her, head the other way and call me.'

'Why? Is she dangerous? She's a detective, isn't she?'

Moone leaned towards her. 'She is, but unfortunately that doesn't always mean that they're a good person. She certainly isn't.'

'What did she do?' Alice's eyes widened.

'All manner of things, but we can't prove any of it. Another detective has gone missing and we think she might have something to do with it.'

'Are you going to arrest her?'

'No proof. No evidence. She's clever…'

'Not as clever as you, Dad, surely?' Alice smiled.

'I've been lucky. She's some kind of… evil mastermind. But we have to find a way to stop her.'

Moone shuddered a little as his phone started ringing in his pocket.

'That'll be work,' Alice said with a sad smile.

Moone took out his phone and saw, as his stomach dived towards his shoes, that DI

Crowne was calling. He looked up at Alice. 'I better go and take this. Will you be OK?'

'Yeah, go on, I'm fine. Go and be clever.'

He smiled, then hurried off and answered the call as he headed out onto Royal Parade. 'DCI Peter Moone.'

'Moone, there you are,' Crowne said.

'All OK?'

'Not really. You haven't heard from DS Maxine Rivers, have you?'

Moone closed his eyes, swallowed and shook his head. 'No, why? What's happened?'

'I don't know. She's not turned up at work and no one can get hold of her. Her phone must be off.'

'Oh, right, that's odd. We haven't heard from her.'

'Strange. I've tried to track her phone and the last time it was used was down there.'

Moone's heart thumped. 'Right, OK. Why did she head this way?'

'I'm not sure. She was thinking of transferring down there, but I don't think she had an interview or anything. I was wondering if DI Butler knows anything.'

'Butler? Why?'

'Well, she came up here to ask some questions about Carthew not long before Rivers went AWOL, and I wondered if there was any connection. I'm clutching at straws really.'

'I see. Well, I'll ask her and see if she knows

anything.'

'I'll ask her. I'm heading your way later.'

'Really? OK. I suppose I'll see you soon.'

'You will. Make sure Butler knows I want a word with her.'

'I will.'

The call ended and Moone was left staring at the traffic that passed through the city centre and the queues of people at the bus stops, his mind racing. He thought about Rivers and Carthew, trying to decide what the best course of action was, and whether there was anything linking him and Butler to Rivers' disappearance. He couldn't think of anything, but they also needed Crowne to link her vanishing to Carthew, for him to put two and two together and come up with an image of Carthew committing murder or at least kidnapping. He hoped Rivers was still alive somewhere. There was always the slim possibility Carthew had talked her round and now Rivers had gone to ground, but he knew Carthew, knew what she was capable of and that was a fact that made his hope fade away.

His phone started ringing and he prayed it wasn't Crowne calling back. It wasn't; this time it was Inspector Pinder, so he answered it and tried not to sound like he was being weighed down by everything.

'Moone,' he said, in what he thought was a cheery manner. 'What's new, Kev?'

'Oh, you sound depressed,' Pinder said. 'Everything all right?'

Moone gave an empty laugh as he walked towards the station. 'Just life. What about you?'

'Well, I might be about to cheer you up.'

Moone stopped walking and stepped under the shelter of one of the bus stops. 'Go on.'

'You know I've been keeping tabs on Lloyd Redrobe?'

'Yep.'

'Well, I've been bunging a couple of my off-duty guys some pocket money to keep an eye on him. They don't know the full story, obviously and they know not to ask any questions...'

'Come on, Kev. What's happened?' Moone moved out of the way to let a mum and her pram get into the shelter.

'Today, Redrobe was picked up again by that scrote Jason Harris, you know, Jim Nair's right-hand man. Anyway, who's in the car as well? None other than the lovely DS Carthew.'

'You're joking?'

'No, I kid you not. Then, Jim Nair turns up on his hog and sits in the car for a bit. They chat then they all leave. Nair goes first, then they leave a little while later.'

Moone stopped outside the station and looked upwards to where the incident room was, his mind reeling and the penny finally dropping. 'We were right, weren't we? She did it, didn't she? At least she got Redrobe to do it.'

'McAllister's murder?' Kev sighed over the line. 'It has to be them, doesn't it? So what's she up to?'

'She's hiring herself out to them, using her police connections and general psychopathy, to help them stay on top. First, she knocks off McAllister, then... well, God knows. But we can't prove it. Did your mate get any photos or anything?'

'No, sorry, he didn't get a chance. So why were they meeting this time? They must have been planning something else.'

Moone nodded and ran a hand down his face. 'Come to the station if you can. We need a council of war.'

'It's my day off, so I'll be there soon.'

When Moone reached the incident room, he found Butler waiting for him, arms folded, resting on her desk, her face tight, no real sign of emotion.

'Everything OK?' he asked, smiling briefly before heading to his desk.

'Most of his alibi checks out,' she said, sitting at her desk. 'He wasn't even in Plymouth when Caroline Abbott was killed.'

Moone nodded. 'So, doesn't look like he's our murderer, then?'

'Unless he's got an accomplice. He swans

off to London for a couple of days, while his mate kills her. Perfect alibi.'

'This killer, he works alone. He's a predator, pretending to be a handyman. He turns up on his own and he enjoys what he does, lets out this rage that's always building inside him...'

Butler sighed. 'Yeah, I know. So, who's our chief suspect? Are we back to Nick Dann? We still don't know what he was up to the night the van was supposedly stolen.'

'That's something we need to follow up on. Why's there no CCTV footage? What's he hiding?'

'I'd say it's because he's moonlighting as a handyman, but we've shown Sarah Launce a few photos and she didn't pick out Dann. In fact, she didn't pick out anyone. So, we're back to nowhere.'

Moone sat back, his mind working a little clearer. 'If he is telling the truth and the van was stolen from his depot, then the killer picked his place to steal from, the businessman who has a connection to most of the victims. Why? This must have something to do with Dann.'

'Then this killer is targeting him in a way. He's targeting the women who Dann has a thing with. But why?'

'Jealously? He's jealous 'cause he can only get off by beating women? Sick bastard.'

'He really hates these women, doesn't he? He beats them until they're unrecognisable, then strangles them with their own tights. He's getting back at them for something.'

'Punishing them,' Butler said.

'Yep. Punishing them.' Moone stood up, staring at the crime scene photos. 'But why women who Dann has been involved with? As far as we knew he targeted just single women of a certain age, befriended them online or put a flyer through their door. But it's not just that, it's the women who Dann has been seeing that he's targeting.'

'Then we need to find out if there's anyone Nick Dann, or the women he's been seeing, has upset. Which means talking to him again.'

Moone blew the air from his cheeks as he stepped closer to the board. 'The problem is, neither Dann nor Boulton is going to like us asking more questions.'

'No.' Butler raised her eyebrows. 'But that's never stopped us before, has it?'

'No, it hasn't.' Moone's mind flashed back to a few minutes earlier. He stepped closer to Butler, lowering his voice so none of the civvies could hear. The rest of the team was out on assignments. 'There's something else. Crowne called me. He was asking about Rivers.'

Butler lowered her head, her lips pursing. 'Shit. What did he say?'

'He tracked her phone down here, but

that's about it. He wants to talk to both of us.'

Butler put her hands to her face. 'Oh, bloody hell. What're we going to say to him?'

Moone shrugged. 'I don't know. Just that we haven't seen her. But he needs to be pointed in the right direction.'

'Carthew.'

'But we can't have him going to see Boulton or anyone else. Speak of the devil.' Moone nodded to the incident room door where DSU Boulton was coming through. Then his eyes jumped to the female uniform behind him, who seemed to be a woman in her late forties, with white bobbed hair. Shit, he thought, realising it had to be the new Chief Superintendent, Kate Hellewell. He straightened himself and saw Butler look at him as if he had blown off.

'What's wrong with you?' she asked and looked towards the glass door as it opened.

'DCI Peter Moone,' Boulton said, smiling. 'The very man we wanted to see. May I introduce you to our new Chief Superintendent, Kate Hellewell. Chief Superintendent, this is DCI Peter Moone.'

'Nice to meet you, ma'am,' Moone said, putting on a smile and offering his hand.

She took it and gave it a gentle shake as she looked around and said, 'So, this is where it all happens? The epicentre of murder investigations in Plymouth. You're working on a major murder inquiry right now, aren't you?'

'Yes, ma'am,' Moone said.

'Two women beaten and strangled,' Boulton said. 'The two deaths seem to be linked to two murders from several years ago.'

'Twenty years,' Butler said, folding her arms. 'Not just linked, but the same killer.'

'Allegedly,' Boulton said, smiling at the Chief Super. 'This is DI Mandy Butler.'

Hellewell smiled and nodded as she shook Butler's hand. 'Good. Nice to see another female DI making headway. What's your take on this case, may I ask?'

Butler looked round at Moone, so he urged her on with his eyes. She cleared her throat and said, 'I'd say it was the same killer, but for some reason he waited twenty years. We've got ourselves a patient psycho this time.'

'I don't think psycho is the term I'd use,' Boulton said, looking uncomfortable.

'It's fine,' the Chief Super said, smiling at Butler. 'Well, I'm sure you'll catch your killer. Isn't there an up-and-coming young DS stationed here too, DSU Boulton?'

'Yes, ma'am, DS Faith Carthew, she's on the fast-track program,' Boulton said as they both stepped away and toured the incident room.

Butler looked at Moone, her eyebrows raised and lowered her voice. 'Did you hear that? We've got to do something about her.'

'I know. Listen, Kev Pinder is coming in to

talk to us. He's seen Carthew meeting up with Redrobe, Jim Nair and someone called Jason Harris...'

'Harris?' Butler huffed out a laugh. 'He's a right little scrote, been in trouble since he was knee high. Get him in an interview room facing some serious charges and he'd piss his pants and go along with whatever we say.'

'That might be true, but we'd need to catch him doing something first. I wonder what they're up to.'

'Well, we know it's not good. Nair and his motorcycle-loving morons teaming up with that psycho-bitch? That means big trouble. For them, I mean.'

The engine of the van wasn't vibrating any more, but his body was still trembling all over. He was parked a couple of streets away, tucked into a cul-de-sac. There were no cameras around, no one with those front doorbells that record whoever knocks on the door, he had checked. He put on his baseball cap, looked at himself in the rearview mirror and felt sick at the sight of himself. It wasn't about him, or how he looked, it was about dishing out the punishment they deserved. He brought a kind of justice. His eyes jumped to the dark shape in the mirror, the outline of the hunched old man and the grey-blue wisps of smoke from his roll-up.

'You ready, bey?' the old man's croaky, grinding voice asked.

He nodded.

'Good, cause you got to take the pleasure in it now, bey. They'll be looking for you soon enough, and they'll probably find you. This is your chance to make them pay.'

He wanted to climb out of the van and head to the house, but he didn't move, his legs didn't want to move.

'Go on, get out,' the old man said. 'What's wrong with you? She's waiting to die in there and you're pissing about in here.'

'I'm going.'

'Go on then, prove you're not a useless shit like all those other kids in that school.'

He looked at the old man in the mirror, the anger making his chest thump even more than it had been. 'I'm not. I'm not like them.'

'Then prove it. Show me.'

He pushed open the door and grabbed his bag of tools as he stepped out onto the bright street. He stopped and looked away when an elderly lady came past walking a little ball of fluff dog. The old man was already standing on the pavement, still smoking when he started towards the front door, watching him with a smirk on his face.

'You won't be able to come in,' he said to the old man as he reached the garden gate.

'Oh, I'm coming in,' he said, half laughing

as the smoke poured out of his mouth. 'You knock on the door, start the show and then you can let me in after a minute. Go on, bey, you owe me for what I did for you all those years ago.'

He looked back at the old caretaker, that same old knowing look in his dark eyes. He nodded, then went up the path carrying his tool bag, the claw hammer poking out. He stared at it, his hands shaking as he pressed the doorbell.

Just as the door began to open, he swung his head round to see where the old man was, but he was gone and there was only the scent of his roll-ups in the air.

'Oh, hello,' the woman said, a brief smile crossing her face. 'Wasn't sure if you'd come back or not. So many builders and tradesmen say they'll come and then they don't turn up.'

As she stepped aside to let him in, he smiled, burying all the doubts, the fear and anger deep inside. 'Not me. I always turn up when I say I will.'

He walked along the hallway that was painted lilac, the pleasant scent of perfume in the air.

'It's the kitchen I want painted,' she said and gestured through the doorway towards the back of the house. Sunlight beamed in through two full-length French windows. He shaded his eyes for a moment as he put his tool bag down.

'I've picked out some colours,' she said, and moved past him and he was engulfed in a scent that he found familiar.

Sarah's scent?

Yes, she smells just like her. You know what you must do.

She picked up a couple of sample pots of paint and put them on the kitchen table. Feeling that he had to do something, he moved over to the table and picked one up to examine it. His hand trembled madly as he lifted it to his eyes.

'Are you all right?' she asked, and when he looked at her, he saw genuine concern.

'Oh, yes...' He put on a bright smile. 'Just not had my afternoon coffee yet.'

'Would you like one now?' She smiled, gesturing to the kettle.

'Thanks. That would be great.'

There was a knock on the front door, two thuds that echoed through the house, making him flinch. Of course, he knew who it would be.

'I'll get that,' he said, forcing another big smile to his lips. His heart pounded, the slow wave of fear and hate and loathing rising like flood water.

'I didn't hear the door,' the woman called out, but he ignored her and hurried to the door and pulled it open.

There the old man was standing, a smile on his face, showing his stained teeth, the roll-up between his dirty fingers. His dark eyes jumped to the hallway behind him, trying to see inside.

'Where is the bitch?' the old man said.

'Shut up, she'll hear you,' he said, lowering his voice. 'She's in the kitchen. You can't come in... it's not the time... I don't think...'

But the old man threw down his cigarette, gave a gruff laugh and barged him out of his way with tremendous force, almost knocking him off his feet. When he'd steadied himself, his heart now rattling in his chest and the blood pounding in his skull, he hurried after him. He stopped dead in the kitchen when he saw the old man had hold of her, his dirty hands gripped around her throat. There was a smile on his face. His mouth was open and wisps of cigarette smoke still leaked out from between his lips and poisoned the air. The woman's hands scrabbled and clawed at his face, but it was no good. For an old man, he was strong, too strong for her. Her face grew red, and her arms became limp. Then he loosened his grip and pushed her backwards, knocking her into the kitchen cupboards. Her head hit the work surface, the sound of it echoing through the room and him as he watched her fall. Her chest was still rising and falling, but only slightly.

The old man straightened himself and turned to look at him, still smiling.

'That was beautiful, eh, bey?' he asked, then looked down at her again. 'Who's going to do the next part? You or me, bey?'

He shook his head, frozen to the spot. He could only watch now, could only witness it all as the old man, now just a dark and sinister shape, laughed and hurried to the tool bag and grabbed the hammer. He sat astride her, then pushed her hands away as she came to.

'Tights!' the old man shouted at him, so he turned, coming out of his dream and hurried up the stairs, searching blindly for her bedroom, his whole body pounding. He could only hear a whine in his ears as he raced from room to room.

He stopped in the doorway of the large bedroom at the front of the house. The scent of perfume, of make-up, of womanly smells engulfed him. His hands trembled as he made his way to the chest of drawers and started yanking them open and searching through. He saw what he was after and grabbed a pair of tights and rushed back down the stairs. When he reached the kitchen, he saw the old man raising the hammer, laughing to himself, and coughing a little.

The hammer came down. Thud. Thud.

He shuddered and dropped the tights.

The old man pounded her head again and again, laughing manically. Then he got to his feet and stepped back, turning his head to one side and then the other, admiring his handiwork.

'Look at this, bey,' the old man said, pointing at the woman.

He could only see her feet from where he was and his heart fluttered at the sight of them as they jerked a little. There was some life left in her yet, but he couldn't bring himself to go over and look at her.

'What's wrong?' the old man asked, just a dark shape on the edge of his vision. He couldn't bear to look at him. It was all so familiar. And he staggered backwards as the memory burned brightly in his mind.

Where was Sarah? The real Sarah, the one who had tortured him at school, who had made his life a living hell?

Dead. Long since dead.

He looked at the old man, his dirty hand now stretching out to him.

'Give me them, bey!' the old man barked.

'You,' he said. 'It was you.'

The old man stared at him, turning to face him properly. 'What're you wittering on 'bout, bey? Just give me those so I can finish the job.'

'No. It was you. I remember now. I'd forgotten until now.' He stepped closer to the old man, who was now starting to smile.

'What was me?'

'In the car park... over the other side of the road, near the school...'

The old man straightened himself, nodding. 'Yeah, go on, bey. Get it off your chest.'

'You did it. You killed Sarah. She's dead. All this time… I've been looking for her, trying to find her to…'

'Have you fuck,' the old man said. 'You knew she was dead. That was an excuse. Just so you could do it over and over again. This is what you do. What we do. Now, give me those tights, so we can finish this and find the next one. You do want to find another, don't you, lad? Another Sarah?'

He trembled as he stared at the woman on the floor, her legs still twitching. 'Yes.'

CHAPTER 24

Late afternoon had crept in mostly unnoticed by Moone. The heat had subsided a little, helped by the greying clouds that had blanketed the sky, threatening a downpour. Then he had been told someone had asked for him at reception but didn't give a name. Said they would be outside. Confused, and more than a little anxious, as he had noticed Carthew had done one of her disappearing acts, he took the stairs down to the main reception and out onto the path outside. He looked around, his eyes focusing towards the ragged and oddball shape of Drake Circus. For a moment, he looked beyond the figure standing on the grass, leaning against a post, and then his eyes took him in. He was built like the proverbial brick shit house, hair shaved and short, signs of damage to the face over the years. He was dressed in jeans and a T-shirt that bulged with all his muscles. He smiled and started moving towards Moone and stopped when he got a few feet away.

'Fuck me,' he said, looking him over, then up at the police station. 'Say it ain't fuckin' true, you fucka. Did little Pete Moone go and become part of the filth's gang?'

Moone stood staring at him for a moment, looking into his eyes before the penny dropped. 'Terry?'

'The one and fuckin' only.' The big man came striding towards him, his big arms spreading wide.

'What're you doing?' Moone said, half deciding to signal for backup.

Terry Hankin wrapped his arms around him, then picked him easily off the ground and squeezed him tight.

'You beautiful man,' he said in his ear, then laughed and plonked him back down.

'How the hell did you find me?' Moone asked, adjusting his suit and tie.

'Eason,' Terry said. 'He gave me a bell and 'ere I am. Still can't believe you're a pig though.'

Moone gave an awkward laugh, knowing full well that Eason had called him out of a kind of revenge. 'Bit of a surprise to you, I bet.'

Hankin raised his boulder-sized shoulders. 'Someone's got to be a fucking pig, I suppose, and you was always so fucking nice. One of the fuckin' good guys. You still being a good boy, Pete?'

He laughed, then nodded. 'I try.'

Terry laughed, shaking his head. 'Look at you, all grown up.'

'Sorry, Terry, but why're you here?'

'Why am I here? To see me old mucka, ain't I? To catch up and get legless. How about we go out for a few beers tonight and paint Plymouth red? Where do all the birds hang out?'

Moone laughed, realising the big, violent, golden hearted, lump hadn't changed. Then he recalled his date and was suddenly glad he wouldn't be available to paint Plymouth red. 'Sorry, Terry, I'm otherwise engaged tonight. Would have been great to catch up...'

'No worries, my son,' Terry said, grinning. 'I'm not leaving until we get legless.'

'Oh, right. Good. Where are you staying?'

'With you, mate, in your gaff, in your house or flat or whatever you live in.'

Moone sighed. 'Well, actually, I live in a mobile home.'

Terry's eyes widened before he began to laugh loudly. 'You live in a bleeding caravan?'

'Mobile home.'

'Sorry, mate. It's just funny. It's fine, just give me the keys and I'll chuck my stuff in there. We can have a chat when you get home.' Terry grinned again as he held out his big hand.

The memory of what Eason had told him about Terry Hankin, in his brief outline of his shady life, came back to Moone as he reached into his pocket for his keys. He hesitated, and

Terry must have seen it, because he said, 'It's all right, Pete, I'm not going to rob your gaff. We're mates, remember. I've always looked up to you. Still do.'

'Even me being a copper?'

Terry laughed, looking over at the red brick station. 'Yeah, even that. Sort of fits ya, know what I mean?'

'Yep.' Moone pulled out his keys and handed them over. 'I'll text you the address.'

'You ain't got my number but I got yours.' Terry took out his mobile and sent a text.

Moone heard his phone beep at him. 'Now I'll text you the address.'

'Nice one. I'll put it in the SatNav. See you later, mate.'

Moone smiled, then lost all expression when the big guy sauntered off, heading across the street. But he couldn't worry about him right now, for he still had three big problems to contend with; Carthew and a psycho who likes to beat and strangle his victims to death. The third was a date that was bound to be awkward. He sighed, then headed back into the station and found Inspector Pinder waiting for him.

'Afternoon,' Pinder said, then nodded towards the entrance. 'Who was that giant you were talking to?'

'No one really, an old friend. Anyway, what did you want?'

Pinder stepped closer, lowering his voice

so the desk sergeant didn't hear. 'I've been putting the feelers out, gathering info on Lloyd Redrobe...'

'And? Please tell me something's come up.'

Pinder smiled. 'Have I ever let you down? Well, don't answer that...'

'You saved my fucking life, Kevin.'

Pinder nodded, looking a little awkward. 'Oh, yeah, I did, didn't I? Well, I've talked to a couple of criminal types I know, and they reckon that the Dark Horses are going to be moving a load of their drugs soon. They heard that they've got some one-man delivery service, some daredevil on a bike who's going to go back and forth.'

'So they won't be risking a load of drugs in a van or something. Makes sense.'

'Guess who they reckon the courier is?'

Moone smiled. 'Redrobe?'

Kevin was about to answer, then looked round at the sergeant on the desk again before returning his eyes to Moone. He gestured to the entrance as he said, 'Let's step outside.'

When they were safely out of the hearing range of anybody, Pinder said, 'Yeah, Redrobe. Normally, this is something I'd be passing along the chain as intelligence. The drugs squad in Plymouth would love to take down the Dark Horses...'

'But then we wouldn't get a chance to talk to Redrobe.'

Kev nodded, then let out a sigh. 'She's got to go down. So, we keep an eye on him, and when he tries to move the drugs, then we grab him and it'll be either talk to us or go to prison. He'll give up Carthew to us rather than do time.'

Moone nodded, feeling the bite of excitement dig into his spine. They were a step closer to nailing her, he could almost taste it. 'That's great, Kev. And any intelligence about the Dark Horses' drug dealings we find out we can pass on to the intelligence department later.'

Pinder nodded. 'OK. Let's just hope no one gets wind of what we're doing, because if they do, then we'd be stuffed. My job, your job... all pissed up the wall.'

Moone nodded. 'I'm not going to let that happen, mate. We're going to get her. I promise.'

Pinder stared at him for a moment, seeming to let the idea ferment before he nodded and stuck out his hand for Moone to shake. 'OK. Let's get her, then. She's long overdue.'

'Agreed. So, let us know when they're moving the stuff.'

'Will do.'

'There you are!' Butler's voice called out as she hurried over to them.

When she got closer, she narrowed her eyes, looking suspiciously between them.

'What're you two up to? You look shifty.'

'I'll tell you later,' Moone said as Kevin scurried away. 'What is it?'

'You're not going to like this,' she said, and by the roll of her eyes he could tell she would be right. 'But Crowne is here and wants a chat.'

'Shit.' Moone enclosed his face in his hands, let out a deep breath and then looked at her again. 'How long can we keep this up? Us knowing, or at least suspecting Carthew's done her in, and not telling anyone?'

'What can we do? We've got nothing above board proving that she's done anything to her. We've got her phone, but we can't get into it.'

Moone nodded, then looked up at the building. 'Then let's put on our best poker faces and go and talk to Crowne.'

Crowne was sitting in the family room, looking relaxed on the grey sofa, a coffee and biscuits on the table in front of him. Moone stood in the doorway for a moment as he nodded a greeting, thinking it all through and trying to keep his face straight. Then he took a breath and went and faced the detective who stood up and shook his hand. Butler followed Moone in and sat down. When they all were seated, Crowne, looking glum, said, 'So, neither of you have heard from her?'

'DS Rivers?' Butler asked. 'No, nothing.'

'Moone?' Crowne stared at him.

She's probably dead, mate, and Carthew has probably killed her, he heard himself saying. But his mouth remained shut. He shook his head. 'No, not a thing. So, you think she was down this way?'

'I know she was,' Crowne said, picking up a biscuit and dunking it in his coffee. 'She told me she was heading down here to see her girlfriend. I pinged her phone, and it showed she was down here.'

'Where?' Butler asked, and Moone felt his whole body stiffen.

'Exeter Street, I think,' Crowne said, then took out his notebook and opened it up. 'Yeah, Exeter Street. What's there?'

'You name it,' Butler said. 'Pubs, takeaways. There's a furniture place. Maybe she was looking for a new sofa.'

Crowne stared at her, a look of annoyance appearing in his eyes. 'Are you making fun of this, DS Butler? This is my partner we're talking about, and my friend. One of the few I've got. And she's missing.'

'What about her girlfriend? Have you got any idea where she might live?' Moone asked, wanting to run out of the room and throw up.

Crowne dragged his angry eyes from Butler and looked at Moone as he said, 'No, not a clue. She was very cagey about it all. I can't even ask her family or friends, because she hasn't got any family or many friends. Who I have managed to contact, haven't been any help. I need to find her girlfriend, but I'm waiting to find out if I can get her phone records. I just don't know what else to do. I mean, I don't know why she would just up and disappear. Things were going well for her, she had a promotion...'

Butler sat forward. 'What about enemies? Someone she banged up?'

Crowne stared at her. 'What? You're thinking someone's got her or... done something to her?'

Moone felt his gut strangle itself. How the hell could they point the finger at Carthew? 'You've got to look into any possibility, I suppose.'

Crowne nodded. 'Yeah, I know, but I can't think of anyone with a grudge to bear. The last big case was Armstrong's murder, but what would the connection be there?'

Butler huffed. 'Well, that was never properly put to bed, was it?'

'You mean you still think Carthew did it?' Crowne asked. 'Even though they put someone else down for it? Maybe we just got it wrong.'

'We didn't,' Butler said, anger in her voice. 'She did it and she got away with it. What about this for a theory...'

Moone stared at her, wanting to jump up and gag her.

'What?' Crowne asked, leaning towards her.

'What if Rivers was still looking into it?' Butler said. 'Just like I was. Maybe that's the real reason she came to Plymouth. Maybe she had a lead.'

Crowne stared at her for a moment, his eyes digging deep into hers. 'Are you sure you haven't talked to her?'

'I'm sure.'

'OK, but Rivers was pretty satisfied with the way things went. She got her promotion from it, remember.'

Butler nodded. 'Yeah, well, maybe that started to eat at her, the fact she might have it wrong. I don't know. But what if it led her to the only possible suspect?'

Crowne gave an empty laugh. 'Carthew, you mean? What, she comes to Plymouth investigating her and then what are you suggesting? That Carthew's got her or...'

'I don't know,' Butler said, while Moone could feel his heart was on the way to an attack. 'But I'd check out Carthew if I was you.'

Crowne slowly looked away from Butler and fixed his eyes on Moone. 'What do you think about this?'

He thought he would like to be anywhere else, even hanging from the viaduct again. He raised his shoulders. 'I honestly don't know, but you've got to look into every possibility and you know she was down here. It's worth looking into.'

Crowne got up suddenly and straightened his clothes. 'Where is Carthew? I'll ask her.'

Moone and Butler got up at the same time, but it was Moone who said, 'You can't just go accusing her...'

'I know,' Crowne said, anger sharp and clear in his voice. 'I know my job. But I can ask if she's seen her, can't I? At least I'd get a feel for it, see if she's hiding something. Where is she?'

'To be honest, we're not totally sure,' Butler said, following Crowne to the door and through it. 'She plays by her own twisted rules these days.'

'Up in your incident room?' Crowne said, heading along the corridor and towards the stairwell.

Moone hurried after them, the sickness invading his stomach again, unsure what the hell was going to happen next. They had to get Lloyd Redrobe to talk and soon before Carthew could cause any more death and destruction.

Crowne stormed into the incident room, with Moone and Butler following behind. As luck would have it, Carthew was putting some files on her desk as they arrived.

'DS Carthew,' Crowne said, standing by her desk, putting on a polite voice. 'Can I have a word in one of the interview rooms?'

Carthew looked up at him with a blank

face, then turned to take in Butler then Moone. 'Sure. Is something wrong?'

Crowne stepped aside as she got up and gestured to the door. 'I just need to clarify something.'

Carthew raised her shoulders, smiled, then carried on through the doors and out into the corridor. Crowne looked at Moone and Butler, his face dark and tight. He let out a harsh breath, then followed Carthew out. When Moone looked round the room, he could see the rest of the team were watching, curiosity bright in their eyes.

'Nothing to see here,' he said, then went into the corridor and along to the interview rooms where Crowne was opening a door for Carthew. When she had gone in, Crowne turned to Moone and said, 'I'm trying to give up the fags, but I could kill for one right about now.'

'You're preaching to the choir,' Moone said.

Crowne nodded, then opened the door and went in. Moone followed him in and sat down next to Crowne when he seated himself. Carthew sat back in her chair, a smile on her lips, her eyebrows raised, the same old look of self-assurance in her eyes.

'I'll cut to the chase,' Crowne said, sitting back and folding his arms. 'Have you heard from DS Rivers?'

Carthew looked confused, not missing a beat, as she said, 'Rivers? Your colleague? No, why would I?'

'She's not been in contact with you lately?'

Carthew leaned forward. 'No. We don't really know each other. Why're you asking? Is she missing?'

Crowne gave a dry, empty and brittle laugh. 'Yeah, she's missing. Thing is, we gave you a pretty tough time when we were looking into the Armstrong murder... murders, actually...'

'It's fine,' Carthew said, flashing a smile. 'Don't apologise, I don't hold grudges.'

Moone looked at Crowne and saw the thunder clouds over his head, the shadow darkening his face. The anger was there in his voice as he spoke.

'Oh,' he said, folding his arms again, but tighter. 'I wasn't going to apologise. No, in fact, I feel pretty sick that we never caught the real murderer.'

'But I thought –' Carthew began.

Crowne held up a silencing hand. 'Shut up for a minute. Let me talk. I know you murdered Armstrong, and probably his wife and her lover. I think you've done a lot of bad things. I don't know why, maybe you weren't cuddled enough when you were a kid. Or maybe you were cuddled too much. Like I said, I don't know why you do it and I don't give a shit really, but when my colleague, my friend, goes missing shortly after arriving here, in Plymouth, then I go to the person who likes to hurt people, the one person who had a reason to hurt her...'

Carthew didn't say anything for a moment, just stared, blank-faced. Then a smile began.

'Oh, I wouldn't smile, if I was you,' Crowne said, a deep anger making his voice crack a little.

'Why not?' Carthew said, smiling even more. 'I'm feeling happy.'

Moone watched as Crowne unfolded his arms, revealing his balled fists.

'Where is she?' Crowne asked. 'What have you done to her?'

'Are we done yet?' Carthew said, blank as she faced Moone. 'I've got work to be getting on with.'

'Yes, we're done,' Moone said, catching Crowne's eye and shaking his head.

Crowne got up after Carthew and followed her out, only a few steps behind her as if he was trying to catch up. Moone hurried after them both, watching for trouble, a bad feeling welling in his chest, making his heart thump. He heard DSU Boulton's voice ahead of them all, coming from the incident room. Then Carthew was turning on the spot, facing Crowne. In slow motion she seemed to lean towards

Crowne, her lips getting close to his ear, her mouth opening.

'You fucking bitch!' Crowne shouted, his right hand grasping her and throwing her around and slamming her against the wall. Moone rushed towards them both as he watched in horror as Crowne had her pinned against the wall by her collars. Carthew smiled.

'Let her go!' Moone said, grasping his wrists. 'Please, Crowne...this is what she wants.'

'What the hell is going on?' Boulton said as he stormed towards them all.

Crowne let her go and stepped back, still seething, eyeing her with more hate than Moone had ever seen in anyone's eyes before.

'Did you just assault one of my officers?' Boulton asked, stepping in front of Crowne. 'Who are you? Who is this man, Moone?'

Moone stepped closer, but he wasn't in his own body any more. He was watching from far away, shaking inside as the horror unfolded. 'DI Vincent Crowne, sir.'

'What are you doing here?' Boulton asked Crowne.

'Trying to find out what DS Carthew has done with one of my colleagues,' Crowne said, the anger making his voice tremble.

Bolton looked at Carthew, who had lost her smile and had affected a look of shock.

'What does he mean, Carthew?' Boulton

asked her.

'I don't know, sir,' she said, straightening her clothes. 'I think, DI Crowne is highly stressed and emotional because his colleague has gone missing.'

Boulton looked back at Crowne. 'Right, DI Crowne, and DS Carthew, my office now. Come on.'

Moone watched as they all filed out, heading to the stairwell and then vanishing. He let out a breath, his hands trembling. Butler appeared, standing watching him, her eyebrows raised.

'What the fuck?' she said, coming closer. 'What the hell just happened?'

'When they were leaving the interview room, she turned and whispered something to him. It must have been bad because Crowne lost it.'

Butler looked towards the stairs. 'Well, he's in the shit now. What the hell do we do now?'

Moone lowered his voice. 'Pinder's got word that Redrobe is going to courier some drugs for the Dark Horses. A lot of drugs, doing a few trips, trying to stay under our radar. When he does, then we grab him, then make him give up his crazy half-sister.'

Butler stared at him. 'That's the plan? Sounds pretty shit to me. If we do catch him, there's no guarantee he'll talk. She's his family.'

'Well, Pinder thinks he'll turn on her. It's the only chance we've got.'

'Well, there's Bob Hope of that working, but like you said, we haven't got much choice. What now?'

Moone took out his phone. 'I've got to leave. Can you take care of things from here?'

'Off out then?' Butler looked unimpressed.

'I'm afraid so.' He smiled.

She nodded. 'Go on then, sling your hook. See you first thing Monday morning.'

'Right then, I'm off.' He grabbed his stuff and got ready to leave.

'Unless something happens before Monday morning,' Butler said, sitting at her desk. 'But I'm sure nothing will. Have fun.'

CHAPTER 25

'What're you shaking for, bey?' The old man was sitting in one of the kitchen chairs, a roll-up cigarette in between his thin, dry lips. He always seemed to be smoking, and he imagined his lungs were just as black and congested as the man's soul seemed to be.

'I'm not,' he said, staring down at the woman on the floor. He looked at his gloved hands and saw that he was right, his hands were trembling. He had positioned her, put her hands on her chest, feeling the coolness of her skin that was already losing all colour. It wasn't the sight of her that was making him shake, it was the memory of that day all those years ago. He had wondered what had become of her and questioned why he couldn't recall if he had ever told her how she had made his life a misery. Now he knew.

She was outside the school, waiting by herself. She said something to him, some derogatory remark. She laughed too.

Then she was crying. Why was she

crying?

'Why didn't you tell me?' He looked at the old man and saw the subtle smile on his lips.

'Tell you what, bey?' The wisps of blue-grey smoke escaped his mouth as he spoke, the way they always did, as if they played on a loop.

'About her.' He stepped over to the table, clenching his fists.

'Her? Who're you talking 'bout now? The dead bitch on the floor?'

'You know who I mean. Don't fucking try and mess with my head. Sarah.'

The old man closed his eyes for a moment, nodding to himself. 'Oh, right. Sarah. That little bitch. I can't help it if you forgot 'bout that, can I? Does it even matter?'

'Of course it matters.' He clasped his hands on the sides of his head. 'She's dead, and I've been searching for her…'

'No, you ain't.' The old man stood up, pointing his cigarette at him. 'You've been looking for bitches just like her.'

'Not just like her!' he shouted. 'Her! Sarah!'

The old man put a dirty finger to his lips. 'Quiet, bey, you don't want one of those nosey neighbours calling the law. Not yet you don't. Just calm yourself down. You don't want to go to prison, do you?'

'You didn't tell me what you did.'

The old man laughed. 'What I did?'

'I watched you. I remember now and it

was you. You did it.'

'She was screaming.' The old man lost his smile, his eyes growing darker as he stepped closer. 'She had said something to you and you got angry. She couldn't be allowed to get away with it. Remember how much she screamed? It echoed all round that car park. But no one came. She was done and she knew it. She cried then, remember that? Cried for her mummy. Wet herself with fear. Oh, how beautiful it was, bey.'

He nodded, recalling it all, watching the old man come out of the shadows to stop her noise, muffling her screams with his dirty hand. Then those terrible hands were round her throat, squeezing. The tights. He trembled as he recalled it all, feeling dizzy, as he saw the old man taking off her tights and tying them around her throat.

'That's where it all started,' the old man said, taking another drag on his cigarette. 'So long ago, so far away. But this is where it'll end, bey.'

The old caretaker stared at him, burrowing his dark eyes into him. 'You know it's coming to an end, don't you?'

He nodded, unable to deny the feeling, the sensation that all was to come to its conclusion soon. 'The blood moon.'

The old man nodded. 'The blood moon. What better way to end it? The tides rolling backwards, the earth all upside down. Full circle we've come. Soon, my lad, you'll bring it all to an end and they won't know what's happened. Not until it's too late.'

After a couple of brief texts to Dr Jenkins, a somewhat nervous Moone headed to her place, a modest semi-detached house in Beacon Park, just on the border of Peverell. Her address said, in fact, Peverell when he looked it up, but he knew Butler would argue that she resided in Beacon Park.

Butler. She was on his mind in the taxi all the way over to Beacon Park, Peverell, whatever it was, and he just couldn't shake the disappointed look in her eye that late afternoon before he left. He also found the evening of her dad's funeral playing over and over in his head, and the look on her face back then, and how, now he came to think of it, she had leaned towards him, her lips brushing his cheek as she came in for a hug. His heart thumped as he recalled the moment, and the brief thought in his mind, the urge to kiss her. He shook his head, dismissed it as a ridiculous notion, and how embarrassing and awkward things would have been if he had taken that chance. He could see Butler slapping his cheek, or worse, and carrying home his testicles in his coat pocket.

As the taxi arrived in her street, Moone's

mind returned to the Crowne incident, and he tried to imagine what Carthew had whispered to him to get him so riled up. He wondered then what Boulton would do and if any of the shit would fall onto Carthew, but he doubted it. She was coated in Teflon. Those thoughts were pushed aside when the taxi pulled up outside Dr Jenkin's house. He told the driver he wouldn't be long, got out of the car and readied himself. But the front door was already opening.

He felt his eyebrows rise, his heart thump harder and a burn of desire rise from deep within him as Dr Jenkins, fully made-up, hair straightened and beautifully styled into a long bob, and adorned in a short summery dress and cardigan, stepped down from her front door and smiled.

'You look...' he said, trying to find the words.

'What?' she asked, narrowing her eyes. 'Like a dog's dinner?'

'No way. You look beautiful.' He hurried to the taxi, opened the door for her, and she climbed in, smiling, her cheeks scarlet under her make-up.

He told the driver to carry on to Marjons and then sat back, trying not to stare at her too much, while grasping for interesting conversation.

'So, Dr Jenkins, how did you end up at

Marjons?' he said.

'You're not going to call me Dr Jenkins all night, are you, Peter?' She raised one eyebrow, a slight smile raising one corner of her mouth. 'It's Dawn, or had you forgotten?'

'No. I hadn't forgotten... Dawn. So, Marjons?'

'I did a teacher training course there a million years ago, but I obviously didn't go into teaching, thank God. Can you imagine?'

'I can and the thought fills me full of dread.' Moone laughed.

'Definitely. At least the dead don't answer back. Anyway, I made some good friends on the course, that was before I went back to Swansea and then went on to do my degree in Medicine.'

'You must have liked Plymouth, then?'

She looked forward, nodding. 'I love it down here. The way of life. Don't get me wrong, I love Wales too. They're similar places in a way. But I've made this place my home for now. How about you? You followed your family down here, didn't you?'

He nodded. 'I did. London, born and bred. Enfield, if you've ever heard of it.'

'I have. So, you're practically a cockney?'

He laughed. 'No, not technically, although loads of East Enders left the East End during the war to avoid the bombs and ended up in North London, including my grandparents.'

'But do you prefer it down here?'

He shrugged. 'It's a different way of life. A bit slower, nicer scenery. But part of me misses London. But not all the stabbings, shootings and terrorist threats.'

'But even so, you never forget where you're from.' She smiled. 'We're nearly at Marjons.'

The taxi took them along the main road, past the Marjons Health Centre and swimming pool, then dropped them off at the Porters Lodge, where Jenkins took his arm with a smile. They walked into the building, and Moone found himself entering a massive reception area with a long desk on one side and glass doors at the far end where party music thumped from within.

'This place has changed a lot since my day,' Jenkins said as they were approached by a young waitress carrying a tray of champagne-filled flutes.

They both took a glass and then carried on into the main building where lots of bodies were already gathered, a few of them dancing away already next to the DJ's booth which had been set up in the far corner.

'Do you want to grab a table?' Jenkins asked, pointing to one of the many on one side of the room. 'I'll just say hi.'

Moone smiled, then looked round the room, catching the eye of some of the other party-goers and nodding before he sat down at a table and sipped his champagne. He watched Jenkins glide across the room, meeting and greeting, trying to decide exactly what he felt for her, apart from the obvious sexual desire. There was no mistaking that. She was a beautiful woman, but all dolled up she was stunning. And of course, she was clever. They were all elements that would normally set him on edge, make him nervous and hardly able to put one word after another. But he didn't feel that. Not really. He did wonder what the end of the evening would bring, what the correct romantic procedure would be, but then Butler came to mind again and he felt that if something did happen with Jenkins, then he would be somehow betraying her. He sipped his champagne, seeing her come back with a flushed smile.

'Sorry,' she said and sat next to him. 'Got to be social. So, what's occurring?'

He laughed. 'Not much. Just drinking champagne.'

'Of course.' She picked up hers and sipped it, eyeing him all the time. 'So, Peter Moone, talk to me about DI Mandy Butler.'

'Butler? What's to say? She's my clever, but quite often grumpy sidekick.'

'Your sidekick? Not sure she'd like that description.'

He made a terrified face. 'No, I think you're right. My partner? That sounds weird, a bit like a Hollywood buddy cop movie.'

'Or that you're in a relationship.' Jenkins raised her eyebrows as she sipped more champagne.

Moone felt his body tighten. 'Oh, no. Nothing like that.'

'I still remember Dr Parry's suggestion that she has feelings for you.'

Moone nodded, his heart sinking a little at the memory of Parry. There was also a little panic too. 'Well, I don't think that's true. We get on, sort of, for the most part, but nothing more than that.'

She nodded, looking across the room. 'Where is she tonight?'

He shrugged. 'Not sure. She said she would be at home alone and nursing a bottle of wine.'

Jenkins stared at him. 'Did she invite you to join her?'

Moone opened his mouth to speak, but he didn't know what to say, fearing some trap awaited him.

'She did, didn't she?' Jenkins nodded. 'Then why are you here?'

'Because… you invited me and I wanted to come. I really wanted to come.'

She made a sound in her throat that told him she wasn't convinced. He could feel the ice slowly breaking under his feet. 'I did. I think you're lovely. Beautiful.'

She narrowed her eyes. 'Then why do I feel like your consolation prize?'

Moone was about to answer when he felt his phone vibrate in his pocket. He looked down, then up at her.

'Your phone?' she asked. 'You'd better answer it. You might be saved by the bell, Peter Moone.'

He smiled apologetically and took out his phone. It was the station calling.

'Boss,' DC Molly Chambers said, not sounding too bright. 'I thought I'd better call you. I know you're out…'

'What is it, Molly?' Moone watched Jenkins as she turned away and finished her champagne.

'There's been another murder. A woman. Beaten and strangled.'

Moone sighed, his stomach and heart sinking. 'OK. Text me the address, I'll be there soon.'

'Another murder?' Jenkins said with a heavy sigh, then downed her champagne.

'I'm afraid so.' Moone put away his phone and smiled sadly at her. 'Maybe we can do this another time.'

She laughed. 'I think we both know that's not going to happen.'

'Why?' He knew exactly why.

'Because, DCI Peter Moone, your heart belongs to another.' The doctor stood up. 'I'd better get my gear and meet you at the scene. Come on, and I'll call us a taxi.'

Moone picked up his champagne, went to take a drink then stopped himself. He stood up, watching Jenkins heading to the reception area. He felt guilty, but then his mind returned to Butler. He should have been thinking about the latest murder, but there she was.

The scene was pretty much the same, as if all the murders were merging into one and playing over again. The sun was sinking below the houses in Lipson. People were gathering, poking their faces out of their front doors. There was a lot of student accommodation in the area, and most of the young tenants seemed to be gathered on the street, some with drinks in their hands, acting almost as if they were at a party. Moone told the uniforms to get them back inside, then walked to the three-bedroom terrace house, and into the front garden, where a tent had been erected over the front door. The SOCOs were inside, still at work, occasionally bringing out equipment and evidence bags. Moone grabbed some overshoes and gloves and put them on, trying to clear his mind of the evening, to concentrate on the matter at hand. But that was made much harder when Dr Jenkins appeared in a light blue forensic outfit, her make-up still in place.

He smiled awkwardly and nodded as they met outside the tent.

'We must stop meeting like this,' she said, then smiled. 'Oh, Peter Moone, you look so downhearted. Sorry, it's probably the dead woman inside, isn't it? God, listen to me.'

Moone shrugged. 'Sorry how the evening went. And now we've got this.'

'Sir,' DC Chambers said behind him, and he turned to see her holding her notebook, her face a little flushed.

'Chambers,' he said, seeing the doctor enter the tent out of the corner of his eye. 'What have you got?'

She looked at her notes. 'Victim appears to be Sarah Metcalf. Forty-five. Single. Never been married. I've talked to some of the neighbours, and they said she keeps herself to herself. Only ever see her in her garden. They think she was retired or something.'

'Retired at forty-five?' Moone said. 'I was about to say she was lucky. Jesus, Chambers, I thought we were close to catching this nutter.'

She nodded. 'Me too. But we will.'

'I wish I had your confidence. The thing is, he's escalating. And bloody fast. I'm starting to feel this is leading to something.'

'He probably knows we're onto him.'

'I think you're right. He knows time's running out.' Moone looked around the dusky street that was quickly getting darker. 'What's the pattern here? I mean, is that it? He targets single women of a certain age.' Moone stopped talking and then pointed at Chambers' notebook. 'What did you say her name was?'

'Sarah Metcalf.'

'Sarah Metcalf. Sarah Lance. Coincidence?' Moone shrugged. 'Probably a coincidence. The others weren't called Sarah.'

Chambers' eyes narrowed as she said, 'I'm sure there was something I read about the name Sarah.'

'What was it?' Moone felt that icy invisible hand playing his spine like a glockenspiel.

She shook her head. 'I can't remember. I'll have to go and read through everything again and look at the notes I've made. I'll head back to the station.'

'Could you? I know it's late.'

'It's fine. I've got nowhere to be.' She smiled. 'By the way, how was your evening? Hope I didn't interrupt anything.'

He shook his head and looked towards the house, thinking of Dr Jenkins inside. Once known briefly as Dawn, now definitely back to being Dr Jenkins. 'No, it's fine. It's probably the best thing that happened. Right, I better take a look.'

A SOCO was bringing out some equipment and held the tent door open for Moone as he went in, taking a few deep breaths and preparing himself for what was to greet him inside. He headed straight for the kitchen, knowing that was where the assault would have taken place. He stood in the hallway, looking at the modern, smart kitchen. His eyes jumped to blood spatters covering one of the white kitchen cupboards, then to the body lying neatly placed as always, the hands on the chest. His eyes widened as his brain suddenly made sense of what he was seeing. He looked away, his stomach churning, ready to bring up whatever was in his stomach, nothing much more than champagne.

'Horrific, isn't it?'

Moone looked round when he heard the familiar Welsh lilting voice. Dr Jenkins was standing, arms folded, decked out in her forensic outfit, staring down at the body, shaking her head.

'This is the worst one so far,' Moone said, avoiding looking at the head again. 'He's getting out of control.'

'He's not going to stop, is he?' Jenkins said with a sigh.

'No. Not this time. He stopped before, somehow... I don't understand how or why, but he can't this time. We have to find him... yesterday.'

'It's just like all the rest,' Jenkins said. 'Beaten and strangled with her tights. Someone must have seen or heard something.'

'DCI Moone,' a female voice said from

down the hall. Moone turned and could only make out a slender female shape near the door, lit up occasionally by the blue lights of the incident response cars. He couldn't see a face. He looked back at Jenkins. 'I have to go.'

'Wait,' Jenkins called out as he turned to leave. 'Forensics found something under the body.'

'What?'

'The dog end of a roll-up,' she said. 'There's nothing here that says the victim smoked.'

Moone nodded. 'So, our killer might be a smoker? Doesn't make sense. Why decide to leave a dog end now when he's been so careful?'

Jenkins shrugged. 'Like you said, maybe he's out of control. Anyway, maybe we'll get some DNA from it.'

'Good. Thanks.' Moone turned away and headed to the female figure who started walking out into the front garden. As Moone reached the woman, who had her back to him, he said, 'Hello. Did you want to speak to me?'

The blonde woman turned to him and he immediately recognised the face of Chief Superintendent Kate Hellewell.

'I'm sorry, ma'am,' he said. 'I didn't realise it was you.'

She held up a hand briefly. 'It's OK, DCI Moone. I'm not in the habit of visiting crime scenes, but when I heard word of what had happened, I decided I should.'

'It's pretty bad.'

The Chief Super looked over his shoulder. 'I can't imagine... listen, the press is obviously now putting two and two together, and people are starting to panic. This is the Yorkshire Ripper all over again, except they didn't have social media and the conspiracy theorists to deal with. We're not looking good at the moment.'

'I'm just trying to do my job, ma'am.'

'I know. The thing is, we're going to need to hit this head-on. Which means we need a press conference and an appeal. You said you've got a sketch of the killer?'

'Well, yes, but it's not great. Could be anyone...'

'And a van?' The Chief Super raised her eyebrows. 'A registration number?'

He nodded. 'Yes, we believe the killer used...'

'Then when you go in front of the cameras tomorrow morning, you show the sketch and the van... do we have any images of the van?'

'Yes, ma'am.'

'Then I want those shown. We'll need the public's help on this and we need to warn the local women that there's a predator out there...'

'But he might go to ground...'

She held up her hand. 'I understand your reservations, Moone, but we need to make sure people are kept safe. Preservation of life, always takes priority, doesn't it?'

He nodded, tiredness and uneasiness clambering up his back and sitting heavy on his shoulders. 'Yes, ma'am. By the way, the SOCOs found a dog end of a roll-up. The victim didn't smoke. Maybe we'll get DNA from it.'

She smiled briefly. 'Good, but that will take a while. Press conference. Tomorrow morning. First thing.'

He nodded.

She went to turn away but stopped and looked at him again, her face tight, her eyes digging into him. 'I've worked on several murder cases. Children and adult victims. Serial offenders. Obsessive killers, every single one, driven by the desire to kill, to relive that pleasure all over again. They're like junkies, I suppose. I don't think your killer will go to ground, Moone. In fact, this might force him to make a mistake. Anyway, I have faith in you and your team.'

'Thank you, ma'am.'

She stared at him for a moment, making him feel a little uncomfortable before she stepped closer and lowered her voice.

'I'd like to ask your opinion on something, DCI Moone,' she said.

'Yes, ma'am.'

'You knew Chief Superintendent Andrew Laptew.'

The muscles in Moone's neck and

shoulders locked together. 'A little. What did you want to know?'

'What he did... what they say he did... do you think he was capable of such a thing?'

Moone hesitated. 'They found his wife...'

'I know the circumstances, but do you believe he did it, and then killed himself?'

Moone let out a breath. 'Honestly? No, ma'am. I don't believe he did any of it.'

'Then who did?' She raised her eyebrows.

He thought for a moment, weighing it all up, trying to decide if he could trust her, and whether she would believe what he had to say. 'I wish I knew, ma'am.'

She nodded. 'OK. Tomorrow morning. First thing. Don't let the victims or your team down, DCI Peter Moone.'

CHAPTER 26

'What the fuck 'appended to you last night?' Terry Hankin said, rubbing his red eyes as Moone stepped out of the shower and wrapped a towel around himself.

'Jesus!' Moone flinched, then took a few deep breaths, his heart thudding. 'Terry! You scared the shit out of me.'

As Moone moved past him, drying himself as he went, Terry followed.

'You never came 'ome!' Terry moaned. 'I had to get pissed by myself.'

Moone hid himself inside his bedroom and hurriedly got dressed. He hadn't had time for sleep and had spent the night in his car, parked down the road, not wanting to have to face a drunken Terry. He had got close to his mobile home last night and had heard the beat of music and loud voices. He'd found he couldn't stomach a late-night party, especially when he had to give a press conference first thing in the morning that he didn't want to give. The thought of facing the press and any TV cameras present, made him want to projectile vomit.

'By yourself?' Moone asked, stepping out of his room as he did up his tie. 'Didn't manage to meet anyone?'

Terry grinned. 'Well, there might have been a couple of birds I met at that shit hole bar they've got here. I tell ya, mate, you could've had the dark-haired one. She was right up your alley.'

Moone smiled politely. 'Well, thanks for the thought, mate, but I've got to get to work...'

'Work? Now? It's Sunday.'

'I know, but murder doesn't stop for the weekends, and I have to give a press conference on a series of murders I'm looking into.'

Terry widened his eyes. 'Murders? What murders? Jesus, mate. When do you sleep?'

'When I can. If you can call it sleep.'

'Well, wish I could catch this bastard for yer, and sort him out.'

Moone laughed. 'Him and all the other trouble I have to deal with.'

Terry's face changed, losing his smile, as he puffed out his chest. 'Someone giving you trouble, mate? You know you only 'ave to ask. I'll fuckin' sort 'em for yer.'

Moone let out a breath. 'Thanks, mate, but it's not a fella.'

'Oh, right. You got romantic trouble, 'ave yer?' Terry nodded.

'Not romantic. But she's serious trouble.'

'A psycho bird, eh?' He frowned, folding his thick arms over his massive chest. 'Don't think it's right to hit a bird, mate.'

'No, it's not right to hit a woman, Terry. That's why I'm after this killer. Right, I better go.' Moone opened the door of the mobile home and felt the warm morning air clasping hold of him already.

'Well, mate, you let me know if there's anyone you need sorted.'

Moone smiled. 'I will, Terry. Don't you worry.'

Moone didn't have a clue what to expect until he was driven by Butler to Crownhill Station, where the large conference room had been set up for the appeal. Butler remained by the door while he was ushered to the long table at the front, facing all the people from the press, phones and cameras out at the ready. The whole world could be looking at him, he thought, shuddering a little, and feeling his face burn. The Chief Super came in, decked out in her best uniform, hair done, and sat beside him with a brief smile and nod. Boulton sat on the other side of him and pushed the script in front of him. Moone looked down at it, reading the words carefully picked out. Then he looked up, scanning the crowd of journalists. He saw one familiar face seated near the front. Carly

Tamms, who had helped him on one of their biggest investigations. She caught his eye and smiled.

'Thank you all for coming,' the Chief Super said, looking over the crowd that soon stopped chattering. 'We won't be taking any questions. This will be a short statement and appeal given by the detective in charge of the investigation, DCI Peter Moone.'

Photos were taken, camera phones held up. He tried to ignore it all as he looked at the words, his heart pounding in his ears.

'As some of you are already aware,' he said, then cleared his throat, 'there have been three recent deaths. Three women, aged in their forties, have been found dead in their homes...'

'Is there a serial killer targeting women?!' someone called out.

'There'll be no questions!' the Chief Super said. 'Please continue.'

Moone cleared his throat again. 'All three victims sustained serious injuries that led to their deaths. We believe that Caroline Abbott, Shena Caballero and Sarah Metcalf were all victims of the same killer. All three of these women had families, loved ones who will miss them. Their lives have been torn apart. We will be handing out an image of a vehicle we believed was used in the crimes, as well as a sketch that our police artist has put together based on the description a witness has given us...'

Moone caught the eye of Tamms again, who gave him an encouraging nod. He looked at the script once more. 'Devon and Cornwall police are appealing to the man in the sketch. Please, whoever you are, hand yourself in at your nearest police station or call the number that will appear at the bottom of the screen. We know you must be going through some traumatic times, and we would like to help you stop all this. We want to help. We'd also like to appeal to the family of the man in the sketch. If you suspect someone in your family may be involved in these crimes, then please contact us at the number below or through the Devon and Cornwall website. This man could be someone's father, brother, husband or uncle... someone knows him. You might recognise him from the sketch or even the vehicle. Please get in touch if you have any suspicions. Ask yourselves, do you know this person? If you do, and you hesitate to call us, in fear that you'll be somehow betraying them... well, you won't be. You will be helping them in the long run and saving lives. Please get in contact. Thank you.' Moone sat back and let out a breath.

'Is it true that you suspect this man is some kind of manual worker or handyman?' someone called out.

'There will be no questions, thank you,' the Chief Super said again as she stood up.

Boulton raised himself and patted Moone's shoulder as a signal for him to do the same. They all hurried out of the room, then all went into a side office. The Chief Super shut the door after them and faced Moone, seeming to look him over.

'You went off script a little,' she said, folding her arms.

'Sorry, I thought…' he started to say, his face heating up.

'No, don't be,' she said, a slight smile appearing. 'It was good. The whole you won't be betraying him, you'll be helping him… very good. I'm guessing you've had some experience of this sort of case before? You were awarded a bravery medal, weren't you?'

Moone looked down, the same old jagged spike of regret sinking through his heart and stomach. 'I was, but it was a mistake. I didn't do anything…'

'That's not what I read.' The Chief Super patted his shoulder. 'I heard you saved quite a few lives.'

'I lost a lot too.'

The Chief nodded, her face becoming a little solemn. 'It can be tough, our job…'

Moone's eyes jumped to the window in the door when he saw Carly Tamms walking past, being taken along by the wave of the press that moved down the corridor.

'Sorry, ma'am,' he said, smiling

apologetically. 'I need to talk to someone.'

She stepped aside. 'Good work, Moone.'

He nodded, then hurried through the door, and found himself submerged by the press. When they realised who he was, they all turned on him like a pack of wild dogs, shouting out questions.

'Carly Tamms?' he called out and saw her turn and start swimming back towards him. Her hand found his and Moone opened another office door, pulled her inside and closed the door.

Tamms smiled and said, 'You nearly got ripped to pieces.'

'Nearly.' He laughed. 'Haven't seen you for a while. I heard you made editor.'

'I did,' she said and nodded. 'I don't usually find myself in these situations, but I was curious and like most of the female population of Devon and Cornwall, a little scared. Is he really targeting women who live alone?'

Moone sighed, weighing it all up, wondering if he could trust her. 'Off the record?'

She smiled. 'Brownie's promise.'

He laughed. 'Were you actually in the Brownies or were you in the Brownies like I was in the Scouts?'

'I was definitely in the Brownies.' Tamms rested her bottom on the desk behind her. 'So come on, spill the beans. How close are you to catching him?'

'We're always close. Yes, he is targeting single women who live alone.'

'What does he do? I mean what's his MO?'

'I can't discuss that. But he's a sadistic killer. One of the worst I've come across. We need to stop him and quickly.'

She nodded, then stepped forward. 'And you need my help, I'm guessing?'

'Kind of. The problem I've got is, I need to preserve life, that's rule number one...'

'Of course, but you also don't want to scare him off, otherwise you can't catch him in the act. He's not left you much to go on, apart from the sketch, who could quite frankly be anyone, and the van... well, he's probably got rid of that by now...'

Moone sighed. 'This killer... he's got a lot of fury that has been building up for a long time.'

'For about twenty years?' Tamms raised her eyebrows.

Moone tried to keep the shock from his face as he said, 'What made you say that?'

'Because there were two murders nearly twenty years ago. Two women who lived alone, and they were about the same age as your latest victims. I was only a kid back then, but I've heard stories about it, and I remember we did a piece on unsolved crimes in Devon and Cornwall. I talked to a former police detective and he happened to spill the beans on a couple of details...'

Moone let out a deep groan. 'Oh, shit. What details?'

'He said the women were beaten, almost unrecognisably, and they found them positioned like they were lying in a coffin.'

Moone covered his face for a moment, almost afraid to ask his next question. 'Did this idiot of a detective let slip anything else?'

'Nothing. He stopped talking after that. I think he realised he'd said too much. But he seemed pretty upset they never caught him.'

'What was this detective's name?'

'Brendon Mitchell. He was a detective sergeant, I think. Is he in trouble?'

Moone shrugged. 'Not really, but he might know something we don't.'

'Oh, there was something else he did say, which I thought was interesting...'

'Go on.'

'He mentioned a dishcloth or towel or something being found draped over the first victim's face. He said it was as if the killer didn't want to look at her.'

Moone felt the old icy hand tease the back of his neck. 'He said that the cloth was draped over her face? Not near her, not on the floor?'

'I'm sure he said it was over her face. Why? Doesn't that usually mean the killer's experiencing regret or that they know the victim?'

Moone stepped closer. 'I don't know, but I need to know where this detective lives. Also, I need you to keep this to yourself. Please.'

She looked horrified for a moment. 'Do you think I'm going to interfere with an ongoing police investigation?'

'I'm hoping not. We need the women of Plymouth to be safe, and you can help with that, but please don't mention the position of the bodies or the cloth.'

She let out a harsh breath as she folded her arms, narrowing her eyes at him. 'I didn't mention those details back when I did the piece on unsolved crimes, so why would I now?'

'I'm sorry. Thank you. If you can tell me where this detective lives, I'd be eternally grateful...'

She smiled. 'I'll look up his address. But you have to promise to give one of my reporters an exclusive interview when this killer's caught.'

Moone nodded and put out his hand. 'It's a deal.'

He was still trembling when he went home and walked into the house, listening out for signs of life, for the sound of the TV. He kept seeing the old man, the roll-up hanging on his dry lips as he stretched out those dirty, almost grey hands to the girl... He shuddered, and almost threw up.

There was no TV sound. He walked into the living area and froze. The TV was off and she was sitting there. She didn't look at him for a moment, just stared ahead. A wave of uneasiness came across the room, thick and oppressive like a storm cloud.

'Where is she?' he asked, his voice coming out weak and strained.

'With her friend.' She turned and looked at him. Her face was red, tight like it always was when she was pissed off with him. 'Where have you been?'

'At work.'

'Where?'

'I had to price a job...'

'There's been another murder. In Lipson this time.'

The world shifted. He almost fell to one side, his heart racing, his emotions rushing about his body, trying to find a way out. Keep calm, he told himself. 'I heard on the radio. It's terrible...'

'Some people think he's a handyman.' She stared at him.

'Really? People are always coming up with crazy theories...'

'I don't think it's just a theory. A friend of mine told me that two of the women were getting ready to have work done in their houses. Next thing... it's horrible.'

He nodded. 'It is. But don't worry, you're safe here... I wouldn't let...'

'Where were you yesterday afternoon?' Her eyes drilled into him as she stood up and came closer.

'Where was I?' His heart thumped as his hands twitched.

She knows. You have to stop her from going to the police.

'Yes, that's what I said. Are you deaf now? Just tell me where you were.' She stepped closer and then started to sniff. 'What's that stink? Is that cigarettes? Have you been smoking?'

He looked down at his clothes, smelling the stench of the old man's roll-ups. 'No, I don't smoke, you know that.'

'Then why do you stink like an ashtray?'

His mind whirred, delving deep for a reasonable explanation. 'I was just at the builders merchants. I was talking to this old builder bloke. He was smoking like a trooper. Roll-ups.'

She stared at him, narrowing her eyes. 'I don't even know why you hang around there...'

'Because it's part of what I do... the job I do.'

'What happened to the websites? I thought you were going to give that another go after the virus and lockdowns. Or have you just given up like you always do?'

Grab her by the throat. Do it now, and you

can end all this, stop her from asking any more difficult questions.

'No.'

'No what?'

'I haven't given up. I'm going to try and get some more clients soon.'

She crossed her arms tight against her chest. 'You'd better. Because you're playing a dangerous game.'

His hands shook.

Kill her. Now.

'What do you mean?'

'Well, no one's going to trust handymen after this, are they? You need to get your old job back or do something else. If you don't, you're not much use to your daughter or me, are you?'

'Why do you say…'

She moved closer, pointing her finger in his face. 'Just get your act together and for God's sake take a shower, because you stink.'

She stormed past him, heading off to her office more than likely, he thought. He looked down at himself, seeing his hands trembling. He gripped them into fists, feeling his heart pounding in his chest, knowing how close he had come to his secret being revealed.

There's one way to stop her from ever revealing your secret to the world.

No.

I can't.

I could never.

You might have no choice.

Moone had just been driven back to Charles Cross station by Butler and was climbing the stairs towards the incident room when he heard DSU Boulton call out his name. He stopped and gave a heavy sigh, before once again pushing an uncomfortable smile to his lips and turning to face his superior.

'Boss?' Moone said.

Boulton pointed a thumb behind him. 'My office. Now.'

Moone trudged behind him, back down the stairs and into Boulton's office where his boss shut the door behind him and then sat at his desk.

'I think the press conference went pretty well,' Moone said and sat down.

Boulton stared at him. 'DI Crowne has been making some pretty wild claims.'

Shit. Moone raised his eyebrows. 'Has he?'

'Yes. Mostly involving DS Faith Carthew. He seems to believe she's involved in the disappearance of his colleague, DS Rivers.'

'I see.'

'Don't play dumb, Moone. You know all about it. Where does this all come from?'

Moone sat back, pausing for a moment and trying to come up with some kind of version of events that didn't put him in the shit. 'Crowne did mention his theory. He seems to think that maybe Rivers came down here to have words with Carthew, something to do with DSU Charlie Armstrong's murder... anyway, he believes Carthew might have her somewhere or... has killed her.'

Boulton let out an incredulous laugh. 'Why? Why does he think Carthew would do something like this?'

'Well, Carthew was at one point a suspect in Armstrong's murder...'

'Yes, but that came to nothing. There was no evidence that she was involved. DC Banerjee committed those murders...'

'On her own?'

Boulton shook his head. 'No. Not on her own. Do you want to know what I think?'

'Yes, sir.'

Boulton leaned towards him. 'I think that DC Banerjee and this DS Rivers were involved in a clandestine relationship. I think they plotted the murders between them in some ill-fated attempt to rise up the ranks down here. It doesn't make much sense to me, but there you go...'

Moone couldn't quite believe what he was hearing. 'What about Rivers' disappearance, sir? Is anyone looking for her?'

'Of course. She's a high-priority missing person, and her bosses are of course very concerned. They're also not too happy with DI Crowne at this moment in time, so they've made him take some leave for the sake of his mental health. Probably for the best as the man seems out of control.'

Moone hesitated to ask his next question. 'Have you talked to DS Carthew about all this?'

He nodded. 'Of course. Those were very serious allegations that Crowne made about her. But after talking to her, I'm satisfied she knows nothing about the disappearance of DS Rivers.'

'So, that's it?'

'Unless you have more information you'd like to share?'

Moone stood up, resisting the urge to grab his boss by the shirt and shake some sense into him. Then he thought on, let his mind wander into a much darker labyrinth, a place where images of Boulton and Carthew flickered into his brain. There they were, entwined. No, it couldn't be. Could it? 'No, sir. No more information. If you excuse me, sir, I better get back to work.'

'Yes, you had better. And I don't want any more of this Rivers business interfering with your investigation. Do I make myself clear?'

'Yes, sir. Very clear.'

CHAPTER 27

'Did I hear you got dragged in by Boulton yesterday?' Butler asked, raising one eyebrow as Moone entered the incident room the next morning. 'Everything all right?'

Moone sighed and carried his coffee to his desk, thinking back to the very depressing chat he'd just had with the clueless, and the possibly blinded-by-sex, DSU Boulton. 'You did. They've done a real number on Crowne.'

'What do you mean?' Butler folded her arms as she rested her backside on the corner of her desk.

'The whole incident between him and Carthew? Remember? It didn't go his way. He ended up making allegations against her, she's made up a load of crap and fed it to them, and they've believed her.'

Butler gave a sickened laugh. 'What is it with her? Can no one else see it, but us?'

'I see it,' Harding said, poking his head over the top of his monitor.

'I know you do,' Butler said with a huff. 'So, looks like Boulton's under her spell, then?'

Moone nodded, feeling sick all over. 'Looks like it. She's put it in his head that maybe Rivers and DC Banerjee were in cahoots and planned the murder of Armstrong and the rest.'

'Well, that's half the truth. But she conveniently leaves herself out.'

Moone rubbed his tired eyes, his heart still thudding a little from the adrenalin burst that the press conference had given him. Once again, he couldn't think straight. Nothing made sense any more and he couldn't see a way to catch out Carthew. He went over to Butler and lowered his voice as he said, 'She's beaten us, hasn't she?'

'No. Don't be soft, Moone. She's only won so far 'cause we keep playing by the rule book…'

'But we've bent the rules a few times and it's got us nowhere.'

Butler looked round the room for a moment, then lowered her voice to a whisper. 'We need to follow her and find out where she's staying and plant Rivers' phone.'

Moone shook his head. 'We can't. For one thing, she will never lead us to where she's staying, and I've got another feeling that wherever she's holed up, probably isn't registered to her. She's not stupid, she knows all our moves before we make them.'

Butler stared at him for a moment, then

nodded. 'Yeah, she seems to. Then what do we do? Let another team try and find Rivers? Hope to hell it somehow leads to bringing down Carthew?'

Moone shrugged. 'I don't know, but we've got a killer to stop at the moment and we're getting closer to tracking him down. We can't let him kill any more women. By the way, the SOCOs found a dog end under the victim last night. The victim didn't smoke. It's been sent out so they can extract the DNA.'

'Well, good. If it's his cigarette, then we've got him.'

'If it's his. Just seems strange that he leaves that behind after being so careful. Anyway, the DNA will take a while.'

'Then what do we do in the meantime? Have you got any bright ideas, London boy?'

'No. Has anything come from the fake profile you and Molly set up?'

Butler sighed. 'No. Nothing. No psychos are biting. But we won't give up.'

Then it came to Moone, the memory of what Carly Tamms had said to him the day before, rising from the cloud his mind had become wrapped in. The detective she had talked to. How could he have forgotten? 'I just remembered, I talked to Carly Tamms after the press conference yesterday.'

'The reporter?'

'She's editor now, but yes... she told me

she talked to a former detective who worked on the original murders. A detective called Brendon Mitchell. I'm waiting for her to let me know where he's living now. Anyway, he told her that when they found Ludlow's body, the dishcloth was over her face.'

'So?'

'What if the first victim was known to her killer? It could be one of her family or friends. It could even be...'

'Nick Dann?' Butler huffed. 'You've got a real thing for him, haven't you?'

'He does seem to be the link in this.'

Butler sighed. 'OK, then I'll find out where Brendon Mitchell resides, you tell the team the latest.'

'Boss,' Chambers said from across the room, and they both turned as she stood up.

'What is it, Molly?' Moone said, walking over and seeing she was holding a printout.

She looked up at him, a glimmer of excitement clear in her eyes. 'It's the Sarah thing...'

'Sarah thing?' Butler asked as she joined Moone.

Moone looked at Butler. 'The last victim was called Sarah, and obviously he targeted Sarah Launce before that. Might be a coincidence, but...'

'I don't think it is,' Molly said. 'Judy Ludlow's middle name was Sarah. Apparently, she used to go by Sarah when she was younger. And our second victim twenty years ago, had an older sister called Sarah but she died when she was in her teens. It can't be a coincidence, can it?'

'Sarah's a pretty common name of women of a certain age,' Butler said and folded her arms. 'Seems like a coincidence to me.'

Moone ignored her doubt and faced Molly. 'Caroline Abbott? Any Sarah connection there?'

'There is,' she said but sounded hesitant. 'Her mum used to own the house she was living in and she was called Sara. I know, a little bit of a stretch.'

Moone smiled. 'No, it's good, Molly. Good work. You may have given us the connection between our victims. The name Sarah.'

Moone went over to the whiteboard and wrote Sarah in large letters at the centre of the board, just below all the victims' photos. He turned to face the team, ignoring a doubtful-looking Butler.

'Listen up, people,' he said. 'DC Chambers has given us a possible lead. The name Sarah. Sarah Metcalf is the name of our latest victim. Sarah Launce, we believe, was the intended victim the time before and not her best friend. The first victim all those years ago, Judy Ludlow, used to go by her middle name when she was younger. Guess what it is?'

'Marjorie?' Harding asked, and a ripple of

laughter travelled around the room.

Moone stared at him and watched him sheepishly lower his head. 'Sarah. She went by the name Sarah. Our second victim, from twenty years ago, Teresa Burrows had an older sister who died when she was only a teenager. She was called Sarah. What if our killer thought Teresa was Sarah or Teresa reminded him of Sarah? Anyway, Caroline Abbott, her home used to be owned by her mother, Sara Abbott. Yes, it could be a coincidence, but when it comes to murder, I think we stop believing in coincidences, don't we? There's something else too. I talked to the reporter Carly Tamms after the press conference yesterday and she reckons she talked to a former detective called Brendan Mitchell who worked the original case. He told her that when they found Judy Ludlow, she had a dishcloth over her face, not beside her. What if the cloth accidentally got moved during the examination of the body? Did the killer put it over her face because he was regretting what he did? Butler and I will talk to Brendan Mitchell, while you lot look into the background of all the victims again with your mind on this Sarah business. Try and find any past cases, unsolved cases involving a victim called Sarah. Anything. Right, let's get back to work.'

Moone went over to the Butler, who was already getting her stuff together, ready to leave. 'Right, did you find Brendan Mitchell?'

'I did. He seems to be living in a nice part of Peverell, in one of those posh new houses they've built. Must've done all right for himself.'

'Right then, let's go.'

Jason left his motorcycle on the end of Mannamead Road, then walked in the direction of the Golden Hind pub, keeping an eye out for anyone who might be following him. He saw no one, so took a few wrong turns then walked back on himself and headed towards the MOT centre that was just off the high street. It was set behind an old petrol station that was now a car wash and valet service, just down a lane a couple hundred yards. He came out into the small yard of the MOT garage, which was chock-a-block with cars waiting to be seen too. He ignored the young and older men of the garage in their overalls and headed for one of the buildings around the back, as instructed. The owner of the MOT centre knew Nair, was an old friend who owed him a favour.

Jason knocked on the door of the large weather-worn garage he came to, then stood back as he took out his cigarettes. The door opened towards him, and Nair stood there, looking him over, then beyond him.

'You weren't followed?' Nair asked as he stepped aside to let Jason into the darkened garage.

'No, I wasn't,' he said as he stepped in and saw the grey van parked a couple of feet away. His eyes then jumped to Carthew who was sitting in a chair, wearing a trouser suit, legs crossed. 'Look at you two, all cosy in here.'

'Shut your trap,' Nair said and walked around him and folded his arms. 'I still don't like this.'

Carthew got up on her feet. 'What don't you like?'

Nair looked at her. 'I don't like that Jason's doing the dirty work. I think you've got him wrapped around your finger.'

'I know what I'm doing,' Jason said.

Nair turned to him, giving him a dead-eye stare. 'Do you, son? You know you've got to take this van and drive it at a man? You've got to kill him with it and not get caught? You all right with that?'

'He's fine,' Carthew said, stepping closer. 'Aren't you, Jason?'

'Yeah, I am.'

Nair shook his head, huffed, and then stepped closer to Jason. 'You'd better not get caught, then. We can't have you being collared and them getting you to spill your guts.'

'I would never tell them anything. No comment, all the way. Anyway, I won't get caught.'

'That's what they all say.' Nair looked at

Carthew. 'You really must want this fella out of your way.'

Carthew smiled. 'I do. I need him gone. Once and for all. Don't worry, once he's out of the way, things will run a lot smoother and we'll make a lot of money together.'

'I hope so. For all our sakes.' Nair pushed past Jason and left the garage, leaving them alone.

'I don't think he likes you,' Jason said and took out a cigarette and lit it.

'I don't care,' Carthew said. 'It's business. We can help each other.'

Jason pointed his fag at the van. 'So, this is the murder weapon?'

'It is. Are you ready to do this?'

He looked at her. 'Would you even be worried if I was having doubts?'

She came close to him and touched his face. 'You know I would. Just say if you've changed your mind.'

'I haven't.'

She leaned in and kissed him, and it was like it always was with her, all the doubt and suspicions burned away as the scent and warmth of her muffled his brain and got his heart hammering. He'd do anything for her, and knowing that scared him. Would she do anything for him? He pushed the question back down and brought up the thought that they could make a lot of money together and he needed that more than anything. He had debts that needed to be paid off, and that's what he had to think of, and not let her cloud his mind.

'Has there been anything on Facebook?' she asked. 'Any messages for Sarah?'

'Nothing. I don't think he's going to take the bait.'

Her face changed, darkness washing over it, and all signs of her former affection dissolved as she moved back from him. 'He has to. I can't let my idiot colleagues get to him first. Hasn't there been any contact from anyone?'

He shook his head. 'No, sorry. But you're clever, you'll figure it out. If you don't catch him…'

Her eyes jumped up to him, now filled with a flicker of annoyance. 'If I don't? Do you know anything about me? Whatever I set out to do, I do. I'll catch him. We just need to find him. I just need to think, to get inside his head.'

He watched her walk off, her fingers rising to her temples and pressing against them. She was determined, and he admired that in her and of course desired her because of what she looked like. But he was definitely scared of her too, and that was riding over any desire he had for her, along with her promise of the future, of himself being in charge of the gang and her heading the police team that might cause them any problems. He looked over at the van, the instrument that she had told him was the best way to remove this man from her life. He had volunteered because she had convinced him to, had persuaded him with her body that he needed to prove himself to her, and this was the only way. She trusted no one else to get this job done. His heart pounded at the thought of what she wanted him to do, to drive full speed at the target and hopefully kill him instantly. His hands trembled as he looked back over at her as she was now sitting on a chair in some kind of pose of meditation. Money. He needed the money desperately and selling his nan's old home would barely cover it. He had no choice but to do what she asked. He just had to do it, get away with it, and he'd be home free.

Butler pulled up in the street in Peverell, just along from one of the side roads filled with nice large terrace houses that fetched over three hundred grand these days, she informed Moone. But it wasn't the terrace houses that interested them as they got out and waited for the traffic along Peverell Park Road to slow down before they crossed. They were headed to a new development of houses a couple of streets up. Two houses in particular interested them, one being a large, three-storey house that had been standing off of Beauchamp Crescent for quite a while, and the other was an equally sized newly built house next door. It was surrounded by a tall brick wall and fronted by large gates.

Moone stood by the intercom and tried to see over the gate with no luck. 'This is where he lives?'

Butler nodded. 'Apparently. This house must have cost a fair bit. Wonder what he does now?'

'Maybe he won the Pools?' Moone shrugged as he got out his ID.

Butler turned to him, pulling a face. 'The Pools? Haven't you heard of the Lottery, Mr Eighties?'

He laughed. 'Let's just buzz him and find out about this cloth business.'

Butler pressed the intercom which started making a beeping noise, followed by an electronic humming sound. Then it was all interrupted by a gruff voice that asked them who they were.

'I'm DCI Peter Moone,' he said, sticking his head towards the intercom. 'We're here to ask you about a murder you worked twenty years ago.'

There was a click and the humming went dead. Moone and Butler stared at each other and exchanged shrugs.

'Is that Brendan Mitchell?' Moone asked, pressing the intercom.

'I haven't got time right now,' the voice came back. 'Come back another time.'

'More women are dying, Brendan,' Butler said before he had a chance to end the conversation. 'We believe you have information that might help stop it. We just need ten minutes of your time.'

The crackling sound and the hum went on for almost a minute before the voice said, 'For fuck's... oh, all right. Ten minutes, but that's it.'

The intercom went off, then shortly after the gate started to groan and whine as it slowly opened. Moone walked across the tarmac driveway and up to the large 1930s style house. The grand front door opened and a man in his sixties, dressed in a beige shirt and grey trousers stared out at them. He had thinning grey hair and matching goatee beard, and a ruddy complexion, which Moone recognised as the tell-tale signs of a possible drink problem.

'You'd better come in, then,' Brendan Mitchell said and stepped back into the magnolia-painted hallway.

'Nice house,' Butler said as she followed Moone inside. 'Must've cost a bomb. You get your police pension, do you?'

'You can sling your hook if you're going to get personal,' he said and pushed past them along the hallway which had a telephone table and a few group family photos on the walls. He went into a large lounge that had a massive wall-mounted TV and a black leather corner sofa. Mitchell sat himself down on the sofa and

Moone saw him snatch a can of lager from the coffee table and hide it behind the chair.

'What's it you wanted to talk about?' the ex-detective asked, eyeing them up and down as they came in. While Butler remained standing as usual, Moone sat down on an armchair and faced Mitchell and said to him, 'Tell us about the first murder.'

The old man sat back, narrowing his eyes. 'Judy Ludlow? What 'bout her?'

'You still remember her name, then?' Butler asked, folding her arms and staring at him.

'Course I do,' the old man snapped like she was stupid. 'You don't forget things like that. Was the first time I'd seen anything like that. I can see it now, as I'm telling you 'bout it. Sticks in your skull. State of her.'

'How was the body found?' Moone asked, sitting forward.

The old detective brought his steely eyes on Moone again, staring right into him. 'Why do you ask that?'

'There seems to be some disagreement on how the body was found.'

'You're talking 'bout the dishcloth,' he said and nodded. 'I'm telling you that cloth was over her face when we found her. Someone must've taken it off. Not me, before you ask. Some forensic idiot or someone. Anyway, when it comes to the photos being taken, well, there she is, nothing on her face. I raise it, but I get told to keep my mouth shut.'

'Who told you to keep your mouth shut?' Butler asked.

Mitchell looked over at her. 'King. Stupid, lapdog. He got word from above to let things lie, not to complicate matters and so there was no cloth on her face...'

'But if there was...' Moone started to say, but Mitchell jumped forward, pointing a finger at him as he barked, 'There was. Other people saw it, uniforms, but they were afraid to say anything. But, yeah, I know what you're going to say. If there was a cloth, it meant the killer might've known her.'

Moone sat back. 'Did you have your suspicions?'

'Of course. I should've been in charge of that case. It was my turn, but King licked so many arses. I said we should be looking for anyone who knew her, family, friends, boyfriends and all that, but I wasn't listened to.'

'Anyone in particular?' Butler asked.

'Someone untouchable,' Mitchell said. 'Best I don't mention them now.'

'A local businessman?' Butler asked before Moone could say anything.

Mitchell's eyes jumped to her. 'I didn't say that. Don't you tell anyone I said anything...'

Moone could see how agitated he had

got. They were getting much closer. He looked round at the house, the nice decor. 'This place must have cost quite a bit.'

Mitchell got up suddenly. 'Right, I think I've said enough. You two, out!'

Butler stepped up to Mitchell. 'Don't suppose a local businessman is financing this, is he? To keep you quiet?'

'You pair of nosey fuckin...' Mitchell pointed a warning finger between them. 'Don't you go telling anyone I said anything to you... I'll deny it.'

'He'd take away the money coming in, would he?' Moone asked. 'Nick Dann? He's financing this, isn't he?'

'I'm not saying anything,' Mitchell said, his face reddening. 'Time you two was gone.'

'We won't say a word,' Butler said. 'As long as you lay it on the line now. Otherwise, we can let it slip to nice generous Mr Dann what you told us.'

Mitchell stared at her. 'Oh, you're one of those bitches they've got working now?'

'That's right. Talk.'

Mitchell looked between them furtively, then sighed. 'It's not just me. It's my niece and nephew. Dann got them nice jobs. Well paid for down here. If he suspects I said anything, then that goes down the pan. Do you want that on your conscience?'

'Do you want more deaths on yours?'

Butler asked. 'Who do you think killed Judy Ludlow? Who put that cloth on her face?'

Mitchell looked down. 'I found out... well, I suspected Nick Dann was seeing Ludlow. Some old dear, long dead now reckons she saw a man in a suit leave her house that day. Mentioned a car, flash one, the same as Dann drove back then. I went to see Dann, and, well...'

'He persuaded you to keep quiet?' Butler asked. 'To not mention the fact that he murdered her.'

Mitchell looked at her. 'He said he didn't, swore he didn't. He said they had a row that morning and he stormed off, then later he went back and found her like that. He put the cloth over her face, then he snuck out.'

'He didn't call the police?' Moone asked.

Mitchell shook his head. 'No, of course the bastard didn't. He was married to a rich cow by then and building up a business and reputation across Plymouth. He wasn't about to risk that, was he?'

'So you kept quiet all these bloody years?' Butler huffed. 'You're as bad as him, if not worse.'

'Oh, fuck you,' Mitchell snapped. 'I'm not the only one who bent the rules...'

'Bent the rules?' Butler gave a disgusted laugh. 'You didn't bend them, you pissed all over them.'

'Yeah, well, I was pretty convinced he didn't do it, and he had alibis for the other murders... and anyway, I wasn't the only one to break the rules! What about King, our boss?'

'What about him?' Moone asked.

'Did you know his son was helping with the investigation on the quiet?' Mitchell nodded, looking pleased with himself.

'What do you mean helping?' Butler asked.

'Putting stuff on computer for him, helping him organise stuff. Not only that...'

Mitchell stopped talking, his expression changing, as if he had caught himself and heard what he was saying. 'Nothing. Forget it.'

'No,' Butler said, stepping closer. 'What were you going to say?'

Mitchell gritted his teeth as he looked up at her. 'You can't intimidate me, love. Fine, go and tell who you like, go running to Dann. I don't care, I'm not being held over a barrel any more. Go on, stroll on. All I'm going to say is go and see King. Ask him about it all.'

Moone looked at Butler and she returned his look of confusion and growing curiosity.

'Come on,' Moone said. 'Let's leave the man to his guilt.'

CHAPTER 28

When they were safely back in the car, Butler, her cheeks red, turned on Moone and snapped, 'Bloody hell, Moone. What was that? Leave the man to his guilt? So he gets to get away with perverting the course of justice?'

Moone sighed. He'd been putting things together all the time they made their way from Mitchell's house and none of it sounded good in his head. 'Look, we've got to tread very carefully...'

'Have we?' Butler glared at him.

'Yes. Think about it. Mitchell is in cahoots with Nick Dann who's all cozied up with our boss. Do you think Mitchell's going to start singing like a canary about Ludlow and the cloth and Dann when he's got so much to lose? We've got little evidence and no one who will back us up.'

Butler seemed to calm down as she looked through the windscreen. 'You might have a point... for once.'

'You know it makes sense,' Moone said.

'All right, Del Boy, keep your sheepskin coat in the boot. So, what do we do, then? I mean, chances are Dann murdered Ludlow…'

'Or he told Mitchell the truth and he just found her and put the cloth over her face?'

Butler grunted. 'Yeah, right. But like you said, we've got nothing. So what now?'

'We go and see King, see what he has to say for himself.'

'Can you believe he had his son helping him with the investigation? No wonder he doesn't see him any more.'

'Well, we'll need to talk to him too, in case he's got any information. Let's go and see King.'

Inspector Pinder parked up in the side street off of Stonehouse, not far from the poky little tavern he was heading for. He looked around when he climbed out and checked the coast was clear and none of the Dark Horse people were about. He could see no one, so walked to the side door of the whitewashed and red-timbered pub, then knocked. The door of the pub was unbolted and a young, suited detective looked out at him, then let him in.

'Everything OK, Paul?' Pinder said to the detective who worked in the intelligence department.

'Yeah, Kev,' Detective Sergeant Paul Lester said and bolted the door behind them, the stench of stale beer that had soaked into the carpet rising to Pinder's nostrils. 'He's in the back room, sweating like a pig.'

Pinder went through to the back bar that housed the pool table and the fruit machines. He could hear the man puffing away on a cigarette as he was sitting at a table in the back corner.

'You can't smoke in here, Steve,' Pinder said and stood in front of the man, who was in his late thirties, with long greying red hair, and an equally untidy beard. Sweat had dampened his forehead and his Iron Maiden T-shirt.

'Give us a break, boss,' Steve said, his eyes pleading with him. 'I could die at any moment, so let me enjoy a fag! I implore you.'

'You implore me?' Pinder shook his head. 'Fancy word. Don't worry, Steve, you're not going to die.'

'I will if Nair finds out we've been talking.' Steve took another desperate suck of his cigarette.

'Cancer will kill you,' Lester said as he stood behind Pinder.

Steve ignored him and stared up at Pinder. 'I can't keep going on like this. I'll have a stroke.'

'Look, you just need to tell us what they're up to. No one will find out.'

'I already said, didn't I? They're getting that weirdo, Redrobe to move the stuff.'

'Just him?' Pinder said, finding it hard to

believe.

'Yeah. They reckon it's best if he takes a bit at a time. Back and forth. Think about it, it's pretty smart. You'd expect a car or van with a load of drugs…'

'When though?'

Steve raised his podgy shoulders. 'I don't know. They don't tell me stuff like that. *Get lost, Steve*, they say when they start talking business…'

'This week? Next week?'

'This week, I reckon. They've been talking more and more and I get the feeling… yeah, I reckon this week.'

Pinder sighed. 'This week? That makes life more difficult.'

'Why?' Lester asked.

'Well, Tuesday is the start of the conference…' Pinder stopped talking, his mind suddenly on fire. He turned to face Lester. 'The conference. That's it. Tuesday and Wednesday all the bigwigs are coming to Cornwall for the political conference, aren't they? Loads of uniforms are heading down there, leaving Plymouth thin on the ground!'

Lester smiled. 'The clever sods. That's when they're planning on moving the stuff. Cheeky bastards. Right, we'd better warn…'

Pinder grabbed his arm as he was about to turn away. Lester stared down at Pinder's hand, then up at his face, frowning.

'What?'

Pinder pushed him across the room, lowering his voice. 'Listen, Paul... this is a delicate operation...'

'I know. But we've got the Dark Horses right where we want them. Do you know how long we've been after them? I've been liaising with DI Anna Jones on this...'

'I know, but there's more at stake...' Pinder stopped talking, pausing, knowing he had to be careful what he said.

'What's at stake? Come on, Kev, what's this all about? When you came to me asking me about the Dark Horses and what intel I had on them, I thought, fine, I get it, they've probably been dealing and causing trouble on his local community patch... but it's not that, is it?'

Pinder shook his head. 'No. I need you to trust me.'

Lester straightened up. 'Right. OK. Spill the beans.'

'I can't. Look, you'll have your eyes on the prize... Redrobe carrying the drugs back and forth. You see where he takes them and then you pounce... we just need a word with him. He'll be in a tight spot and we hope he'll give us someone...'

'Who?'

'I can't say. But believe me, mate, this is vital. Please, trust me.'

Lester stared at him, the sums going on in

his head. 'You want a word with him after we nick him? That's all? And we get the bust?'

Pinder nodded. 'Just a word. A few minutes with him.'

Lester let out a breath and put out his hand. 'It's a deal. Just don't fuck me over.'

Former Detective Inspector King appeared in the untidy street right on cue, carrying a couple of heavy-looking carrier bags stuffed with food. He took them to his door, put them down, and then struggled to unlock his door. In the meantime, Moone and Butler climbed out and approached his house.

'Having a party, Gary?' Butler asked, making the old man flinch and grab his chest.

'Jesus, fuck...' he said, shaking his head. 'You nearly gave an old man a coronary. What do you pair want now?'

'Can we come in?' Moone asked, smiling, doing a pretty good job of hiding his annoyance and suspicions.

King looked between them. 'I suppose so. How's the case going? Any closer? Na, 'course you're not. Me and my team couldn't solve it, so you lot aren't...'

Moone and Butler followed him into the house as the old man put the shopping in the kitchen. They went into the living room and waited, stood up, both with their arms folded, looking at each other.

When King came in, he stopped dead and examined them carefully. 'What's happened? Something's happened, hasn't it?'

'We've been to see Brendan Mitchell,' Butler said. 'Your old colleague.'

Darkness fell over King's face as he sat down in his armchair and reached for a pack of cigarettes that was on the coffee table. He lit one and took a lungful. 'I know who he is, love. I ain't daft. You don't want to believe half of what comes out of his mouth.'

'Why not?' Moone asked and sat down on the sofa.

King blew out some smoke and stared at Moone. 'See any cans lying around the house?'

'He likes a drink.' Moone nodded.

'He was always like that. That's what finished his career. He talks out of his arse.'

'He says you had your boy helping on the case,' Butler said.

King stared up at her, his mouth falling open, a plume of smoke escaping his lips. 'He what? Oh, fuck me. See, I told you, only lies come out of his mouth. He's just bitter that he got kicked off the team.'

'So, you didn't have your son helping?' Moone asked.

'Course not.' King sat back, taking another puff. 'What sort of amateur do you take me for?'

'Tell us about the cloth again,' Butler said.

'The cloth?' King nodded, then laughed. 'I see. Right, yeah, Brendan, the moron was always harping on 'bout that dishcloth being over her face. But you look at the crime scene photos. It wasn't.'

'What if someone moved it?' Butler asked. 'What if she murdered by was someone who knew her?'

'We believe Nick Dann was having an affair with Judy Ludlow,' Moone said.

'Nick Dann?' King said and let out a breath full of smoke. 'The up-and-coming businessman? Yeah, I remember hearing rumours. I sent some of our lads to talk to him, but he had an alibi if I remember right.'

'Who did you send?' Butler asked. 'Brendan Mitchell?'

King looked at her suspiciously. 'Yeah, I think I did. Why? What's he said?'

'Nothing,' Moone said. 'When we talked to Mitchell, he hinted at the fact that you might have broken some rules back then.'

King stared at Moone, taking a lungful. 'Like I said, he's full of it. Full of booze.'

'Anything involving your son we should know about?' Butler asked.

'No. Leave my son out of it.'

'Where is he?' Moone asked. 'We might need to contact him.'

'I don't know. Haven't seen him for ages. Heard he got married, but that's the last I heard. Good luck finding him.'

Moone stood up. 'If you happen to find out where your son is now, let us know.'

King stood up with a heavy grunt. 'Michael's probably miles from here. Well, I hope he is. So, let me get this right. You're thinking this Nick Dann was seeing Ludlow, the first victim, and he beat and strangled her to death? Why?'

'We can't discuss that with you,' Butler said as they walked away.

King followed them to the door. 'And what? He did Teresa Burrows too? Why?'

'Sorry,' Moone said, opening the door and looking back at King. 'Just let us know if you remember where Michael is.'

'I might.' King watched them leave, and stood in the doorway, smoking.

They went back to the car and sat in silence for a moment.

'Well, he was telling fibs,' Butler said, breaking the silence.

'Yep, he was,' Moone said and looked at her. 'We need to find his son.'

'What do we do about Nick Dann? If he did murder Ludlow, we can't let him get away with it. You and I both know the top brass will try and pile it on the handyman's kill list and he'll get to walk away, with no stains on his character.'

'I know. But we've got no proof at

the moment. We need to find something concrete...' Moone stopped talking as his phone rang in his jacket pocket. He took it out and saw Inspector Pinder was calling.

'Hello, Kevin,' he said, putting on a happier tone than he felt. 'What's new?'

'Tuesday or Wednesday this week,' Kev said.

'Tuesday or Wednesday for what?'

'Your sex change operation.' Pinder laughed. 'No, seriously though, that's when they're planning on moving the stuff.'

'Why then?'

'I'll explain when I come see you at the station in half an hour.'

Moone and Butler slipped into the small office on the top floor that wasn't being used for much except storing some tables, chairs and stationery. Pinder was already there, sitting at a desk and staring down at his phone, a coffee at his side. He looked up, then past them, as if he expected someone to be entering with them. Seeming satisfied, he got up and picked up his coffee.

'So, Tuesday or Wednesday?' Moone asked and rested his back on the wall, while Butler grabbed an office chair and sat down. 'Tomorrow's Tuesday'

'You're on fire, Moone,' Butler said and sighed.

Pinder nodded. 'Guess how I know?'

Moone exchanged a perplexed look with Butler then shrugged. 'I don't know. You've got psychic powers?'

Pinder laughed. 'I wish. No, do you know what's happening tomorrow and Wednesday?'

Butler let out a sigh that turned into a dry laugh. 'The bloody political conference thing.'

'That's right,' Pinder said, pointing at her. 'Tomorrow morning, all the posh sods and their secretaries and PAs and all that lot come rushing down here for their political piss-up.'

Moone nodded. 'I don't think they get pissed, but I get it. Loads of our people go down there to protect them, leaving us thin on the ground. It's the perfect time to move a stash of drugs.'

'A lot less bloody risky,' Butler said. 'Clever. One guess who came up with that idea.'

'Only she could,' Moone said. 'So, when do we swoop?'

'I'd say later in the first day,' Pinder said. 'Let them think things are running smoothly, then bang, we grab him.'

Moone smiled and looked at Butler. 'She thinks she's being clever, but she's just played right into our hands.'

But Butler pulled a face that said she wasn't convinced. 'I don't know. She's always a few moves ahead. Always expect the unexpected with that one.'

'Don't worry,' Moone said, rubbing his hands. 'She or her brother won't know we're coming.'

As soon as he stepped into the old house, he could smell the old man, could smell the foul stench of him, the acrid scent of his cigarettes. He was always there lately, and he had told him to stay away in fear that his wife might make an impromptu visit and find him living there. But he wouldn't leave. He couldn't force him out, because the old man knew too much, had too much hold over him.

He walked into the back room where all the computers were and found the old man still wearing the same clothes, smoking the same spitty little roll-ups. He was sitting in the office chair, legs crossed, staring back at him.

'You look like shit, bey,' the old man said and gave a gravel-filled laugh that turned into a deep cough.

'I think she suspects,' he said and shut the door behind him.

'Who?'

'My wife. The police have given a press conference and they've got a sketch of me and they've got a photo of the van.'

'It doesn't look anything like you,' the old man said, not seeming to have a care in the world. 'You got rid of that van, didn't you?'

'Yeah. Dumped it. Burned it.'

'There you go, bey. Nothing tying it to you, then. Nothing to worry about.'

'What about my wife?'

The old man tapped his ash on the floor. 'You know what I reckon about that little problem.'

'I can't… I couldn't do that.'

'Well, then, you'd better work fast. You haven't got long until the tides roll back. You better make it count.'

'There's no time.'

The old man sighed, shaking his head then faced him. 'There's plenty of time. You just have to act quickly. You've got a few days until the blood moon. That's the time to do it. Get on that machine of yours and pick out a few. Get their addresses, make a list, bey, and they can be the last.'

He looked down at his hands. 'Maybe…'

'What?'

He looked up. 'Maybe this is the time to stop.'

The old man gave another rattling laugh. 'Stop? You can never stop, bey. You know that.'

'I stopped once before. Twenty years without doing any of it…'

The old man stood up and stepped closer, bringing that vomit-inducing stench with him. 'You can't stop. You never stopped. Is that what you think? That you put it all to bed for twenty years? You little prick. You stupid fool.'

'I did...'

'Remember when you worked up in Scotland? On the oil rigs? What do you think you did when you were on leave? And in Manchester when you were labouring? There are plenty of unsolved murders all over the country, lad. You've been real busy, even if you didn't realise it.'

He shook his head, stepping back, the whole room seeming to jerk sideways, his heart thundering in his chest. 'No, I was... I was good. I behaved myself.'

'Did you? Did you really?'

'You?' He lifted his trembling hand, pointing at the old man, who smiled at him, grinning. 'You. It was you. Not me. It was you, you've been following me and you've been doing them! Making it look like it was me!'

The old man laughed. 'Oh, you going to cry? Go crying to your mummy 'cause a little bitch didn't want to go out with you?'

'What?'

'Her, the bitch. That's where it all started. Did you really think she'd go out with you?'

'Why are you saying that?' He fought back the tears as he stood frozen, back in that school hall, his heart pounding with fury.

'You need to man up, bey. Grow some balls. Finish what we started.'

'It's what you started. You've been trying to make me look bad, doing all those others...'

'Me? Making you look bad? What does it matter now? It's you and me, bey. You go down, I go down. You've still got time to finish this game. There's still time to punish them.'

He nodded, his mind clearing, his fury rising at the thought of any of the bitches getting away with it.

'So, what's it to be?' the old man asked, taking another drag of his roll-up.

'I'll finish it. On the blood moon. I'll do as many as I can.'

'Good boy. Good boy.'

CHAPTER 29

It was late into the day and Moone was staring at the whiteboard, then looking down at the murder book he held in his hand, trying to absorb it all, as if the crimes might be solved by osmosis. He let out a laugh, a hollow laugh directed at himself and his ridiculous effort to try and make sense of something that made no sense; it was just some mentally deranged person with a fixation with the name Sarah. They had looked for similar crimes far and wide involving victims called Sarah, or some kind of Sarah link. He had to have started somewhere, something ignited his rampage, some moment in time when everything became broken.

Abuse. Bullying. All manner of mental and physical torture could force a child, then a young adult, off onto a dark path. He had seen it all before. *Who was Sarah?*

'Who's Sarah?' he said out loud.

It was Molly who looked up from her desk;

he could see her out of the corner of his eye.

'Sorry, boss?' Molly asked.

He looked at her. 'Who is this Sarah he's so fixated on?'

'Ex-girlfriend? Wife? Could be anyone. We've looked at all kinds of similar cases...'

'Eason mentioned this childhood rage... how he probably never released it and now he carries it around.'

Molly came over and joined him at the board. 'But he managed to stop all that time. He must have some kind of control over it.'

Something stirred in Moone's seemingly decaying brain. 'Did he? What if he didn't?'

'We haven't found anything...'

'Similar? What if it isn't? What if his mind is so messed up, he doesn't even know he's been carrying on all this time? What if there are other crimes he's committed, but they're different, not like what he does to these... Sarahs?'

Molly gave a heavy sigh. 'Then what are we looking for?'

'Unsolved crimes. Probably women. What if he's moved around the country? Fred West did, and they reckon he probably killed loads more.'

'I'll start looking,' she said and walked away.

He nodded, absently, his mind trying to get a grip on the killer, imagining all those years ago, and the Sarah who must have seriously fucked with his head.

Ex-girlfriend? No, it didn't sit right. He would have been an angry young man, probably incapable of a relationship back then. What if he had some kind of crush on a girl called Sarah? He turned to Molly. 'Definitely not any unsolved murders of girls called Sarah?'

'No,' she said as she sat at her desk. 'No murders. There was a missing young girl called Sarah...'

Moone froze, the icy hand creeping up his spine. 'When was this?'

'About twenty-five years ago. Young girl went missing after school. Never came home. She was thirteen.'

'What school was this?' Moone walked over.

'That's the thing, I ruled it out. It was in London. South London.'

Moone closed his eyes for a moment, once again trying to make sense of it. 'London? Did he used to live in London?'

'Who used to live in London?' Butler asked, entering the incident room. 'Only deviant I know from London, is you, Peter Moone.'

'Our killer.' Moone turned to Butler. 'The only slightly similar case we've found is a girl called Sarah who went missing nearly twenty-five years ago. In South London.'

Butler sat at her desk. 'Probably no connection, but we'd better check it out.'

'Can you, Molly?' Moone asked her. 'See if any of our few suspects went there and then moved here?'

'OK, will do, but I suspect there'll be a lot to get through. It's a big school by the looks, so might take a little while.'

Moone looked over at Harding's desk and saw him staring off into space, looking pretty glum. 'Harding? Everything all right?'

The DC didn't seem to register him, so Moone went over and knocked on his desk, snapping Harding out of his dream.

'Sorry, boss,' Harding said, flinching. 'Did you need something?'

'You OK?'

Harding nodded and smiled, but there was something in it that didn't convince Moone, even when he said, 'Yeah, boss. Top of the world.'

'Right, OK, could you help Molly check the records of a school in South London against our suspects? Keep an eye out for anything unusual, obviously.'

'Will do, boss,' he said and headed over to Molly's desk.

Moone looked at Butler as he headed to his desk. 'Any news on the DNA from the roll-up?'

'No. But it's going to take a while.' She signalled for him to come over, her eyes looking furtively round the room.

Moone walked over and lowered his voice. 'What is it?'

'I hear that they've started an official missing persons case on Rivers,' Butler whispered. 'We need to do something with her phone and fast.'

He let out a harsh breath. 'We can't. It's too risky. Anyway, we still don't know where Carthew's living. Pinder's had people on her and the Dark Horses, but she always manages to shake them off.'

'Then we try and slip it into her car.' Butler raised her eyebrows. 'But she's always changing her work car, and we never see her own car. She's not like us...' Butler stopped talking and seemed to stare off into space.

'You all right?' Moone waved a hand in front of her face. 'Earth calling Butler.'

She looked at him, her eyes now ignited by something. 'Our bloody car. We always use the same work cars. Always.'

'Because we know their condition and they never let us down,' Moone said, frowning.

'Yeah, but she knows that, doesn't she?'

'Carthew?' Then the penny dropped into his brain with a crash. 'She could've put some tracker on our car? Is that what you're thinking?'

Butler looked away, laughing a little. 'That bitch. That's how she knew where we were when Parry took his own life. She didn't have any evidence, because she wasn't there, she just put some bug on our bloody car.'

'Really?'

Butler spun round and stormed towards the doors, so Moone hurried after her and tried to catch up with her in the stairwell. She was moving too quickly, taking a couple of steps at a time until they reached the door to the car park. Moone slowed down, letting her go ahead, not convinced by her theory, although it would make sense in the grand scheme of things. By the time he reached their usual car, the dark blue Peugeot, Butler was crouched down, her hand reaching underneath the car and the wheel arches.

Then she stopped moving and looked at him, shaking her head. She stood up and turned to him, holding out a tiny black device that had a red light flashing on it. 'Bingo. That crafty bitch.'

Moone stared at it for a moment, his eyes not really believing what he was looking at, and suddenly filled with the urge for a smoke.

'Jesus.'

'Is that all you can say?' Butler asked. 'Bet we won't find her prints on this?'

'Doubtful. And how do we check anyway? Who do we ask to examine it and what do we say when they ask where it came from?'

Butler shook her head. 'At least she won't

be able to keep tabs on us now. Gives us a slight advantage.'

'Right then. Let's get back to work.'

'But we can't let her get away with this.' Butler held out the tracker.

'Like I said before, we've just got to nick Redrobe, and the rest will fall into place. I can feel it.'

Butler huffed as she started walking back to the entrance. 'I hope you're bleeding right? By the way, someone called Terry left a message here for you. Sounded like another cockney. Who's Terry?'

'An old friend staying at mine,' Moone said as they went inside and back up the stairs.

'You've got friends?'

'Very funny. I do have a past.'

Footsteps echoed from above, hurrying steps coming down towards them. Molly appeared, a little red-faced.

'I've just taken a report of a sighting of the white van we've been after,' Molly said, a little out of breath.

'Where?' Moone asked.

'Apparently, they saw it parked near the shops and the allotments at Peverell Park Road.'

'Did they leave a name or number?' Moone asked.

'Yeah, Allen Kelvin,' Molly said. 'He said he's at the allotments now.'

Allen Kelvin was a red-cheeked, chubby man in his late fifties with a head of wiry grey hair, which was the way he had pretty much described himself to Molly, she had said to Moone in a text. The man in question was talking to an elderly lady who had a small furry white dog on a lead, both of them stood close to the entrance to the allotments, opposite the large and colourful mural that Moone had noticed on the few occasions he had visited Pounds Park. The sun had emerged from the clouds and sent down warmth to the back of his neck as he and Butler approached the gates.

'See you tomorrow, Lynda,' the man said to the woman with the dog as she headed towards the park.

Moone took out his ID and showed it to the man he suspected as being Kelvin, and said, 'DCI Peter Moone. This is DI Mandy Butler. You reported the sighting of the white van we're looking for?'

Kelvin scratched at his wiry hair as he solemnly examined Moone's ID. 'I did, that's right. Been involved in that murder, ain't it?'

'Possibly,' Moone said and put away his ID. 'Where did you see it?'

Kelvin pointed back the way they had just come, towards Peverell Park Road. 'Parked just up there. I saw it a handful of times. Shouldn't be parked there really. That's why I took note of the registration number. It's the one you've been looking for.'

'When was this?' Butler asked.

'A few weeks back,' Kelvin said, seeming to mull it over. 'Ain't seen it lately.'

'Did you see the driver?' Moone asked.

'Na, didn't see them,' Kelvin said and laughed. 'I say them. That's what it is these days, ain't it? They, them, not she or he. I can't keep up.'

'Well, I'm definitely a she,' Butler said with a huff. 'Least I was the last time I looked. Anyway, have you seen anyone else about, or seen anything strange?'

Kelvin laughed again, his face reddening even more. 'Oh, love, I see plenty of strange stuff round here. Couples come here trying to get some alone time, if you know what I mean?'

'We do,' Moone said. 'Anyone else?'

Kelvin squinted, then looked through the gated entrance of the allotments. 'You know what, there has been a new fella about, but I haven't seen him for a few days. Maybe a week. He's been in and out of old Phil's shed. Phil died a year ago, bless him. I asked the fella if he was related to Phil and he mumbled something about family, so I left him to it. I probably should have said something to someone.'

'What did he look like?' Butler said, fishing out her phone, and Moone guessed she was bringing up the sketch of their suspect.

Kelvin shrugged. 'Don't rightly know, love. He was wearing a baseball cap and had a face mask on. Some of the young people still wear 'em, like they're still afraid of catching the Covid. I don't bother.'

'So, you didn't get a good look?' Butler held up the sketch.

Kelvin leant in, staring at it. 'Could've been him. Not sure. You think this murderer's been here, do you?'

'We can't comment on that,' Butler said and gestured to the gate. 'Can you let us in to take a look?'

'I suppose,' he said, taking out a chain loaded with keys. He found the right one and then opened the gate for them. 'Long as no one complains.'

'They won't,' Butler said over her shoulder as she hurried in. 'Which shed?'

'It's the green one, over there,' Kelvin pointed to an old weather-beaten shed and Butler made a beeline for it.

'Thanks, we won't be long,' Moone said.

By the time he caught up with her, Butler was holding a large padlock in her hands and looking over the door of the shed. Nearby a few chickens clucked and pecked at the ground in a fenced-off compound.

'Locked,' Moone said. 'And we haven't got a warrant.'

Butler turned and looked past him. 'Is

Kelvin watching?'

Moone looked around but couldn't see their witness. 'Can't even see him.'

When he looked back, Butler was holding a small black case, about the size of one that glasses come in. She opened it and took out a couple of small tools.

'What's that?' he asked, a little worried that he already knew the answer.

'What does it look like, moron?' She sighed and started picking the lock.

'We can't do this.' Moone looked back to see if their witness was witnessing another crime. 'This is an illegal search. We don't have a warrant or reasonable suspicion.'

'No, we don't. But if he is using this shed, then it's not going to be rented or whatever in his name, is it? He's using some dead old fella's shed, so he's got deniability. Whatever we find, we wouldn't be able to use in court anyway.'

Moone sighed, still keeping dog as he heard the click of the lock opening. He looked at Butler again in time to see her opening the shed door that squeaked painfully loudly.

'Come on, don't faff,' she said and pulled him inside and shut the door.

Moone blinked when a strip light flickered on above him, the musty smell of damp and peat filling his nostrils. Tools lined the walls, all neat and well-used. There was a small table and garden chair too.

'Look at this.' Butler was crouching down opposite a small electronic safe. 'What's the betting he keeps all his weird little bits in here?'

Moone went over. 'Doesn't matter. We can't use any of it. Anyway, that could've been the old man's.'

'An old man with an electronic safe in his shed? Not very likely. No, this is his.' Butler straightened up, took out some gloves and snapped them on. Moone watched her examine some magazines that lay on a nearby dusty shelf. On top, there was a calendar that she picked up and started to look through.

'That's interesting,' Butler said.

'What is?'

'This calendar's got days marked off, but only on this month. Hang on, yeah, these are the days of the murders...'

'Where?' Moone looked over her shoulder and saw what she meant. His eyes travelled down. 'There's one more day marked off. Saturday. Jesus...'

'Blood moon?' Butler looked at him. 'What's that when it's at home?'

'I think I read about that,' Moone said. 'It's something to do with a lunar eclipse, and the sun's rays hitting the moon, making it appear blood red. Some weirdos think it brings strong energy, a good time to cast spells and such.'

'And howl at the moon?' Butler said.

'I think that's a full moon.'

'This guy's a psycho, an angry one at that. I'm betting he's waiting for the fabled Blood Moon energy so he can strike again. So, what's he got planned for the blood moon, Moone?'

'I don't know. But we can't use this.'

Butler took out her phone and took a snap of the marked calendar page before placing it back where she found it. 'No, but we can pretend we're smarter than we are. All the murders so far, judging by that calendar, have been on days where the phases of the moon affect the earth, all building towards this blood moon thing... all we have to say is, we put two and two together.'

Moone sighed. 'And got twenty-six? OK, you can be the one who comes up with the great idea, then. Leave me out of it. Let's go.'

Moone walked out into the fresh air, listening to the chickens clucking and watching them pecking at the ground, wondering why he couldn't have been born a chicken, or even a dog, a dumb animal that didn't have to worry about killers and rules and regulations. Then he looked at Butler, another of God's so-called creatures that disregarded the rule book. But he liked that about her, liked that she didn't take any nonsense from anyone, among the many other things he liked about her. Or was it more than liked?

'What?' She caught his eye. 'Why're you looking so weird at me?'

He noticed her blush a little. 'Nothing. Just thinking about how we're going to present all this.'

She smiled awkwardly, then locked the padlock and walked past him, heading for the gate. 'Leave it to me, cockney boy.'

'Saturday's the day, bey,' the old man said as he was sitting at the desk in front of the computer monitors, still smoking.

He ignored him for a moment and put the larger of his rucksacks on the floor and opened it. It smelled musty inside. It had been stored in a cupboard for who knows how long. It didn't matter, nothing else mattered any more. He looked at the table where he had laid out his tools and the kitchen knives. His hands trembled as he stepped closer to them, while his knees shook, threatening to fail him.

'Don't go all weak on me now, bey.'

'I'm not.' He pulled on a glove, picked up the claw hammer and held it in front of his eyes. He closed them, feeling the weight of it in his grip.

'You'll do some damage with that, all right.' The old man laughed, clouds of grey smoke escaping his repugnant mouth.

He looked away from him and placed the hammer into the rucksack, then went back to the table and stared at the knives, his hand shaking as he reached out for one of the larger ones.

'You sure 'bout that, bey?' the old man asked and came over. 'That's quite a change. You never stabbed no one before, have you?'

He shrugged.

'Na, you never have. Stabbing's a different matter, my lad. Beatings is one thing, but stabbing, using knives, is another. You got the stomach for it?'

He shrugged again but picked up the knife and put it in the bag.

'I suppose we'll find out in a few days, eh, bey?' The old man took another drag, then looked down at his roll-up. He laughed, then held it out to him. 'You want a smoke, lad? Settle your nerves?'

He shook his head.

'What's wrong? Wife got your tongue and your balls?'

His head swung round to the smiling old man, his fist drawing back as he trembled all over. The old man didn't move, just kept smiling as he took another drag on his fag.

'There he is,' he said. 'The same old angry little boy I met all those years ago. He can do it, that little fucker can do all this. You wait and see.'

There was the sound of a key in the lock, the door opening. 'Shit.'

'Looks like the missus has made a surprise visit,' the old man laughed. 'Better hide that bag.'

He picked up the bag and hid it behind the computer desk, then hurried out of the room and shut the door behind him. When he turned, she was there, halfway down the dusty hallway, staring at him, looking pale.

'What have you been doing?' she asked, her voice quiet, not as harsh as it usually was.

'Just… you know, working on some quotes.' He tried to smile, but it crumbled. 'What are you…'

'That's not what I meant.' It was only then he realised she had been holding one hand behind her back. She brought it out and clenched in her fist was a copy of the Evening Herald.

'What's that for?' he asked, his heart pounding.

'It's you, isn't it?'

'What's me?'

She knows. Don't be stupid, she knows.

'The man in the paper.' She unfolded it and showed him the photo fit. 'This is you. At first, I thought, no it can't be. He couldn't… but the more I thought about it…'

'You know me, you know I wouldn't…'

'I know you. That's right.' She nodded, tears in her eyes. 'I know you. I've seen it. I tried to pretend it wasn't there, this… I can't even say what it is…'

She'll go to the police. You have to stop her.

'What're you going to do?' He stepped closer to her. She moved back towards the door.

'See, you're not even bothering to deny it. You just want to know if I'm going to go to the police.'

'Are you?' He took another step.

'What else am I supposed to do?' Tears poured out of her eyes, her body shuddering.

You can't let her go to the police. You have to stop her.

'No.'

She stared at him, wiping her eyes with the back of her hand. 'What do you mean, no?'

'You can't go to the police.'

'I have to. These things you've done…'

'I couldn't help it. I tried not to. I really tried. You've got to listen to me, I…'

'No! I don't want to listen to you! What is our little girl going to think? Our beautiful little girl!'

She swung round and made for the door.

'You can't let her go, bey,' the old man appeared in the doorway. 'You know you can't.'

As he ran after her, he heard a deep growl, echoing everywhere, seeming to come from all around. No, it was him, a growl coming from deep within that almost became a scream as he wrenched out his hand and grasped hold of her hair. He yanked her backwards and she fell to the floor, kicking and screaming as he dragged her down the hallway and into the kitchen. Her fingernails dug into his hand, her mouth trying to bite at his skin until he dropped her. She immediately flipped herself over and scrabbled to get to her feet.

'She's a fighter, bey,' the old man said, laughing.

He grabbed her shoulder and swung her round, then hurled his fist into her jaw. Her head and hair snapped sideways, and everything seemed to go into slow motion as she fell, millimetre by millimetre until she hit the lino floor. He stood over her, his fist still clenched, panting.

'That was quite a punch,' the old man said, looking down at her. 'No better than she deserved though. Now, looks like she's still breathing. So, you'd better finish her off or tie her up. What's it to be, bey?'

CHAPTER 30

Moone stifled a yawn, then opened up his takeaway coffee and looked at the team that he had gathered together that morning. They were noisily moving chairs closer to the whiteboard, where he stood waiting. Butler was standing by her desk, her face blank, not looking one bit guilty about what they were going to lie about. They had cut corners again and bent the rules one more time, but it didn't seem to bother her, while his stomach tied itself in knots. He didn't want to be like Carthew, didn't want to stoop to her level, but then he recalled someone once saying that you have to be more ruthless than your enemy if you stand a chance of winning. But that wasn't him.

Then his mind jumped to Pinder and the fact that he now had eyes on Lloyd Redrobe, preparing to give them the heads up when he started transporting the drugs. It was the only bit of light in an otherwise stormy and grey day, the hope that they might soon have something on Carthew. He couldn't help but look over to the corner desk where Carthew was sitting, unusually present for once. She caught his eye and smiled. He looked away. He prayed to whoever might listen, that she would soon be out of their hair.

Moone was about to step forward and clap his hands together, to quieten the chatting team, when Butler did it before him.

'Listen up,' she said and flashed a strange look at him. 'We've got some news. We believe we know something about our handyman's timeline...'

Eyes widened and there was more positive and excited chatter before Butler held up her hands and continued.

'Last night, DCI Moone and myself were looking over the dates, trying to figure out what his ultimate goal is. Then we noticed something...'

Butler turned and pointed to a copy of a map that illustrated the upcoming moon phases. 'If you look at these, you'll see that each of the murders has occurred on a particular phase of the moon, leading up to this one...'

'The blood moon,' Carthew said aloud.

Everyone looked at her, including Butler who was now scowling.

'You had figured this out?' Butler asked her, the grit clear in her voice.

Carthew stood up and came around so she could see the board. 'No, of course not. But I heard something about the blood moon or super blue moon, they call it. The tides change direction and all sorts. Some people believe the moon dictates the state of people's minds, and that mad people commit acts of violence in relation to the moon. Moon, lunar, loony.'

'Yes, thank you, Carthew,' Moone said. 'Anyway, we believe that our handyman is probably planning some kind of big event on this blood moon. So we need to be prepared...'

'But we don't know where or when he'll strike,' Harding chipped in.

'No, we don't,' Moone agreed, 'so, we have to be ready this weekend. We're going to have response teams ready to speed to any reports of... well, anything violent.'

'He could have his targets already picked out,' Carthew said. 'He's obsessed with the name Sarah... so, perhaps we need to concentrate...'

'Yes, thank you, Carthew,' Butler said. 'We'll give high priority to any incidents that have any connection to that name, but that's going to be touch and go. The key here is to protect lives. We're going to issue a warning before the weekend for women to not let anyone into their homes that they don't know, especially workmen.'

'But how are we going to catch him?'

Carthew asked, staring, her eyebrows raised.

Moone cleared his throat and stepped forward. 'We possibly have his DNA, and we're still waiting for that to come back, and in the meantime, we're going through the employees or students or anyone who has a connection to a school in South London, where a young girl called Sarah disappeared almost twenty-five years ago. She was never found and presumed dead. Basically, we're looking at any crimes or murders linked...'

'So, the DNA is our only real lead?' Carthew asked, eyebrows still raised. 'Let's hope it's our killer's. But it won't be back before Saturday when he's probably going to kill again on a bigger scale.'

Butler huffed. 'Thank you for stating the bloody obvious, Detective Sergeant. Right, we've got actions for you all. Most of which is visiting women called Sarah in the same geographical area that he's already struck in. The chances are he lives in that area or has links to it. So, visit these women and ask them the questions we've put down for you and warn them to stay home and not to open the door to anyone this weekend. Right, get to work.'

'Carthew!' Moone called, the irritation he felt for her now digging into his back muscles. 'A word.'

She smiled as she came over, folding her arms over her chest.

'Have I got any special duties?' she asked.

'No, you don't,' Butler growled, then lowered her voice. 'It's CCTV duty for you and don't go swanning off. Oh, and by the way, we know how you've been keeping tabs on us.'

She smiled brighter. 'I don't know what you mean.'

'Yes, you do.' Butler pointed a finger at her and Moone saw it trembling.

Carthew stepped closer. 'Well, it's a good job I do keep an eye on things. Like your boyfriend here, having a date with Dr Jenkins. Although it was cut short when another victim turned up. Anyway, I'd better go and do my duties.'

Butler kept staring at where she had been, her face growing redder by the second.

Moone's stomach took a nosedive. 'She wanted me to go with her to a...'

Butler held up a hand. 'I don't want to know. What you do or who you date is none of my business. I hope you're very happy together.'

'We're not...'

Butler walked away and sat at her desk, her eyes fixed on the screen as she started to work, and all he could do was stare at her, knowing a chasm had just opened up between them.

Her head jerked up for a moment, then fell

again as she moaned through the tape on her mouth. He let out a sigh of relief as he realised she wasn't dead. He had tied her to a kitchen chair using some spare cables from some of the computers he'd collected, then strapped her hands together with cable ties. He shook his head, tears coming to his eyes. How had it come to this?

'It was always going to happen, bey,' the old man said, sitting at the kitchen table, watching with his usual smirk, a cigarette in his mouth as always. 'If that makes you feel any better.'

'It doesn't,' he said, quietly and then turned and stared at the old man, the stinking, unwashed old man. He found himself lurching towards him, jabbing a finger at him as he shouted, *'This is your fault. If you hadn't turned up.'*

The old man laughed, plumes of grey-blue smoke escaping his dark mouth. 'Oh, this is me, is it, bey? I don't think so. Without me, where would you be?'

He could only whimper, shaking his head, flashes of everything he had done over the years exploding into his brain until it hurt to think.

'You'd be in prison if it wasn't for me.' The old man pointed at his wife. 'That bitch needs to go.'

'No! I can't! I can't.'

The old man stood up. 'Why not? What's another bitch to add to the list?'

'I have a daughter.'

The old man laughed again. 'Another fucking mistake. You just keep making them, don't you, bey?'

'It's you! You fucking... you're the... devil. It was you that did that to her! Sarah. You did that...'

'Which Sarah?'

'At school. You killed her. You started all this.'

'You're remembering it all wrong, lad. Your mind's all messed up.'

He looked away from the old man when his wife groaned and lifted her head, her eyelids fluttering open, then closing again. He watched her coming to, slowly realising where she was, the fog lifting until her eyes widened and took him in.

'I'll leave the pair of you to it,' the old man said and left the room.

There was the anger first from her, the wild fury, the muffled screams before she spouted more words, a little calmer.

He put a finger to his lips. 'Shhh. You have to be quiet.'

Then more harsh, muffled words, her eyes screaming out to him.

'I'm sorry, I really am, but I can't let you go. I need you to understand that this isn't me. Not the real me. I'm still the man you married…'

She mumbled more words, tears streaming down her face.

'It's OK,' he said, crouching down. 'I'm not going to hurt you. I just need you to stay calm for a while. I have stuff to do. Things I've got to see to.'

There were more tears, more muffled pleading. He stood up, smiling down at her, thinking it all through. He thought of his little girl. 'I'll look after her. Don't worry about our little girl. She'll be safe with me.'

Then came more angry and desperate words, and the tears pouring out of her eyes.

'I wouldn't hurt a hair on her head,' he said. 'I'm not a monster.'

He walked out of the kitchen, shut the door and pressed his back to it, breathing hard, his chest tight, his head pounding.

'Not a monster?' the old man said, standing smoking by the front door. 'Who're you trying to convince, bey? Her? You? Funny. Listen, we ain't got long. You've got to be ready for the blood moon.'

He looked down. 'I can't think about that right now. I've got to go and see my girl. I've got to be with her.'

He headed out the door, ignoring the old man's shouts for him to come back. He had to go to her and make sure she was OK before all the bad things happened.

The next couple of hours passed painfully slowly as Moone was sitting at his desk and trying to concentrate on the paperwork he had to do. Now and again, he would look up and see that Butler was also working away, keeping her hurt eyes on the screen. There had to be a way back into her good books, he thought, but he couldn't think of one, couldn't solve the puzzle of Butler, in the same way as he couldn't solve the mystery of why a man starts to beat and strangle women called Sarah. To pass the time, he contacted the forensic people to see if the DNA on the roll-up had come back yet. No luck yet. The blood moon was coming, and if they were right, then this weekend he was planning a blood bath. Moone covered his face and groaned quietly into his hands.

Then his phone rang and he saw Pinder was calling.

'How's it going?' Pinder asked when Moone answered the call.

'Terrible.'

'Why, what's happened now?'

'Nothing. Doesn't matter. Anyway, what's happening your end?'

'It's started. Me and my pal who works in the intelligence department have been watching Redrobe and he's started going to and fro. When do you want to launch the attack?'

Moone sat back and sighed, his eyes

jumping to Butler. 'Fuck it. Let's do it now. Let us know when he's picked up his latest consignment and text the address.'

'Will do. See you soon.'

Moone ended the call, his eyes immediately jumping to Butler, thinking all the time, trying to grasp for a way into her good books. He felt a dreadful feeling come over him, a kind of hopelessness, a sense that he had somehow lost what they once had. No, there had to be a way back. He stood up and slowly went over and stood close to her desk, trying to find the right words, some magical phrase that would let him back...

'What?' Butler glared at him for a second, then went back to her work, her face just as rigid and scarlet as it always was when she was upset with him. No, that wasn't true, he realised. There was something different this time, something deeper.

'Are you just going to stand there all bloody day?'

He flinched and cleared his throat. 'Pinder called. I think it's time to make a move on Redrobe.'

Butler snapped up out of her chair and started getting her stuff together. 'Right then, let's go and get the bugger.'

'I can do this if you don't...'

'Why wouldn't I? If it means putting an end to her, then that's all that matters. Anyway,

I'd better drive. You're a terrible driver.'

Nearly an hour later, Moone and Butler were parked in an unmarked car that wouldn't be recognised by Nair, Carthew or any of their merry people. They were parked opposite an industrial estate filled with mostly building merchants and kitchen places. There were also a few lock-ups, and that was where Lloyd Redrobe had taken his motorbike, to undoubtedly pick up his latest consignment. Butler had parked so they were out of Redrobe's line of sight, but so they could get a good view of him coming and going. Somewhere Pinder and his mate from the Intelligence department were holed up, watching and feeding back information.

Moone opened up his takeaway coffee and listened to the Airwaves radio lying in his lap that crackled with the clipped voices of officers communicating with each other. Moone looked over to Butler, the air between them as thick as butter. He delved around inside for the right words, but nothing came. He felt dry inside, just a husk. He couldn't help but feel he had lost her.

'Is he going to hurry up or what?' Butler said and gave a huff. 'I hope there's no other way out.'

Moone picked up the radio that was set to the same channel as Pinder's and said,

'Kilo-four, come in, Kilo-four. This is Echo-one. Over.'

'Kilo-four,' Pinder's crackly voice said. 'Go ahead.'

'Kilo-four, how sure are we there's no other way out, over?'

'Echo-one, there's no other way out. The suspect has to come your way, over.'

'Received. Understood. Over.' Moone put the radio down and picked up his coffee again. 'Don't worry, we'll get him, then we'll get her.'

'Do I look worried?' she snapped, still looking ahead.

'No.'

'No.' She sighed. 'You know, I've been thinking…'

'What?'

'I'm not sure it's such a good idea us working together…'

He turned to her, lost for words, his heart pounding. 'Why? Look, I'm sorry…'

Then the radio beeped and crackled to life again.

'Come in, Echo-one, over,' Pinder's voice said, but Moone was frozen.

'You'd better answer that.'

Moone picked up the radio, his hand trembling a little. 'Go ahead, Kilo-four.'

'Got eyes on Redrobe. He's loaded up and heading your way. Over.'

'Received. We're ready to go. Over and

out.' Moone put the radio down on the floor and pulled on his seatbelt as Butler started the engine. His mind swam, his heart still thumping, a strange kind of desperation gripping him. He needed to say something to her. Words rose in him, ready to blurt out, to admit how he really felt, but then the roar of a motorbike came in their direction and Redrobe streaked past, clad in leathers and a red crash helmet. The car moved, Butler keeping them back so as not to draw any suspicion. Moone tried to concentrate, to observe the motorbike as it headed towards traffic. The roads weren't too busy as they headed away from Plympton and back towards the city.

Slowly, the traffic moved in around them, swarming, making life more difficult. But Pinder had eyes on him too, and kept feeding back information. But by now they knew pretty much where he was heading. The destination was Devonport, where there were some storage units behind a blocks of flats. As Redrobe went on, it became clear that's where they were heading as he joined Albert Road and sped up a little. There were only a couple of cars ahead, but Butler was being cautious.

'We've got that bugger now,' Butler said. 'And that bitch.'

Then suddenly Redrobe was racing, speeding up, his engine roaring as he was coming up to the next junction.

'He's trying to get away from us!' Butler growled. 'He knows we're onto him. We need to take him.'

'I'm not sure,' Moone said, picking up the radio.

'Fuck that!' Butler put her foot down, the engine opening up, the gap between them and Redrobe's bike closing. 'Better put the siren on.'

Moone was about to reach for the siren after putting down the radio, his head lifting in time to see a dark shape roaring into view. His head spun to his right, past Butler as a large van came speeding out of a side street and hurtled past the front of them, then smashed into Redrobe's bike, taking him with them. Butler spun the wheel, trying to control the car as it was clipped and knocked around. The air was filled with the engine roaring, skidding, and Moone gripped the sides of the seat, his heart pounding, the blood smashing around in his skull. Then there was a bang, metal hitting metal, and a thud as they were both jerked sideways. His head spun to look at Butler but all he saw was her white hands still gripped to the wheel and her hair whipping towards him.

The world seemed to turn in slow motion as the airbags deployed, then deflated, Moone's head flying backwards as they turned over, rolling, flashes of tarmac and shards of glass flying through the air. Then it all stopped.

Moone's eyes flickered open and he saw the cracked glass in the windscreen. There was a whining in his ears and the thump of a pulse in his neck. He could feel himself being pulled downwards and realised the car was upside down. Something wet was travelling down his face.

Butler.

His head turned and he saw her, hanging upside down like him, her hair covering one side of her face. His heart jumped at the sight of the blood pouring down her pale cheek. Her eyes were closed.

'Hey!' he tried to call, but his voice broke up. 'Hey! Wake up! Butler! Can you hear me?! Butler! You've got to wake up!'

She didn't move. He looked around and saw movement, figures moving towards their car. There were sirens too, getting louder. He looked over at Butler again, feeling the tears reaching his eyes.

'Butler!' he shouted. 'Please. Wake up!'

There was nothing. No movement from her. He closed his eyes, then opened them again, trying to think straight. The sirens were louder and he thought he saw something red entering the street. The fire brigade was here.

'Butler,' he said, quieter. 'They'll get us out. Come on, Butler. Come on... Mandy. Mandy. Mand... I know you hate being called

Mand. You always say what you mean, how you're feeling but I never do. I'm too scared. So… here we are… Mandy. You and me. I should've told you this ages ago…'

He saw more movement, heavy boots upside down hitting the tarmac, voices calling.

He looked at her and saw her closed eyes. 'I love you, Mandy Butler.'

Then his head seemed to swim again as voices called to him from beyond the glass. The darkness edged in, and he let himself fall.

CHAPTER 31

There was a blurry kind of light hanging over his head and it seemed to be sharp somehow, piercing into his brain and making his whole skull throb. He blinked, trying to focus and bringing the blurry light into a shape, an actual object. There were sounds too, muffled at first, as if lots of people were talking through masks from miles away. It was kind of peaceful for a moment, just a brief flicker in time where his mind didn't rampage on.

Then the volume got turned up and the constant battle of voices and beeping machines filled his brain and made his head hurt even more. He looked around and saw he was in a curtained-off cubicle, and close by was a shape, a dark figure stood there and he flinched when he saw a face staring at him.

'It's all right, Pete,' Pinder said, looking concerned as he came towards the bed Moone was lying on. 'It's just me. How're you feeling?'

He was in a hospital. Probably Derriford. He looked through the gap in the curtain and saw the staff racing past and the corridor full of gurneys with patients on.

'Pete? Can you hear me? I'd better get someone.' Pinder went to turn round.

'Wait.' Moone sat up a little, his head throbbing with every movement. 'What happened?'

Pinder pulled up a chair and sat down. 'You don't remember the crash?'

A bolt of memory smashed into his brain, making him close his eyes. He saw the van hurtling past their car. He opened his eyes. 'Redrobe?'

Pinder shook his head. 'Dead on impact. He was... well, a mess.'

He saw her hanging upside down, the blood, another lightning bolt into his brain, panic making his chest tight. 'Butler!'

Pinder took a breath. 'She's still with us. She's in Intensive Care. She took the worst of it, but you know Butler, she's tough, stubborn... I think she'll be OK.'

Moone tried to move, but his body screamed out, his ribs and arms begging him to stay still. 'I need to see her...'

'Not at the moment. She's in good hands. She's not conscious they tell me. They're going to give her a CT so they can see what's going on in her head.'

Moone dropped his head, shaking it. 'She's got to be all right. She has to be. The last conversation we had... it wasn't good. I need to talk to her.'

Pinder patted his leg. 'You will. Don't worry.'

Moone looked at him, a terrible loneliness absorbing him. 'What if she's not OK? I don't know what I'd do without her.'

Pinder stared at him for a moment, then sat back. 'Oh, right. It's like that, is it?'

Moone nodded, and then another much darker thought came burrowing into his brain. 'Carthew.'

Pinder stared at him, his face losing any sign of mirth. 'You think this was her?'

'This is her taking out Redrobe. It was her or her bloody brother. Half-brother. A witness to all the bad things she's done lately. Her crimes. He had to go.'

'Her brother?' Pinder let out an exhausted breath.

Moone gave an empty laugh. 'I used to think... I don't know what I thought. Maybe I thought that I could beat her by adhering to the rules, to be somehow better than her. Be a good boy and beat her. But I can't, can I?'

Pinder shrugged. 'I don't know.'

'I used to work with this DCI. He was one of my closest friends, but he'd bend and break all the rules, he'd walk the line and sometimes do some pretty bad things to get the right result. DCI Jairus, he's called. I don't know where he is now, but it used to scare the hell out of me, terrify me to watch him doing all the wrong things for the right reasons. But I get it now. I really get it.'

'What does that mean?'

Moone looked at his hands, thinking. 'She's got to be stopped. I have to stop her.'

Pinder blew out the air from cheeks. 'How? She's always one step ahead.'

'The van. Who was driving the van?'

'Jason Harris. One of the Dark Horses, Nair's right-hand man. God knows how they talked him into doing that... money, I would guess. He's always up to his eyes in debt I hear. Gambling, bikes...'

'Is he dead?'

'No. Very much alive and in custody at Devonport. A doctor's coming to take a look at him, but his injuries are minor. He was caught doing a runner.'

Moone sat up, ignoring the pain that dug its steel claws into his back and sides.

Pinder pushed him gently backwards. 'I don't think you're going anywhere for a while. Anyway, Harris is a dead end.'

'Why?'

'Nair will send his expensive solicitor and he'll tell Harris to say No Comment to everything we ask. He'll go inside for manslaughter, maybe murder if we're lucky, but he knows if he dobs anyone in, then he's dead.'

Moone let his head fall back, feeling hopeless. Then he thought again, leaving the rule book out of it. He looked at Pinder. 'We can do this, but it's going to be dodgy.'

'How dodgy?'

'Very. So, Harris is at Devonport? Can we get him moved to Charles Cross tomorrow at some point?'

Pinder shrugged. 'Possibly. Why?'

'Get it arranged. We need to ask him some questions, massage a few necks.'

'I'll give a few hand shandies if I have to.' Pinder laughed, then lost his smile. 'That was a joke.'

'Right, you do that. And there's something else you can do. Have you got Butler's possessions?'

'Yeah.'

'Go to her flat. Search it. She'll have a phone hidden somewhere. A Galaxy Smartphone. We'll need it. Handle it with gloves.'

Pinder's expression had changed, taking on a look as if someone had started examining his prostate. 'A phone? What bloody phone?'

'I'll tell you later. Find it. We'll need it. Now, I need to get out of here.'

'Are we really going to take her down?' Pinder stood up.

Moone looked him in the eyes. 'Yes, we are.

Scout's honour.'

He stepped into the house and heard the TV and the kids' programme blaring out. He went into the front room and saw his daughter hunched over the coffee table, all her pens and crayons everywhere. Next to her, with a cup of tea in her hand, was his wife's cousin. She sat up and smiled awkwardly.

'I wasn't expecting you,' she said. 'Where is Sarah?'

Of course, his wife was called Sarah too, and he had found her one night. But it had been different, she had been different, and somehow the rage had left him.

But she's not different. She hates you like all the other Sarahs do.

His daughter sprung up from her drawing, breaking into a big smile. 'Daddy! Look what I'm drawing!'

She held up a piece of her artwork that he couldn't make head nor tail of. 'It's beautiful, my angel.'

'Sarah said she'd come back soon.' Her cousin got up, her eyes digging into him. Her family disliked him.

'I'm here now. You can go.'

'Where's Sarah?'

'She had some work meeting. Last minute thing.'

'Is Mummy coming home?' his daughter

asked.

'She is. Soon. She's just busy.'

'I'd better give her a ring.' Her cousin took out her phone and started moving towards the kitchen.

'Better text her. She's in some important, last-minute meeting,' he called out.

After a moment, he felt the vibration in his pocket and took out his wife's phone. He opened the text messages. There was one from her cousin.

'Where r u? He's here, being weird as always. R u OK? Xx'

He huffed, the fury bellowing in his chest. He clenched his fist, then took a few breaths and got ready to send a message back. He looked at his wife's sent messages, then copied her style.

'Sorry. Got caught up. Last minute meeting. Just ignore him. As long as Clare's OK. Let me know. Be back soon xx'

He quickly put the phone away and sat down next to Clare, watching her draw but not really seeing anything, his heart a thunderous storm of rage and hate. A voice in his head kept talking to him, whispering dark words.

Kill them. Kill all the bitches. Everything will be OK if the bitches are punished.

'Right, I'd better go.' The cousin came back in, then came over and kissed Clare's head. 'Right, gorgeous, I'll see you soon. Stay cute.

Don't grow up any more.'

'I'll try not to,' Clare sang.

'Bye,' the cousin said to him, the same old look of loathing in her eyes.

Get up and smash her skull in.

He smiled, gave a wave and listened to her tap her way to the front door and out of it. He let out a breath.

'Where's Mummy?' Clare looked up at him with her big brown eyes.

'She's... she's got a lot of work stuff on, darling. But she'll be home soon. It's just me and you for the moment. OK?'

She nodded and seemed to happily go back to drawing.

He sat back, his mind rampaging in every direction as always. He didn't have long and soon the blood moon would be here, and he had so much work to do.

There came a banging on the clubhouse door. Nair signalled for Steve to open it up. He knew who would be there already, he'd have to be thick, stupid like Jason to not know. The door opened and DS Carthew came strolling in and looked the place over.

'Where is he now?' Nair asked, picking up the coffee by his chair.

Carthew sat down, her eyes as cold as the Antarctic as always. 'Devonport Police station. They've got a doctor looking him over, then they'll question him.'

'He won't say anything,' Nair said. 'My solicitor is on the way to see him and he'll advise him to keep his mouth shut.'

'I hope you're right.'

Nair leaned forward. 'You knew this would happen.'

Carthew nodded. 'Of course.'

'You said you could get him to do it, to volunteer to commit murder for you. You're a mind reader.'

'No. Just clever and I know how predictable people are. Sex and money. That's what really drives people.'

Nair laughed. 'Well, he'll keep his mouth shut and go to prison. He knows that we can get to him on the inside if he grasses.'

'Then what?'

'We send someone after him anyway. We can't risk him having a change of heart, can we? He was planning on usurping my throne anyway, cheeky fucker. What's happened to your colleagues?'

She smiled. 'One has minor injuries, which I'm kind of glad of, as it's fun to mess with his head. The other is in critical condition. If I'm really lucky, she'll die.'

Nair stood up, then went over to the cupboard where he kept the booze. He took out a bottle of vodka and a bottle of whisky, then turned around and held them up. 'Want to celebrate?'

'Do you have any wine?'

'No, but I'll send out for some.'

'No comment,' Jason Harris said, leaning back in his chair, smirking. Sitting next to him was David Samms-Jones, a slender, peppery-haired man in his late forties, wearing a pinstripe suit and square glasses. The pricey solicitor was paid for by Jim Nair.

DI Anna Jones had been brought in for the interview out of politeness, seeing as she had been working tirelessly to find out who killed Stuart McAllister. Next to her was DS Toby Blaine. Moone watched it all going on from the interview room next door, observing it on a monitor, topped up with painkillers, having done a runner from the hospital with the help of Pinder. He had checked up on Butler and found out she was critical but stable. She was in a coma. After he had talked to a doctor who told him the lay of the land, he had rushed outside and let out a few tears. Then he had shook himself out of it and let the hatred and determination take the place of his worry and fear.

Pinder entered the interview room Moone was in and stood next to him, both of them facing the screen.

'Have you got it?' Moone asked.

'Oh, yeah, baby, I got it, I got the moves

like Jagger.' Pinder was smiling.

'The phone?'

'Sorry, just trying to lighten the mood. Yeah, I got the phone in an evidence bag in a locker. I'm frightened to ask whose phone it is.'

'Then don't ask.'

Pinder nodded. 'I won't.'

'Good.'

'Is it Carthew's?'

Moone stared at him, not able to find one part of him that was amused by Pinder that day. There was now nothing in him of the old Moone, the light-hearted, jokey, friendly detective. He was inside somewhere, watching it all from a distance. He felt like someone else, another copper, and one prepared to go to any lengths for the right result. 'No, it's not.'

'OK. Well, it's in my locker. What now?'

'You might as well talk to us, Jason,' DI Anna Jones said on the monitor. 'We have plenty of witnesses who saw you running from the van you crashed into Lloyd Redrobe's motorcycle, killing him outright.'

'No comment.' Jason flashed a smile.

The solicitor leaned forward. 'DI Jones, you know my client has already presented a written statement in which he says, yes, he was driving the said vehicle, which he borrowed from a friend, and admits, quite freely that he was driving too fast as he pulled out of the junction. He is very shaken up over the death of the young man who he hit on the motorcycle, but he is willing to admit to reckless driving.'

'A man who has links to your client's rival gang?' Jones said and shook her head. 'We found several bags of what we initially thought was drugs, Jason, on Lloyd Redrobe's motorbike, but we now know they only contain baby powder. It's as if someone was setting him up.'

'No comment.' Jason let out a tired breath and shrugged.

DI Jones looked down at her notes as she tapped the table with her pen. 'Tell us about Stuart McAllister.'

'No comment.'

'Your boss, Nair, had him murdered, didn't he?'

'No comment.'

'You're going to go away for a long time, even longer when we prove you were ordered to kill Redrobe to shut him up. Who paid for that hit, Jason?'

Jason stared at her for a moment, then leaned towards her, blank-faced. He smiled and said, 'No... comment.'

'Why don't we take a break there?' the solicitor said, looking at everyone in turn. 'I'm sure my client would appreciate a cup of tea.'

Jones rolled her eyes and got up. 'Pausing the interview there. Jason, don't get too comfortable. I'll get someone to bring you a tea.'

Moone was waiting out in the corridor, biting his nails, chewing the inside of his mouth, things he hadn't done for years and never thought he would again. He didn't know who he was any more and he could see a dark path opening up and spreading before him, and a deep voice urging him on, promising it was the only way to go now. And he couldn't stop himself. There was no way back from this now, the force of nature, of every bad event that had happened was propelling him forward. Just when he thought he might be doing something terrible, unforgivable, his mind would be filled with the sight of Butler in her ICU bed, machines surrounding her, while a group of masked doctors and nurses treated her and called out commands to each other. She was in good hands, he told himself and looked down at his hands that sweated and trembled.

The door to the interview room opened and DI Jones and her colleague came out and chatted briefly, not seeming too happy. Then Jones saw Moone and told her colleague to fetch her a coffee.

She came over with a sad smile. 'Sir, I didn't expect to see you here.'

'It's just Moone,' he said, looking to the door of the interview room. 'He's never going to say more than no comment, is he?'

She sighed. 'I wished I could be more positive about it, but I don't think so, no. He knows what's waiting for him in prison if he does.'

'But he's going inside?'

'Undoubtedly. Reckless driving, maybe manslaughter, murder if we can prove it. The van's stolen.'

'Where from?'

'Not from down here. Somewhere far north of here. Why?'

Moone nodded. 'Nothing. Just another unrelated case I've got going on. Listen, I need to ask you a favour.'

Jones looked at him suspiciously. 'OK, this sounds like it might be dodgy.'

He smiled, but inwardly his mind screamed and ran and hid. 'Not dodgy. We'd like a word with Jason…'

'He's not going to talk, you know that, but you're welcome to go in there and try.'

Moone nodded. 'Thing is, this is related to a case that my team have been working hard on. I sort of promised them we'd bring Jason to them, to Charles Cross.'

She frowned. 'I'm sorry, but that's not going to happen. He's staying in our custody for the duration and until he's put before a magistrate.'

'I know, I get it. But I promised them…'

'I'm sorry, but there's nothing you can say

that'll persuade me…'

'Celine Dion.' Moone stared at her, watching her face change, her eyes fixing on him as she stepped closer.

'Did you say what I thought you said?'

Moone nodded. 'I've got a mate, who's got a friend who knows someone who can get a signed copy of any album of hers you want.'

Jones stared at him. 'Are you joking?'

'No. And a signed photo. And a letter from her.' Moone raised his eyebrows, his hands and back and armpits dripping with icy sweat.

She slowly shook her head. 'How long would you have him for?'

'An hour, maybe two, tops. Inspector Pinder and I will even transport him to Charles Cross.'

She let out a harsh, doubtful breath, then looked at him. 'You also pay for tickets for the next time she performs anywhere. And I mean anywhere!'

He smiled and stuck out his hand. 'Done. I'll get our car ready. Thanks for this, DI Jones, my love for you will go on.'

'Wrong lyrics, but I'll let you off. Now hurry up, the clock is ticking.'

'Yep, it really is.'

He walked away and found a quiet corner. He took his phone out and brought up a number, his mind travelling again, a headless chicken kind of movement. He pressed call.

'Terry Hankin here,' the gruff, cockney voice said.

'Terry, it's Moone. Peter.'

'Alright, Pete, my son. What's 'appening?'

'I need your help with something.'

'You name it.'

'It's delicate. Definitely illegal. But morally correct. I think.'

'You had me at illegal. What do yer want me to do?'

CHAPTER 32

Within half an hour, Jason Harris was being questioned by one of the custody suite officers as he was processed, and all the paperwork was filled out. All the time they stood in the custody suite, all three of them, Moone, Pinder and Harris, were observed by the bespectacled and watchful eyes of the Sergeant at the desk. Moone knew that it was their realm and they were gods when it came to the prisoners in their care; whatever they said, was carved in stone.

'Right, I'm satisfied that you are to be released into these officers' protection,' the custody officer said. 'Make sure he's back safe and sound, gentlemen.'

'We will,' Moone said as Pinder manoeuvred the cuffed Harris towards the door to the car park.

Moone watched them both ahead of him, going through the security door and then out into the car park where Pinder's response car was waiting. Moone helped by opening the back door then stepped away and let the Inspector direct Harris onto the back seat.

'Ow!' Jason complained. 'At least take the cuffs off and let me put my hands in front! They're digging into my back.'

'Rule one,' Pinder said, climbing in the driver's seat. 'Never cuff a prisoner's hands in front of him.'

'Why not?' Harris asked as Moone climbed in the passenger seat.

'You could use your hands and cuffs as a weapon,' Moone said as the engine rumbled to life and Pinder started taking them towards the large gates.

'I'm not going to do that,' Harris said with an exasperated breath. 'At least let me smoke.'

'Not in my car,' Pinder said. 'I don't want you stinking it out.'

Jason shook his head. 'Have they got more comfortable cells in this place we're going?'

'Oh, yeah, four-star accommodation.' Kev laughed, then slowed up as they came to a pedestrian crossing.

There was a tap on the window, so Moone climbed out and opened the back passenger door and let Terry Hankin in, then climbed back in. Pinder drove them on, all in silence for a moment. In the rearview mirror, Moone could see Harris staring at Terry, looking him up and down.

'Who the fuck're you?' Harris asked Terry. 'Who the fuck is this?'

'Just relax,' Pinder said. 'Enjoy the ride.'

After a few minutes, Pinder took a turn into a narrow side street and drove them to the old, battered-looking pub on the corner. He parked up and turned off the engine, leaving the interior of the car in silence.

'What the fuck?' Harris said, leaning over and looking up at the pub. 'What's happening? I thought we were off to another nick?'

Moone climbed out and looked up and down the street, making sure no nosey neighbours were watching as they removed Harris from the vehicle. Pinder got out and opened up the back door and helped Harris out and pushed him towards the entrance of the pub that had a chain and padlock through the door handles. Moone took out a key and undid the padlock and let them inside the dusty and dank interior.

'Right then,' Hankin said, rolling his shoulders and doing a few practice boxing punches as he walked into the pub. 'Let's have him.'

'Oi, Terry, remember, we can't have claret all over him,' Moone said. 'He's already got bruising on his body, so try and keep to that area.'

'No worries, mate. I'll do my best.'

'Is someone going to tell me what exactly

the fuck's going on?' Harris looked panicked as he stood near a dusty bar at the centre of the square room, the thick stench of the toilets overriding any other smells. 'What am I doing in this shithole?'

Pinder grabbed an old chair and placed it near Harris. 'Sit down.'

'Hang on, what's…'

'Sit the fuck down,' Hankin said and stood looking down at Harris, staring at him until he did as he was told.

'Who the fuck are you?' Harris said, staring up at him.

Hankin grinned as Moone closed the door of the pub, leaving them in the cool gloom, only beams of sunlight dancing through the mostly barred windows.

'I'm the geezer who's gonna hurt yer, mate,' Terry said and balled his fists.

Harris looked at Pinder. 'You're a fucking copper. You can't do this.'

Pinder shrugged. 'I'm not. I'm not even here. You're not even here, mate. Are you here, Moone?'

Moone shook his head, trying to appear calm even though his heart was racing and all he wanted to do was leave and run. 'No, I'm not here. I'm sunning myself in Spain.'

Harris laughed, but it was dry and empty as he looked at them in turn, perhaps half expecting a joke was happening. 'Fuck off.'

'What's she up to?' Moone asked.

'Who?' Harris asked.

'Carthew.'

'I don't know.'

Terry sprung forward, jabbing his hand at Harris' neck. The suspect shouted and groaned.

'What the hell was that?' Harris yelled. 'Jesus, that fucking hurt.'

Terry laughed. 'I worked as a bouncer for a long time, then I ended up meeting this bird. Tanya. She convinced me to do this bodyguard course. Anyway, it was run by two ex-SAS lads, hard nuts they were. Half the size of me, but I wouldn't fuck with them. But they taught us how to hurt someone. Really hurt someone without leaving a mark.'

'Fuck off.'

Hankin sent his hand jabbing again, this time at Harris' throat, making him choke and gasp for air.

'That's one of the best ones they taught us,' Hankin said. 'Do you know there's nerves on the side of your neck, and if you hit them hard enough, then you can incapacitate someone pretty fucking fast. Hit them too hard and they're dead. Thing is, I'm not very good at pulling my punches.'

'Don't let him near me!' Harris tried to drag his chair backwards.

'Then tell us where she is.' Moone folded his arms. 'Where does she live these days?'

'I don't know!'

Moone bent down, staring at him. 'My partner is in hospital thanks to you and her. I've just about reached my limit with her. She's crossed a line and now I don't care what I do. I don't care who I have to step on to get her. I swear, I will make your life hell if you don't start talking, Scout's Honour. Now, listen, Terry here has connections…'

'Underworld connections,' Terry said. 'My uncle, Ray, nutter he was. Didn't have fear. He'd do anything. He worked for this crime boss who liked to rob bullion and all that malarkey. He'd get my uncle to take a train up north where they would get him to hijack a truck full of goods and bring it back down south. He had massive balls, my uncle Ray. Well, I'm still very much in with that lot and they have a long reach. You go to prison and they can either fuck you up or make sure you're protected from the likes of Jim Nair.'

Moone nodded. 'Terry's right. If Nair hears of this, you know your life will be over. We can protect you. And when you get out, I'll help you get away. I swear. Just tell me what Carthew is up to.'

Harris stared up at him, seemingly frozen for a while, swallowing, making calculations, weighing it all up. 'Fucking hell. That fucking bitch… right, alright. She's at my place…'

'Try again, we've searched your place

already,' Kev said.

'Na, me nan's old place. Near King's Tamerton. She's there. You can grab her there.'

'What's she up to? What's her big plan?' Moone asked.

Harris shrugged. 'I don't know. She wanted us to take over running the Dark Horses, said she could keep us protected, that she was going to work her way up the ranks. That's it.'

'We guessed all that,' Pinder said.

'Oh, and she's got a bee in her bonnet about this killer bloke you're after. The one attacking those women in their homes. She wants to find him before you lot. Make him disappear to mess with your heads.'

'How?'

'She got me to set up a fake profile online. She pretends to be this woman called Sarah, and hopes this nutter contacts her.'

Moone looked at Pinder who shook his head and let out a harsh breath.

'Right, Kev, write down all the details, his nan's address and everything.' Moone started to turn away, heading to the doors, his mind already working something out.

'Hang on,' Harris said. 'Listen, if you go to my nan's place… there's… well, there's quite a bit of… stuff there.'

'You've got a lot of gear there, haven't yer, you naughty boy?' Hankin laughed.

'It's not mine.' Harris' eyes pleaded with them.

Moone laughed. 'Of course not. Now, the most important question. Will you go on the record that Carthew put you up to killing her half-brother, Lloyd Redrobe?'

Harris shook his head. 'I can't. You know I can't. They'll kill me.'

'I'm talking about you in a court of law, testifying that DS Carthew paid you to kill her half-brother. That's it. No mention of the Dark Horses.'

'Oh come on,' Harris said.

'I can keep you safe inside,' Hankin said. 'Or I can help fuck you up.'

Harris hung his head. 'OK. Whatever. I'm fucked anyway.'

'Right,' Moone said. 'Let's hurry up and get him to Charles Cross.'

Moone left the pub and stood out in the sunshine, and stretched, still thinking and formulating a plan. Pinder stepped out and joined him as they surveyed the empty street.

'So?' Pinder asked. 'Do you think a jury will take his word against a detective?'

Moone shrugged. 'I don't know. It's worth a try. But I have another idea.'

'What?'

'Drugs. His nan's place. Carthew. Let's go over it later when Jason Harris is safely in the cells.'

'This Terry fella. Was he lying about the underworld... stuff?'

'No, unfortunately not. But he's a pussycat really. Right, let's move it and get to work.'

He watched his little girl being put in the back seat of the car, then Sarah's cousin doing up her seatbelt and closing the back door. Then her cousin walked closer to him, staring at him and he could see she had doubts and questions in her eyes.

'Has something happened?' she asked.

'What do you mean?'

'With Sarah? She hardly replies to my texts. Have you two...'

He stared at her, his right fist, which was hidden behind the front door, balled up as the fury pounded around his body. 'We're fine. She's just... busy with work. You know what she's like.'

But the questions seemed to remain in her eyes as she looked at the car and his little girl in the back. 'OK, well, she can come and collect her tomorrow or Saturday.'

He nodded. 'Thank you for this.'

'I'm doing it for Sarah.'

Then she got back in her car and drove off, his daughter waving from the back seat. He closed the door, then turned around and flinched. The old man was standing there, smoking as always.

'That bitch asks too many questions,' the old man said. 'She needs to be seen to.'

'No, she doesn't. She doesn't. I can't... it's bad enough that I've...'

'You're talking 'bout your bitch of a wife?' The old man shook his head, smoke puffing out of his mouth as he grunted.

'Don't call her that!'

'That's what she is. A bitch like the rest. Just another bitch called Sarah.'

'Get out!' He jerked his hand towards the door, his body trembling. 'Go on, leave me alone. This is all your fault. I didn't want all this.'

'You need me, bey.' The old man's voice softened. 'You know you do. We've got a big day ahead of coming up, a lot of work to do. You don't want to be caught, do you, bey?'

He shook his head, tears in his eyes.

'No, so you need me. It's the big day soon. The blood moon. The day we've been waiting for, my lad. My boy. You're like a son to me, and I'm not just saying that.'

He let out a sob, his body convulsing with the tears.

'There, there, bey. Don't cry. Only little weaklings cry. Be a man and punish the bitches. You and me. Together. You've got the first one picked out, ain't yer?'

He nodded.

The old man took a puff of his cigarette,

nodding. 'Good. Then soon we knock on her door and she gets it. Then we find the rest and the world will know what we've done.'

Moone was looking through the glass at the bed that she was lying on. He had driven to the hospital in a dream and found himself in the car park opposite the Costa coffee, the place they always parked in. Then he'd somehow trudged all the way to the room she was recovering in. She was stable, they said. She'd had internal bleeding, and a head injury, but there was no sign of anything majorly wrong on the scans. She was in a coma, but hopefully, she would wake up soon.

He was in the car, upside down, the belt cutting into him, her hair covering her face, sirens getting louder, voices calling to him. His heart was pounding, racing like never before.

But there had been another time when his heart had raced like that. It was after her father's funeral, when she smelt of wine and perfume, and they had hugged before he had put her in a taxi. There was that moment, her face close to his, her lips brushing his cheek. He thought... perhaps... nothing happened, but his heart had still hammered against his ribcage.

'You can go in for a moment,' a voice said behind him and he turned to see a smiling, dark-skinned nurse looking at him.

'It's OK, I'm fine.'

'Is she your wife?'

He laughed, but his heart was being squeezed. 'No. My colleague.'

'Well, hopefully she'll be awake soon.'

He smiled. 'Thank you. Thank you for taking care of her.'

'It's our pleasure.' The nurse went off.

Moone looked at her again, then went in and shut the door behind him and stood at the end of the bed.

'Butler,' he whispered. 'I'm going to get her. I'm doing everything I can to finish this. I promise you. By the time you wake up, she'll be gone from our lives for good.'

He stayed for a few minutes, listening to the constant beeping of the machines, and counting himself more than lucky that she hadn't died in the crash. He had the urge to hug her lifeless body, to kiss her forehead, but instead, he wiped his tears away. He had work to do.

'I'll get the cow, I promise,' he said, walked away and headed out of the hospital, his mind awash with what he was prepared to do.

He took out his phone when he was close to his car and phoned Terry. When he had answered and Moone had said his piece, then there would be no going back.

'Alright, mate?' Terry said. 'How is she?'

'The same, but hopefully she'll be awake soon.'

'Nice one. Can't wait to meet her.'

'Listen.' Moone closed his eyes. 'I need you to go to an address. I need you to...' Moone looked around, making sure he wasn't being listened to. He decided to climb into his car, where he couldn't be overheard. He turned on the radio, shut the door and started telling Terry exactly what to do.

CHAPTER 33

Saturday came with a great wave of apprehension, and Moone could almost taste his team's misgivings as he entered the incident room and tried to sit at his desk with as little fuss as possible. He had even toyed with hiding in his newly appointed office but realised that would be no good for morale.

As soon as he sat down, he found himself boxed in by Molly and Harding, their faces drawn.

'You OK, boss?' Harding asked, an awkward smile on his face.

'I'm doing all right, thanks.' Moone nodded, his chest tightening.

'I went to see her last night,' Molly said. 'They say she'll be OK, and she's tough.'

'Tough as old boots is our Mandy.' Harding laughed.

'She'd kill you if she heard you say that,' Molly said.

Moone looked down at the work on his desk, feeling tired from getting little sleep. His conversation with Terry kept playing over and over in his head, wondering when he would do what he had asked him to do.

'Anything back about the DNA?' Moone asked.

'Nothing yet,' Molly said. 'I'll go and chase it up.'

He watched her go off but noticed Harding was still standing behind him. 'Everything all right, Harding?'

'Yeah, boss. Just… a bit worried about…'

'She'll be OK,' Moone said. 'That's what they said. She'll be awake and giving us aggro very soon.'

'I know. I know.'

'Anything from the school list?'

Harding sighed. 'So far, I haven't found any of our suspects attended the school. By the way, on Monday we've got a scan, a baby scan thing at Derriford…'

'It's fine. Just come in after or before. It's OK.'

Moone breathed out a sigh of relief when Harding thanked him and then sloped off to his desk. He turned his head, daring to look over at the desk where DS Carthew would normally be sitting. It was Saturday and she had the day off. He had thought about cancelling all leave as they needed all hands on deck in case the handyman did strike, but he needed her not to be here.

Blood moon. He stood up and walked over to the board, looking at the faces of the victims, the ones they had failed. He rubbed his eyes, tired all over, ready to throw in the towel. What would the killer do? What was his plan for this holy day in his calendar? They had put out the warning, reiterating the need for everyone to be vigilant, not to answer the door to strangers and not to arrange appointments. He prayed that they were listened to.

But where was the killer? Would he go to ground for the day? No, it was an important, once-in-a-lifetime chance to strike out at the world. The special response team, which Pinder was in charge of, was ready to go, waiting for any reports of... well, anything out of the ordinary. He looked at the time. It was passing slowly. He wondered again where Terry was.

He heaved the rucksack onto his back and swung it around and adjusted the straps until it was comfortable. He felt a little dizzy as he slipped on the gloves, then the baseball cap and then the face mask. He looked at himself in the bedroom mirror, shaking all over.

'You look great, bey.' The old man stood in the doorway, watching him with his dark eyes, the eyes that seemed even darker than ever, glistening. 'This is the big day.'

He turned around and picked up the claw hammer from the bed and gripped it in his hand.

'You know what to do.' The old man took a drag of his roll-up.

He nodded, picked up his van keys and started down the stairs, his heart now thudding, the beat of rage still in the distance, somewhere behind him but coming closer, running towards him. He went out the front door.

'Do me proud, bey!' the old man shouted before the door closed.

He unlocked the van, sweeping his eyes over the street and seeing only a few people about, a couple of dog walkers. He climbed in, put the hammer on the dashboard and put the keys in the ignition. He turned the key and the van's engine rumbled to life. He sat there breathing for a moment, recalling what had happened all those years ago, and he felt it, the rage grasping hold of him in a fiery hug. He put the van into first gear with a trembling hand and then steered it into the street.

He didn't have an exact destination but knew he had to get as far away from his own home as possible. After half an hour, he found a parking space in the high street, near St Budeaux. He turned off the engine and watched the people on the streets, kids, women and men all going somewhere, unaware of him. He grasped the hammer, pushed open the door and stood on the pavement, watching the people go past. He waited.

Then his eyes jumped to two women coming towards him, chatting and laughing about something.

Bitches. Laughing at you. The bitches.

He took a couple of steps and lifted the hammer. The two women froze. One of them shrieked. He took aim at the blonde bitch, smiling as the hammer smacked into her skull and she went crumpling to the pavement. The other bitch was screaming now.

He looked around and saw people were either frozen in horror or running away.

He swung again, hitting the friend who cowered and held her hands over her head. He batted them away and struck her again and again until she dropped to her knees and fell flat on her face.

It was enough, he said to himself and strode towards the van, climbed in and started the engine. He pulled away, the sound of traffic mingling with the shouts and screams behind him.

He kept driving, smiling to himself, the old man's voice in his ears, imagining what he would be saying. He soon pulled up in the road where she lived. Sarah. Another Sarah.

He pushed open the door and pulled the backpack on, then looked around to make sure no one was waiting for him. There was no one around, but he imagined the chaos that was starting up somewhere, the police alerted and heading for a location where he was not. The old man had come up with the plan and he had to admit it was genius.

He walked to the door, pressed the doorbell and waited, his hands trembling.

DS Faith Carthew stopped what she was doing and looked across the room towards the stairs. The doorbell still echoed, and she checked the time. She took a step and listened. The bell rang again. He was early. The handyman, who had been recommended through a woman she had befriended online, was early. She looked at her bag that was on the bed, half filled with the stuff she had left at this house, Jason Harris' home. She was going to stay there longer and wait for the potential killer to turn up and show his hand, but now Harris was locked up, she decided it was time to move on. Peter Moone, the weakling, would have undoubtedly failed to get any information from him, but she didn't want to take the risk. A little while ago, she might have found herself being concerned by Butler, who although a lot more stupid than

Moone, was more likely to do something out of the blue that might interfere with her plans. But no, she thought and laughed to herself, knowing the cow was in ICU, tubes sticking out of her, machines keeping her alive. Fingers crossed, she hoped, she might suddenly take a turn for the worse.

The doorbell rang again.

She had made the appointment with the handyman at the last minute, a final attempt to capture him before she had to give up on it all. After all, she had other plans to deal with. She picked up her Casco baton and pepper spray then slipped them into her pockets. She hurried down the stairs and headed for the front door and opened it a crack.

'Hello,' the man said, through the face mask he wore. 'I'm the handyman. Dave. Mrs Riley recommended me.'

Carthew looked him over, quickly. He wore a face mask, which could have just been paranoia left over from the whole Covid affair, but then she saw the gloves, the light blue surgical gloves pulled tight over his hands. She buzzed inside as she opened the door wide, her free hand reaching into her pocket for her Casco baton.

'Yes, come in,' she said, putting on a bright smile, then watched him enter.

'You've got a nice home,' he said and faced her, his eyes seeming quite blank. 'Your name's

Sarah, isn't it?'

'It is.' Her eyes jumped to the kitchen, the place she knew he liked to carry out his work. 'It's the kitchen. I'm thinking about having it painted and maybe some new units put in.'

He nodded and turned and faced the kitchen. He seemed to pause, then started towards it.

'Sorry, about the mask,' he said, once he reached the kitchen and stood by the table. 'It's just… after Covid… you can't be too careful.'

She smiled and stepped closer to him. 'No, you can't.'

'Do you live alone?' he asked and put down his bag, his eyes scanning the room.

'Is it important that my name is Sarah?' she asked and his eyes jumped to her.

'Why do you ask that?'

'Do you like the name Sarah?' She pulled the Casco baton from her pocket and flicked it to full length as she took out the pepper spray and shot it towards his eyes. He made a yelping noise as his gloved hands grasped at his face. She swept the baton, cracking him on his ankle and making him scream out as he collapsed to the floor.

'Echo one!' he yelled. 'Go!'

She swung round when she heard the thud at the door. She saw the dark figures outside, battering to get in. She dropped the baton just as the door flung open and hit the wall of the porch. An armed officer came rushing in, pointing a handgun at her as she shouted, 'Stay where you are! Drop your weapons! Now!'

She looked down to see the pepper spray in her hand and dropped it on the carpet.

'This man came into my home and then tried to attack me!' Carthew said, realising that the situation was a little trickier than she first thought. But there was always a way out.

'I'm a DS from Devonport,' the man on the floor said as he grunted. 'Can someone get me some water? I'm pretty much blind here.'

'This isn't your house, is it?'

She heard his voice before she saw him come in, the armed officer blocking her view. Her first response was to grab the baton and take a swipe at Moone as he came in. Then she saw the armed officer's gun again, so smiled calmly. She would get out of this, there was nothing incriminating in the house, nothing linked to her, anyway.

'Peter, thank heaven you're here,' she said. 'Can you tell these morons that I'm a police detective?' She looked at them. 'I'm a police officer, you idiots.'

'Oh, they know.' Moone smiled. 'This was Jason Harris' nan's place. Harris, of Dark Horse gang fame. Why are you staying here?'

She looked around the walls. 'Jason Harris? His nan? Weird, I had no idea. Anyway, it's not my house. I'm sorry I injured your colleague, but I thought he was our killer. A simple case of mistaken identity.'

Moone nodded. 'That's right. It's not your home. We know there are drugs hidden in this house...'

'Not mine.' She raised her eyebrows and smiled. 'Nice try.'

'Is that your car outside?' He pointed a thumb behind him.

She found herself looking to the doorway, thinking, wondering what he was up to. There was nothing. Yes, it was her car but there was nothing incriminating in the car. She would never keep anything incriminating in her car. She hesitated. 'Yes, that's my car.'

He smiled. 'Yes, I know it is. Registered to you. We're going to search it.'

'You don't have any right to.'

'Faith Carthew, I'm placing you under arrest for the murder of Lloyd Redrobe and for the suspected murder of DS Maxine Rivers. You do not have to say anything. But, it may harm your defence if you do not mention when questioned something which you later rely on in court. Anything you do say may be given in evidence. Do you understand?'

'Of course I understand. You won't find anything.'

Moone turned and walked to the front door. 'You can search the car now!'

When Moone turned back to face her, he was trembling a little, unable to quite believe he had her. She still looked confident, blank almost, not fearing that anyone could be cleverer than her.

'So, we just wait?' She raised her eyebrows.

'Yep. Turn around.'

She did as she was told, so he put the restraints on her. By the time he had and was moving her to the front door, Pinder was coming up the front path carrying an evidence bag.

'Look what we found hidden underneath her car seat,' he said. 'An android phone.'

Moone looked at Carthew and saw the slow burning anger that was filling her eyes. 'I suspect that might belong to DI Maxine Rivers. DI Crowne knows her password.'

'You corrupt bastards,' she said. 'You planted that there. When you were searching...'

'No,' Pinder said. 'The search was carried out by another team, not us. We didn't plant anything.'

She stared at them, her eyes sharpening, her teeth showing. 'I hope she fucking dies! That fucking bitch you love so fucking much! I hope she fucking dies!'

'You two!' Moone called to a couple of uniforms close by. 'Take Faith Carthew into custody.'

The uniforms came over, hooked their arms through Carthew's and marched her down the path. She struggled against them, fought to turn round and face Moone.

'Peter!' she called, a mad look in her eyes, a strange smile on her lips. 'Don't worry, darling, sweetheart, I'll be back. I'll soon be back.'

'But you won't ever be my boss. I told you, I warned you to stop.'

She stared at him. 'This isn't over, Peter Moone.'

Moone watched her for a moment as she was taken away, absorbing her words with a shudder, but then comforted himself with the fact that she was wrong, she was fucked. They hadn't bothered to tell her that drugs were also found in her car. A large amount of drugs.

He walked to Pinder's response car and waited for him to unlock it, then climbed in and put on his seatbelt, his mind still not quite accepting what had just happened. He'd done it, he'd won the battle and the war.

Pinder climbed in, and they remained in silence for a moment, perhaps both contemplating recent events.

'OK, I've got to ask,' said Pinder. 'How the hell did you get that stuff in her car?'

Moone looked at him. 'I didn't. They were in there. I had nothing to do with it. They were hidden in her car and the search team found them.'

Pinder stared at him, nodding, a slight smile creeping onto his face as he started the engine. 'Right, OK. I still can't believe it's over.'

'We've still got a killer to find. Let's get back to the station.'

Then Pinder's radio beeped and a voice began to squawk at them. He took the call, and they listened as the attack on two young women in St Budeaux was reported to them. The suspect had then fled in a van, but no one had got the registration number. The young women were quite badly injured but stable at Derriford. When the radio call ended, Moone put his face in his hands and let out a deep groan.

'Fuck,' he said, taking away his hands. 'He's done it again and here we were chasing that fucking cow!'

'They're alive.'

Moone sighed. 'Yeah, but they shouldn't have had to go through that. We need to trawl through CCTV and find that van. Jesus, he could be heading anywhere. Come on, let's get to the station.'

When Moone walked back into the incident room, every member of his team was busy on the phones or writing up reports. He stood there for a moment, watching them, feeling a little elated that at last Carthew was out of the picture, and sick at the same time that his plan to respond to any violent attacks had failed. He had failed the women of Plymouth.

'Is it true, boss?' Harding asked when he put down his phone. 'Did they arrest DS Carthew?'

He nodded. 'Yep. They did. I'm sorry to say it, but one of our own officers has been working with the Dark Horses and probably murdered DS Rivers. It's a sad day.'

The team started to cheer and clap, and he stood there numb, watching them punch the air, someone even singing a few bars of 'The Wicked Witch Is Dead' before he held up his hands.

'There's nothing to celebrate,' he said, sickened to his core. 'There's been another attack. Two young women were badly injured, because we failed to find him. I want that CCTV around St Budeaux, I want to know where he's heading next.'

Molly stood up. 'Sir, apparently a report came in that a man with a hammer tried to break into the home of a woman called Sarah Wise in Mount Gould Road. He didn't get in and then left before a response team got there.'

Moone closed his eyes, let out a breath and then looked them all over, the frustration biting into him. 'Does anyone have any idea where the fuck this bastard's going?'

They all looked at him blankly.

'Boss,' Molly said quietly, and by her expression, he could tell she had more bad news.

'Yes, Chambers?'

'I'm afraid I contacted the DNA forensic service, and they said that there was a technical error with the cigarette roll-up we sent.'

'You're joking?'

'No, I'm afraid not. They think maybe there was improper handling of the evidence and bacteria contamination occurred, and so they can't interpret the results. They send their apologies.'

Moone could only stare at her for a moment, a voice screaming in his head. He tried to scramble to find something, some thread of hope that their killer might be found through some scrap of evidence. Only one thing came to mind. 'What about the school list? Anything there? Harding?'

Harding shrugged. 'I've been through it, and I can't find any of our suspects on it.'

'Where is it?' Moone went round his desk.

Harding brought up the list and started going through it, bringing up hundreds of male names. Moone scanned through it, flickering eyes over them. Just names, none that meant anything. Then one name caught his eye.

'Go back,' he said, so Harding did.

Moone leaned in. 'Michael King. DI King has a son called Michael. Michael King. This can't be a coincidence.' He looked at Harding, a little irritation growing in his head. 'Didn't you notice the name? King?'

Harding looked a little broken as he shrugged. 'Sorry. I didn't think…'

Moone sighed. 'Right, let's go and see Gary King and ask him about this. Molly, come on, you're with me.'

CHAPTER 34

When they were close to Gary King's house in Ernesettle, Molly indicated, turned the wheel and said, 'I can hardly believe Carthew's gone.'

Moone was looking out the window, picturing Butler lying on the hospital bed. 'I know. Feels like it was a long road, but we got there.'

'Do you think she'll go down for murder?'

'Hopefully, the jury will take Jason Harris' testimony seriously. I'm not sure about Maxine Rivers' murder. We haven't even got a body.'

Molly nodded. 'By the way, sorry about the list, the school list, I mean. I should've checked…'

'Harding should have picked up on it. But I think he's got a lot going on at home. I'll let him off with a caution.'

'We're here.' Molly pulled in and then they left the car and knocked on his door.

Former DI King answered the door, looking a little surprised to see them.

'You caught the bastard yet?' he asked,

stepping aside to let them in.

'No,' was all Moone said as he went through to the living room, his eyes scanning the room for familiar photos. There weren't many, none of a boy or a man who might be King's son.

When King came in, followed by Molly, Moone said, 'Tell us about your boy.'

King narrowed his eyes. 'Michael? What about him?'

'Did he go to a school in South London for a while?'

'Yeah, that's right. I was stationed there for a couple of years. I was still married then, but the wife didn't want to stay, so we came back. Why? What's happened? Has something happened to him?'

'No. I'm just trying to put something together.' Moone sighed, trying to work it out. 'A young girl called Sarah went missing back then. From the same school Michael went to.'

King stared at him, his eyes slowly widening as he looked at Molly too. 'What? What the hell're you trying to say? Do you think Michael had something to do with that? You can fuck yourself. Go on, get out...'

'No.' Moone stood firm. 'Prove me wrong. Have you got a photo of him?'

King kept staring at him, venom in his eyes. 'No. Not a recent one. Only one from about ten years ago. Somewhere, hang on.'

The old man started searching through a sideboard across the room, pulling out drawers, and muttering to himself. A terrible feeling entered Moone's stomach.

'Here,' King said and shoved the old, dog-eared photo into his hand. It was an old school photo of a young man, with dark brown hair, a slight resemblance to DI King about the eyes and mouth. There was something familiar about the young lad. He turned the photo over and saw a name scribbled there and froze, his chest tightening, the realisation coming over him. He read the name again and looked up at King.

'Jon Michael King?' Moone said. 'But you called him Michael?'

'Yeah, he never liked being called Jon. We preferred Michael. Why, what of it?'

Moone held out the photo to Molly but kept his eyes on King. 'Where is Michael?'

'I've already told you, I don't know. Somewhere far from here, I hope. He's not part of all this. He's not some nutter.'

Moone rubbed his face for a moment, trying to find the right words. 'I think he might be part of this. Your son was there when the body of Teresa Burrows was found.'

'No, he wasn't. What're you talking about?'

'He called himself Jon Reagan and he was living with his Aunt Carol.'

King stared at him, slowly shaking his head. 'Me and the wife had split up by then and she wouldn't let me see him. She got ill and he went off to live with some relatives but I never knew where he was. You mean to tell me when I sent off one of my people to talk to the old lady and the boy who found Burrows, it was him?'

'I'm sorry, but yes. But I don't think Michael just found her...'

'No, no, no, you're wrong. No way. He wouldn't... he couldn't. Not my boy. You lot get out. You're wrong. Get out. Leave me alone.'

Moone didn't know what to say, so he just nodded and said, 'OK. Fine. We'll leave you to it.'

He signalled to Molly for them to head to the door and they went out, with King following them, calling out to Moone, telling him he was wrong. But they left him standing on his doorstep and drove off.

'We need to find Jon Michael Reagan, and fast,' Moone said.

'Oh God,' Molly said, putting her foot down. 'Reagan. Doesn't that mean King?'

'I think so. Jesus Christ. He was right there. Right there in front of us and I never saw it. I was thinking the killer would be older. What an idiot.'

'None of us saw it, boss. They even had him down as a witness all those years ago, but no one put two and two together.'

Moone nodded. 'Because King didn't deal with it himself, just sent someone off to talk to him and Mrs Harris. And by then he was calling himself something else. Now we need to find him.'

Jon Michael King entered his family home and stood there for a moment, the hammer in his hand. There was still blood on it. He saw it, almost as if for the first time and flinched and dropped it.

'What the fuck're you doing back here, bey?' the old man appeared down the stairs, smoking like a trooper as always. 'Go and find them, fucking get those bitches, you weak little bastard.'

'No.' He shook his head.

'What did you say?'

'No. I can't. Not anymore. This isn't me. I'm a family man. You did all this! You put this in my head.'

'I put it in your head?' The old man came down the stairs, laughing, the smoke bellowing from his black, cavernous mouth. 'Oh, fuck me, bey. This is you. All you. They're coming for you.'

'Good.' He went into the kitchen and found his phone and dialled the police.

'What the fuck're you doing, you piece of shit? Look at you, weak as the day I saw you outside the headmaster's office. Crying like a little girl. Just like the little bitches. Are you going to cry for your mummy? Your mummy, who was a little bitch too?'

He ignored him and told the operator he needed the police. Then he was put through to someone, so he said, 'My name is Jon Michael King. I've done some bad things... I've hurt people, but it wasn't my fault...'

The old man laughed again, shaking his head. 'They'll come and kill you, bey.'

'Please come and get me. Please. I need help.' He ended the call and left his phone on. They would trace the call, he was sure of that.

Molly had been driving them back to the station when the call came in, the news that Jon Michael King had called the police. They had his address and an armed response team had been dispatched. Molly took the next turn, heading for the same address.

By the time they got there, the armed response team had the house covered. They rang the bell and shouted for Jon Michael King to come out and surrender.

What happened next, surprised Moone, as he witnessed their suspect open the door and walk out, his hands in the air. The armed response team ordered him to kneel, then pinned him to the ground and cuffed him. More of the team went into the house and cleared it. It was empty.

Nearly four hours later, after King was arrested and transported to the station, and was examined by a doctor and then booked in at the custody suite, Moone found himself alongside DC Molly Chambers, facing the prisoner across the interview table.

King was looking down, his face pale, his body trembling.

'Do we call you Jon or Michael? King or Reagan?' Moone asked, after all the official business was recorded.

King shrugged. 'Michael, I guess. I've always been Michael. Or Mike.' He looked up, facing Moone. 'I know I've done some terrible things, but I didn't want to. I want you to believe me.'

Moone took a breath. 'Who made you do them, then, Michael?'

'He did.'

'He? Who's he?'

Michael looked down at the desk, swallowing. 'The old man. The caretaker.'

'The caretaker?' Moone exchanged confused looks with Molly.

'Yeah, he was the caretaker of my school. The one in London. There was this day, when this girl I liked... she... she made a fool of me. Everyone was laughing. I hit this boy and then ended up being sent to the headmaster. But the caretaker sat with me, and talked to me, he was the only person who seemed to understand me.'

'What was his name?' Molly asked, ready to write it down.

Michael looked blank for a moment. 'I don't know. He's just... the caretaker.'

'You never knew his name?' Moone asked.

'No. Never. He turned up again, recently. Got inside my head and made me start doing it all over again. For so long I managed to stop...'

'You started with Judy Ludlow... why her?'

Michael's eyes widened and sat forward. 'No! I didn't. I had nothing to do with that.'

'Then who?' Moone couldn't believe the excuses now pouring out of his mouth.

'That was that bastard,' he said. 'Nick Dann. He killed her.'

Moone looked at Molly and saw she shared his surprise. 'You're saying Dann killed Ludlow? How do you know this?'

Michael looked down. 'I saw him. I'd been following him.'

'Why?' Moone asked.

'He'd been seeing my mum behind my dad's back when I was a kid. I didn't find out until I was older, my Auntie Carol let it slip. I think they met at some charity thing. My aunt told me my dad knew too but he didn't do anything. He's weak. Fucking weak. I started following Dann, meaning to have it out with him. Then I saw him leave her house... Ludlow.

He left the door ajar and drove off. I went in and there she was. He'd put a cloth over her face. But I saw it and I couldn't forget what I'd seen.'

'So you started doing the same? Copying him? Why?'

Michael looked up, tears in his eyes. 'I didn't want to, I told you. The old man, the caretaker made me. I'm not sure I did do those things. I think maybe it was him.'

'You think it was him who killed Teresa Burrows? She was living in the same street as your aunt, wasn't she? The old lady knocked on your aunt's door and there you happened to be. But you gave a false name to the police and no one bothered to check up on it.'

Michael gripped his face, shaking his head. 'He must've done it. He knew I was staying with my aunt and he did it to frame me.'

'The caretaker?'

Michael's eyes lit up as he leaned forward. *'It was him who killed Sarah. The girl at school. He did it to punish her for me.'*

'So, Sarah's dead?' Molly asked.

'Yeah... she's dead. Oh God. I watched him. He beat her, then strangled her with her tights.'

'Like Ludlow and Burrows and the others?' Moone sat back, trying to make sense of it all.

'Yeah.' Michael nodded. 'You've got to find him. He might kill again.'

'The caretaker?' Moone asked.

Michael nodded. 'Yeah. He's evil.'

'What does he look like?'

Michael shrugged. 'I don't know. Old. He's always looked old. And dark. Dark skin.'

'He's black?' Molly said.

'No, no, he's white. Just… dark. I don't know.'

'You met him in London?' Moone asked.

'Yeah, London.'

'So, he's from London?'

Michael shook his head. 'No, he's proper Plymouth. Always calls me bey. Always smoking roll-ups. Please, there's something else. My wife, she's tied up in a house. I'll give you the address. Please go and get her before he kills her. I'm begging you.'

They had paused the interview and headed back to the incident room, still trying to put it all together. Molly had organised officers to go to the address Michael had given them, in the hopes of releasing his poor wife, then she had started investigating the whereabouts of the mysterious caretaker.

In the meantime, Moone sat at his desk and stared at the whiteboard and all the poor women who were dead or injured. He had failed them. Jon Michael King had handed himself in. But where was this old man who had convinced him to murder so many women?

Molly got off the phone and walked over to

him.

'So?' he asked.

Molly looked bewildered. 'I asked the school if they'd ever had someone from down here working there, but they said no. The caretakers they had there didn't match this old man Michael said about. So who is he?'

Moone stood up, an idea forming, a little burning in the pit of his stomach. 'Sarah. He said the old man beat and strangled her with her tights. Just like the others.'

'That's right.'

Moone looked at her. 'What if it wasn't the old man who killed Sarah? What if it was Michael? What if years later, seeing what Nick Dann did to Judy Ludlow, set something off? What if he started killing, after all those years, after he killed that poor young girl? Then for some reason he stops, somehow gets it under control…'

'I've been looking into his background, his job history,' Molly said. 'He moved around a lot, worked a few jobs in Scotland, the north of England, all over before he came back here and got married.'

'Jesus, Molly. Are you thinking he never actually stopped?'

'I don't know. But they don't just stop, do they?'

'No, they don't,' Moone said.

'But what about this old man, the

caretaker?'

'I don't think he exists. He describes him as a dark man. What if Michael has a personality disorder, like schizophrenia? The old man tells him to kill, or he convinces himself that the old man does the killing. Maybe he doesn't even know he's been doing all this.'

Molly let out a harsh breath. 'Makes sense. Sort of. That's why we can't find him. But we found that roll-up.'

Moone nodded. 'I bet Michael smoked that himself. Any word on his wife?'

'She's safe. Her name's Sarah, by the way.'

Moone shook his head. 'Of course it is.'

Then a phone started ringing on one of desks and Molly answered the call. 'Charles Cross incident room…Oh, hello. Yes, he's here. Oh, that's amazing. I'll tell him.'

When Molly ended the call, her face lit up, she said, 'DI Butler's awake.'

'She is?' Moone found himself almost crying. 'Jesus. I better get over there.'

Michael was alone in the interview room, staring down at his hands, praying they found the old man in time.

'You stupid, weak, idiot.'

Michael's head shot up. There he was, the old man, smoking, staring at him with loathing stamped into his dark skin. 'What are you doing here?'

The old man shook his head. *'You really are thick, bey. They get you, they get me. Don't you get it?'*

'I'm glad they got you. You're evil.'

The old man laughed. *'Oh, Michael. You really don't understand. You've fucked it all up, bey. Now no more bitches will get the punishment they deserve.'*

'Good.' Michael started crying.

'Good? Look at you, pretending you didn't do it. Lying to yourself and to them that you didn't get your thrill from doing those things.'

Michael gripped his head, humming, not listening.

'You loved it, bey, you know you did. You got all excited when they got scared, and oh, didn't you love it when they were lying there black and blue? But you wanted someone else to blame, didn't you, bey? Listen to me!'

Michael buried his head in his arms. 'No, no, no. Go away. Go away.'

'I'm not going anywhere. I'll always be here, bey. It doesn't matter what they tell you, I'll always be here.'

CHAPTER 35

Moone hesitated as he reached the room in the ICU, the same one where he had stood outside, looking in at Mandy Butler, praying she would be OK. Now she was going to be fine and his stomach was in all kinds of knots knowing he was about to talk to her again for the first time since she'd learned that he'd lied to her about his date with Dr Jenkins. He took a deep breath, listening to the chatter inside, mostly made up of Pinder and Molly gossiping away.

He took a deep breath and stood in the doorway, the nerves gripping him. There she was, sitting propped up on some pillows, with Pinder on one side, looking strange in his civvies and Molly on the other.

'Oh, there he is,' Butler said, her voice sounding hoarse. 'I wondered when you'd show your face.'

He stepped in, trying to raise a smile.

Pinder stood up and said, 'Come on, Molly, let's go and get a coffee, and leave these two to catch up. Molly got up too, but not before squeezing Butler's hand and grinning at her.

As they both slipped out, Pinder flashed him a look, but Moone wasn't sure exactly what it meant.

'Sit down then,' Butler said, looking at the chair that Pinder had been sat in. 'Sorry, my voice is rough as anything. I've had a tube stuck down my throat.'

'How do you feel?' he asked and sat down.

'Oh, you know, like I was in a car crash.'

They both laughed until Butler grimaced in pain. 'I've got a few broken ribs and bruising and everything else,' she said, then she stared at him. 'Is it true?'

'What?'

'That the wicked witch is gone?'

Moone nodded and smiled. 'She's going before a magistrate tomorrow. Then, well, there'll be a trial... and at the very least, she'll no longer be a police officer.'

Butler closed her eyes and rested her head back on the pillow. 'Oh, praise the fucking Lord. I wish I could've seen the look on her face.'

'It was priceless.'

Butler looked at him. 'I'm guessing you... well, you had to bend a few rules?'

'Me?' He put on a look of surprise. 'You know me, I'm straight down the line. Always by the book.'

'Yeah, right. I'm surprised you weren't too

busy faffing to get around to arrest the cow.'

He laughed.

Then her face took on a more serious look. 'Are you alright? I mean, I know we were in a crash, but I don't remember much else. You seem in all right shape.'

He nodded, looking down at himself. 'Yeah, I think everything's still there. Just about. My knees are where my balls used to be, but apart from that, I'm Ok.'

Butler let out a groan of pain again. 'Don't make me laugh. It hurts!'

'Sorry. I'm just glad you're OK. I was really worried. When we were in the car... waiting to be rescued... you were out cold and I thought...'

'God, that must've been bleeding scary. What did you do?'

He shrugged. 'Nothing much.'

'Go on, tell me, Peter Moone.'

'I talked to you, tried to see if you could hear me.'

'Really? Bless you. Thanks. I can't remember anything. What did you say?'

Moone looked down, his heart thudding, flashing back to being upside down in the car, remembering his words. He swallowed, then looked up at her. He wanted to say it all over again, knowing he had come so close to losing her.

'Go on,' she said, staring at him.

'I said... well, you know, come on Butler,

don't leave me now. Who's going to tell me to stop faffing? Wake up, you lazy sod. That sort of thing.'

She smiled. 'Typical bloody Moone, poetic even in the face of death.'

'That's me. Oh, by the way, we caught our killer too. Well, he handed himself in actually. He's messed up in the head, thinks some old man that doesn't even exist did it all.'

'Don't they all?'

'It's good to have you back.' He reached out and took her hand and squeezed it.

'Any other news?'

He shrugged. 'Oh, my daughter is staying in Plymouth, but my wife is heading back to London. Looks like Alice will be living with me.'

'Living with you? You'll cramp her style. She should move into my place. We can have girly nights and slag you off.'

'Really?'

'Yeah. Why not?'

He laughed. 'OK. I'll tell her. Anyway, I better go and let you rest.'

'Come back tomorrow.'

He smiled. 'I will. See you then.'

When Moone got outside, he saw Pinder was there waiting, sipping a coffee. He saw Moone and shook his head sagely.

'What was that?' Pinder asked.

'What?' Moone started heading out with Pinder following.

'You were meant to tell her how you feel.'

'I couldn't. I just want her back with me... you know. If I told her how I felt, she might not reciprocate. And then things would get awkward... and I don't want to lose her.'

Pinder patted him on the back. 'Good for you, Moone. Whatever that bollocks all meant, I have no idea.'

A few weeks later, as the summer cooled and the leaves started to desert the trees, Butler drove them towards Central Park where they parked close to the Life Centre and Plymouth Argyle. They climbed out and strolled all the way along the path running through that piece of pleasantness at the centre of their crazy and beautiful city. They passed the cafe and the children's playground that was swarming with screaming kids.

Then they carried on to the baseball diamond at the end of the park.

'I've seen this baseball diamond here a few times,' Moone said as they reached the ground where a baseball game was in full swing. 'I've never known where it came from.'

'The Plymouth Mariners,' Butler said. 'That's whose diamond it is. They play in the Westcountry Baseball league.'

Moone stared at her as one of the players swung his bat and hit the ball high into the air. 'There's a Westcountry Baseball league?'

Butler sighed. 'You've got a lot to learn about Plymouth, Moone. Look, they're playing the Newton Brewers.'

Moone watched a player running through the bases, and not really understanding what was going on. But he looked at Butler and was glad she was enjoying the game. He was glad she was alive.

'We'd better do what we came to do,' he said and gestured to where Nick Dann was sitting watching the game. They had learned that he sponsored the Plymouth Mariners, buying them equipment occasionally. They had found this out during their investigation of him, and while questioning the police officers who his wife had bribed twenty years earlier. During it all, one of his colleagues had come up with the CCTV footage that had mysteriously disappeared the night the van was allegedly stolen from Dann's depot. It showed him talking heatedly with Jon Michael King, who had come to have it out with him. Then King had taken one of his vans and the businessman had let him. Perverting the course of justice was just one of the minor charges he was facing compared to the big one.

Moone walked up to him and caught the businessman's eye. Nick Dann nodded, then with a heavy breath got to his feet and walked over.

'It's a good game, isn't it?' Dann said,

looking over at the action.

'So I hear,' Moone said, then cleared his throat. 'Nick Dann, I'm arresting you for the murder of Judy Ludlow. You do not have to say anything, but, it may harm your defence if you do not mention when questioned something which you later rely on in court. Anything you do say may be given in evidence. Do you understand?'

Nick Dann nodded, then looked at Butler. 'I understand. I've got a good team of lawyers. I'm not worried.'

'Good for you,' Butler said, then turned him round and put on the cuffs. 'Right, let's get him booked in.'

Moone smiled at her, watching her for a moment, that deep sense of longing buried in his chest somewhere, the feeling he was getting better at hiding. He looked over at Plymouth, across the baseball field, the sound of the crowd yelling and the crack of ball on bat filling his ears, then out over at the sun that was getting lower in the sky, turning it a deep shade of orange. It looked peaceful over this beautiful city, he thought. The place he called home and always would. He buried the bad things he had done alongside his yearnings and walked on, hoping the peace would last.

He knew at some point, not long from now, the peace would end and more bad moments would come. But with Butler by his

side, and his team ready, they would be OK.
At least he hoped.

GET TWO FREE AND EXCLUSIVE CRIME THRILLERS

I think building a relationship with the readers of my books is something very important, and makes the writing process even more fulfilling. Sign up to my mailing list and you'll receive two exclusive crime thrillers for FREE! Get SOMETHING DEAD- an Edmonton Police Station novella, and BITER- a standalone serial killer thriller.

Just visit markyarwood.co.uk

or you can find me here:

https://www.bookbub.com/authors/mark-yarwood

facebook.com/MarkYarwoodcrimewriter/

DID YOU ENJOY THIS BOOK?
YOU COULD MAKE A DIFFERENCE.

Because reviews are critical to the success of an author's career, if you have enjoyed reading this novel, please do me a massive favour by leaving one on Amazon.

Thank you.

Reviews increase visibility. Your help in leaving one would make a massive difference to this author. Thank you for taking the time to read my work.

Printed in Great Britain
by Amazon